Present-Day Stories

Present-Day Stories

Selected by

JOHN T. FREDERICK

CHARLES SCRIBNER'S SONS

New York · Chicago · Boston · Atlanta
San Francisco · Dallas

PREFACE

In the '20's and early '30's moods of cynicism, disillusionment and denial were inescapably reflected in the work of prominent writers, and tended to dominate the character of collections of contemporary work. Today the trend of our literature is positive. Preoccupation with morbid psychology, with frustration and perversion, is replaced by assertion of the lasting values of human courage, integrity, and fidelity.

The vitality of present-day short stories proceeds from their extraordinary variety and the freedom enjoyed by writers in this field.

In this book I have collected stories which I believe interestingly and truthfully represent the positive tone and rich range of the short story as we find it today. I have faith in the fruitfulness of literary study when it gives pleasure to the student. Therefore, I have put into this book stories which I believe students will enjoy.

A large measure of the merit which the book may possess is due to the generous help of friends. Especially, I wish to thank Paul Fenlon, of the department of English of the University of Notre Dame, for helpful suggestions and general assistance; Maxwell E. Perkins and William C. Weber of Charles Scribner's Sons, for the suggestion of stories; Thomas J. B. Walsh, of the college department of Charles Scribner's Sons, for valuable help from first to last.

JOHN T. FREDERICK

Contents

vii

viii   *Contents*

Present-Day Stories

The Dark City

CONRAD AIKEN

Conrad Aiken was born at Savannah, Georgia, in 1889. Since his graduation from Harvard in 1912 he has made literature his profession, and has published twenty volumes of poetry, five novels, and three volumes of short stories. His poems are noteworthy for musical quality and strong evocation of mood, and often for philosophic depth. His prose is distinguished by a style at once fluent and precise, and by psychological penetration. Many of his short stories reveal to a remarkable degree the dramatic significance of seemingly commonplace incidents and relationships. He has lived much abroad, in England, France, and Italy. He is married and the father of three children. Among his books are *Selected Poems,* which was awarded the Pulitzer Prize for 1929; *Conversation* (1940), a novel; *Among the Lost People* (1934), a collection of short stories; and *And in the Human Heart* (1940), a volume of poems.

HIS greatest pleasure in life came always at dusk. Its prelude was the reading of the evening paper in the train that took him out of the city. By long association the very unfolding of the grimy ink-smelling sheets was part of the ritual: his dark eyes dilated, he felt

From *Bring, Bring,* by Conrad Aiken (Liveright, 1925). Copyright, 1925, by Conrad Aiken. Reprinted by permission of the author.

himself begin to "grin," the staggering load of business detail, under which he had struggled all day in the office, was instantly forgotten. He read rapidly, devoured with rapacious eyes column after column—New York, London, Paris, Lisbon—wars, revolutions, bargains in umbrellas, exhibitions of water colors. This consumed three-quarters of the journey. After that he watched the procession of houses, walls, trees, reeling past in the mellow slant light, and began already to feel his garden about him. He observed the flight of the train unconsciously, and it was almost automatically, at the unrealized sight of a certain group of trees, oddly leaning away from each other, like a group of ballet dancers expressing an extravagance of horror, that he rose and approached the door.

The sense of escape was instant. Sky and earth generously took him, the train fled shrieking into the vague bright infinity of afternoon. The last faint wail of it, as it plunged into a tunnel, always seemed to him to curl about his head like a white tentacle, too weak to be taken seriously. Then, in the abrupt silence, he began climbing the long hill that led to his house. He walked swiftly, blowing tattered blue clouds of smoke over his shoulders, revolving in his mind the items of news amusing enough to be reported to Hilda; such as that Miss Green, the stenographer, who had for some time been manifesting a disposition to flirt with him, today, just after closing, when everybody else had gone out, had come to him, blushing, and asked him to fasten the sleeve of her dress. A delicious scene! He smiled about the stem of his pipe, but exchanged his smile for a laugh when, looking in through a gap in his neighbor's hedge, he found himself staring into the depraved eyes of a goat. This would add itself to the episode of Miss Green, for these eyes were precisely hers. He turned the corner and saw his house before him, riding on the hill like a small ship on a long green wave. The three children were playing a wild game of croquet, shrieking. Louder sounds arose at his appearance, and as he strode across the lawn they danced about him chattering and quarreling.

"Daddy, Martha won't play in her turn, and I say——"

"Marjorie takes the heavy mallet——"

The chorus rose shrill about him, but he laughed and went into the house, shouting only, "Out of the way! I'm in a hurry! The beans are dying, the tomatoes are clamoring for me, the peas are holding out their hands!"

"Daddy says the beans are dying. Isn't he silly?"

"Let's get to the garden before daddy does."

As he closed the door he heard the shrieks trailing off round the corner of the house, diminuendo. He hung up coat and hat with a rapid gesture and hurried to the kitchen. Hilda, stirring the cocoa with a long spoon, looked round at him laconically.

"Chocolate!" he shouted, and pulled a cake of chocolate out of his pocket. He was astonished, he rolled his eyes, for it appeared to have been sat upon—"in the train." Hilda shrieked with laughter. He thrust it into her apron pocket and fled up the stairs to change.

He could not find his old flannel trousers. Not in the cupboard—not in the bureau. He surrendered to an impulse to comic rage. "Not under the bed!" he cried. He thrust his head out of the window that overlooked the garden and addressed his children.

"Martha! Bring my trousers here this instant!"

He drew in his head again from the shower of replies that flew up at him like missiles and going to the door roared down to his wife.

"I've lost my trousers!"

Then he found them in the closet behind the door and, laughing, put them on.

II

He ran out of the side door, under the wistaria-covered trellis, and down the slippery stone steps to the vegetable garden.

"Here comes daddy, now," shrilled to him from Martha.

He lighted his pipe, shutting his left eye, and stood in profound meditation before the orderly, dignified, and extraordinarily vigorous rows of beans. They were in blossom—bees were tumbling the delicate lilac-pink little hoods. Clouds of fragrance came up from them. The crickets were beginning to tune up for the evening. The sun was poised above the black water tower on the far hill.

Martha and Marjorie began giggling mysteriously behind the lilacs.

"My hoe!" he wailed.

The hoe was thrust out from behind the lilacs.

"If anybody should drive up in a scarlet taxi," he said to Martha, accepting the hoe, "and inform you that your soul is free, don't believe him. Tell him he's a liar. Point me out to him as a symbol of the abject slavery that all life is. Say that I'm a miserable thrall to wife, children, and beans—particularly beans. I spend my days on my knees before my beans."

"I'll do nothing of the sort," said Martha.

He held his hoe under his arm and walked solemnly among the beans. The two girls followed him.

"Here's a caterpillar, daddy!"

"Kill him!"

"Here's another—a funny green one with red sparkles on his back. Oh, look at him!"

"Don't look at him! Kill him!"

"He squirts out like green toothpaste."

"Don't, Martha!" he cried, pained. "Don't say such things! Spare your neurotic father."

He shrank visibly and strode off to the corner where his peas were planted and started methodically hoeing the rows, turning the rich loam up about the pale stalks. Now and again a pebble clinked, he stooped and threw it off into the meadow. Mary, the youngest, came to the top of the steps and cried. Martha and Marjorie went to her, and he forgot them. The rising and falling of the hoe-blade, shiny with much polishing in the brown soil, hypnotized him, and his thoughts fell into a sort of rhythm, came and went without his interference. "Ridiculous!" he thought, "that this solemn singular biped, whom other bipeds for convenience call Andrew, should stand here with a stick and scratch the skin of this aged planet. What does he expect to get for it? It pleases the aged planet. She stretches herself in the twilight, purrs like an old cat, and expresses her pleasure in the odd and useful effluvium we call peas. And this biped wears clothes. Think of it! He wears clothes; things made out of plant-fiber and sheep's wool cunningly and hideously made to fit his arms and legs. He has in his pocket—a small pouch made in these singular garments—a watch, a small shiny round object in which he has reduced to feeble but regular iambics the majestic motions of the sun, earth and stars. He takes it out and looks at it with an air of comprehension and puts it back again. Why doesn't he laugh at himself?" . . . He chuckled. . . . "This object tells him that he has time for two more rows before dinner. Clink, clink. Damn these pebbles. My antediluvian anthropoid ape of an ancestor had to walk round them, they were so huge. He sat on them, cracked nuts against them, chattered with his family. He had no watch, and his trousers grew like grass. . . . Thank the Lord they've become pebbles."

He sighed, and for a moment rested his chin on the hoe-handle, peering out towards the tree-encircled swamp. The hylas were beginning to jingle their elfin bells. A red-winged blackbird sailed in the last sunlight from one apple-tree to another.

"All a vicious circle and all fascinating. Utterly preposterous and futile, but fascinating."

He dropped the hoe and trundled the wheelbarrow to the edge of the strawberry-bed.

"Why can't you stay where you're put?" he said. "Why do you grow all over the place like this?"

With a trowel he began digging up the runners and placing them on the wheelbarrow. It delighted him to part the soft cool soil with his fingers, to thrust them sensitively among the finely filamented roots. The delicate snap, subterranean, of rootlets gave him a delicious pang. "Blood flows—but it's all for the best; in the best of all possible worlds. Yield to me, strawberries, and you shall bear. I am the resurrection and the life." When he had a sufficient pile of plants, he trundled the wheelbarrow to the new bed, exquisitely prepared, rich, warm, inviting. With the hoe he made a series of holes, and then, stooping, thrust the hairy roots back into the earth, pressing the soil tenderly about them. Then he rose, stretched his back, and lighted his pipe, shutting his left eye, and enshrining the flame, which danced, in the hollow of his stained hands. The cloud of smoke went up like incense.

"Water!" he cried. "Water! Water!"

Martha appeared, after a moment, bringing the watering-pot. She held it in front of her with both hands.

"Quick, Martha, before they die. Their tongues are turning black."

"Silly!" Martha replied.

The earth about each plant was darkened with the tilted water, and the soiled leaves and stems were brightened.

"Listen, daddy! They're smacking their lips."

"They are pale, they have their eyes shut, they are reaching desperately down into the darkness for something to hold on to. They grope and tickle at atoms of soil, they shrink away from pebbles, they sigh and relax."

"When the dew falls, they'll sing."

"Ha! ha! what fools we are!"

He flung the hoe across the wheelbarrow and started wheeling it towards the toolhouse.

"Bring the watering-pot."

Martha ran after him and put it in the wheelbarrow.

"That's right—add to my burden—never do anything that you can make somebody else do."

Martha giggled in response and skipped towards the house. When she reached the stone steps she put her feet close together and with dark seriousness hopped up step after step in that manner. He watched her and smiled.

"O Lord, Lord," he said, "what a circus we are!"

He trundled the bumping wheelbarrow and whistled. The red sun, enormous in the slight haze, was gashing itself cruelly on a black pine tree. The hylas, by now, had burst into full shrill-sweet chorus in the swamp, and of the birds all but a few scraping grackles were still. "Peace—peace—peace," sang the hylas, a thousand at once. Silver bells, frailer than thimbles, ringing under a still and infinite sea of ether. . . . "Peace—peace," he murmured. Then he dropped the wheelbarrow in horror, and put his hands to his ears. "The enemy!" he cried. "Martha! Hurry! Martha!" This time Martha seemed to be out of earshot, so he was obliged to circumvent the enemy with great caution. The enemy was a toad who sat by preference near the toolhouse door: obese, sage, and wrinkled like a Chinese god. "Toad that under cold stone." Marvelous compulsion of rhythm. . . . He thrust the wheelbarrow into the cool pleasant-smelling darkness of the toolhouse, and walked towards the kitchen door, which just at that moment Hilda opened.

"Hurry up," she said. Her voice had a delicious mildness in the still air and added curiously to his already overwhelming sense of luxury. He had, for a moment, an extraordinary satisfying sense of space.

III

He lifted his eyes from the pudding to the Hokusai print over the mantel.

"Think of it with shame! We sit here again grossly feeding our insatiable bellies, while Fujiyama, there, thrusts his copper-colored cone into a cobalt sky among whipped-cream clouds! Pilgrims, in the dusk, toil up his sides with staves. Pilgrims like ants. They struggle upwards in the darkness for pure love of beauty."

"I don't like bread-pudding," ejaculated Mary solemnly, "it's beany."

Martha and Marjorie joined in a silvery cascade of giggles.

"Where *did* she get that awful word!" said Hilda.

"Tom says it, mother."

"Well, for goodness' sake forget it."

Mary stared gravely about the table, spoon in mouth, and then, removing the spoon, repeated, "It's beany."

He groaned, folding his napkin.

"What an awful affliction a family is! Why did we marry, Hilda? Life is a trap."

"Mrs. Ferguson called this afternoon and presented me with a basket of green strawberries. I'm afraid she thought I wasn't very appreciative. I hate to be interrupted when I'm sewing. Why under the sun does she pick them before they're ripe?"

"That's a nice way to treat a neighbor who gives you a present! . . . You *are* an ungrateful creature."

Hilda was languid.

"Well, I didn't ask her for them."

Her eyes gleamed with a slow provocative amusement.

"They're beany," said Mary.

He rolled his eyes at Mary.

> "Our kids are too much with us. Bib and spoon,
>   Feeding and spanking, we lay waste our powers!"

They all pushed back their chairs, laughing, and a moment later, as he lighted his cigar, he heard, from the music-room, Hilda's violin begin with tremulous thin notes, oddly analogous to the sound of her voice when she sang, playing Bach to a methodical loud piano accompaniment by Martha. Melancholy came like a blue wave out of the dusk, lifted him, and broke slowly and deliciously over him. He stood for a moment, made motionless by the exquisite, intricate melody, stared, as if seeking with his eyes for the meaning of the silvery algebra of sound, and then went out.

The sun had set, darkness was at hand. He walked to the top of the stone steps and looked across the shallow valley towards the fading hill and the black water-tower. The trees on the crest, sharply silhouetted against a last band of pale light, looked like marching men. Lights winked at the base of the hill. And now, as hill and water-tower and trees became obscure, he began to see once more the dim phantasmal outlines of the dark city, the city submerged under the infinite sea, the city not inhabited by mortals. Immense, sinister and black, old and cold as the moon, were the walls that surrounded it. No gate gave entrance to it. Of a paler stone were the houses upon houses, tiers upon tiers of shadowy towers, which surmounted the walls. Not a light was to be seen in it, not a motion: it was still. He stared and stared at it, following with strained eyes the faint lines which might indicate its unlighted streets, seeking in vain, as always, to discover in the walls of it any sign of any window. It grew darker, it faded, a profound and vast secret, an inscrutable mystery.

"She is older than the rocks," he murmured.

He turned away and walked over the lawn in the darkness, listening to the hylas, who seemed now to be saturating the hushed night with sound. "Peace—peace—peace—" they sang. *Pax vobiscum*. He gathered the croquet mallets and leaned them against the elm tree, swearing when he tripped over an unseen wicket. This done, he walked down the pale road, blowing clouds of smoke above him with uplifted face, and luxuriated in the sight of the dark tops of trees motionless against the stars. A soft skipping sound in the leaves at the road's edge made him jump. He laughed to himself. . . . "He had no watch, and his trousers grew like grass. . . ." He took out his watch and peered closely at it. The children were in bed, and Hilda was waiting for a game of chess. He walked back with his hands deep in his pockets. Pawn to king-four.

"Hilda! Wake up!"

Hilda opened her candid eyes without astonishment and sat up over the chessboard, on which the tiny men were already arranged.

"Goodness! How you scared me. What took you so long? I've been dreaming about Bluebeard."

"Bluebeard! Good Heavens! I hope he didn't look like me."

"He did—remarkably!"

"A *nice* thing to say to your husband. . . . Move! Hurry up! . . . I'm going to capture your queen. Queens die young and fair."

He smoked his pipe. Hilda played morosely. Delicious, she was, when she was half asleep like this! She leaned her head on one hand, her elbow on the table. . . . When she had been checkmated at the end of half an hour she sank back wearily in her chair. She looked at him intently for a moment and began to smile.

"And how about the dark city tonight?" she asked. He took slow puffs at his pipe and stared meditatively at the ceiling.

"Ah—the dark city, Hilda! The city submerged under an infinite sea, the city not inhabited by mortals! . . . It was there again—would you believe it? . . . It was there. . . . I went out to the stone steps, smoking my cigar, while you played Bach. I hardly dared to look—I watched the hill out of the corner of my eyes and pretended to be listening to the music. . . . And suddenly, at the right moment of dusk, just after the street lamps had winked along the base of the hill, I saw it. The hill that we see there in the daylight, with its water-tower and marching trees, its green sloping fields and brook that flashes in the sun, is unreal, an illusion, the thinnest of disguises—a cloak of green velvet which the dark city throws over itself at the coming of the first ray of light. . . . I saw it distinctly. Immense, smooth and black, old and cold as the moon, are the walls that surround it. No gate gives entrance to it. Of a paler stone are the houses upon houses, tiers upon tiers of shadowy towers that surmount those sepulchral walls. No motion was perceptible there—no light gleamed there—no sound, no whisper rose from it. I thought: perhaps it is a city of the dead. The walls of it have no windows, and its inhabitants must be blind. . . . And then I seemed to see it more closely, in a twilight which appeared to be its own, and this closer perception gave way in turn to a vision. For first I saw that all the walls of it are moist, dripping, slippery, as if it were bathed in a deathlike dew; and then I saw its people. Its people are maggots—maggots of perhaps the size of human children; their heads are small and wedge-shaped, and glow with a faint bluish light. Masses of them swarm within those walls. Masses of them pour through the streets, glisten on the buttresses and parapets. They are intelligent. What horrible feast is it that nightly they celebrate there in silence? On what carrion do they feed? It is the universe that they devour; and they build above it, as they devour it, their dark city like a hollow tomb. . . . Extraordinary that this city, which seen from here at dusk has so supernatural a beauty, should hide at the core so vile a secret. . . ."

Hilda stared at him.

"Really, Andrew, I think you're going mad."

"Going? I'm gone! My brain is maggoty."

They laughed and rattled the chessmen into their wooden box. Then they began locking the doors and windows for the night.

The Devil and Daniel Webster

STEPHEN VINCENT BENÉT

Stephen Vincent Benét was born in 1898 at Bethlehem, Pennsylvania, a descendant of three generations of army officers. His childhood included years in California and in Georgia. He had published two volumes of poetry before his graduation from Yale, and was chairman of the *Yale Literary Magazine* in his senior year, 1919. His most popular and influential book is *John Brown's Body,* the narrative poem of the Civil War which received the Pulitzer Prize for 1928. It was written during the two years which Benét spent in France on a Guggenheim fellowship. His short stories, collected in *Thirteen O'Clock* (1937) and *Tales Before Midnight* (1939), are widely varied in substance, and are marked by admirable structure and characterization and often by a boldly imaginative quality. He lives in New York City.

IT'S a story they tell in the border country, where Massachusetts joins Vermont and New Hampshire.

Yes, Dan'l Webster's dead—or, at least, they buried him. But every time there's a thunderstorm around Marshfield, they say you can hear his rolling voice in the hollows of the sky. And they say that if you go to his grave and

From *Thirteen O'Clock,* by Stephen Vincent Benét (Farrar and Rinehart, Inc., 1937). Copyright, 1936, 1937 by Stephen Vincent Benét. Reprinted by permission of the author and of Farrar and Rinehart, Inc.

speak loud and clear, "Dan'l Webster—Dan'l Webster!" the ground'll begin to shiver and the trees begin to shake. And after a while you'll hear a deep voice saying, "Neighbor, how stands the Union?" Then you better answer the Union stands as she stood, rock-bottomed and copper-sheathed, one and indivisible, or he's liable to rear right out of the ground. At least, that's what I was told when I was a youngster.

You see, for a while, he was the biggest man in the country. He never got to be President, but he was the biggest man. There were thousands that trusted in him right next to God Almighty, and they told stories about him that were like the stories of patriarchs and such. They said, when he stood up to speak, stars and stripes came right out in the sky, and once he spoke against a river and made it sink into the ground. They said, when he walked the woods with his fishing rod, Killall, the trout would jump out of the streams right into his pockets, for they knew it was no use putting up a fight against him; and, when he argued a case, he could turn on the harps of the blessed and the shaking of the earth underground. That was the kind of man he was, and his big farm up at Marshfield was suitable to him. The chickens he raised were all white meat down through the drumsticks, the cows were tended like children, and the big ram he called Goliath had horns with a curl like a morning-glory vine and could butt through an iron door. But Dan'l wasn't one of your gentlemen farmers; he knew all the ways of the land, and he'd be up by candle-light to see that the chores got done. A man with a mouth like a mastiff, a brow like a mountain and eyes like burning anthracite—that was Dan'l Webster in his prime. And the biggest case he argued never got written down in the books, for he argued it against the devil, nip and tuck and no holds barred. And this is the way I used to hear it told.

There was a man named Jabez Stone, lived at Cross Corners, New Hampshire. He wasn't a bad man to start with, but he was an unlucky man. If he planted corn, he got borers; if he planted potatoes, he got blight. He had good-enough land, but it didn't prosper him; he had a decent wife and children, but the more children he had, the less there was to feed them. If stones cropped up in his neighbor's field, boulders boiled up in his; if he had a horse with the spavins, he'd trade it for one with the staggers and give something extra. There's some folks bound to be like that, apparently. But one day Jabez Stone got sick of the whole business.

He'd been plowing that morning and he'd just broke the plowshare on a rock that he could have sworn hadn't been there yesterday. And, as he stood looking at the plowshare, the off horse began to cough—that ropy kind of cough that means sickness and horse doctors. There were two children down with the measles, his wife was ailing, and he had a whitlow on his thumb. It was about the last straw for Jabez Stone. "I vow," he said, and he looked around him kind of desperate—"I vow it's enough to make a man want to sell his soul to the devil! And I would, too, for two cents!"

Then he felt a kind of queerness come over him at having said what he'd said; though, naturally, being a New Hampshireman, he wouldn't take it back. But, all the same, when it got to be evening and, as far as he could see, no notice had been taken, he felt relieved in his mind, for he was a religious man. But notice is always taken, sooner or later, just like the Good Book says. And, sure enough, next day, about suppertime, a soft-spoken, dark-dressed stranger drove up in a handsome buggy and asked for Jabez Stone.

Well, Jabez told his family it was a lawyer, come to see him about a legacy. But he knew who it was.

He didn't like the looks of the stranger, nor the way he smiled with his teeth. They were white teeth, and plentiful —some say they were filed to a point, but I wouldn't vouch for that. And he didn't like it when the dog took one look at the stranger and ran away howling, with his tail between his legs. But having passed his word, more or less, he stuck to it, and they went out behind the barn and made their bargain. Jabez Stone had to prick his finger to sign, and the stranger lent him a silver pin. The wound healed clean, but it left a little white scar.

After that, all of a sudden, things began to pick up and prosper for Jabez Stone. His cows got fat and his horses sleek, his crops were the envy of the neighborhood, and lightning might strike all over the valley, but it wouldn't strike his barn. Pretty soon, he was one of the prosperous people of the county; they asked him to stand for selectman, and he stood for it; there began to be talk of running him for state senate. All in all, you might say the Stone family was as happy and contented as cats in a dairy. And so they were, except for Jabez Stone.

He'd been contented enough, the first few years. It's a great thing when bad luck turns; it drives most other things out of your head. True, every now and then, especially in rainy weather, the little white scar on his finger would give him a twinge. And once a year, punctual as clockwork, the stranger with the handsome buggy would come driving by. But the sixth year, the stranger lighted, and, after that, his peace was over for Jabez Stone.

The stranger came up through the lower field, switching his boots with a cane—they were handsome black boots, but Jabez Stone never liked the look of them, particularly the toes. And, after he'd passed the time of day, he said, "Well, Mr. Stone, you're a hummer! It's a very pretty property you've got here, Mr. Stone."

"Well, some might favor it and others might not," said Jabez Stone, for he was a New Hampshireman.

"Oh, no need to decry your industry!" said the stranger, very easy, showing his teeth in a smile. "After all, we know what's been done, and it's been according to contract and specifications. So when—ahem—the mortgage falls due next year, you shouldn't have any regrets."

"Speaking of that mortgage, mister," said Jabez Stone, and he looked around for help to the earth and the sky, "I'm beginning to have one or two doubts about it."

"Doubts?" said the stranger, not quite so pleasantly.

"Why, yes," said Jabez Stone. "This being the U. S. A. and me always having been a religious man." He cleared his throat and got bolder. "Yes, sir," he said, "I'm beginning to have considerable doubts as to that mortgage holding in court."

"There's courts and courts," said the stranger, clicking his teeth. "Still, we might as well have a look at the original document." And he hauled out a big black pocketbook, full of papers. "Sherwin, Slater, Stevens, Stone," he muttered. "I, Jabez Stone, for a term of seven years— Oh, it's quite in order, I think."

But Jabez Stone wasn't listening, for he saw something else flutter out of the black pocketbook. It was something that looked like a moth, but it wasn't a moth. And as Jabez Stone stared at it, it seemed to speak to him in a small sort of piping voice, terrible small and thin, but terrible human. "Neighbor Stone!" it squeaked. "Neighbor Stone! Help me! For God's sake, help me!"

But before Jabez Stone could stir his hand or foot, the stranger whipped out a big bandanna handkerchief, caught the creature in it, just like a butterfly, and started tying up the ends of the bandanna.

"Sorry for the interruption," he said. "As I was saying——"

But Jabez Stone was shaking all over like a scared horse. "That's Miser Stevens' voice!" he said, in a croak. "And you've got him in your handkerchief!"

The stranger looked a little embarrassed.

"Yes, I really should have transferred him to the collecting box," he said with a simper, "but there were some rather unusual specimens there and I didn't want them crowded. Well, well, these little contretemps will occur."

"I don't know what you mean by contertan," said Jabez Stone, "but that was Miser Stevens' voice! And he ain't dead! You can't tell me he is! He was just as spry and mean as a woodchuck, Tuesday!"

"In the midst of life—" said the stranger, kind of pious. "Listen!" Then a bell began to toll in the valley and Jabez Stone listened, with the sweat running down his face. For he knew it was tolled for Miser Stevens and that he was dead.

"These long-standing accounts," said the stranger with a sigh; "one really hates to close them. But business is business."

He still had the bandanna in his hand, and Jabez Stone felt sick as he saw the cloth struggle and flutter.

"Are they all as small as that?" he asked hoarsely.

"Small?" said the stranger. "Oh, I see what you mean. Why, they vary." He measured Jabez Stone with his eyes, and his teeth showed. "Don't worry, Mr. Stone," he said. "You'll go with a very good grade. I wouldn't trust you outside the collecting box. Now, a man like Dan'l Webster, of course—well, we'd have to build a special box for him, and even at that, I imagine the wing spread would astonish you. But, in your case, as I was saying——"

"Put that handkerchief away!" said Jabez Stone, and he began to beg and to pray. But the best he could get at the end was a three years' extension, with conditions.

But till you make a bargain like that, you've got no idea of how fast four years can run. By the last months of those years, Jabez Stone's known all over the state and there's talk of running him for governor—and it's dust and ashes in his mouth. For every day, when he gets up, he thinks, "There's one more night gone," and every night when he lies down, he thinks of the black pocketbook and the soul of Miser Stevens, and it makes him sick at heart. Till, finally, he can't bear it any longer, and, in the last days of the last year, he hitches up his horse and drives off to seek Dan'l Webster. For Dan'l was born in New Hampshire, only a few miles from Cross Corners, and it's well known that he has a particular soft spot for old neighbors.

It was early in the morning when he got to Marshfield, but Dan'l was up already, talking Latin to the farm hands and wrestling with the ram, Goliath, and trying out a new trotter and working up speeches to make against John C. Calhoun. But when he heard a New Hampshireman had come to see him, he dropped everything else he was doing for that was Dan'l's way. He gave Jabez Stone a breakfast that five men couldn't eat, went into the living history of every man and woman in Cross Corners, and finally asked him how he could serve him.

Jabez Stone allowed that it was a kind of mortgage case. "Well, I haven't pleaded a mortgage case in a long time, and I don't generally plead now, except before the Supreme Court," said Dan'l, "but if I can, I'll help you."

"Then I've got hope for the first time in ten years," said Jabez Stone, and told him the details.

Dan'l walked up and down as he listened, hands behind his back, now and then asking a question, now and then plunging his eyes at the floor, as if they'd bore through it like gimlets. When Jabez Stone had finished, Dan'l puffed out his cheeks and blew. Then he turned to Jabez Stone and a smile broke over his face like the sunrise over Monadnock.

"You've certainly given yourself the devil's own row to hoe, Neighbor Stone," he said, "but I'll take your case."

"You'll take it?" said Jabez Stone, hardly daring to believe.

"Yes," said Dan'l Webster. "I've got about seventy-five other things to do and the Missouri Compromise to straighten out, but I'll take your case. For if two New Hampshire-men aren't a match for the devil, we might as well give the country back to the Indians."

Then he shook Jabez Stone by the hand and said, "Did you come down here in a hurry?"

"Well, I admit I made time," said Jabez Stone.

"You'll go back faster," said Dan'l Webster, and he told 'em to hitch up Constitution and Constellation to the carriage. They were matched grays with one white forefoot, and they stepped like greased lightning.

Well, I won't describe how excited and pleased the whole Stone family was to have the great Dan'l Webster for a guest, when they finally got there. Jabez Stone had lost his hat on the way, blown off when they overtook a wind, but he didn't take much account of that. But after supper he sent the family off to bed, for he had most particular business with Mr. Webster. Mrs. Stone wanted them to sit in the front parlor, but Dan'l Webster knew front parlors and said he preferred the kitchen. So it was there they sat, wait-ing for the stranger, with a jug on the table between them and a bright fire on the hearth—the stranger being sched-uled to show up on the stroke of midnight, according to specifications.

Well, most men wouldn't have asked for better company than Dan'l Webster and a jug. But with every tick of the clock Jabez Stone got sadder and sadder. His eyes roved round, and though he sampled the jug you could see he couldn't taste it. Finally, on the stroke of 11:30 he reached over and grabbed Dan'l Webster by the arm.

"Mr. Webster, Mr. Webster!" he said, and his voice was shaking with fear and a desperate courage. "For God's sake, Mr. Webster, harness your horses and get away from this place while you can!"

"You've brought me a long way, neighbor, to tell me you don't like my company," said Dan'l Webster, quite peaceable, pulling at the jug.

"Miserable wretch that I am!" groaned Jabez Stone. "I've brought you a devilish way, and now I see my folly. Let him take me if he wills. I don't hanker after it, I must say, but I can stand it. But you're the Union's stay and New Hampshire's pride! He mustn't get you, Mr. Webster! He mustn't get you!"

Dan'l Webster looked at the distracted man, all gray and shaking in the firelight, and laid a hand on his shoulder.

"I'm obliged to you, Neighbor Stone," he said gently. "It's kindly thought of. But there's a jug on the table and a case in hand. And I never left a jug or a case half finished in my life."

And just at that moment there was a sharp rap on the door.

"Ah," said Dan'l Webster, very coolly, "I thought your clock was a trifle slow, Neighbor Stone." He stepped to the door and opened it. "Come in!" he said.

The stranger came in—very dark and tall he looked in the firelight. He was carrying a box under his arm—a black, japanned box with little air holes in the lid. At the sight of the box, Jabez Stone gave a low cry and shrank into a corner of the room.

"Mr. Webster, I presume," said the stranger, very polite, but with his eyes glowing like a fox's deep in the woods.

"Attorney of record for Jabez Stone," said Dan'l Webster,

but his eyes were glowing too. "Might I ask your name?"

"I've gone by a good many," said the stranger carelessly. "Perhaps Scratch will do for the evening. I'm often called that in these regions."

Then he sat down at the table and poured himself a drink from the jug. The liquor was cold in the jug, but it came steaming into the glass.

"And now," said the stranger, smiling and showing his teeth, "I shall call upon you, as a law-abiding citizen, to assist me in taking possession of my property."

Well, with that the argument began—and it went hot and heavy. At first, Jabez Stone had a flicker of hope, but when he saw Dan'l Webster being forced back at point after point, he just scrunched in his corner, with his eyes on that japanned box. For there wasn't any doubt as to the deed or the signature—that was the worst of it. Dan'l Webster twisted and turned and thumped his fist on the table, but he couldn't get away from that. He offered to compromise the case; the stranger wouldn't hear of it. He pointed out the property had increased in value, and state senators ought to be worth more; the stranger stuck to the letter of the law. He was a great lawyer, Dan'l Webster, but we know who's the King of Lawyers, as the Good Book tells us, and it seemed as if, for the first time, Dan'l Webster had met his match.

Finally, the stranger yawned a little. "Your spirited efforts on behalf of your client do you credit, Mr. Webster," he said, "but if you have no more arguments to adduce, I'm rather pressed for time"—and Jabez Stone shuddered.

Dan'l Webster's brow looked dark as a thundercloud.

"Pressed or not, you shall not have this man!" he thundered. "Mr. Stone is an American citizen, and no American citizen may be forced into the service of a foreign prince. We fought England for that in '12 and we'll fight all hell for it again!"

"Foreign?" said the stranger. "And who calls me a foreigner?"

"Well, I never yet heard of the dev—of your claiming American citizenship," said Dan'l Webster with surprise.

"And who with a better right?" said the stranger, with one of his terrible smiles. "When the first wrong was done to the first Indian, I was there. When the first slaver put out for the Congo, I stood on her deck. Am I not in your books and stories and beliefs, from the first settlements on? Am I not spoken of, still, in every church in New England? 'Tis true the North claims me for a Southerner and the South for a Northerner, but I am neither, I am merely an honest American like yourself—and of the best descent—for, to tell the truth, Mr. Webster, though I don't like to boast of it, my name is older in this country than yours."

"Aha!" said Dan'l Webster, with the veins standing out in his forehead. "Then I stand on the Constitution! I demand a trial for my client!"

"The case is hardly one for an ordinary court," said the stranger, his eyes flickering. "And, indeed, the lateness of the hour——"

"Let it be any court you choose, so it is an American judge and an American jury!" said Dan'l Webster in his pride. "Let it be the quick or the dead; I'll abide the issue!"

"You have said it," said the stranger, and pointed his finger at the door. And with that, and all of a sudden, there was a rushing of wind outside and a noise of footsteps. They came, clear and distinct, through the night. And yet, they were not like the footsteps of living men.

"In God's name, who comes so late?" cried Jabez Stone, in an ague of fear.

"The jury Mr. Webster demands," said the stranger, sipping at his boiling glass. "You must pardon the rough appearance of one or two; they will have come a long way."

And with that the fire burned blue and the door blew open and twelve men entered, one by one.

If Jabez Stone had been sick with terror before, he was blind with terror now. For there was Walter Butler, the loyalist, who spread fire and horror through the Mohawk Valley in the times of the Revolution; and there was Simon Girty, the renegade, who saw white men burned at the stake and whooped with the Indians to see them burn. His eyes were green, like a catamount's, and the stains on his hunting shirt did not come from the blood of the deer. King Philip was there, wild and proud as he had been in life, with the great gash in his head that gave him his death wound, and cruel Governor Dale, who broke men on the wheel. There was Morton of Merry Mount, who so vexed the Plymouth Colony, with his flushed, loose, handsome face and his hate of the godly. There was Teach, the bloody pirate, with his black beard curling on his breast. The Reverend John Smeet, with his strangler's hands and his Geneva gown, walked as daintily as he had to the gallows. The red print of the rope was still around his neck, but he carried a perfumed handkerchief in one hand. One and all, they came into the room with the fires of hell still upon them, and the stranger named their names and their deeds as they came, till the tale of twelve was told. Yet the stranger had told the truth—they had all played a part in America.

"Are you satisfied with the jury, Mr. Webster?" said the stranger mockingly, when they had taken their places.

The sweat stood upon Dan'l Webster's brow, but his voice was clear.

"Quite satisfied," he said. "Though I miss General Arnold from the company."

"Benedict Arnold is engaged upon other business," said the stranger, with a glower. "Ah, you asked for a justice, I believe."

He pointed his finger once more, and a tall man, soberly clad in Puritan garb, with the burning gaze of the fanatic, stalked into the room and took his judge's place.

"Justice Hathorne is a jurist of experience," said the stranger. "He presided at certain witch trials once held in Salem. There were others who repented of the business later, but not he."

"Repent of such notable wonders and undertakings?" said the stern old justice. "Nay, hang them—hang them all!" And he muttered to himself in a way that struck ice into the soul of Jabez Stone.

Then the trial began, and, as you might expect, it didn't look anyways good for the defense. And Jabez Stone didn't make much of a witness in his own behalf. He took one look at Simon Girty and screeched, and they had to put him back in his corner in a kind of swoon.

It didn't halt the trial, though; the trial went on, as trials do. Dan'l Webster had faced some hard juries and hanging judges in his time, but this was the hardest he'd ever faced, and he knew it. They sat there with a kind of glitter in their eyes, and the stranger's smooth voice went on and on. Every time he'd raise an objection, it'd be "Objection sustained," but whenever Dan'l objected, it'd be "Objection denied." Well, you couldn't expect fair play from a fellow like this Mr. Scratch.

It got to Dan'l in the end, and he began to heat, like iron in the forge. When he got up to speak he was going to flay that stranger with every trick known to the law, and the judge and jury too. He didn't care if it was contempt of court or what would happen to him for it. He didn't care any more what happened to Jabez Stone. He just got madder and madder, thinking of what he'd say. And yet, curiously enough, the more he thought about it, the less he was able to arrange his speech in his mind.

Till, finally, it was time for him to get up on his feet, and he did so, all ready to bust out with lightnings and denunciations. But before he started he looked over the judge and jury for a moment, such being his custom. And he noticed the glitter in their eyes was twice as strong as before, and they all leaned forward. Like hounds just before they get the fox, they looked, and the blue mist of evil in the room thickened as he watched them. Then he saw what he'd been about to do, and he wiped his forehead, as a man might who's just escaped falling into a pit in the dark.

For it was him they'd come for, not only Jabez Stone. He read it in the glitter of their eyes and in the way the stranger hid his mouth with one hand. And if he fought them with their own weapons, he'd fall into their power; he knew that, though he couldn't have told you how. It was his own anger and horror that burned in their eyes; and he'd have to wipe that out or the case was lost. He stood there for a moment, his black eyes burning like anthracite. And then he began to speak.

He started off in a low voice, though you could hear every word. They say he could call on the harps of the blessed when he chose. And this was just as simple and easy as a man could talk. But he didn't start out by condemning or reviling. He was talking about the things that make a country a country, and a man a man.

And he began with the simple things that everybody's known and felt—the freshness of a fine morning when you're young, and the taste of food when you're hungry, and the new day that's every day when you're a child. He took them up and he turned them in his hands. They were good things for any man. But without freedom, they sickened. And when he talked of those enslaved, and the sorrows of slavery, his voice got like a big bell. He talked of the early days of America and the men who had made those days. It wasn't a spread-eagle speech, but he made you see it. He admitted all the wrong that had ever been done. But he showed how, out of the wrong and the right, the suffering and the starvations, something new had come. And everybody had played a part in it, even the traitors.

Then he turned to Jabez Stone and showed him as he was—an ordinary man who'd had hard luck and wanted to change it. And, because he'd wanted to change it, now he was going to be punished for all eternity. And yet there was good in Jabez Stone, and he showed that good. He was hard and mean, in some ways, but he was a man. There was sadness in being a man, but it was a proud thing too. And he showed what the pride of it was till you couldn't help feeling it. Yes, even in hell, if a man was a man, you'd know it. And he wasn't pleading for any one person any more, though his voice rang like an organ. He was telling the story and the failures and the endless journey of mankind. They got tricked and trapped and bamboozled, but it was a great journey. And no demon that was ever foaled could know the inwardness of it—it took a man to do that.

The fire began to die on the hearth and the wind before morning to blow. The light was getting gray in the room when Dan'l Webster finished. And his words came back at the end to New Hampshire ground, and the one spot of land that each man loves and clings to. He painted a picture of that, and to each one of that jury he spoke of things long forgotten. For his voice could search the heart, and that was his gift and his strength. And to one, his voice was like the forest and its secrecy, and to another like the sea and the storms of the sea; and one heard the cry of his lost nation in it, and another saw a little harmless scene he hadn't remembered for years. But each saw something. And when Dan'l Webster finished he didn't know whether or not he'd saved Jabez Stone. But he knew he'd done a miracle. For the glitter was gone from the eyes of judge and jury, and, for the moment, they were men again, and knew they were men.

"The defense rests," said Dan'l Webster, and stood there like a mountain. His ears were still ringing with his speech, and he didn't hear anything else till he heard Judge Hathorne say, "The jury will retire to consider its verdict."

Walter Butler rose in his place and his face had a dark, gay pride on it.

"The jury has considered its verdict," he said, and looked the stranger full in the eye. "We find for the defendant, Jabez Stone."

With that, the smile left the stranger's face, but Walter Butler did not flinch.

"Perhaps 'tis not strictly in accordance with the evidence," he said, "but even the damned may salute the eloquence of Mr. Webster."

With that, the long crow of a rooster split the gray morning sky, and judge and jury were gone from the room like a puff of smoke and as if they had never been there. The stranger turned to Dan'l Webster, smiling wryly.

"Major Butler was always a bold man," he said. "I had not thought him quite so bold. Nevertheless, my congratulations, as between two gentlemen."

"I'll have that paper first, if you please," said Dan'l Webster, and he took it and tore it into four pieces. It was queerly warm to the touch. "And now," he said, "I'll have you!" and his hand came down like a bear trap on the stranger's arm. For he knew that once you bested anybody like Mr. Scratch in fair fight, his power on you was gone. And he could see that Mr. Scratch knew it too.

The stranger twisted and wriggled, but he couldn't get out of that grip. "Come, come, Mr. Webster," he said, smiling palely. "This sort of thing is ridic—ouch!—is ridiculous. If you're worried about the costs of the case, naturally, I'd be glad to pay——"

"And so you shall!" said Dan'l Webster, shaking him till his teeth rattled. "For you'll sit right down at that table and draw up a document, promising never to bother Jabez Stone nor his heirs or assigns nor any other New Hampshireman till doomsday! For any hades we want to raise in this state, we can raise ourselves, without assistance from strangers."

"Ouch!" said the stranger. "Ouch! Well, they never did run very big to the barrel, but—ouch!—I agree!"

So he sat down and drew up the document. But Dan'l Webster kept his hand on his coat collar all the time.

"And, now, may I go?" said the stranger, quite humble, when Dan'l had seen the document was in proper and legal form.

"Go?" said Dan'l, giving him another shake. "I'm still trying to figure out what I'll do with you. For you've settled the costs of the case, but you haven't settled with me. I think I'll take you back to Marshfield," he said, kind of reflective. "I've got a ram there named Goliath that can butt through an iron door. I'd kind of like to turn you loose in his field and see what he'd do."

Well, with that the stranger began to beg and to plead. And he begged and he pled so humble that finally Dan'l, who was naturally kindhearted, agreed to let him go. The stranger seemed terrible grateful for that and said, just to show they were friends, he'd tell Dan'l's fortune before leaving. So Dan'l agreed to that, though he didn't take much stock in fortune-tellers ordinarily. But, naturally, the stranger was a little different.

Well, he pried and he peered at the lines in Dan'l's hands. And he told him one thing and another that was quite remarkable. But they were all in the past.

"Yes, all that's true, and it happened," said Dan'l Webster. "But what's to come in the future?"

The stranger grinned, kind of happily, and shook his head.

"The future's not as you think it," he said. "It's dark. You have a great ambition, Mr. Webster."

"I have," said Dan'l firmly, for everybody knew he wanted to be President.

"It seems almost within your grasp," said the stranger, "but you will not attain it. Lesser men will be made President and you will be passed over."

"And, if I am, I'll still be Daniel Webster," said Dan'l. "Say on."

"You have two strong sons," said the stranger, shaking his head. "You look to found a line. But each will die in war and neither reach greatness."

"Live or die, they are still my sons," said Dan'l Webster. "Say on."

"You have made great speeches," said the stranger. "You will make more."

"Ah," said Dan'l Webster.

"But the last great speech you will make will turn many of your own against you," said the stranger. "They will call you Ichabod; they will call you by other names. Even in New England, some will say you have turned your coat and sold your country, and their voices will be loud against you till you die."

"So it is an honest speech, it does not matter what men say," said Dan'l Webster. Then he looked at the stranger and their glances locked.

"One question," he said. "I have fought for the Union all my life. Will I see that fight won against those who would tear it apart?"

"Not while you live," said the stranger, grimly, "but it

will be won. And after you are dead, there are thousands who will fight for your cause, because of words that you spoke."

"Why, then, you long-barreled, slab-sided, lantern-jawed, fortune-telling note shaver!" said Dan'l Webster, with a great roar of laughter, "be off with you to your own place before I put my mark on you! For, by the thirteen original colonies, I'd go to the Pit itself to save the Union!"

And with that he drew back his foot for a kick that would have stunned a horse. It was only the tip of his shoe that caught the stranger, but he went flying out of the door with his collecting box under his arm.

"And now," said Dan'l Webster, seeing Jabez Stone beginning to rouse from his swoon, "let's see what's left in the jug, for it's dry work talking all night. I hope there's pie for breakfast, Neighbor Stone."

But they say that whenever the devil comes near Marshfield, even now, he gives it a wide berth. And he hasn't been seen in the state of New Hampshire from that day to this. I'm not talking about Massachusetts or Vermont.

Bloodhound

JAMES BOYD

James Boyd was born in Pennsylvania in 1888. When he was thirteen, his family—of southern origin—moved to North Carolina. He studied at Princeton and at Trinity College, Cambridge, and worked as a newspaper reporter and in a book publisher's office. During 1917 he served as an officer on the Italian front and in France. When he returned to this country after the war, doctor's orders to go south and live on his grandfather's plantation led to his development as a writer of fiction. He is a permanent resident of Southern Pines, North Carolina, and has found much of his material for writing in the history of the surrounding region and in the lives of its present inhabitants—their varied occupations, habits of mind, and patterns of speech. His novels are *Drums* (1925); *Marching On* (1927); *Long Hunt* (1930); *Roll River* (1935); and *Bitter Creek* (1939).

THE crowd of black felt hats moved from the track.

"Hyer she comes. Hark to her whistle."

"That's good. They tell me with a bloodhound every minute counts."

"That nigger's had four hours' start right now."

"Reckon it was a nigger."

"It's a nigger. All this stealing around town's nigger

work. And what white man would take a purple suit with yellow stripes?"

"All I hope, this dog can smell him. They tell me it costs the town fifty dollars to bring it here."

"Heyo, Will, you got a bloodhound aboard?"

"Sure have. Hyer's the man with him."

"Gentlemen, how you all?"

"Howdy."

"Now, gentlemen, stand back and give this dog room. Too many folks is liable to mess him up."

"Look at them great ears. A man could tie them under his chin."

"Now, gentlemen, whereabouts do we start?"

"Right yonder. See that sign 'Bullteel's Clothing Store'? Nigger taken the suit right off the hanger."

"That dog knows what he come for. Don't he walk proud, though?"

"He's a severe dog."

"They tell me, though, a bloodhound's gentle."

"Well, doggone if I'd love to hear one belling on my track."

"They tell me, though, he don't do nothing but smell and holler."

"That's all right, but, as the fellow says, does the dog say it? Yes, sir, I want to hear it from the dog, else I'm gone right now, I——"

"Now, gentlemen, stand back. Don't mess up the sidewalk. You Mr. Bullteel?"

"Yes, sir. Bring in your dog."

"Never mind that. Bring out the hanger the suit was on."

"You reckon he keeps the harness on that dog all the time?"

"I expect so."

"Sure he keeps it on. How could he stay with him else?"

"Yes, sir, without that harness that dog would fly."

"Watch him snuff that hanger."

"Hark to him snuff."

"Now, gentlemen, stand back."

"He's working the ground now. Now he's whimpering."

"Man, he's off."

"Come on, boys."

"Now, gentlemen, keep back."

"Doggone, he's bound to catch that nigger. He's straining in the collar."

"Man, hark to him. I'd love mighty well to hear that tongue on a fox."

"Now he's hushed."

"Hold on, boys, don't push him. This cross street has him bothered."

"Stand still. Let's us see what he will do."

"There he goes. Round the corner and down the hill. Right for Jim Crowtown."

"Didn't I say it was a nigger?"

"Bill, you and some others cut around ahead. Don't let any nigger leave on the other side. You all got guns?"

"We all got guns."

"Now, gentlemen, stay back. All these nigger tracks keeps him studying."

"Look at all the niggers disappear."

"Nothing but dust and doors a-slamming."

"Niggers sure despise a bloodhound."

"They say, though, a bloodhound's gentle."

"That's all right, but does the bloodhound say it? Yes, sir, I want to hear it from the bloodhound."

"Hush, he's hit off his loss. Come on."

"Now, gentlemen, keep back."

"If he branches off yonder they ain't but one house it can be."

"Well, there he goes. It's Sis Highpocket's."

"He's straining on it now."

"It's Sis Highpocket's. Look at him jump at that door."

"Stand back, gentlemen. Nigger, open that door."

"Come out, Sis."

"Sis, open that door."

"Take a run at it, Lon. Pull out your guns, boys, and go right in behind him."

"Hold on, gentlemen, till I get my dog away."

"All right, let's go. Everybody in."

"Oh, my sweet God, gentlemens, oh, my——"

"Hush your fuss, Sis. Who you got with you?"

"God is my judge and witness, gentlemens. They ain't been a man in this house since my man went on the roads."

"What you got under that green wrapper, Sis?"

"Gentlemens, let me tell you the truth. I was just changing my closes to step over to town for my Saturday rations. I was——"

"What man you got here, Sis?"

"Gentlemens, I——"

"Look under the bed, Jeff."

"Oh, my sweet God, gentlemens."

"Yonder he is. I can see his feet. Come out, nigger. Grab his leg."

"Who's got the handcuffs? Nigger, hold out your hands. Anybody know this nigger?"

"Looks like one of them south Georgia niggers that's come in."

"That's what he is. It's them south Georgia niggers been raising all the fuss around here."

"Sis, what ails you? This is as sorry a nigger as ever I saw."

"He's yellow and he's puny."

"Can't you do no better than that, Sis?"

"Gentlemens, God is my judge and witness. I never seen this person before. He must have crope under my bed when I was sleeping. Black boy, don't you grin at me. I'll slap your head in, ape. Gentlemens, let me tell you the truth. This is a mighty big surprise. I declare——"

"Anybody find the suit? Cut open the mattress."

"Done cut it open. Pillows as well."

"Let's get out. Between nigger and feathers I'm about to lose my breath."

"Never mind the suit. We got the nigger."

"So long, Sis."

"Sis, you better tread light. When your Lundy gets off the roads he'll cut your liver."

"Gentlemens, ain't I told you——"

"We ought to tie a rope on this nigger."

"You know what we ought to do? We ought to tie this nigger up and whip him good."

"Road gang don't mean nothing to him. He'll get fat on the roads."

"Nigger, you want to be whipped?"

"No, suh."

"Heyo, here comes Hugh Dave. His face is afire and he's stepping high."

"Look at him raise his knees. That scoundrel sure loves his liquor."

"Howdy, Hugh Dave."

"Hi, boys, howdy. How you all come on? What's the fuss?"

"Nigger yonder been stealing."

"Nigger, you been stealing? Doggone my hide, you ought to be whipped. If they's anything I despise it's a stealing nigger. For two cents I'd lay onto you with a bull whip till you had the gospel in your soul. You hear me? Who caught him?"

"Bloodhound from Twelve Oaks."

"Bloodhound, come here. Rise up, dog. You and me will finish this bottle together. Rise up, dog. Only don't mess up my clothes. They're new."

"Man, keep your liquor away from my dog."

"Whereabouts did you get that suit, Hugh Dave?"

"Taken it out of Bullteel's store. He was gone and I aimed to go on that Birmingham excursion, only I needed a suit and I was drunk."

"You're drunk now, Hugh Dave."

"Then I went to sleep and missed the excursion. And now look at my fix. I've the suit to pay for and I've slept in it already and my liquor is give out and it's a sorry bluegum nigger suit, anyways."

"Doggone if that ain't the suit."

"Sure enough, that's the suit."

"Well, boys, it looks like this is the suit. Nigger, you listen. You can go this time, but mind how you carry on around here."

"Yes, suh."

"Man, what ails your bloodhound that we paid fifty dollars for?"

"You lay off this dog. He's caught twenty-nine niggers and a white man in the last three years. And two of them was hung."

"Looks like they hung the wrong niggers if this fyce dog caught them."

"You call my dog a fyce, you——"

"Now gentlemen, gentlemen——"

"Well, then, let him lay off my dog."

"Friend, they is no complaint about your dog. Ain't that a fact, boys?"

"Sure is. A dog can't always be right."

"And it's a mighty good thing for this community—to bring in a bloodhound."

"Yes, sir. It will keep the niggers quiet for some little time."

"Why, man, this bloodhound has done a thousand dollars' worth of good."

"What this town needs is a bloodhound."

"Well, gentlemen, times are hard with me. For three hundred dollars——"

"Well, boys, I reckon we better be getting back to town."

Dorothy

ERSKINE CALDWELL

Erskine Caldwell was born in 1903 at White Oak, Georgia. His father was a Presbyterian minister. He attended the University of Virginia, but found more immediate preparation for his writing in experience as farm hand and mill laborer. His novels *Tobacco Road* (1932) and *God's Little Acre* (1933) and many of his short stories express his deep interest in social and economic problems, particularly in the South. His short stories are collected in the volume *Jackpot* (1940).

WHEN I saw her for the first time she was staring several hundred miles away. She was standing on the other side of the street near the corner holding a folded newspaper in front of her. It had been folded until the want ads were the only print showing, and it looked like a paper printed without headlines. Suddenly she blinked her eyes several times and looked at the paper she was holding. Her knees and legs were rigidly stiff but her body swayed backward and forward like some one weak from hunger. Her shoulders dropped downward and downward until they seemed to be merely the upper part of her arms.

She glanced at the ads every few moments and then searched half-heartedly for a number on one of the doors behind her. Once she opened her pocketbook and read something written on the back of an envelope. There were numbers on most of the doors, but either she could not see the numerals plainly enough or she could not find the one she was looking for—I didn't know what the trouble was. I couldn't see her face. Her head had dropped forward, and her chin sank to the collar of her waist. She would look up for a moment and then her head would suddenly drop downward again and hang there until she could raise it. She looked like a young mother weeping over the body of her child.

She was standing across the street within reach of one of the whiteway poles. She could have leaned against the pole or else found a place to sit down. I don't know why she did neither. I don't suppose she knew herself.

I was standing on the shady side of the street waiting for something. I didn't know what I was waiting for. It wasn't important, anyway. I didn't have anything to do, and I wasn't going anywhere. I was just standing there when I looked across the street and saw her with the folded paper in her hands. There were hundreds of other people in the street, all of them hurrying somewhere. She and I were the only ones standing still.

It was between one and two o'clock in the afternoon. Men and women were coming out of the restaurants on both sides of the street, hurrying back to work. I had a quarter in my pocket but I had not eaten any lunch. I was hungry but I was saving it. I wanted to get up to Richmond, where I was sure I could find a job. Things were quiet in New Orleans, and I had tried Atlanta. Now I wanted to get up to Richmond. It was July, and there were not many jobs anywhere. I had always been lucky in Richmond, though.

The girl on the other side of the street turned the paper over and read down another column of the close print. There were several office buildings and a few banks on the street. Everywhere else were retail stores of some kind. Most of them had displays of women's wear in the windows. It was hard for a man to find a job, and not much easier for a woman. Especially a girl, unless she was wearing the right kind of clothes.

The girl put the newspaper under her arm and started across the street. I was standing a few steps from the corner. She came across, holding the paper tightly under her arm and looking down at the pavement all the time. When she reached the curb, she came down the street in my direction. She still did not look up. She held her head down all the time as if she were looking at her slippers.

The pavement was hot. It was July.

She walked past me, behind. I could hear the gritty sand and dust grind under her shoes. It made a sound like the sandpapering of an iron pipe. Then suddenly the sound stopped. I looked around and saw her standing almost beside me. She was so close I could have touched her with my hand. Her face was pale and her lips were whiter than her forehead. When she looked up at me she did not raise her head, only her eyes saw me. Her eyes were damp. They were very blue. She did not want me to know that she had been crying.

I turned all the way around and looked at her. I did not know what to do. Until she spoke to me she held her mouth tight against her teeth, but she could not stop her lips from quivering.

"Can you tell me where No. 67 Forsythe Street is?" she asked me.

I looked down at her. Her hands were clinched so tightly I could see only the backs of her fingers. They were stained as if she had been handling freshly printed newspapers all day. They were not dirty. They were just not clean. A sort of blackish dust had settled on the backs of her hands. Dust is in the air of every city, and some people wash their hands five or six times a day to keep them clean. I don't know, but maybe she had not had a chance to wash her hands for several days. Her face was not soiled, but it looked as if she had tried to keep it clean with a dampened handkerchief and a powdered chamois skin.

She had asked me where No. 67 Forsythe Street was. She had said, "Pardon me," when she asked me. I knew she would say, "Thank you very much," when I told her where the address was.

I had to swallow hard before I could say anything at all. I knew where the number was. It was an employment agency. I had been there myself two or three times a day all that week. But there were no jobs there for anybody. It was July. I could look across the street and see the number in large gilt numerals on the door. The door was being constantly opened and closed by people going in and coming out again.

"What?" I asked her. It didn't sound like that, though, when I said it. When you talk to a girl who is very beautiful, you say things differently.

I knew what she said but I could not remember hearing her say it. I had been looking at her so long I forgot the question she asked.

She opened her pocketbook and put her hand inside, feeling for the envelope on which she had written the address. Her eyes were staring at me with the same far-away vagueness they had when I saw her for the first time on the other side of the street. She searched for the envelope without once looking at what she was doing. It had fallen to the pavement the moment she unclasped the pocketbook.

I picked up the letter. It was addressed to Dorothy—I couldn't read the last name. It had been sent in care of general delivery at the main post-office from some little town down near the Florida border. It might have been from her mother or sister. It was a woman's handwriting. She jerked it from me before I could hand it to her. There was something in the way she reached for it that made me wonder about it. Maybe her father had died and she was trying to find a job so she could support her mother—I don't know. Things like that happen all the time. Or all of her family could have been killed in an accident and she had to leave home to make a living—things like that happen everywhere.

People were turning around to look at us. They walked past us and then turned around and stared. Peachtree Street was only around the corner from where we stood. It was a fashionable section.

I don't know what made me say what I did. I knew where No. 67 Forsythe Street was. I had been there myself only half an hour before. It was an employment agency. They said come in again tomorrow morning. They told everybody the same thing—both men and women. It was the dull season. It was July.

I said, "No. 67 is about three blocks down the street, on the other side of the viaduct." I pointed down there, my arm over her head. She was very small beside me.

She looked down the street to the other side of the viaduct. There were half a dozen cheap hotels down there. They were the cheapest kind. Everybody has seen them. A lot of us know what they are like inside. There are some in every city. They charge seventy-five cents and up. . . . I thought I was doing right. There was no money in her pocketbook. Not a cent. I saw everything she had in it. I had a quarter, and I would have to go all the way to Richmond before I found a job. There were no jobs across the street at No. 67. It was the dull season. Everybody was out of town for the summer. There were no jobs in July. And she was hungry. She had been trying to sleep in railroad-stations at night, too. . . . On the other side of the viaduct there were at least seven or eight hotels. The cheap kind. I had seen women in them, running down the corridors in kimonos after midnight. They always had some money, enough to buy something to eat when they were hungry. I know what it is to be hungry. A man can stand it for a while—a week, ten days, two weeks—but a woman—if you have ever seen the body of a starving woman you'll know why I thought I was doing right.

She had not moved.

"It's about three blocks down the street, on the other side of the viaduct," I told her again. She knew what I said the first time.

She did not move.

She was standing there, looking at the dirty red brick buildings. She knew the kind they were. Some of them had signs that could be read across the viaduct. Hotel—75¢ & $1. She was reading the signs. My hand was in my pocket holding the quarter between the fingers. I don't know what she could have done with the money. I was ashamed to give it to her—it was only a quarter.

"All right," she said.

It was as if she was making up her mind about something of great importance, like a decision of life and death. It was as if she had said, "All right, I'll go." She was not thanking me for telling her where she could find the number. She knew No. 67 was on this side of the viaduct.

"All right," she said.

She turned and walked down the street toward the dirty red brick hotels. The heels of her slippers had worn sideways. She tried to stand erectly on her feet and she had to walk stiffly so her ankles would not turn. If her legs had relaxed for a second she would have sprained her ankles.

She did not look back at me. Her blue flannel skirt was wrinkled far out of shape. It looked as if she had slept in it for several nights, maybe a week. It was covered with specks of dust and lint. Her white silk waist was creased and discolored. The dust had lodged in the folds and the creases made horizontal smudges across her shoulders. Her hat looked as if it had been in a hard rain for several hours and then dried on a sharp peg of some kind. There was a peak in the crown that drew the whole hat out of shape.

I couldn't stand there any longer. She had gone almost a block toward the dirty red brick buildings. I crossed over and ran down an alley toward Alabama Street. At the end of the alley I found a drain sewer. I dropped the quarter in it. I didn't want the money in my pocket.

I went to a garage on Alabama Street. A mechanic had told me there was a good chance of getting a ride to Richmond if I would stay there long enough and wait until a car came along that was going through.

When I got to the garage, there was a car inside being greased. The man in the garage nodded at me and pointed toward the automobile. It was a big car. I knew it wouldn't take long to make the trip in a car like that. I asked the man who was driving it if he would take me to Richmond with him. He asked the man in the garage about me. They talked awhile in the office and then he came out and said he would take me up with him. He was leaving right away.

We drove up to Richmond. I started out to find a job somewhere. There's a wholesale district under the elevated railway-tracks between the State Capitol and the river. I had been there before.

But there was something the matter with me. I didn't

have the patience to look up a job. I was nervous. I had to keep moving all the time. I couldn't stand still.

A few days later I was in Baltimore. I applied for a job in an employment agency. They had plenty of jobs but they took their time about giving them out. They wanted you to wait a week or two to see if you would stick. Most everybody went on to Philadelphia. That's the way it is in summer. Everybody goes up. When the weather begins to get cold they come down again, stopping in Baltimore until the weather catches up, and then they move to the next city. Everybody ends up in New Orleans.

I couldn't stay. I couldn't stand still. I went on up to Philadelphia like everybody else. From Philadelphia you move up into Jersey. But I didn't. I stayed in Philadelphia.

Then one day I was standing on Market Street, near the city hall, watching a new skyscraper go up. I saw a woman on the other side of the street who looked like the girl I had seen in Atlanta. She was not the same one, of course. But there was a resemblance.

I could not think about anything else. I stood there all the afternoon thinking about the girl in Atlanta and wondering what I could do. I knew I had to figure out some way to get to Atlanta and find her. I had sent her down Forsythe Street, across the viaduct. She knew where she was going, but she would not have gone if it had not been for me. I sent her down there. . . . God, if I had only pointed across the street to No. 67! She knew where it was. She had been standing in front of it when I first saw her with the newspaper folded back at the want ads. But she knew it would have been useless to go inside. They would have told her to come in again the next morning. That's what they told everybody. Maybe she thought I would give her some money. I don't know what she thought, to tell the truth. But she was up against it, just as I was. She was too proud to ask for money to buy something to eat, and yet she thought I might give her some. I had a quarter, but I was ashamed to offer it to her after I sent her down the street toward those hotels. She had tried to find a job somewhere so she could have something to eat and a place to sleep. She knew there was always one way. She knew about Forsythe Street on the other side of the viaduct. Somebody had told her about it. A woman in one of the railroad-stations, perhaps. Somebody told her, because she knew all about it.

I didn't send her there, she would have gone anyway. . . . That's what I think sometimes—but it's a lie! I told her to go down the street and cross the viaduct.

A Wedding-Dress

Morley Callaghan was born in 1903 in Toronto, graduated from St. Michael's College of the University of Toronto, and worked as a reporter on *The Toronto Daily Star*.
He studied law and is a member of the Canadian Bar. His
stories first appeared in *transition, This Quarter, The Exile,
The American Caravan,* and *Scribner's Magazine*. Both his
short stories and his novels are markedly simple and natural in style and structure. His characters and situations are
drawn from the everyday life of ordinary men and women
in Canada and the United States, and present a remarkably
wide range of occupations and personalities. Although objective to the point of detachment, his fiction expresses a
deep and understanding sympathy for harassed and bewildered humanity.

FOR FIFTEEN years Miss Lena Schwartz had waited
for Sam Hilton to get a good job so they could get
married. She lived in a quiet boarding-house on Wel-
lesley Street, the only woman among seven boarders. The
landlady, Mrs. Mary McNab, did not want woman boarders;
the house might get a bad reputation in the neighborhood;
but Miss Schwartz had been with her a long time. Miss
Schwartz was thirty-two, her hair was straight, her nose
turned up a little and she was thin.

From *Present-Day American Stories* (Scribners, 1929). Copyright,
1929, by Charles Scribner's Sons. Reprinted by permission.

Sam got a good job in Windsor and she was going there to marry him. She was glad to think that Sam still wanted to marry her, because he was a Catholic and went to church every Sunday. Sam liked her so much he wrote a cramped homely letter four times a week.

When Miss Schwartz knew definitely that she was going to Windsor, she read part of a letter to Mrs. McNab, who was a plump, tidy woman. The men heard about the letter at the table and talked as if Lena were an old maid. "I guess it will really happen to her all right," they said, nudging one another. "The Lord knows she waited long enough."

Miss Schwartz quit work in the millinery shop one afternoon in the middle of February. She was to travel by night, arrive in Windsor early next morning and marry Sam as soon as possible.

That afternoon the downtown streets were slushy and the snow was thick alongside the curb. Miss Schwartz ate a little lunch at a soda fountain, not much because she was excited. She had to do some shopping, buy some flimsy underclothes and a new dress. The dress was important. She wanted it charming enough to be married in and serviceable for wear on Sundays. Sitting on the counter stool she ate slowly and remembered how she had often thought marrying Sam would be a matter of course. His love making had become casual and good-natured in the long time; she could grow old with him and be respected by other women. But now she had a funny aching feeling inside. Her arms and legs seemed almost strange to her.

Miss Schwartz crossed the road to one of the department stores and was glad she had on her heavy coat with the wide sleeves that made a warm muff. The snow was melting and the sidewalks steaming near the main entrance. She went lightheartedly through the store, buying a little material for a dress on the fourth floor and curling tongs in the basement. She decided to take a look at the dresses.

She took an elevator to the main floor and got on an escalator because she liked gliding up and looking over the squares of counters, the people in the aisles, and over the rows of white electric globes hanging from the ceiling. She intended to pay about twenty-five dollars for a dress. To the left of the escalators the dresses were displayed on circular racks in orderly rows. She walked on the carpeted floor to one of the racks and a salesgirl lagged on her heels. The girl was young and fair-haired and saucy-looking; she made Miss Schwartz uncomfortable.

"I want a nice dress, blue or brown," she said, "about twenty-five dollars."

The salesgirl mechanically lifted a brown dress from the rack. "This is the right shade for you," she said. "Will you try it on?"

Miss Schwartz was disappointed. She had no idea such a plain dress would cost twenty-five dollars. She wanted something to keep alive the tempestuous feeling in her body, something to startle Sam. She had never paid so much for a dress, but Sam liked something fancy. "I don't think I like these," she said. "I wanted something special."

The salesgirl said sarcastically, "Maybe you were thinking of a French dress. Some on the rack in the French room are marked down."

Miss Schwartz moved away automatically. The salesgirl did not bother following her. "Let the old maid look around," she said to herself, following with her eyes the tall commonplace woman in the dark coat and the oddly shaped purple hat as she went into the gray French room. Miss Schwartz stood on a blue pattern on the gray carpet and guardedly fingered a dress on the rack, a black Canton crepe dress with a high collar that folded back forming petals of burnt orange. From the hem to the collar was a row of buttons, the sleeves were long with a narrow orange trimming at the cuff, and there was a wide corded silk girdle. It was marked seventy-five dollars. She liked the feeling it left in the tips of her fingers. She stood alone at the rack, toying with the material, her mind playing with thoughts she guiltily enjoyed. She imagined herself wantonly attractive in the dress, slyly watched by men with bold thoughts as she walked down the street with Sam, who would be nervously excited when he drew her into some corner and put his hands on her shoulders. Her heart began to beat heavily. She wanted to walk out of the room and over to the escalator but could not think clearly. Her fingers were carelessly drawing the dress into her wide coat sleeve, the dress disappearing steadily and finally slipping easily from the hanger, drawn into her wide sleeve.

She left the French room with a guilty feeling of satisfied exhaustion. The escalator carried her down slowly to the main floor. She hugged the parcels and the sleeve containing the dress tight to her breast. On the street-car she started to cry because Sam seemed to have become something remote, drifting away from her. She would have gone back with the dress but did not know how to go about it.

When she got to the boarding-house she went straight upstairs and put on the dress as fast as she could, to feel that it belonged to her. The black dress with the burnt orange petals on the high collar was short and loose on her thin figure.

And then the landlady knocked at the door and said that a tall man downstairs wanted to see her about something important. Mrs. McNab waited for Miss Schwartz to come out of her room.

Miss Schwartz sat on the bed. She felt that if she did not move at once she would not be able to walk downstairs. She walked downstairs in the French dress, Mrs. McNab watching her closely. Miss Schwartz saw a man with a wide heavy face and his coat collar buttoned high on his neck complacently watching her. She felt that she might just as well be walking downstairs in her underclothes; the dress was like something wicked clinging to her legs and her body. "How do you do," she said.

"Put on your hat and coat," he said steadily.

Miss Schwartz, slightly bewildered, turned stupidly and went upstairs. She came down a minute later in her coat and hat and went out with the tall man. Mrs. McNab got red in the face when Miss Schwartz offered no word of explanation.

On the street he took her arm and said, "You got the dress on and it won't do any good to talk about it. We'll go over to the station."

"But I have to go to Windsor," she said, "I really have to. It will be all right. You see, I am to be married tomorrow. It's important to Sam."

He would not take her seriously. The street lights made the sidewalks glassy. It was hard to walk evenly.

At the station the sergeant said to the detective, "She might be a bad egg. She's an old maid and they get very foxy."

She tried to explain it clearly and was almost garrulous. The sergeant shrugged his shoulders and said the cells would not hurt her for a night. She started to cry. A policeman led her to a small cell with a plain bed.

Miss Schwartz could not think about being in the cell. Her head, heavy at first, got light and she could not consider the matter. The detective who had arrested her gruffly offered to send a wire to Sam.

The policeman on duty during the night thought she was a stupid silly woman because she kept saying over and over, "We were going to be married. Sam liked a body to look real nice. He always said so." The unsatisfied expression in her eyes puzzled the policeman, who said to the sergeant: "She's a bit of a fool, but I guess she was going to get married, all right."

At half past nine in the morning they took her from the cell to the police car along with a small wiry man who had been quite drunk the night before, a colored woman who had been keeping a bawdy house, a dispirited fat man arrested for bigamy, and a Chinaman who had been keeping a betting house. She sat stiffly, primly in a corner of the car and could not cry. Snow was falling heavily when the car turned into the city hall courtyard.

Miss Schwartz appeared in the Women's court before a little Jewish magistrate. Her legs seemed to stiffen and fall away when she saw Sam's closely cropped head and his big lazy body at a long table before the magistrate. A young man was talking rapidly and confidently to him. The magistrate and the crown attorney were trying to make a joke at each other's expense. The magistrate found the attorney amusing. A court clerk yelled a name, the policeman at the door repeated it and then loudly yelled the name along the hall. The colored woman who had been keeping the bawdy house appeared with her lawyer.

Sam moved over to Miss Schwartz. He found it hard not to cry. She knew that a Salvation Army man was talking to a slightly hard-looking woman about her, and she felt strong and resentful. Sam held her hand but said nothing.

The colored woman went to jail for two months rather than pay a fine of $200.

"Lena Schwartz," said the clerk. The policeman at the door shouted the name along the hall. The young lawyer who had been talking to Sam told her to stand up while the clerk read the charge. She was scared and her knees were stiff.

"Where is the dress?" asked the magistrate.

A store detective with a heavy mustache explained that she had it on and told how she had been followed and later on arrested. Everybody looked at her, the dress too short and hanging loosely on her thin body, the burnt orange petals creased and twisted. The magistrate said to himself: "She's an old maid and it doesn't even look nice on her."

"She was to be married today," began the young lawyer affably. "She was to be married in this dress," he said and good-humoredly explained that yesterday when she stole it she had become temporarily a kleptomaniac. Mr. Hilton had come up from Windsor and was willing to pay for the dress. It was a case for clemency. "She waited a long time to be married and was not quite sure of herself," he said seriously.

He told Sam to stand up. Sam haltingly explained that she was a good woman, a very good woman. The crown attorney seemed to find Miss Schwartz amusing.

The magistrate scratched away with his pen and then said he would remand Miss Schwartz for sentence if Sam still wanted to marry her and would pay for the dress. Sam could hardly say anything. "She will leave the city with you," said the magistrate, "and keep out of the department stores for a year." He saw Miss Schwartz wrinkling her nose and blinking her eyes and added, "Now go out and have a quiet wedding." The magistrate was quite satisfied with himself.

Miss Schwartz, looking a little older than Sam, stood up in her dress that was to make men slyly watch her and straightened the corded silk girdle. It was to be her wedding-dress, all right. Sam gravely took her arm and they went out to be quietly married.

similarity of characterization between "dress" & "her"

The Net

ROBERT M. COATES

Robert M. Coates was born at New Haven, Connecticut, in 1897, and is a graduate of Yale. He has contributed many stories and articles to magazines, and is the author of *The Eater of Darkness* (a novel) and *The Outlaw Years* (history). He is a member of the editorial staff of *The New Yorker*.

WALTER had just turned the corner of Charles Street into Seventh when he saw her. She was standing a little way up the block talking to a fellow in a black overcoat and a black felt hat, and just the way they were standing—the fellow leaning back against th: wall of the building there and she crowded close against him, looking up at him—was enough to let Walter know the kind of talk they were having. Almost without thinking, he stopped and stepped back a pace down Charles, out of sight around the corner.

This was the way things went, then; this was what she had left him for. He had known it, but this was the first time he had ever had sight of it, and it sent a queer feeling through him, as if more air than he could breathe had been forced into him. He was a tall man, with a pale, solemn,

From *Short Stories from the New Yorker* (Simon and Schuster, 1940). Copyright, 1940, by Simon and Schuster. Reprinted by permission of the author and of Simon and Schuster, Inc.

heavy-jawed face and a slow, slightly awkward manner of movement. He placed himself against the railing of an areaway and stood there, looking down Seventh Avenue, waiting. He knew she would have to come around the corner when she started home, and whether she was alone or the fellow was still with her, he would have a right to speak to her then. Till then he would wait. He had time.

It was growing late and the evening had been cold; there were few people walking. Down by Christopher Street there was a cluster of bright signs and illuminated buildings, but up where he was the houses were mostly dark, and the only sound was the rough, shuffling whir of the tires on pavement as the cars went flying by. Then the traffic lights changed and the cars stopped, at Charles, at Tenth, at Christopher; at Charles, a black truck crawled out across the avenue and went slowly on down the street past Walter, toward Hudson.

That was all the cross traffic there was, but for a few seconds longer the avenue was still. Then the lights went green and the headlights moved forward, sifting past each other as the cars took up their varying speeds. A moment later, Walter heard the tap of her heels on the sidewalk, coming around the corner, and she passed him.

"Hello, Ann," he said softly.

She hadn't noticed him till then; he could tell that from the way her head snapped around and the look that came over her face. Then she turned her head away. She kept on walking. "Hello, Walter," she said wearily.

He was walking along beside her. "Where you been, Ann?" he asked. "I was at your people's house and they said you'd went to the movies."

"I did."

"Yeah. The movies."

She glanced up at him, and he could see her face pinching up in the way it did when she got angry. But she didn't say anything; she just turned her face forward again, tucked her chin down in the fur collar of her coat, and walked on. He kept pace with her. "I saw you talking to that fellow back there, Ann," he went on in his slow, insistent voice. "I saw you."

"Well," she said. "So you saw me. Can't a girl meet a friend on the street?"

"Yeah. But the movies."

He knew she didn't like to be prodded like that about things, even when she was telling the truth, and he half expected her to burst out with something then and there. He could feel his chest tightening already, in that mixture of fear and excitement and stubbornness that always came over him when they got into an argument. But she just kept on walking. After a few steps she turned to him again. "You was up to the folks'?" she asked, her voice very innocent and offhand. "Who'd you see? Was Ma there?"

"Yes, your mother was there," he said. "As you doubtless know. I know what you're thinking, Ann, but I didn't think it would give you pleasure. She didn't give me no nice reception. But that don't bother me, either; that I expected. I'm not blind, and I know who it was that turned you against me and broke up our marriage. But there's an old saying, Ann, that marriages are made in heaven, and I believe it, and I believe she will get her punishment, too, for what she's done—turning a man's wife against her lawful husband. If not now, then she'll surely get it in the hereafter. But it's not her I'm worried about; I leave her to her own devices. It's you, Ann. Listen," he said. "What you don't get is, I'd take you back tomorrow. Like that. I don't care who you been with, what you done—even that fellow back there, Ann, whoever he is. I don't ask. But a fellow you got to meet on street corners, can't even show to your folks—

but even him, Ann; I'd forget everything. Just so long as you'd tell me, come clean about things. But this lying and hiding. Listen, Ann—" He had thought a good deal about this meeting and had planned for it, and this was one of the things he had figured on saying, so he found himself talking faster and faster. But just then a crazy thing happened.

They were passing a series of old-fashioned houses with high-stooped entrances, and the steps running down from them made the sidewalk narrow. And there was a couple, a man and a girl, walking up the street toward them; in his excitement, Walter didn't notice them until he was upon them, and then there wasn't room for them all to pass. The man bumped him, and Walter stumbled, trying to sidestep them, but all the time his eyes were on Ann. She had walked on, never varying her pace, as if she had nothing to do with him at all, and at the sight of her tan-stockinged legs flicking briskly away beneath her black coat a kind of panic took hold of him. "I'm your husband, Ann!" he yelled suddenly. He could see both the man's and the girl's faces turned toward him, but for the moment he didn't care. He shoved past them and ran after Ann, grabbing at her arm. "I'm your husband," he repeated, his voice still loud. "Don't that mean anything to you? For better or for worse." Then he saw that she was laughing, and he let go of her arm.

It was only a little way farther on to her family's apartment house. When they reached it, she ran up the three or four steps to the entrance. Walter followed her, letting the street door swing shut behind him. They were alone in the dim vestibule. She bent her head for a moment, fumbling in her bag for the key, then she glanced up. "Well, Walter," she said. She wasn't laughing now, but she might just as well have been; he could tell from the look on her

face that she was only waiting to get on upstairs to start in
again. "Well, it's been a enjoyable little walk."

He could feel the air crowding into his lungs again, so
hard that it made his whole chest feel hot inside. "Maybe it
ain't finished yet," he said.

"Well, it is for me. I'm going up."

"I'm coming up too."

"No you won't."

"Why won't I?" Without his meaning it to, he could hear
his voice getting louder. "What you got to conceal up
there?"

"Oh, Walter! It ain't that and you know it. But you know
what'll happen. You and Ma." He hadn't realized that he
had moved closer to her, but he must have, for suddenly
she stepped back a pace and stared up at him. "Walter,"
she said. "You been drinking?"

"I have not been drinking," he said, and he let his voice
go louder still when he said it. Let her scare a little, he was
thinking; at least she wasn't laughing at him any more.
She was paying attention to him now. "Well, then," she
said, and she began talking faster. "Listen, Walter. This
kind of chasing around ain't getting us anywhere, you hiding around corners and laying for me and all that. Why
don't we get together some other way, sometime? I could
come up to your place sometime, even. You still got the
apartment, haven't you? We could talk."

"You come up there," he said, "and maybe you wouldn't
never leave it again." He hadn't meant to put it like that;
what he'd meant was that if she came up, it would have
to be because she wanted to stay there and be with him
again, but the way it came out it sounded threatening, even
to him, and she must have thought so too, for she stared
at him blankly a moment. Then, suddenly, she made a
kind of a dive out of the corner where he had crowded

her. "Then go home then! Get out of here!" he heard her cry, and she began pushing with both hands against his chest. He grabbed her wrists and she screamed. When she screamed, his hands went directly to her throat.

He had only intended to stop her screaming, but as soon as he touched her a strange kind of strength flowed into his hands, a strength that came from somewhere inside him and that once released could not be recalled, so that he couldn't have let go if he'd tried. For a while she struggled, jerking her body this way and that and pulling at his arms with her hands. It didn't bother him. He had shoved her back against the wall, so hard that her head bumped against it and her hat tipped over sidewise. He just stiffened his legs and stood there, his hands locked hard in the flesh of her throat; he was surprised at how strongly he stood there, meeting and conquering every move she made. "Laugh now," he said once, not loud, but almost gently.

Her knee worked up somehow between them until it was pressing against his thigh, but there was no strength in it; the strength was all in him, and soon the knee slipped harmlessly down again. Then her body lashed back and forth once or twice, fast and violently, and stopped, and her eyelids, which had been tight shut, opened so that he could see through her lashes the blue of her eyes, glittering in the dim light overhead. A kind of shudder ran through her. It was some time after that before he realized that she was not struggling any more.

It was the strain on his arms that told him of the change. Her body was just so much weight now, almost more than he could hold, and he let her slide slowly down along the wall until she was sitting on the floor, her back propped against the corner of the vestibule. Well, I did it, he thought, I did it; and for a moment he stood looking down at her uncertainly, not knowing what he ought to do next. One leg was crooked awkwardly sidewise, he noticed, so that the skirt was pulled up above the stocking top, and he bent down and pulled the hem over the knee. Then he turned and went out the door.

At the top of the steps he stopped and looked up and down the street. At first glance it seemed there was no one in sight at all, not a soul; then he noticed a couple of people standing in front of a house farther down the block—a man and a girl, he thought, though he couldn't be sure; about all he could see was their faces, and these were no more than pale spots in the shadows where they were standing. Farther still, down almost to Hudson, he sighted two others, two men, dark against the light from a shop window on the corner. And now there was a girl clipping quickly along on the opposite sidewalk; it was amazing how silently they all moved, and how easy it was not to notice them in the darkness. He stood where he was for a while, watching them, trying to determine if there was any sign of concerted scheme in their actions. He had a feeling that they were only moving as they did in order to set a trap for him; at a signal they might all turn and begin running to surround him.

But none of them paid any attention to him. The couple down the block just stood there, the two men walked onward, the girl hurried around the corner and disappeared. Walter went down the steps and turned up toward Seventh Avenue. Well, I did it, he thought again, and as before, the thought carried no emotion with it except relief. It had to be done, it was coming to her; that was the way his thoughts ran, and what little guilt he had was submerged in a kind of careless irresponsibility, the feeling that a drunken man has when he knows he has done something wrong, admits it, and doesn't care. The emotion was so close to that of drunkenness that even Walter recognized it. I could say I was drunk, he thought, his mind momentarily occupied with stratagems. But as soon as the idea came to him, he rejected it. I've got better reasons than that, he decided; her laughing at me, cheating on me, chasing at every corner. As he neared Fourth Street, another man, a new one, sprang up suddenly before him, a short, heavy-set fellow stepping out of the shadows and striding directly toward him.

The man passed without giving him a second glance, but after the man had gone by, Walter stopped and stepped back against a house wall, watching his progress down the street; suppose he was headed for her house, he was thinking, and the fear became so strong that he almost set out in pursuit of the stranger. I could ask him for a match, get him talking, lead him on past the door, he thought. As he hesitated, the man went by; he went three or four doors farther before he turned in.

Walter walked on. He didn't hurry, and when he reached the end of the block he even stopped for a moment, glancing, as if idly, up and down before crossing the street. The night was a net, he realized, with its streets and its people walking this way and that along them; what he had to do was to find his way out without disturbing anything or any one. The thing that worried him most now was his breathing; he discovered that it had been bothering him for some time. He would find himself breathing fast and hard, so hard that it hurt his chest, and then he would take a deep breath, so long and so deep that when he let it out he could feel the flesh of his body shrinking away from his clothes, leaving the skin damp and prickly and cool. Then the hard, quick breathing would begin again.

Like a man that's been running, he thought. That was one thing he mustn't do; without even thinking about it, he knew he mustn't run. Or talk. For a while he had had the notion of going up to his brother-in-law's place. It was just a notion, or really it was more like a picture that had come into his mind; somehow, he didn't want to go home, and suddenly he had seen himself sitting with Frank and Ethel in their warm apartment, and then he had thought how pleasant it would be, it would rest him; they'd send out for some beer even, maybe. But he saw now that it wouldn't do. He'd get to talking, and there was no way of knowing how they'd take it. At the thought, the picture in his mind changed in a way that made him go cold all over; from seeing their faces smiling at him, friendly and companionable, he had seen them go white and staring, and hard with horror as they looked at him.

It was an awful thing he had done, all right, and the funny part was that he hadn't meant to. "God sakes!" he said. For the moment he was arguing with Frank and Ethel, and he found himself talking out loud. "If I'd meant to do it, wouldn't I have planned the thing different? Me here with no more than a couple of bucks in my pocket." If it had been Friday, even, when his pay came through at the shop; then he'd have had a matter of thirty-five dollars in his hand, enough to start out with, anyway. But maybe Frank would lend him some money; he'd done as much for him on occasion.

"I swear, Frank, it's the first time I ever even laid hands on her. I never meant to harm a hair of her head." He had stopped talking out loud, but he was still arguing to himself when he remembered that Frank was Ann's brother; he had had an idea all along that his mind was running too fast for him, sort of, so that he was overlooking things. And maybe important things. This proved it. If Frank was Ann's brother, that left him out, of course; he was the last man to turn to now. It was late, too. His mind had been racing ahead, full of confidence, but now it was swarming with doubts and uncertainties: how could he expect to burst in on them now, at this hour, asking for money, without them asking questions? And even if he did get some money, where would he go? It would mean quitting his job, leaving every one he knew, everything. "Me a man that's near forty," he thought.

It was just that Frank was the only one in the family that had ever had a decent word for him.

And the thing was, he hadn't meant to do it. All the time back there in the vestibule it had seemed like all the dozens of times in the past when he and Ann would have arguments; and she'd slump down in a chair or a sofa, so mad that she couldn't keep from crying but still trying to hide it; and he'd shout something, slam the door, and go out. And then, like as not, she'd get up, slam the door too, and go off to see one of her girl friends or something. But not now. Now she would lie where she was, in the dim hallway, until some one came in from the street or down from the apartments above, and stumbled over her.

It would happen any minute now, if it hadn't happened already, and at the thought a vast sorrow rose up slowly inside him and filled him—sorrow for himself and for Ann, but mostly for himself. "What I've got myself in for," he kept thinking. A whole group of people, men and women all talking and laughing, were coming down the steps of a house ahead of him, and he slowed his pace so as not to get tangled up with them on the sidewalk. But they just stood there, and finally he had to brush past them. As he did so, he shoved one of the men and gave the whole group such a fierce look that they must have noticed it; he was sure he saw their faces change.

"I could tell you something that would stop your giggling," he thought, and this time, when he thought of the terror he could bring to their faces, he felt an odd sort of satisfaction; it would serve them right, he thought. When he had gone a few paces farther on, he looked back. They were all trailing off down the street, and on an impulse he stopped and leaned against an areaway railing, watching them. It would happen any minute now, he thought.

How long he stood there he didn't know, but it couldn't have been long, and the thing that made him conscious of time again was a thin knife of sound like a scream or a siren; then a car's headlights turned into the street from away down at Hudson. He watched them, and it was some seconds before he realized what was the matter with them; the car was heading up the wrong way, against traffic.

Only a police car would do that, he thought, and as if in confirmation he saw it swing in toward the curb and stop, just about where the entrance to Ann's house would be. Well, then, the police were coming, he thought; that was right, it was proper, and if the old woman—he realized that one of the things he had been worrying about was Ann's mother; he'd known she'd be mixed up in the scene down there some way. But if the police were there and she started her ranting and screaming—well, they'd know how to stop her. Slowly, he pushed himself away from the railing.

He'd go on up to Frank's, he thought, but it was only when he started walking on up the street, toward Seventh, that he realized how tired he was. So maybe, after all, he'd go home. "It's too much," he thought. "It's too much to expect of a man." He was still arguing about this question of packing up and leaving town for good. But he was almost too tired, and too lonely, to bother about it. Unexpectedly, as he walked, a picture came into his mind of the couple he had bumped into when Ann and he were walking home. Down this very block, it had been, and he could see them again, their faces turning in surprise as he shoved past them shouting; somehow, the recollection only added to his feeling of lonely helplessness.

If he could only talk to them, he thought, he could explain everything; they were the only people in the world, perhaps, who would understand. But they had gone, and the thought vanished too, almost as soon as it had come to him. He walked on up to Seventh and then turned north, toward the subway. Maybe he'd go up to Frank and Ethel's after all; if there had been a reason against going there, he had forgotten it, and anyway it wasn't worth bothering about now. Most of all, now, he felt tired.

Adam and Eve and Pinch Me

A. E. COPPARD

A. E. Coppard was born at Folkestone, England, in 1878.
He left school at the age of nine to earn his own living,
eventually becoming a clerk. He had passed the age of forty
before his stories won recognition for their sensitiveness
and beauty of style, their humor, and their extraordinary
variety—from exuberant fantasy to somber realism. Among
the volumes of his collected stories are *Fishmonger's Fiddle,
The Black Dog, The Field of Mustard,* and *Adam and
Eve and Pinch Me.*

AND in the whole of his days, vividly at the end of
the afternoon—he repeated it again and again to
himself—the kind country spaces had never absorbed quite so rich a glamour of light, so miraculous a
bloom of clarity. He could feel streaming in his own mind,
in his bones, the same crystalline brightness that lay upon
the land. Thoughts and images went flowing through him
as easily and amiably as fish swim in their pools; and as
idly, too, for one of his speculations took up the theme of
his family name. There was such an agreeable oddness
about it, just as there was about all the luminous sky today,
that it touched him as just a little remarkable. What did

such a name connote, signify, or symbolize? It was a rann
of a name, but it had euphony! Then again, like the fish,
his ambulating fancy flashed into other shallows, and he
giggled as he paused, peering at the buds in the brake.
Turning back towards his house again he could see, beyond
its roofs, the spire of the church tinctured richly as the
vane; all round him was a new grandeur upon the grass
of the fields, and the spare trees had shadows below that
seemed to support them in the manner of a plinth, more
real than themselves, and the dykes and any chance heave
of the level fields were underlined, as if for special emphasis,
with long shades of mysterious blackness.

With a little drift of emotion that had at other times
assailed him in the wonder and ecstasy of pure light, Jaffa
Codling pushed through the slit in the back hedge and
stood within his own garden. The gardener was at work.
He could hear the voices of the children about the lawn
at the other side of the house. He was very happy, and the
place was beautiful, a fine white many-windowed house
rising from a lawn bowered with plots of mould, turreted
with shrubs, and overset with a vast walnut tree. This house
had deep clean eaves, a roof of faint colored slates that,
after rain, glowed dully, like onyx or jade, under the red
chimneys, and halfway up at one end was a balcony set
with black balusters. He went to a French window that
stood open and stepped into the dining room. There was
no one within, and, on that lonely instant, a strange feeling
of emptiness dropped upon him. The clock ticked almost
as if it had been caught in some indecent act; the air was
dim and troubled after that glory outside. Well, now, he
would go up at once to his study and write down for his
new book the ideas and images he had accumulated—beautiful rich thoughts they were—during that wonderful afternoon. He went to mount the stairs and he was passed by

one of the maids; humming a silly song she brushed past
him rudely, but he was an easy-going man—maids were
unteachably tiresome—and reaching the landing he sauntered towards his room. The door stood slightly open and
he could hear voices within. He put his hand upon the
door . . . it would not open any further. What the devil
. . . he pushed—like the bear in the tale—and he pushed,
and he pushed—was there something against it on the other
side? He put his shoulder to it . . . some wedge must be
there, and that was extraordinary. Then his whole apprehension was swept up and whirled as by an avalanche—
Mildred, his wife, was in there; he could hear her speaking
to a man in fair soft tones and the rich phrases that could
be used only by a woman yielding a deep affection to him.
Codling kept still. Her words burned on his mind and
thrilled him as if spoken to himself. There was a movement
in the room, then utter silence. He again thrust savagely at
the partly open door, but he could not stir it. The silence
within continued. He beat upon the door with his fists, crying: "Mildred, Mildred!" There was no response, but he
could hear the rocking armchair commence to swing to
and fro. Pushing his hand round the edge of the door he
tried to thrust his head between the opening. There was not
space for this, but he could just peer into the corner of a
mirror hung near, and this is what he saw: the chair at one
end of its swing, a man sitting in it, and upon one arm of
it Mildred, the beloved woman, with her lips upon the man's
face, caressing him with her hands. Codling made another
effort to get into the room—as vain as it was violent. "Do you
hear me, Mildred?" he shouted. Apparently neither of them
heard him; they rocked to and fro while he gazed stupefied.
What, in the name of God, . . . what this . . . was she be-
witched . . . were there such things after all as magic-
devilry!

He drew back and held himself quite steadily. The chair stopped swaying, and the room grew awfully still. The sharp ticking of the clock in the hall rose upon the house like the tongue of some perfunctory mocker. Couldn't they hear the clock? . . . Couldn't they hear his heart? He had to put his hand upon his heart, for, surely, in that great silence inside there, they would hear its beat! Then in a queer way he found himself reflecting, observing, analyzing his own actions and intentions. He found some of them to be just a little spurious, counterfeit. He felt it would be easy, so perfectly easy to flash in one blast of anger and annihilate the two. He would do nothing of the kind. There was no occasion for it. People didn't really do that sort of thing, or, at least, not with a genuine passion. There was no need for anger. His curiosity was satisfied, quite satisfied, he was certain, he had not the remotest interest in the man. A welter of unexpected thoughts swept upon his mind as he stood there. As a writer of books he was often stimulated by the emotions and impulses of other people, and now his own surprise was beginning to intrigue him, leaving him, O, quite unstirred emotionally, but interesting him profoundly.

He heard the maid come stepping up the stairway again, humming her silly song. He did not want a scene, or to be caught eavesdropping, and so turned quickly to another door. It was locked. He sprang to one beyond it; the handle would not turn. "Bah! what's up with 'em?" But the girl was now upon him, carrying a tray of coffee things. "O, Mary!" he exclaimed casually, "I . . ." To his astonishment the girl stepped past him as if she did not hear or see him, tapped upon the door of his study, entered, and closed the door behind her. Jaffa Codling then got really angry. "Hell! were the blasted servants in it!" He dashed to the door again and tore at the handle. It would not even turn, and, though he wrenched with fury at it, the room was utterly sealed against him. He went away for a chair with which to smash the effrontery of that door. No, he wasn't angry, either with his wife or this fellow—Gilbert, she had called him—who had a strangely familiar aspect as far as he had been able to take it in; but when one's servants . . . faugh!

The door opened and Mary came forth smiling demurely. He was a few yards further along the corridor at that moment. "Mary!" he shouted, "leave the door open!" Mary carefully closed it and turned her back on him. He sprang after her with bad words bursting from him as she went towards the stairs and flitted lightly down, humming all the way as if in derision. He leaped downwards after her three steps at a time, but she trotted with amazing swiftness into the kitchen and slammed the door in his face. Codling stood, but kept his hands carefully away from the door, kept them behind him. "No, no," he whispered cunningly, "there's something fiendish about door handles today, I'll go and get a bar, or a butt of timber," and, jumping out into the garden for some such thing, the miracle happened to him. For it was nothing else than a miracle, the unbelievable, the impossible, simple and laughable if you will, but having as much validity as any miracle can ever invoke. It was simple and laughable because by all the known physical laws he should have collided with his gardener, who happened to pass the window with his wheelbarrow as Codling jumped out on to the path. And it was unbelievable that they should not, and impossible that they did not collide; and it was miraculous, because Codling stood for a brief moment in the garden path and the wheelbarrow of Bond, its contents, and Bond himself passed apparently through the figure of Codling as if he were so much air, as if he were not a living breathing man, but just a common ghost. There was no impact, just a momentary breathlessness. Codling stood and looked at the retreating figure going on utterly unaware

of him. It is interesting to record that Codling's first feelings were mirthful. He giggled. He was jocular. He ran
along in front of the gardener, and let him pass through him
once more; then after him again; he scrambled into the
man's barrow, and was wheeled about by this incomprehensible thick-headed gardener who was dead to all his
master's efforts to engage his attention. Presently he dropped
the wheelbarrow and went away, leaving Codling to cogitate
upon the occurrence. There was no room for doubt, some
essential part of him had become detached from the obviously
not less vital part. He felt he was essential because he was
responding to the experience, he was reacting in the normal
way to normal stimuli, although he happened for the time
being to be invisible to his fellows and unable to com-
municate with them. How had it come about—this queer
thing? How could he discover what part of him had cut
loose, as it were? There was no question of this being death;
death wasn't funny, it wasn't a joke; he had still all his
human instincts. You didn't get angry with a faithless wife
or joke with a fool of a gardener if you were dead, certainly
not! He had realized enough of himself to know he was the
usual man of instincts, desires, and prohibitions, complex and
contradictory; his family history for a million or two years
would have denoted that, not explicitly—obviously impossible—but suggestively. He had found himself doing things
he had no desire to do, doing things he had a desire not to
do, thinking thought that had no contiguous meanings, no
meanings that could be related to his general experience. At
odd times he had been chilled—aye, and even agreeably
surprised—at the immense potential evil in himself. But still,
this was no mere Jekyll and Hyde affair; that a man and his
own ghost should separately inhabit the same world was a
horse of quite another color. The other part of him was
alive and active somewhere . . . as alive . . . as alive . . .

yes, as he was, but dashed if he knew where! What a lark when they got back to each other and compared notes! In his tales he had brooded over so many imagined personalities, followed in the track of so many psychological enigmas that he had felt at times a stranger to himself. What if, after all, that brooding had given him the faculty of projecting this figment of himself into the world of men. Or was he some unrealized latent element of being without its natural integument, doomed now to drift over the ridge of the world for ever. Was it his personality, his spirit? Then how was the dashed thing working? Here was he with the most wonderful happening in human experience, and he couldn't differentiate or disinter things. He was like a new Adam flung into some old Eden.

There was Bond tinkering about with some plants a dozen yards in front of him. Suddenly his three children came round from the other side of the house, the youngest boy leading them, carrying in his hand a small sword which was made, not of steel, but of some more brightly shining material; indeed it seemed at one moment to be of gold, and then again of flame, transmuting everything in its neighborhood into the likeness of flame, the hair of the little girl Eve, and part of Adam's tunic; and the fingers of the boy Gabriel as he held the sword were like pale tongues of fire. Gabriel, the youngest boy, went up to the gardener and gave the sword into his hands, saying: "Bond, is this sword any good?" Codling saw the gardener take the weapon and examine it with a careful sort of smile; his great gnarled hands became immediately transparent, the blood could be seen moving diligently about the veins. Codling was so interested in the sight that he did not gather in the gardener's reply. The little boy was dissatisfied and repeated his question, "No, but Bond, is this sword any good?" Codling rose, and stood by invisible. The three beautiful children were grouped about the great angular figure of the gardener in his soiled clothes, looking up now into his face, and now at the sword, with anxiety in all their puckered eyes. "Well, Marse Gabriel," Codling could hear him reply, "as far as a sword goes, it may be a good un, or it may be a bad un, but, good as it is, it can never be anything but a bad thing." He then gave it back to them; the boy Adam held the haft of it, and the girl Eve rubbed the blade with curious fingers. The younger boy stood looking up at the gardener with unsatisfied gaze. "But, Bond, can't you say if this sword's any good?" Bond turned to his spade and trowels. "Mebbe the shape of it's wrong, Marse Gabriel, though it seems a pretty handy size." Saying this he moved off across the lawn. Gabriel turned to his brother and sister and took the sword from them; they all followed after the gardener and once more Gabriel made enquiry: "Bond, is this sword any good?" The gardener again took it and made a few passes in the air like a valiant soldier at exercise. Turning then, he lifted a bright curl from the head of Eve and cut it off with a sweep of the weapon. He held it up to look at it critically and then let it fall to the ground. Codling sneaked behind him and, picking it up, stood stupidly looking at it. "Mebbe, Marse Gabriel," the gardener was saying, "it ud be better made of steel, but it has a smartish edge on it." He went to pick up the barrow, but Gabriel seized it with a spasm of anger, and cried out: "No, no, Bond, will you say, just yes or no, Bond, is this sword any good?" The gardener stood still and looked down at the little boy, who repeated his question—"just yes or no, Bond!" "No, Marse Gabriel!" "Thank you, Bond!" replied the child with dignity: "That's all we wanted to know," and, calling to his mates to follow him, he ran away to the other side of the house.

Codling stared again at the beautiful lock of hair in his

hand, and felt himself grow so angry that he picked up a strange-looking flower pot at his feet and hurled it at the retreating gardener. It struck Bond in the middle of the back and, passing clean through him, broke on the wheel of his barrow, but Bond seemed to be quite unaware of this catastrophe. Codling rushed after, and, taking the gardener by the throat, he yelled, "Damn you, will you tell me what all this means?" But Bond proceeded calmly about his work unnoticing, carrying his master about as if he were a clinging vapor, or a scarf hung upon his neck. In a few moments, Codling dropped exhausted to the ground. "What . . . O Hell . . . what, what am I to do?" he groaned. "What has happened to me? What shall I do? What can I do?" He looked at the broken flowerpot. "Did I invent that?" He pulled out his watch. "That's a real watch, I hear it ticking, and it's six o'clock." Was he dead or disembodied or mad? What was this infernal lapse of identity? And who the devil, yes, who was it upstairs with Mildred? He jumped to his feet and hurried to the window; it was shut; to the door; it was fastened; he was powerless to open either. Well! well! this was experimental psychology with a vengeance, and he began to chuckle again. He'd have to write to McDougall about it. Then he turned and saw Bond wheeling across the lawn towards him again. "Why is that fellow always shoving that infernal green barrow around?" he asked, and, the fit of fury seizing him again, he rushed towards Bond, but, before he reached him, the three children danced into the garden again, crying, with great excitement, "Bond, O, Bond!" The gardener stopped and set down the terrifying barrow; the children crowded about him, and Gabriel held out another shining thing, asking: "Bond, is this box any good?" The gardener took the box and at once his eyes lit up with interest and delight. "O, Marse Gabriel, where'd ye get it? Where'd ye get it?" "Bond," said the boy impatiently, "Is the box any good?" "Any good?" echoed the man, "Why, Marse Gabriel, Marse Adam, Miss Eve, look yere!" Holding it down in front of them he lifted the lid from the box and a bright colored bird flashed out and flew round and round above their heads. "O," screamed Gabriel with delight, "it's a kingfisher!" "That's what it is," said Bond, "a kingfisher!" "Where?" asked Adam. "Where?" asked Eve. "There it flies—round the fountain—see it? see it!" "No," said Adam. "No," said Eve.

"O, do, do, see it," cried Gabriel, "here it comes, it's coming!" And, holding his hands on high, and standing on his toes, the child cried out as happy as the bird which Codling saw flying above them.

"I can't see it," said Adam.

"Where is it, Gaby?" asked Eve.

"O, you stupids," cried the boy. "There it goes. There it goes . . . there . . . it's gone!"

He stood looking brightly at Bond, who replaced the lid.

"What shall we do now?" he exclaimed eagerly. For reply, the gardener gave the box into his hand, and walked off with the barrow. Gabriel took the box over to the fountain. Codling, unseen, went after him, almost as excited as the boy; Eve and her brother followed. They sat upon the stone tank that held the falling water. It was difficult for the child to unfasten the lid; Codling attempted to help him, but he was powerless. Gabriel looked up into his father's face and smiled. Then he stood up and said to the others:

"Now, do watch it this time."

They all knelt carefully beside the water. He lifted the lid and, behold, a fish like a gold carp, but made wholly of fire, leaped from the box into the fountain. The man saw it dart down into the water, he saw the water bubble up behind it, he heard the hiss that the junction of fire and water produces, and saw a little track of steam follow the bubbles about the tank until the figure of the fish was consumed and disappeared. Gabriel, in ecstasies, turned to his sister with blazing happy eyes, exclaiming:

"There! Evey!"

"What was it?" asked Eve, nonchalantly; "I didn't see anything."

"More didn't I," said Adam.

"Didn't you see that lovely fish?"

"No," said Adam.

"No," said Eve.

"O, stupids," cried Gabriel, "it went right past the bottom of the water."

"Let's get a fishin' hook," said Adam.

"No, no, no," said Gabriel, replacing the lid of the box. "O no."

Jaffa Codling had remained on his knees staring at the water so long that, when he looked around him again, the children had gone away. He got up and went to the door, and that was closed; the windows, fastened. He went moodily to a garden bench and sat on it with folded arms. Dusk had begun to fall into the shrubs and trees, the grass to grow dull, the air chill, the sky to muster its gloom. Bond had overturned his barrow, stalled his tools in the lodge, and gone to his home in the village. A curious cat came round the house and surveyed the man who sat chained to his seven-horned dilemma. It grew dark and fearfully silent. Was the world empty now? Some small thing, a snail perhaps, crept among the dead leaves in the hedge, with a sharp, irritating noise. A strange flood of mixed thoughts poured through his mind until at last one idea disentangled itself, and he began thinking with tremendous fixity of little Gabriel. He wondered if he could brood or meditate, or "will" with sufficient power to bring him into the garden again. The child had just vaguely recognized him for a moment at the waterside. He'd try that dodge, telepathy was a mild kind of a trick after so much of the miraculous. If he'd lost his blessed body, at least the part that ate and smoked and talked to Mildred. . . . He stopped as his mind stumbled on a strange recognition. . . . What a joke, of course . . . idiot . . . not to have seen that. He stood up in the garden with joy . . . of course, he was upstairs with Mildred, it was himself, the other bit of him, that Mildred had been talking to. What a howling fool he'd been.

He found himself concentrating his mind on the purpose of getting the child Gabriel into the garden once more, but it was with a curious mood that he endeavored to establish this relationship. He could not fix his will into any calm intensity of power, or fixity of purpose, or pleasurable mental ecstasy. The utmost force seemed to come with a malicious threatening splenetic "entreaty." That damned snail in the hedge broke the thread of his meditation; a dog began to bark sturdily from a distant farm; the faculties of his mind became joggled up like a child's picture puzzle, and he brooded unintelligibly upon such things as skating and steam engines, and Elizabethan drama so lapped about with themes like jealousy and chastity. Really now, Shakespeare's Isabella was the most consummate snob in . . . He looked up quickly to his wife's room and saw Gabriel step from the window to the balcony as if he were fearful of being seen. The boy lifted up his hands and placed the bright box on the rail of the balcony. He looked up at the faint stars for a moment or two, and then carefully released the lid of the box. What came out of it and rose into the air appeared to Codling to be just a piece of floating light, but as it soared above the roof he saw it grow to be a little ancient ship, with its hull and fully set sails and its three masts all of faint primrose flame color. It cleaved through the air, rolling slightly as a ship through the waves, in widening circles above the house, making a curving ascent until it lost the shape of a vessel and became only a moving light hurrying to some sidereal shrine. Codling glanced at the boy on the balcony, but in that brief instant something had happened, the ship had burst like a rocket and released three colored drops of fire which came falling slowly, leaving beautiful gray furrows of smoke in their track. Gabriel leaned over the rail with outstretched palms, and, catching the green star and the blue one as they drifted down to him, he ran with a rill of laughter back into the house. Codling sprang forward just in time to catch the red star; it lay vividly blasting his own palm for a monstrous second, and then, slipping through, was gone. He stared at the ground, at the balcony, the sky, and then heard an exclamation . . . his wife stood at his side.

"Gilbert! How you frightened me!" she cried, "I thought you were in your room; come along in to dinner." She took his arm and they walked up the steps into the dining room together. "Just a moment," said her husband, turning to the door of the room. His hand was upon the handle, which turned easily in his grasp, and he ran upstairs to his own room. He opened the door. The light was on, the fire was burning brightly, a smell of cigarette smoke about, pen and paper upon his desk, the Japanese book-knife, the gilt match-box, everything all right, no one there. He picked up a book from his desk . . . *Monna Vanna.* His bookplate was in it— *Ex Libris*—Gilbert Cannister. He put it down beside the green dish; two yellow oranges were in the green dish, and two most deliberately green Canadian apples rested by their side. He went to the door and swung it backwards and forwards quite easily. He sat on his desk trying to piece the thing together, glaring at the print and the book-knife and the smart matchbox, until his wife came up behind him exclaiming: "Come along, Gilbert!"

"Where are the kids, old man?" he asked her, and, before she replied, he had gone along to the nursery. He saw the two cots, his boy in one, his girl in the other. He turned whimsically to Mildred, saying, "There are only two, are there?" Such a question did not call for reply, but he confronted her as if expecting some assuring answer. She was staring at him with her bright beautiful eyes.

"Are there?" he repeated.

"How strange you should ask me that now!" she said. . . . "If you're a very good man . . . perhaps. . . ."

"Mildred!"

She nodded brightly.

He sat down in the rocking chair, but got up again saying to her gently—"We'll call him Gabriel."

"But, suppose——"

"No, no," he said, stopping her lovely lips, "I know all about him." And he told her a pleasant little tale.

Geese Flying South

AUGUST DERLETH

August Derleth was born in 1909 at Sauk City, Wisconsin, where his family has lived for almost a century, and has made his home town and region the field of his already extensive work as a writer. He planned his "Sac Prairie Saga" while still a student at the University of Wisconsin, where he graduated in 1930. He has completed a dozen volumes—novels, short stories, poetry, journals—of the fifty or more projected for this series. A regionalist in the best sense, avid student of local history and sensitive observer of nature and of human nature in his immediate environment, he stresses constantly attitudes and experiences which are universal in significance. He lives at Sauk City, and lectures for a few weeks each winter on regional literature at the University of Wisconsin.

NEITHER my grandfather nor my grandmother would go to bed that night. They sat looking at each other and all the time my Aunt Cella was getting more nervous. I suspected from the start that the old folks might guess what it was all about. Anyway, I knew from the way he looked that my grandfather didn't think it was natural for the family to be gathered around looking so uneasy.

Aunt Cella had said that something would have to be done about grandmother, who was losing her faculties, losing her mind, Aunt Cella said candidly. We were surprised to hear it, but we thought Aunt Cella ought to know since she lived with the old folks. There we were, every part of the family represented, my grandparents, Aunt Cella, Uncle Burdace, Uncle Frank, and I. My father could not come and sent me instead.

My grandfather sat across the table from my grandmother, one hand resting laxly on his knee, palm upward, the other grasping his cane, fondling the handle gently from time to time. My grandmother sat with her hands clasped in her lap, her dimming eyes fixed on my grandfather, her thin, sharp face slightly pale. Aunt Cella, whose gaunt, hollow eyes seemed to be everywhere at once, kept moving around the room, fidgeting here and there with little things, and my uncles talked to one another and to my grandparents. I sat back and waited for them to do something, or to hint to my grandparents to go to bed. Several times I wished Aunt Cella would stop braiding her hands together and do something else with them.

Uncle Burdace was saying something about blacksmithing in the old days when suddenly my grandmother said, "There's a big flock of geese flying around the house. They're lost. I can hear them."

For a moment no one said anything.

Then Aunt Cella nodded significantly and said, "Now, Ma, if you hear anything, it's probably a dog barking somewhere."

My grandmother looked at Aunt Cella and smiled. Then she said with a very detached air, "No, they're geese. I've heard them often enough before. I can't imagine any one mistaking a dog's barking for the honking of geese." Then she settled together a little and looked back at my grandfather.

"I can remember," he said, "how we heard them that night at your brother's place in Eau Claire. All night long. It was a night like this. Dark and rainy."

"Yes," said my grandmother. "I remember that very well."

For a few moments everyone was quiet. Aunt Cella kept nodding dolefully and let her fingers push nervously at her hair, which was straggling down one side of her head.

Then my grandmother said, "There must be near five hundred of them."

Aunt Cella trembled and got up and went out of the room. I followed her. We went outside and stood on the porch, and there, sure enough, were the geese, hundreds of them, flying in circles against the gray sky, so low that we could see them clearly despite the murky night. They were honking confusedly, loudly. Aunt Cella pressed her thin body against the porch rail and looked up at them. She stood there for a while, her face gray in the mist, her eyes dark and lost. She jerked nervously around and looked at me. She didn't say anything.

When we came back to the front room, my grandmother was talking. "Most likely the streetlights are confusing them," she was saying.

"Or perhaps they lost their leader," my grandfather said.

The old folks were talking just to each other; they were ignoring the rest of us as if we weren't there at all. I wondered whether they were doing it on purpose.

"I remember that night in Eau Claire," my grandmother went on, "how low they were that night. Almost right up against the streetlights. And what a noise they made. Pretty near all night, too. My, but that was a sight and a thing to remember."

My grandfather smiled and nodded at her.

"There *are* wild geese," said Aunt Cella with the helpless air of giving the point to grandmother.

"Yes, of course, there are," said my grandmother, very detached.

Aunt Cella looked uncertainly from Uncle Burdace to Uncle Frank. She began to twist her fingers nervously, and a worried look grew on her face.

Uncle Burdace pulled out his watch and looked at it. "Nine-thirty," he said slowly. "A little after already." He looked irritated.

Uncle Frank said something about watches, and Aunt Cella said that nobody could beat grandfather's old watch for accuracy. "What does your watch say, Pa?" she asked.

My grandfather took out his watch and said, "Nine twenty-nine." Then he put it back into his pocket and looked speculatively out of the window into the glow shed by the streetlight beyond.

"Likely that honking will go on all night," said my grandmother.

My grandfather smiled at her. "I guess it will," he said.

"They don't seem to be flying any too well," my grandmother went on. "Must be they lost their leader. Likely shot. Seems they're making pretty small circles."

"Now, Ma," protested Aunt Cella. "You can't tell that by sitting here. You know you can't. You shouldn't put on that way."

My grandmother looked at her. Her eyes were tired, but she took in Aunt Cella and smiled at her as if she were a little child. "Pa and I have heard wild geese before," she said gently. "Pa and I have heard them lost at night."

"But you can't tell that, Ma," continued Aunt Cella, looking toward my uncles for support. "You can't tell it just by sitting here like this."

"When you've heard wild geese before," continued my grandmother patiently, "you learn their cries, yes, you do,

and the sounds they make, and what they mean. Your Pa
and I have heard them often enough before. It's knowing
what they say to each other."

Aunt Cella looked from Uncle Burdace to Uncle Frank.
Neither of them said anything. She looked at me and sighed.
She made as if to get up but changed her mind.

"I guess I'll go out and watch them," I said.

I went out on the porch and watched the geese wavering
around against the dark sky. Sometimes I couldn't see them
at all, and sometimes they were whitish against the black
clouds, and sometimes dark against light fleece-like clouds
behind which the moon was shining somewhere. They were
flying in widening circles, but every little while some of the
geese would break the circle and it would have to be started
all over again. They had been following the river down, and
they were only about a third of a mile from the river, but
they couldn't see it because of the lights, which blinded
them. They were still honking loudly when I turned and
went back into the front room.

My grandmother said, "Well, August, they were flying
in circles, weren't they?"

"*Ja,*" I said. "Small circles."

She nodded, smiling. Aunt Cella didn't know what to
make of it. I thought of my grandmother's guessing like that
and pretty soon it came to me that if the geese had been flying in a straight line in any direction except west, or even
in a large circle, they would have got to see the river because
the river went around east of the town from the northwest
to the southwest.

I began to smile, too, and my grandmother looked at me
and her eyes twinkled.

Aunt Cella got up and began to move nervously about;
she went into an adjoining room and stood there for a while
in the dark. Uncle Burdace said something under his breath

and went to the telephone and called up my Aunt Josephine to say that he would be home pretty soon, but if he was delayed, she shouldn't worry about it.

Uncle Frank pulled out his watch and said, "After ten already. My, but you two are keeping late hours." He said this jokingly, but he sounded anxious.

My grandmother said, "I remember once your Pa and I stayed up for two nights in a row and weren't tired enough to speak of the third night. That was at the World's Fair in Chicago, I guess."

My grandfather nodded.

Uncle Frank's face fell, and he looked at Uncle Burdace, and together the two of them looked at Aunt Cella.

"It isn't always," my grandmother went on, "that we can have our children around us like this, is it, Pa?"

"No, I guess not," my grandfather said.

I had the feeling that they were laughing behind their faces.

"My, how these geese do honk," my grandmother said suddenly. "I remember one night before we were married, Pa, when we got caught in a shower at Grell's Mill, how we heard the geese go honking by over us, and how they honked and honked. I remember that we sat in the buggy under that old elm tree right near the bridge, remember that, Pa?"

"I remember it well," said my grandfather.

"And how the rain let up after a while," my grandmother went on. "I remember after I was home that night how I heard the geese flying over all night long. Cold weather came right after—a long spell."

My grandfather nodded and smiled and my grandmother nodded and smiled, and they looked at each other, saying nothing. I began to feel rather foolish.

"I'm going outside for a cigarette," I said.

I went out on the porch again. The geese were still flying endlessly around. If there were five hundred of them before, there were over a thousand now. They were flying this way and that, around and across, hopelessly mixed up. Their honking came louder because there were more of them. The rain had stopped and the leaves on the ground smelled richly. There was a faint smell of burning leaves, of smudging smoke, in the air, too. The moon was coming a little clearer behind the thinning clouds. If it came out, the geese might be able to find the river again. I went back into the front room after I had finished the cigarette.

"What a noise they make!" I said into the silent room.

"There'll be no sleep for most of us tonight," said my grandmother. "I've been woke up every year now by the geese flying south in fall. I got so I expect them."

Suddenly Uncle Frank pulled out his watch again and said, "I guess I'll make that ten-forty train."

Aunt Cella jumped and said, "But, Frank!" She looked hopelessly at my grandparents.

Uncle Frank looked at her irritably and said, "I got business to attend to. Anyway, I promised Ella and the kids I'd be home tonight."

My grandfather said, "You hardly come but you go. I kind of thought you might take Cella with you for a week or so. She needs a rest, running her legs off for us all the time. A week in Milwaukee would do her good."

Aunt Cella looked at my grandfather as if she had not heard right.

"That's right," said Uncle Frank. "You ought to go out more, Cella."

"Why, you know I can't," said Aunt Cella indignantly.

My grandparents looked at each other.

Uncle Burdace got up and went out into the kitchen. Aunt Cella went after him, closing the door behind her.

They began to talk heatedly. "Pa's right," said Uncle Burdace. "What you need's a rest, Cella."

Uncle Frank got up and opened the door and went into the kitchen. I heard Uncle Burdace say, "I'll drive you down to the station, Frank."

My grandparents looked at each other and smiled.

"Well, I guess we can go to bed, mother," my grandfather said.

My grandmother turned to me and said, "August, open the window a little."

I got up and opened the window.

"My, but I like to hear those geese honking," she said.

Spotted Horses

WILLIAM FAULKNER

William Faulkner was born in Mississippi in 1897, attended the University of Mississippi, and has spent most of his life at the rural town of Oxford in his native State. He served in the British Royal Air Force in France during the World War, and has worked as carpenter, clerk in a bookstore, stoker in a power plant, and film writer in Hollywood. Particularly in the novels *The Sound and the Fury* (1929) and *As I Lay Dying* (1930), he revealed new possibilities in fiction, both in his realistic portrayal of psychological experience and in his parallel development of large numbers of contrasting characters. *The Hamlet* (1940), his most mature work, portrays, with patient attention to details of speech and action and candid realism of effect, the lives of farm and village people of Mississippi.

YES, SIR. Flem Snopes has filled that whole country full of spotted horses. You can hear folks running them all day and all night, whooping and hollering, and the horses running back and forth across them little wooden bridges ever now and then kind of like thunder. Here I was this morning pretty near half way to town, with the team ambling along and me setting in the buckboard about half asleep, when all of a sudden something come swurging up outen the bushes and jumped the road clean, without touching hoof to it. It flew right over my team, big as a billboard and flying through the air like a hawk. It taken me thirty minutes to stop my team and untangle the harness and the buckboard and hitch them up again.

That Flem Snopes. I be dog if he ain't a case, now. One morning about ten years ago, the boys was just getting settled down on Varner's porch for a little talk and tobacco, when here come Flem out from behind the counter, with his coat off and his hair all parted, like he might have been clerking for Varner for ten years already. Folks all knowed him; it was a big family of them about five miles down the bottom. That year, at least. Sharecropping. They never stayed on any place over a year. Then they would move on to another place, with the chap or maybe the twins of that year's litter. It was a regular nest of them. But Flem. The rest of them stayed tenant farmers, moving ever year, but here come Flem one day, walking out from behind Jody Varner's counter like he owned it. And he wasn't there but a year or two before folks knowed that, if him and Jody was both still in that store in ten years more, it would be Jody clerking for Flem Snopes. Why, that fellow could make a nickel where it wasn't but four cents to begin with. He skun me in two trades, myself, and the fellow that can do that, I just hope he'll get rich before I do; that's all.

All right. So here Flem was, clerking at Varner's, making a nickel here and there and not telling nobody about it. No, sir. Folks never knowed when Flem got the better of somebody lessen the fellow he beat told it. He'd just set there in the store-chair, chewing his tobacco and keeping his own business to hisself, until about a week later we'd find out it was somebody else's business he was keeping to hisself—provided the fellow he trimmed was mad enough to tell it. That's Flem.

We give him ten years to own ever thing Jody Varner had. But he never waited no ten years. I reckon you-all know that gal of Uncle Billy Varner's, the youngest one; Eula. Jody's sister. Ever Sunday ever yellow-wheeled buggy and curried riding horse in that country would be hitched to Bill Varner's fence, and the young bucks setting on the porch, swarming around Eula like bees around a honey pot. One of these here kind of big, soft-looking gals that could giggle richer than plowed new-ground. Wouldn't none of them leave before the others, and so they would set there on the porch until time to go home, with some of them with nine and ten miles to ride and then get up to-morrow and go back to the field. So they would all leave together and they would ride in a clump down to the creek ford and hitch them curried horses and yellow-wheeled buggies and get out and fight one another. Then they would get in the buggies again and go on home.

Well, one day about a year ago, one of them yellow-wheeled buggies and one of them curried saddle-horses quit this country. We heard they was heading for Texas. The next day Uncle Billy and Eula and Flem come into town in Uncle Bill's surrey, and when they come back, Flem and Eula was married. And on the next day we heard that two more of them yellow-wheeled buggies had left the country. They mought have gone to Texas, too. It's a big place.

Anyway, about a month after the wedding, Flem and Eula went to Texas, too. They was gone pretty near a year. Then one day last month, Eula come back, with a baby. We figgered up, and we decided that it was as well-growed a three-months-old baby as we ever see. It can already pull up on a chair. I reckon Texas makes big men quick, being a big place. Anyway, if it keeps on like it started, it'll be chewing tobacco and voting time it's eight years old.

And so last Friday here come Flem himself. He was on

a wagon with another fellow. The other fellow had one of these two-gallon hats and a ivory-handled pistol and a box of gingersnaps sticking out of his hind pocket, and tied to the tail-gate of the wagon was about two dozen of them Texas ponies, hitched to one another with barbed wire. They was colored like parrots and they was quiet as doves, and ere a one of them would kill you quick as a rattlesnake. Nere a one of them had two eyes the same color, and nere a one of them had ever seen a bridle, I reckon; and when that Texas man got down offen the wagon and walked up to them to show how gentle they was, one of them cut his vest clean offen him, same as with a razor.

Flem had done already disappeared; he had went on to see his wife, I reckon, and to see if that ere baby had done gone on to the field to help Uncle Billy plow, maybe. It was the Texas man that taken the horses on to Mrs. Littlejohn's lot. He had a little trouble at first, when they come to the gate, because they hadn't never see a fence before, and when he finally got them in and taken a pair of wire cutters and unhitched them and got them into the barn and poured some shell corn into the trough, they durn nigh tore down the barn. I reckon they thought that shell corn was bugs, maybe. So he left them in the lot and he announced that the auction would begin at sunup to-morrow.

That night we was setting on Mrs. Littlejohn's porch. You-all mind the moon was nigh full that night, and we could watch them spotted varmints swirling along the fence and back and forth across the lot same as minnows in a pond. And then now and then they would all kind of huddle up against the barn and rest themselves by biting and kicking one another. We would hear a squeal, and then a set of hoofs would go Bam! against the barn, like a pistol. It sounded just like a fellow with a pistol, in a nest of catty-mounts, taking his time.

It wasn't ere a man knowed yet if Flem owned them things or not. They just knowed one thing: that they wasn't never going to know for sho if Flem did or not, or if maybe he didn't just get on that wagon at the edge of town, for the ride or not. Even Eck Snopes didn't know, Flem's own cousin. But wasn't nobody surprised at that. We knowed that Flem would skin Eck quick as he would ere a one of us.

They was there by sunup next morning, some of them come twelve and sixteen miles, with seed-money tied up in tobacco sacks in their overalls, standing along the fence, when the Texas man come out of Mrs. Littlejohn's after breakfast and clumb onto the gate post with that ere white pistol butt sticking outen his hind pocket. He taken a new box of gingersnaps outen his pocket and bit the end offen it like a cigar and spit out the paper, and said the auction was open. And still they was coming up in wagons and a horse- and mule-back and hitching the teams across the road and coming to the fence. Flem wasn't nowhere in sight.

But he couldn't get them started. He begun to work on Eck, because Eck holp him last night to get them into the barn and feed them that shell corn. Eck got out just in time. He come outen that barn like a chip on the crest of a busted dam of water, and clumb into the wagon just in time.

He was working on Eck when Henry Armstid come up in his wagon. Eck was saying he was skeered to bid on one of them, because he might get it, and the Texas man says, "Them ponies? Them little horses?" He clumb down offen the gate post and went toward the horses. They broke and run, and him following them, kind of chirping to them, with his hand out like he was fixing to catch a fly, until he got three or four of them cornered. Then he jumped into them, and then we couldn't see nothing for a while because of the dust. It was a big cloud of it, and them blare-eyed, spotted things swoaring outen it twenty foot to a

jump, in forty directions without counting up. Then the
dust settled and there they was, that Texas man and the
horse. He had its head twisted clean around like a owl's
head. Its legs was braced and it was trembling like a new
bride and groaning like a saw mill, and him holding its
head wrung clean around on its neck so it was snuffing sky.
"Look it over," he says, with his heels dug too and that
white pistol sticking outen his pocket and his neck swole
up like a spreading adder's until you could just tell what
he was saying, cussing the horse and talking to us all at
once: "Look him over, the fiddle-headed son of fourteen
fathers. Try him, buy him; you will get the best—" Then
it was all dust again, and we couldn't see nothing but
spotted hide and mane, and that ere Texas man's boot-heels
like a couple of walnuts on two strings, and after a while
that two-gallon hat come sailing out like a fat old hen
crossing a fence.

When the dust settled again, he was just getting outen
the far fence corner, brushing himself off. He come and
got his hat and brushed it off and come and clumb onto the
gate post again. He was breathing hard. He taken the
gingersnap box outen his pocket and et one, breathing hard.
The hammerhead horse was still running round and round
the lot like a merry-go-round at a fair. That was when
Henry Armstid come shoving up to the gate in them
patched overalls and one of them dangle-armed shirts of
hisn. Hadn't nobody noticed him until then. We was all
watching the Texas man and the horses. Even Mrs. Littlejohn; she had done come out and built a fire under the
wash-pot in her back yard, and she would stand at the
fence a while and then go back into the house and come
out again with a arm full of wash and stand at the fence
again. Well, here come Henry shoving up, and then we
see Mrs. Armstid right behind him, in that ere faded wrap-

per and sunbonnet and them tennis shoes. "Git on back to that wagon," Henry says.

"Henry," she says.

"Here, boys," the Texas man says; "make room for missus to git up and see. Come on, Henry," he says; "here's your chance to buy that saddle-horse missus has been wanting. What about ten dollars, Henry?"

"Henry," Mrs. Armstid says. She put her hand on Henry's arm. Henry knocked her hand down.

"Git on back in that wagon, like I told you," he says.

Mrs. Armstid never moved. She stood behind Henry, with her hands rolled into her dress, not looking at nothing. "He hain't no more despair than to buy one of them things," she says. "And us not five dollars ahead of the pore house, he hain't no more despair." It was the truth, too. They ain't never made more than a bare living offen that place of theirs, and them with four chaps and the very clothes they wears she earns by weaving by the firelight at night while Henry's asleep.

"Shut your mouth and git on back to that wagon," Henry says. "Do you want I taken a wagon stake to you here in the big road?"

Well, that Texas man taken one look at her. Then he begun on Eck again, like Henry wasn't even there. But Eck was skeered. "I can git me a snapping turtle or a water moccasin for nothing. I ain't going to buy none."

So the Texas man said he would give Eck a horse. "To start the auction, and because you holp me last night. If you'll start the bidding on the next horse," he says, "I'll give you that fiddle-head horse."

I wish you could have seen them, standing there with their seed-money in their pockets, watching that Texas man give Eck Snopes a live horse, all fixed to call him a fool if he taken it or not. Finally Eck says he'll take it. "Only

I just starts the bidding," he says. "I don't have to buy the next one lessen I ain't overtopped." The Texas man said all right, and Eck bid a dollar on the next one, with Henry Armstid standing there with his mouth already open, watching Eck and the Texas man like a mad-dog or something. "A dollar," Eck says.

The Texas man looked at Eck. His mouth was already open too, like he had started to say something and what he was going to say had up and died on him. "A dollar?" he says. "One dollar? You mean, one dollar, Eck?"

"Durn it," Eck says; "two dollars, then."

Well, sir, I wish you could a seen that Texas man. He taken out that gingersnap box and held it up and looked into it, careful, like it might have been a diamond ring in it, or a spider. Then he throwed it away and wiped his face with a bandanna. "Well," he says. "Well. Two dollars. Two dollars. Is your pulse all right, Eck?" he says. "Do you have ager-sweats at night, maybe?" he says. "Well," he says, "I got to take it. But are you boys going to stand there and see Eck get two horses at a dollar a head?"

That done it. I be dog if he wasn't nigh as smart as Flem Snopes. He hadn't no more than got the words outen his mouth before here was Henry Armstid, waving his hand. "Three dollars," Henry says. Mrs. Armstid tried to hold him again. He knocked her hand off, shoving up to the gate post.

"Mister," Mrs. Armstid says, "we got chaps in the house and not corn to feed the stock. We got five dollars I earned my chaps a-weaving after dark, and him snoring in the bed. And he hain't no more despair."

"Henry bids three dollars," the Texas man says. "Raise him a dollar, Eck, and the horse is yours."

"Henry," Mrs. Armstid says.

"Raise him, Eck," the Texas man says.

"Four dollars," Eck says.

"Five dollars," Henry says, shaking his fist. He shoved up right under the gate post. Mrs. Armstid was looking at the Texas man too.

"Mister," she says, "if you take that five dollars I earned my chaps a-weaving for one of them things, it'll be a curse onto you and yourn during all the time of man."

But it wasn't no stopping Henry. He had shoved up, waving his fist at the Texas man. He opened it; the money was in nickels and quarters, and one dollar bill that looked like a cow's cud. "Five dollars," he says. "And the man that raises it'll have to beat my head off, or I'll beat hisn."

"All right," the Texas man says. "Five dollars is bid. But don't you shake your hand at me."

It taken till nigh sundown before the last one was sold. He got them hotted up once and the bidding got up to seven dollars and a quarter, but most of them went around three or four dollars, him setting on the gate post and picking the horses out one at a time by mouth-word, and Mrs. Littlejohn pumping up and down at the tub and stopping and coming to the fence for a while and going back to the tub again. She had done got done too, and the wash was hung on the line in the back yard, and we could smell supper cooking. Finally they was all sold; he swapped the last two and the wagon for a buckboard.

We was all kind of tired, but Henry Armstid looked more like a mad-dog than ever. When he bought, Mrs. Armstid had went back to the wagon, setting in it behind them two rabbit-sized, bone-pore mules, and the wagon itself looking like it would fall all to pieces soon as the mules moved. Henry hadn't even waited to pull it outen the road; it was still in the middle of the road and her setting in it, not looking at nothing, ever since this morning.

Henry was right up against the gate. He went up to the Texas man. "I bought a horse and I paid cash," Henry says. "And yet you expect me to stand around here until they are all sold before I can get my horse. I'm going to take my horse outen that lot."

The Texas man looked at Henry. He talked like he might have been asking for a cup of coffee at the table. "Take your horse," he says.

Then Henry quit looking at the Texas man. He begun to swallow, holding onto the gate. "Ain't you going to help me?" he says.

"It ain't my horse," the Texas man says.

Henry never looked at the Texas man again, he never looked at nobody. "Who'll help me catch my horse?" he says. Never nobody said nothing. "Bring the plowline," Henry says. Mrs. Armstid got outen the wagon and brought the plowline. The Texas man got down offen the post. The woman made to pass him, carrying the rope.

"Don't you go in there, missus," the Texas man says.

Henry opened the gate. He didn't look back. "Come on here," he says.

"Don't you go in there, missus," the Texas man says.

Mrs. Armstid wasn't looking at nobody, neither, with her hands across her middle, holding the rope. "I reckon I better," she says. Her and Henry went into the lot. The horses broke and run. Henry and Mrs. Armstid followed.

"Get him into the corner," Henry says. They got Henry's horse cornered finally, and Henry taken the rope, but Mrs. Armstid let the horse get out. They hemmed it up again, but Mrs. Armstid let it get out again, and Henry turned and hit her with the rope. "Why didn't you head him back?" Henry says. He hit her again. "Why didn't you?" It was about that time I looked around and see Flem Snopes standing there.

It was the Texas man that done something. He moved

fast for a big man. He caught the rope before Henry could hit the third time, and Henry whirled and made like he would jump at the Texas man. But he never jumped. The Texas man went and taken Henry's arm and led him outen the lot. Mrs. Armstid come behind them and the Texas man taken some money outen his pocket and he give it into Mrs. Armstid's hand. "Get him into the wagon and take him on home," the Texas man says, like he might have been telling them he enjoyed his supper.

Then here comes Flem. "What's that for, Buck?" Flem says.

"Thinks he bought one of them ponies," the Texas man says. "Get him on away, missus."

But Henry wouldn't go. "Give him back that money," he says. "I bought that horse and I aim to have him if I have to shoot him."

And there was Flem, standing there with his hands in his pockets, chewing, like he had just happened to be passing.

"You take your money and I take my horse," Henry says. "Give it back to him," he says to Mrs. Armstid.

"You don't own no horse of mine," the Texas man says. "Get him on home, missus."

Then Henry seen Flem. "You got something to do with these horses," he says. "I bought one. Here's the money for it." He taken the bill outen Mrs. Armstid's hand. He offered it to Flem. "I bought one. Ask him. Here. Here's the money," he says, giving the bill to Flem.

When Flem taken the money, the Texas man dropped the rope he had snatched outen Henry's hand. He had done sent Eck Snopes's boy up to the store for another box of gingersnaps, and he taken the box outen his pocket and looked into it. It was empty and he dropped it on the ground. "Mr. Snopes will have your money for you to-morrow," he says to Mrs. Armstid. "You can get it from him tomorrow. He don't own no horse. You get him into the wagon and get him on home." Mrs. Armstid went back to the wagon and got in. "Where's that ere buckboard I bought?" the Texas man says. It was after sundown then. And then Mrs. Littlejohn come out on the porch and rung the supper bell.

I come on in and et supper. Mrs. Littlejohn would bring in a pan of bread or something, then she would go out to the porch a minute and come back and tell us. The Texas man had hitched his team to the buckboard he had swapped them last two horses for, and him and Flem had gone, and then she told that the rest of them that never had ropes had went back to the store with I. O. Snopes to get some ropes, and wasn't nobody at the gate but Henry Armstid, and Mrs. Armstid setting in the wagon in the road, and Eck Snopes and that boy of hisn. "I don't care how many of them fool men gets killed by them things," Mrs. Littlejohn says, "but I ain't going to let Eck Snopes take that boy into that lot again." So she went down to the gate, but she come back without the boy or Eck neither.

"It ain't no need to worry about that boy," I says. "He's charmed." He was right behind Eck last night when Eck went to help feed them. The whole drove of them jumped clean over that boy's head and never touched him. It was Eck that touched him. Eck snatched him into the wagon and taken a rope and frailed the tar outen him.

So I had done et and went to my room and was undressing, long as I had a long trip to make next day; I was trying to sell a machine to Mrs. Bundren up past Whiteleaf; when Henry Armstid opened that gate and went in by hisself. They couldn't make him wait for the balance of them to get back with their ropes. Eck Snopes said he tried to make Henry wait, but Henry wouldn't do it. Eck said Henry walked right up to them and that when they broke, they run clean over Henry like a hay-mow breaking down. Eck said he snatched that boy of hisn out of the way just in time and that them things went through that gate like a creek flood and into the wagons and teams hitched side the road, busting wagon tongues and snapping harness like it was fishing-line, with Mrs. Armstid still setting in their wagon in the middle of it like something carved outen wood. Then they scattered, wild horses and tame mules with pieces of harness and singletrees dangling offen them, both ways up and down the road.

"There goes ourn, paw!" Eck says his boy said. "There it goes, into Mrs. Littlejohn's house." Eck says it run right up the steps and into the house like a boarder late for supper. I reckon so. Anyway, I was in my room, in my underclothes, with one sock in my hand, leaning out the window when the commotion busted out, when I heard something run into the melodeon in the hall; it sounded like a railroad engine. Then the door to my room come sailing in like when you throw a tin bucket top into the wind and I looked over my shoulder and see something that looked like a fourteen-foot pinwheel a-blaring its eyes at me. It had to blare them fast, because I was already done jumped out the window.

I reckon it was anxious, too. I reckon it hadn't never seen underclothes before, or maybe it was a sewing-machine agent it hadn't never seen. Anyway, it swirled and turned to run back up the hall and outen the house, when it met Eck Snopes and that boy just coming in, carrying a rope. It swirled again and run down the hall and out the back door just in time to meet Mrs. Littlejohn. She had just gathered up the clothes she had washed, and she was coming onto the back porch with a armful of washing in one hand and a scrubbing-board in the other, when the horse skidded up to her, trying to stop and swirl again. It never taken Mrs. Littlejohn no time a-tall.

"Git outen here, you son," she says. She hit it across the face with the scrubbing-board; that ere scrubbing-board split as neat as ere a axe could have done it, and when the horse swirled to run back up the hall, she hit it again with what was left of the scrubbing-board, not on the head this time. "And stay out," she says.

Eck and that boy was half-way down the hall by this time. I reckon that horse looked like a pinwheel to Eck too. "Git to hell outen here, Ad!" Eck says. Only there wasn't time. Eck dropped flat on his face, but the boy never moved. The boy was about a yard tall maybe, in overhalls just like Eck's; that horse swoared over his head without touching a hair. I saw that, because I was just coming back up the front steps, still carrying that ere sock and still in my underclothes, when the horse come onto the porch again. It taken one look at me and swirled again and run to the end of the porch and jumped the banisters and the lot fence like a hen-hawk and lit in the lot running and went out the gate again and jumped eight or ten upside-down wagons and went on down the road. It was a full moon then. Mrs. Armstid was still setting in the wagon like she had done been carved outen wood and left there and forgot.

That horse. It never missed a lick. It was going about forty miles a hour when it come to the bridge over the creek. It would have had a clear road, but it so happened that Vernon Tull was already using the bridge when it got there. He was coming back from town; he hadn't heard about the auction; him and his wife and three daughters and Mrs. Tull's aunt, all setting in chairs in the wagon bed, and all asleep, including the mules. They waked up when the horse hit the bridge one time, but Tull said the first he knew was when the mules tried to turn the wagon around in the middle of the bridge and he seen that spotted varmint run right twixt the mules and run up the wagon tongue like a squirrel. He said he just had time to hit it across the face with his whipstock, because about that time the mules turned the wagon around on that ere one-way bridge and that horse clumb across one of the mules and jumped down onto the bridge again and went on, with Vernon standing up in the wagon and kicking at it.

Tull said the mules turned in the harness and clumb back into the wagon, too, with Tull trying to beat them out again, with the reins wrapped around his wrist. After that he says all he seen was overturned chairs and women-folks' legs and white drawers shining in the moonlight, and his mules and that spotted horse going on up the road like a ghost.

The mules jerked Tull outen the wagon and drug him a spell on the bridge before the reins broke. They thought at first that he was dead, and while they was kneeling around him, picking the bridge splinters outen him, here come Eck and that boy, still carrying the rope. They was running and breathing a little hard. "Where'd he go?" Eck says.

I went back and got my pants and shirt and shoes on just in time to go and help get Henry Armstid outen the trash in the lot. I be dog if he didn't look like he was dead, with his head hanging back and his teeth showing in the moonlight, and a little rim of white under his eye-lids. We could still hear them horses, here and there; hadn't none of them got more than four-five miles away yet, not knowing the country, I reckon. So we could hear them and folks yelling now and then: "Whooey. Head him."

We toted Henry into Mrs. Littlejohn's. She was in the

hall; she hadn't put down the armful of clothes. She taken one look at us, and she laid down the busted scrubbing board and taken up the lamp and opened a empty door. "Bring him in here," she says.

We toted him in and laid him on the bed. Mrs. Little-john set the lamp on the dresser, still carrying the clothes. "I'll declare, you men," she says. Our shadows was way up the wall, tiptoeing too; we could hear ourselves breath-ing. "Better get his wife," Mrs. Littlejohn says. She went out, carrying the clothes.

"I reckon we had," Quick says. "Go get her, somebody."

"Whyn't you go?" Winterbottom says.

"Let Ernest git her," Durley says. "He lives neighbors with them."

Ernest went to fetch her. I be dog if Henry didn't look like he was dead. Mrs. Littlejohn come back, with a kettle and some towels. She went to work on Henry, and then Mrs. Armstid and Ernest come in. Mrs. Armstid come to the foot of the bed and stood there, with her hands rolled into her apron, watching what Mrs. Littlejohn was doing, I reckon.

"You men get outen the way," Mrs. Littlejohn says. "Go outside," she says. "See if you can't find something else to play with that will kill some more of you."

"Is he dead?" Winterbottom says.

"It ain't your fault if he ain't," Mrs. Littlejohn says. "Go tell Will Varner to come up here. I reckon a man ain't so different from a mule, come long come short. Except maybe a mule's got more sense."

We went to get Uncle Billy. It was a full moon. We could hear them, now and then, four mile away: "Whooey. Head him." The country was full of them, one on ever wooden bridge in the land, running across it like thunder: "Whooey. There he goes. Head him."

We hadn't got far before Henry begun to scream. I

reckon Mrs. Littlejohn's water had brung him to; anyway, he wasn't dead. We went on to Uncle Billy's. The house was dark. We called to him, and after a while the window opened and Uncle Billy put his head out, peart as a pecker-wood, listening. "Are they still trying to catch them durn rabbits?" he says.

He come down, with his britches on over his nightshirt and his suspenders dangling, carrying his horse-doctoring grip. "Yes, sir," he says, cocking his head like a wood-pecker; "they're still a-trying."

We could hear Henry before we reached Mrs. Little-john's. He was going Ah-Ah-Ah. We stopped in the yard. Uncle Billy went on in. We could hear Henry. We stood in the yard, hearing them on the bridges, this-a-way and that: "Whooey. Whooey."

"Eck Snopes ought to caught hisn," Ernest says. "Looks like he ought," Winterbottom said.

Henry was going Ah-Ah-Ah steady in the house; then he begun to scream. "Uncle Billy's started," Quick says. We looked into the hall. We could see the light where the door was. Then Mrs. Littlejohn come out.

"Will needs some help," she says. "You, Ernest. You'll do." Ernest went into the house.

"Hear them?" Quick said. "That one was on Four-Mile Bridge." We could hear them; it sounded like thunder a long way off. It didn't last long:

"Whooey."

We could hear Henry: "Ah-Ah-Ah-Ah-Ah."

"They are both started now," Winterbottom says. "Ernest too."

That was early in the night. Which was a good thing, because it taken a long night for folks to chase them things right and for Henry to lay there and holler, being Uncle Billy never had none of this here chloryfoam to set Henry's leg with. So it was considerate in Flem to get them started early. And what do you reckon Flem's com-ment was? That's right. Nothing. Because he wasn't there. Hadn't nobody see him since that Texas man left.

That was Saturday night. I reckon Mrs. Armstid got home about daylight, to see about the chaps. I don't know where they thought her and Henry was. But lucky the oldest one was a gal, about twelve, big enough to take care of the little ones. Which she did for the next two days. Mrs. Armstid would nurse Henry all night and work in the kitchen for hern and Henry's keep, and in the afternoon she would drive home (it was about four miles) to see to the chaps. She would cook up a pot of victuals and leave it on the stove, and the gal would bar the house and keep the little ones quiet. I would hear Mrs. Littlejohn and Mrs. Armstid talking in the kitchen. "How are the chaps making out?" Mrs. Littlejohn says.

"All right," Mrs. Armstid says.

"Don't they git skeered at night?" Mrs. Littlejohn says.

"Ina May bars the door when I leave," Mrs. Armstid says. "She's got the axe in bed with her. I reckon she can make out."

I reckon they did. And I reckon Mrs. Armstid was waiting for Flem to come back to town; hadn't nobody seen him until this morning; to get her money the Texas man said Flem was keeping for her. Sho. I reckon she was.

Anyway, I heard Mrs. Armstid and Mrs. Littlejohn talking in the kitchen this morning while I was eating breakfast. Mrs. Littlejohn had just told Mrs. Armstid that Flem was in town. "You can ask him for that five dollars," Mrs. Littlejohn says.

"You reckon he'll give it to me?" Mrs. Armstid says.

Mrs. Littlejohn was washing dishes, washing them like a man, like they was made out of iron. "No," she says. "But asking him won't do no hurt. It might shame him. I don't reckon it will, but it might."

"If he wouldn't give it back, it ain't no use to ask," Mrs. Armstid says.

"Suit yourself," Mrs. Littlejohn says. "It's your money." I could hear the dishes.

"Do you reckon he might give it back to me?" Mrs. Armstid says. "That Texas man said he would. He said I could get it from Mr. Snopes later."

"Then go and ask him for it," Mrs. Littlejohn says. I could hear the dishes.

"He won't give it back to me," Mrs. Armstid says.

"All right," Mrs. Littlejohn says. "Don't ask him for it, then."

I could hear the dishes; Mrs. Armstid was helping. "You don't reckon he would, do you?" she says. Mrs. Littlejohn never said nothing. It sounded like she was throwing the dishes at one another. "Maybe I better go and talk to Henry about it," Mrs. Armstid says.

"I would," Mrs. Littlejohn says. I be dog if it didn't sound like she had two plates in her hands, beating them together. "Then Henry can buy another five-dollar horse with it. Maybe he'll buy one next time that will out and out kill him. If I thought that, I'd give you back the money, myself."

"I reckon I better talk to him first," Mrs. Armstid said. Then it sounded like Mrs. Littlejohn taken up all the dishes and throwed them at the cook-stove, and I come away.

That was this morning. I had been up to Bundren's and back, and I thought that things would have kind of settled down. So after breakfast, I went up to the store. And there was Flem, setting in the store chair and whittling, like he might not have ever moved since he came to clerk for Jody Varner. I. O. was leaning in the door, in his shirt sleeves and with his hair parted too, same as Flem was before he turned the clerking job over to I. O. It's a funny thing about them Snopes: they all look alike, yet there ain't ere a two of them that claims brothers. They're always just cousins, like Flem and Eck and Flem and I. O. Eck was there too, squatting against the wall, him and that boy, eating cheese and crackers outen a sack; they told me that Eck hadn't been home a-tall. And that Lon Quick hadn't got back to town, even. He followed his horse clean down to Samson's Bridge, with a wagon and a camp outfit. Eck finally caught one of hisn. It run into a blind lane at Freeman's, and Eck and the boy taken and tied their rope across the end of the lane, about three foot high. The horse come to the end of the lane and whirled and run back without ever stopping. Eck says it never seen the rope a-tall. He says it looked just like one of these here Christmas pinwheels. "Didn't it try to run again?" I says.

"No," Eck says, eating a bite of cheese offen his knife blade. "Just kicked some."

"Kicked some?" I says.

"It broke its neck," Eck says.

Well, they was squatting there, about six of them, talking, talking at Flem; never nobody knowed yet if Flem had ere a interest in them horses or not. So finally I come right out and asked him. "Flem's done skun all of us so much," I says, "that we're proud of him. Come on, Flem," I says, "how much did you and that Texas man make offen them horses? You can tell us. Ain't nobody here but Eck that bought one of them; the others ain't got back to town yet, and Eck's your own cousin; he'll be proud to hear, too. How much did you-all make?"

They was all whittling, not looking at Flem, making like they was studying. But you could a heard a pin drop. And I. O. He had been rubbing his back up and down on the door, but he stopped now, watching Flem like a pointing dog. Flem finished cutting the sliver offen his stick.

He spit across the porch, into the road. " 'Twarn't none of my horses," he says.

I. O. cackled, like a hen, slapping his legs with both hands. "You boys might just as well quit trying to get ahead of Flem," he said.

Well, about that time I see Mrs. Armstid come outen Mrs. Littlejohn's gate, coming up the road. I never said nothing. I says, "Well, if a man can't take care of himself in a trade, he can't blame the man that trims him."

Flem never said nothing, trimming at the stick. He hadn't seen Mrs. Armstid. "Yes, sir," I says. "A fellow like Henry Armstid ain't got nobody but hisself to blame."

"Course he ain't," I. O. says. He ain't seen her, neither. "Henry Armstid's a born fool. Always is been. If Flem hadn't a got his money, somebody else would."

We looked at Flem. He never moved. Mrs. Armstid come on up the road.

"That's right," I says. "But, come to think of it, Henry never bought no horse." We looked at Flem; you could a heard a match drop. "That Texas man told her to get that five dollars back from Flem next day. I reckon Flem's done already taken that money to Mrs. Littlejohn's and give it to Mrs. Armstid."

We watched Flem. I. O. quit rubbing his back against the door again. After a while Flem raised his head and spit across the porch, into the dust. I. O. cackled, just like a hen. "Ain't he a beating fellow, now?" I. O. says.

Mrs. Armstid was getting closer, so I kept on talking, watching to see if Flem would look up and see her. But he never looked up. I went on talking about Tull, about how he was going to sue Flem, and Flem setting there, whittling his stick, not saying nothing else after he said they wasn't none of his horses.

Then I. O. happened to look around. He seen Mrs. Armstid. "Psssst!" he says. Flem looked up. "Here she

comes!" I. O. says. "Go out the back. I'll tell her you done
went to town today."

But Flem never moved. He just set there, whittling, and
we watched Mrs. Armstid come up onto the porch, in that
ere faded sunbonnet and wrapper and them tennis shoes
that made a kind of hissing noise on the porch. She come
onto the porch and stopped, her hands rolled into her dress
in front, not looking at nothing.

"He said Saturday," she says, "that he wouldn't sell Henry
no horse. He said I could get the money from you."

Flem looked up. The knife never stopped. It went on
trimming off a sliver same as if he was watching it. "He
taken that money off with him when he left," Flem says.

Mrs. Armstid never looked at nothing. We never looked
at her, neither, except that boy of Eck's. He had a half-et
cracker in his hand, watching her, chewing.

"He said Henry hadn't bought no horse," Mrs. Armstid
says. "He said for me to get the money from you today."

"I reckon he forgot about it," Flem said. "He taken that
money off with him Saturday." He whittled again. I. O.
kept on rubbing his back, slow. He licked his lips. After
a while the woman looked up the road, where it went on
up the hill, toward the graveyard. She looked up that way
for a while, with that boy of Eck's watching her and I. O.
rubbing his back slow against the door. Then she turned
back toward the steps.

"I reckon it's time to get dinner started," she says.

"How's Henry this morning, Mrs. Armstid?" Winterbottom says.

She looked at Winterbottom; she almost stopped. "He's
resting, I thank you kindly," she says.

Flem got up, outen the chair, putting his knife away.
He spit across the porch. "Wait a minute, Mrs. Armstid,"
he says. She stopped again. She didn't look at him. Flem

went on into the store, with I. O. done quit rubbing his back now, with his head craned after Flem, and Mrs. Armstid standing there with her hands rolled into her dress, not looking at nothing. A wagon come up the road and passed; it was Freeman, on the way to town. Then Flem come out again, with I. O. still watching him. Flem had one of these little striped sacks of Jody Varner's candy; I bet he still owes Jody that nickel, too. He put the sack into Mrs. Armstid's hand, like he would have put it into a hollow stump. He spit again across the porch. "A little sweetening for the chaps," he says.

"You're right kind," Mrs. Armstid says. She held the sack of candy in her hand, not looking at nothing. Eck's boy was watching the sack, the half-et cracker in his hand; he wasn't chewing now. He watched Mrs. Armstid roll the sack into her apron. "I reckon I better get on back and help with dinner," she says. She turned and went back across the porch. Flem sat down in the chair again and opened his knife. He spit across the porch again, past Mrs. Armstid where she hadn't went down the steps yet. Then she went on, in that ere sunbonnet and wrapper all the same color, back down the road toward Mrs. Littlejohn's. You couldn't see her dress move, like a natural woman walking. She looked like a old snag still standing up and moving along on a high water. We watched her turn in at Mrs. Little-john's and go outen sight. Flem was whittling. I. O. begun to rub his back on the door. Then he begun to cackle, just like a durn hen.

"You boys might just as well quit trying," I. O. says. "You can't git ahead of Flem. You can't touch him. Ain't he a sight, now?"

I be dog if he ain't. If I had brung a herd of wild catty-mounts into town and sold them to my neighbors and kinfolks, they would have lynched me. Yes, sir.

Babylon Revisited

F. SCOTT FITZGERALD

F. Scott Fitzgerald was born in 1896 at St. Paul, Minnesota. He spent much of his boyhood in Syracuse and Buffalo, New York, and at the Newman School in Hackensack, New Jersey. At Princeton he was active in amateur theatricals, but left the university to enter the army in 1917. After the war he wrote advertising copy and magazine stories until the success of his first novel, *This Side of Paradise* (1920). In this novel and *The Beautiful and Damned* (1922) and in his short stories of the early '20s Fitzgerald recorded with brilliant facility the more sensational aspects of the times, particularly the lives of idle and wealthy young people. His later novels, *The Great Gatsby* (1925) and *Tender Is the Night* (1934), and the short stories collected in *Taps at Reveille* (1935) reveal maturing powers and poignantly sympathetic comprehension of tragic experience. He died in December, 1940.

AND where's Mr. Campbell?" Charlie asked.

"Gone to Switzerland. Mr. Campbell's a pretty sick man, Mr. Wales."

"I'm sorry to hear that. And George Hardt?" Charlie inquired.

"Back in America, gone to work."

"And where is the Snow Bird?"

"He was in here last week. Anyway, his friend, Mr. Schaeffer, is in Paris."

Two familiar names from the long list of a year and a half ago. Charlie scribbled an address in his notebook and tore out the page.

"If you see Mr. Schaeffer, give him this," he said. "It's my brother-in-law's address. I haven't settled on a hotel yet."

He was not really disappointed to find Paris was so empty. But the stillness in the Ritz bar was strange and portentous. It was not an American bar any more—he felt polite in it, and not as if he owned it. It had gone back into France. He felt the stillness from the moment he got out of the taxi and saw the doorman, usually in a frenzy of activity at this hour, gossiping with a *chausseur* by the servants' entrance.

Passing through the corridor, he heard only a single, bored voice in the once-clamorous women's room. When he turned into the bar he travelled the twenty feet of green carpet with his eyes fixed straight ahead by old habit; and then, with his foot firmly on the rail, he turned and surveyed the room, encountering only a single pair of eyes that fluttered up from a newspaper in the corner. Charlie asked for the head barman, Paul, who in the latter days of the bull market had come to work in his own custom-built car—disembarking, however, with due nicety at the nearest corner. But Paul was at his country house today and Alix giving him information.

"No, no more," Charlie said. "I'm going slow these days."

Alix congratulated him: "You were going pretty strong a couple of years ago."

"I'll stick to it all right," Charlie assured him. "I've stuck to it for over a year and a half now."

"How do you find conditions in America?"

"I haven't been to America for months. I'm in business in Prague, representing a couple of concerns there. They don't know about me down there."

Alix smiled.

"Remember the night of George Hardt's bachelor dinner here?" said Charlie. "By the way, what's become of Claude Fessenden?"

Alix lowered his voice confidentially: "He's in Paris, but he doesn't come here any more. Paul doesn't allow it. He ran up a bill of thirty thousand francs, charging all his drinks and his lunches, and usually his dinner, for more than a year. And when Paul finally told him he had to pay, he gave him a bad check."

Alix shook his head sadly.

"I don't understand it, such a dandy fellow. Now he's all bloated up—" He made a plump apple of his hands.

Charlie watched a group of strident queens installing themselves in a corner.

"Nothing affects them," he thought. "Stocks rise and fall, people loaf or work, but they go on forever." The place oppressed him. He called for the dice and shook with Alix for the drink.

"Here for long, Mr. Wales?"

"I'm here for four or five days to see my little girl."

"Oh-h! You have a little girl?"

Outside, the fire-red, gas-blue, ghost-green signs shone smokily through the tranquil rain. It was late afternoon and the streets were in movement; the *bistros* gleamed. At the corner of the Boulevard des Capucines he took a taxi. The Place de la Concorde moved by in pink majesty; they crossed the logical Seine, and Charlie felt the sudden provincial quality of the left bank.

Charlie directed his taxi to the Avenue de l'Opéra, which was out of his way. But he wanted to see the blue hour spread over the magnificent façade, and imagine that the cab horns, playing endlessly the first few bars of *La Pluie que Lent,* were the trumpets of the Second Empire. They were closing the iron grill in front of Brentano's Bookstore, and people were already at dinner behind the trim little bourgeois hedge of Duval's. He had never eaten at a really cheap restaurant in Paris. Five-course dinner, four francs fifty, eighteen cents, wine included. For some odd reason he wished that he had.

As they rolled on to the Left Bank and he felt its sudden provincialism, he thought, "I spoiled this city for myself. I didn't realize it, but the days came along one after another, and then two years were gone, and everything was gone, and I was gone."

He was thirty-five, and good to look at. The Irish mobility of his face was sobered by a deep wrinkle between his eyes. As he rang his brother-in-law's bell in the Rue Palatine, the wrinkle deepened till it pulled down his brows; he felt a cramping sensation in his belly. From behind the maid who opened the door darted a lovely little girl of nine, who shrieked "Daddy!" and flew up, struggling like a fish, into his arms. She pulled his head around by one ear and set her cheek against his.

"My old pie," he said.

"Oh, daddy, daddy, daddy, daddy, dads, dads, dads!"

She drew him into the salon, where the family waited, a boy and girl his daughter's age, his sister-in-law and her husband. He greeted Marion with his voice pitched carefully to avoid either feigned enthusiasm or dislike, but her response was more frankly tepid, though she minimized her expression of unalterable distrust by directing her regard toward his child. The two men clasped hands in a friendly way and Lincoln Peters rested his for a moment on Charlie's shoulder.

The room was warm and comfortably American. The three children moved intimately about, playing through the yellow oblongs that led to other rooms; the cheer of six o'clock spoke in the eager smacks of the fire and the sounds of French activity in the kitchen. But Charlie did not relax; his heart sat up rigidly in his body and he drew confidence from his daughter, who from time to time came close to him, holding in her arms the doll he had brought.

"Really extremely well," he declared in answer to Lincoln's question. "There's a lot of business there that isn't moving at all, but we're doing even better than ever. In fact, damn well. I'm bringing my sister over from America next month to keep house for me. My income last year was bigger than it was when I had money. You see, the Czechs——"

His boasting was for a specific purpose; but after a moment, seeing a faint restiveness in Lincoln's eye, he changed the subject:

"Those are fine children of yours, well brought up, good manners."

"We think Honoria's a great little girl too."

Marion Peters came back from the kitchen. She was a tall woman with worried eyes, who had once possessed a fresh American loveliness. Charlie had never been sensitive to it and was always surprised when people spoke of how pretty she had been. From the first there had been an instinctive antipathy between them.

"Well, how do you find Honoria?" she asked.

"Wonderful. I was astonished how much she's grown in ten months. All the children are looking well."

"We haven't had a doctor for a year. How do you like being back in Paris?"

"It seems very funny to see so few Americans around."

"I'm delighted," Marion said vehemently. "Now at least you can go into a store without their assuming you're a millionaire. We've suffered like everybody, but on the whole it's a good deal pleasanter."

"But it was nice while it lasted," said Charlie. "We were a sort of royalty, almost infallible, with a sort of magic around us. In the bar this afternoon"—he stumbled, seeing his mistake—"there wasn't a man I knew."

She looked at him keenly. "I should think you'd have had enough of bars."

"I only stayed a minute. I take one drink every ᵔfternoon, and no more."

"Don't you want a cocktail before dinner?" Lincoln asked.

"I take only one drink every afternoon, and I've had that."

"I hope you keep to it," said Marion.

Her dislike was evident in the coldness with which she spoke, but Charlie only smiled; he had larger plans. Her very aggressiveness gave him an advantage, and he knew enough to wait. He wanted them to initiate the discussion of what they knew had brought him to Paris.

At dinner he couldn't decide whether Honoria was most like him or her mother. Fortunate if she didn't combine the traits of both that had brought them to disaster. A great wave of protectiveness went over him. He thought he knew what to do for her. He believed in character; he wanted to jump back a whole generation and trust in character again as the eternally valuable element. Everything else wore out.

He left soon after dinner, but not to go home. He was curious to see Paris by night with clearer and more judicious eyes than those of other days. He bought a *strapontin* for the Casino and watched Josephine Baker go through her chocolate arabesques.

After an hour he left and strolled toward Montmartre, up the Rue Pigalle into the Place Blanche. The rain had stopped and there were a few people in evening clothes disembarking from taxis in front of cabarets, and *cocottes* prowling singly or in pairs, and many Negroes. He passed a lighted door from which issued music, and stopped with the sense of familiarity; it was Bricktop's, where he had parted with so many hours and so much money. A few doors farther on he found another ancient rendezvous and incautiously put his head inside. Immediately an eager orchestra burst into sound, a pair of professional dancers leaped to their feet and a maître d'hôtel swooped toward him, crying, "Crowd just arriving, sir!" But he withdrew quickly.

"You have to be damn drunk," he thought.

Zelli's was closed, the bleak and sinister cheap hotels surrounding it were dark; up in the Rue Blanche there was more light and a local, colloquial French crowd. The Poet's Cave had disappeared, but the two great mouths of the Café of Heaven and the Café of Hell still yawned—even devoured, as he watched, the meager contents of a tourist bus—a German, a Japanese, and an American couple who glanced at him with frightened eyes.

So much for the effort and ingenuity of Montmartre. All the catering to vice and waste was on an utterly childish scale, and he suddenly realized the meaning of the word "dissipate"—to dissipate into thin air; to make nothing out of something. In the little hours of the night every move from place to place was an enormous human jump, an increase of paying for the privilege of slower and slower motion.

He remembered thousand-franc notes given to an orchestra for playing a single number, hundred-franc notes tossed to a doorman for calling a cab.

But it hadn't been given for nothing.

It had been given, even the most wildly squandered sum, as an offering to destiny that he might not remember the things most worth remembering, the things that now he would always remember—his child taken from his control, his wife escaped to a grave in Vermont.

In the glare of a *brasserie* a woman spoke to him. He bought her some eggs and coffee, and then, eluding her encouraging stare, gave her a twenty-franc note and took a taxi to his hotel.

II

He woke up on a fine fall day—football weather. The depression of yesterday was gone and he liked the people on the streets. At noon he sat opposite Honoria at Le Grand Vatel, the only restaurant he could think of not reminiscent of champagne dinners and long luncheons that began at two and ended in a blurred and vague twilight.

"Now, how about vegetables? Oughtn't you to have some vegetables?"

"Well, yes."

"Here's *épinards* and *chou-fleur* and carrots and *haricots.*"

"I'd like *chou-fleur.*"

"Wouldn't you like to have two vegetables?"

"I usually have only one at lunch."

The waiter was pretending to be inordinately fond of children. *"Qu'elle est mignonne la petite? Elle parle exactement comme une française."*

"How about dessert? Shall we wait and see?"

The waiter disappeared. Honoria looked at her father expectantly.

"What are we going to do?"

"First, we're going to that toy store in the Rue Saint-Honoré and buy you anything you like. And then we're going to the vaudeville at the Empire."

She hesitated. "I like it about the vaudeville, but not the toy store."

"Why not?"

"Well, you brought me this doll." She had it with her. "And I've got lots of things. And we're not rich any more, are we?"

"We never were. But today you are to have anything you want."

"All right," she agreed resignedly.

When there had been her mother and a French nurse he had been inclined to be strict; now he extended himself, reached out for a new tolerance; he must be both parents to her and not shut any of her out of communication.

"I want to get to know you," he said gravely. "First let me introduce myself. My name is Charles J. Wales, of Prague."

"Oh, daddy!" her voice cracked with laughter.

"And who are you, please?" he persisted, and she accepted a rôle immediately: "Honoria Wales, Rue Palatine, Paris."

"Married or single?"

"No, not married. Single."

He indicated the doll. "But I see you have a child, madame."

Unwilling to disinherit it, she took it to her heart and thought quickly: "Yes, I've been married, but I'm not married now. My husband is dead."

He went on quickly, "And the child's name?"

"Simone. That's after my best friend at school."

"I'm very pleased that you're doing so well at school."

"I'm third this month," she boasted. "Elsie"—that was her cousin—"is only about eighteenth, and Richard is about at the bottom."

"You like Richard and Elsie, don't you?"

"Oh, yes. I like them all right."

Cautiously and casually he asked: "And Aunt Marion and Uncle Lincoln—which do you like best?"

"Oh, Uncle Lincoln, I guess."

He was increasingly aware of her presence. As they came in, a murmur of ". . . adorable" followed them, and now the people at the next table bent all their silences upon her, staring as if she were something no more conscious than a flower.

"Why don't I live with you?" she asked suddenly. "Because mamma's dead?"

"You must stay here and learn more French. It would have been hard for daddy to take care of you so well."

"I don't really need much taking care of any more. I do everything for myself."

Going out of the restaurant, a man and a woman unexpectedly hailed him.

"Well, the old Wales!"

"Hello there, Lorraine . . . Dunc."

Sudden ghosts out of the past: Duncan Schaeffer, a friend from college. Lorraine Quarles, a lovely, pale blonde of thirty; one of a crowd who had helped them make months into days in the lavish times of three years ago.

"My husband couldn't come this year," she said, in answer to his question. "We're poor as hell. So he gave me two hundred a month, and told me I could do my worst on that. . . . This your little girl?"

"What about coming back and sitting down?" Duncan asked.

"Can't do it." He was glad for an excuse. As always, he felt Lorraine's passionate, provocative attraction, but his own rhythm was different now.

"Well, how about dinner?" she asked.

"I'm not free. Give me your address and let me call you."

"Charlie, I believe you're sober," she said judicially. "I honestly believe he's sober, Dunc. Pinch him and see if he's sober."

Charlie indicated Honoria with his head. They both laughed.

"What's your address?" said Duncan skeptically.

He hesitated, unwilling to give the name of his hotel.

"I'm not settled yet. I'd better call you. We're going to see the vaudeville at the Empire."

"There! That's what I want to do," Lorraine said. "I want to see some clowns and acrobats and jugglers. That's just what we'll do, Dunc."

"We've got to do an errand first," said Charlie. "Perhaps we'll see you there."

"All right, you snob. . . . Good-by, beautiful little girl."

"Good-by."

Honoria bobbed politely.

Somehow, an unwelcome encounter. They liked him because he was functioning, because he was serious; they wanted to see him, because he was stronger than they were now, because they wanted to draw a certain sustenance from his strength.

At the Empire, Honoria proudly refused to sit upon her father's folded coat. She was already an individual with a code of her own, and Charlie was more and more absorbed by the desire of putting a little of himself into her before she crystallized utterly. It was hopeless to try to know her in so short a time.

Between the acts they came upon Duncan and Lorraine in the lobby where the band was playing.

"Have a drink?"

"All right, but not up at the bar. We'll take a table."

"The perfect father."

Listening abstractedly to Lorraine, Charlie watched Honoria's eyes leave their table, and he followed them wistfully about the room, wondering what they saw. He met her glance and she smiled.

"I liked that lemonade," she said.

What had she said? What had he expected? Going home in a taxi afterward, he pulled her over until her head rested against his chest.

"Darling, do you ever think about your mother?"

"Yes, sometimes," she answered vaguely.

"I don't want you to forget her. Have you got a picture of her?"

"Yes, I think so. Anyhow, Aunt Marion has. Why don't you want me to forget her?"

"She loved you very much."

"I loved her too."

They were silent for a moment.

"Daddy, I want to come and live with you," she said suddenly.

His heart leaped; he had wanted it to come like this.

"Aren't you perfectly happy?"

"Yes, but I love you better than anybody. And you love me better than anybody, don't you, now that mummy's dead?"

"Of course I do. But you won't always like me best, honey. You'll grow up and meet somebody your own age and go marry him and forget you ever had a daddy."

"Yes, that's true," she agreed tranquilly.

He didn't go in. He was coming back at nine o'clock and he wanted to keep himself fresh and new for the thing he must say then.

"When you're safe inside, just show yourself in that window."

"All right. Good-by, dads, dads, dads, dads."

He waited in the dark street until she appeared, all warm and glowing, in the window above and kissed her fingers out into the night.

III

They were waiting. Marion sat behind the coffee service in a dignified black dinner dress that just faintly suggested mourning. Lincoln was walking up and down with the animation of one who had already been talking. They were as anxious as he was to get into the question. He opened it almost immediately:

"I suppose you know what I want to see you about—why I really came to Paris."

Marion played with the black stars on her necklace and frowned.

"I'm awfully anxious to have a home," he continued. "And I'm awfully anxious to have Honoria in it. I appreciate your taking in Honoria for her mother's sake, but things have changed now"—he hesitated and then continued more forcibly—"changed radically with me, and I want to ask you to reconsider the matter. It would be silly for me to deny that about three years ago I was acting badly——"

Marion looked up at him with hard eyes.

"—but all that's over. As I told you, I haven't had more than a drink a day for over a year, and I take that drink deliberately, so that the idea of alcohol won't get too big in my imagination. You see the idea?"

"No," said Marion succinctly.

"It's a sort of stunt I set myself. It keeps the matter in proportion."

"I get you," said Lincoln. "You don't want to admit it's got any attraction for you."

"Something like that. Sometimes I forget and don't take it. But I try to take it. Anyhow, I couldn't afford to drink in my position. The people I represent are more than satisfied with what I've done, and I'm bringing my sister over from Burlington to keep house for me, and I want awfully to have Honoria too. You know that even when her mother and I weren't getting along well we never let anything that happened touch Honoria. I know she's fond of me and I know I'm able to take care of her—well, there you are. How do you feel about it?"

He knew that now he would have to take a beating. It would last an hour or two hours, and it would be difficult, but if he modulated his inevitable resentment to the chastened attitude of the reformed sinner, he might win his point in the end.

Keep your temper, he told himself. You don't want to be justified. You want Honoria.

Lincoln spoke first: "We've been talking it over ever since we got your letter last month. We're happy to have Honoria here. She's a dear little thing, and we're glad to be able to help her, but of course that isn't the question——"

Marion interrupted suddenly. "How long are you going to stay sober, Charlie?" she asked.

"Permanently, I hope."

"How can anybody count on that?"

"You know I never did drink heavily until I gave up business and came over here with nothing to do. Then Helen and I began to run around with——"

"Please leave Helen out of it. I can't bear to hear you talk about her like that."

He stared at her grimly; he had never been certain how fond of each other the sisters were in life.

"My drinking only lasted about a year and a half—from the time we came over until I—collapsed."

"It was time enough."

"It was time enough," he agreed.

"My duty is entirely to Helen," she said. "I try to think what she would have wanted me to do. Frankly, from the night you did that terrible thing you haven't really existed for me. I can't help that. She was my sister."

"Yes."

"When she was dying she asked me to look out for Honoria. If you hadn't been in a sanitarium then, it might have helped matters."

He had no answer.

"I'll never in my life be able to forget the morning when Helen knocked at my door, soaked to the skin and shivering, and said you'd locked her out."

Charlie gripped the sides of the chair. This was more difficult than he expected: he wanted to launch out into a long expostulation and explanation, but he only said: "The night I locked her out—" and she interrupted, "I don't feel up to going over that again."

After a moment's silence Lincoln said: "We're getting off the subject. You want Marion to set aside her legal guardianship and give you Honoria. I think the main point for her is whether she has confidence in you or not."

"I don't blame Marion," Charlie said slowly, "but I think she can have entire confidence in me. I had a good record up to three years ago. Of course, it's within human possibilities I may go wrong again. But if we wait much longer I'll lose Honoria's childhood and my chance for a home." He shook his head. "I'll simply lose her, don't you see?"

"Yes, I see," said Lincoln.

"Why didn't you think of all this before?" Marion asked.

"I suppose I did, from time to time, but Helen and I were getting along badly. When I consented to the guardianship, I was flat on my back in a sanitarium, and the market had cleaned me out. I knew I'd acted badly, and I thought if it would bring any peace to Helen, I'd agree to anything. But now it's different. I'm functioning, I'm behaving damn well, so far as——"

"Please don't swear at me," Marion said.

He looked at her, startled. With each remark the force of her dislike became more and more apparent. She had built up all her fear of life into one wall and faced it toward him. This trivial reproof was possibly the result of some trouble with the cook several hours before. Charlie became increasingly alarmed at leaving Honoria in this atmosphere of hostility against himself; sooner or later it would come out, in a word here, a shake of the head there, and some of that distrust would be irrevocably implanted in Honoria. But he pulled his temper down out of his face and shut it up inside him; he had won a point, for Lincoln realized the absurdity of Marion's remark, and asked her lightly since when she had objected to the word "damn."

"Another thing," Charlie said: "I'm able to give her certain advantages now. I'm going to take a French governess to Prague with me. I've got a lease on a new apartment——"

He stopped, realizing that he was blundering. They couldn't be expected to accept with equanimity the fact that his income was again twice as large as their own.

"I suppose you can give her more luxuries than we can," said Marion. "When you were throwing away money we were living along watching every ten francs. . . . I suppose you'll start doing it again."

"Oh, no," he said. "I've learned. I worked hard for ten years, you know—until I got lucky in the market, like so many people. Terribly lucky. It didn't seem any use working any more, so I quit. It won't happen again."

There was a long silence. All of them felt their nerves straining, and for the first time in a year Charlie wanted a drink. He was sure now that Lincoln Peters wanted him to have his child.

Marion shuddered suddenly; part of her saw that Charlie's

feet were planted on the earth now, and her own maternal feeling recognized the naturalness of his desire; but she had lived for a long time with a prejudice—a prejudice founded on a curious disbelief in her sister's happiness, which, in the shock of one terrible night, had turned to hatred for him. It had all happened at a point in her life where the discouragement of ill health and adverse circumstances made it necessary for her to believe in tangible villainy and a tangible villain.

"I can't help what I think!" she cried out suddenly. "How much you were responsible for Helen's death, I don't know. It's something you'll have to square with your own conscience."

An electric current of agony surged through him; for a moment he was almost on his feet, an unuttered sound echoing in his throat. He hung on to himself for a moment, another moment.

"Hold on there," said Lincoln uncomfortably. "I never thought you were responsible for that."

"Helen died of heart trouble," Charlie said dully.

"Yes, heart trouble." Marion spoke as if the phrase had another meaning for her.

Then, in the flatness that followed her outburst, she saw him plainly and she knew he had somehow arrived at control over the situation. Glancing at her husband, she found no help from him, and as abruptly as if it were a matter of no importance, she threw up the sponge.

"Do what you like!" she cried, springing up from her chair. "She's your child. I'm not the person to stand in your way. I think if it were my child I'd rather see her—" She managed to check herself. "You two decide it. I can't stand this. I'm sick. I'm going to bed."

She hurried from the room; after a moment Lincoln said: "This has been a hard day for her. You know how strongly she feels—" His voice was almost apologetic: "When a woman gets an idea in her head."

"Of course."

"It's going to be all right. I think she sees now that you—can provide for the child, and so we can't very well stand in your way or Honoria's way."

"Thank you, Lincoln."

"I'd better go along and see how she is."

"I'm going."

He was still trembling when he reached the street, but a walk down the Rue Bonaparte to the quais set him up, and as he crossed the Seine, fresh and new by the quai lamps, he felt exultant. But back in his room he couldn't sleep. The image of Helen haunted him. Helen whom he had loved so until they had senselessly begun to abuse each other's love, tear it into shreds. On that terrible February night that Marion remembered so vividly, a slow quarrel had gone on for hours. There was a scene at the Florida, and then he attempted to take her home, and then she kissed young Webb at a table; after that there was what she had hysterically said. When he arrived home alone he turned the key in the lock in wild anger. How could he know she would arrive an hour later alone, that there would be a snowstorm in which she wandered about in slippers, too confused to find a taxi? Then the aftermath, her escaping pneumonia by a miracle, and all the attendant horror. They were "reconciled," but that was the beginning of the end, and Marion, who had seen with her own eyes and who imagined it to be one of many scenes from her sister's martyrdom, never forgot.

Going over it again brought Helen nearer, and in the white, soft light that steals upon half sleep near morning he found himself talking to her again. She said that he was perfectly right about Honoria and that she wanted Honoria to be with him. She said she was glad he was being good and doing better. She said a lot of other things—very friendly things—but she was in a swing in a white dress, and swinging faster and faster all the time, so that at the end he could not hear clearly all that she said.

IV

He woke up feeling happy. The door of the world was open again. He made plans, vistas, futures for Honoria and himself, but suddenly he grew sad, remembering all the plans he and Helen had made. She had not planned to die. The present was the thing—work to do, and some one to love. But not to love too much, for he knew the injury that a father can do to a daughter or a mother to a son by attaching them too closely; afterward, out in the world, the child would seek in the marriage partner the same blind tenderness and, failing probably to find it, turn against love and life.

It was another bright, crisp day. He called Lincoln Peters at the bank where he worked and asked if he could count on taking Honoria when he left for Prague. Lincoln agreed that there was no reason for delay. One thing—the legal guardianship. Marion wanted to retain that a while longer. She was upset by the whole matter, and it would oil things if she felt that the situation was still in her control for another year. Charlie agreed, wanting only the tangible, visible child.

Then the question of a governess. Charlie sat in a gloomy agency and talked to a cross Bernaise and to a buxom Breton peasant, neither of whom he could have endured. There were others whom he would see tomorrow.

He lunched with Lincoln Peters at Griffons, trying to keep down his exultation.

"There's nothing quite like your own child," Lincoln said. "But you understand how Marion feels too."

"She's forgotten how hard I worked for seven years there," Charlie said. "She just remembers one night."

"There's another thing," Lincoln hesitated. "While you and Helen were tearing around Europe throwing money away, we were just getting along. I didn't touch any of the prosperity because I never got ahead enough to carry anything but my insurance. I think Marion felt there was some kind of injustice in it—you not even working toward the end, and getting richer and richer."

"It went just as quick as it came," said Charlie.

"Yes, a lot of it stayed in the hands of *chasseurs* and saxophone players and maîtres d'hôtel—well, the big party's over now. I just said that to explain Marion's feeling about those crazy years. If you drop in about six o'clock tonight before Marion's too tired, we'll settle the details on the spot."

Back at his hotel, Charlie found a *pneumatique* that had been redirected from the Ritz bar where Charlie had left his address for the purpose of finding a certain man.

Dear Charlie: You were so strange when we saw you the other day that I wondered if I did something to offend you. If so, I'm not conscious of it. In fact, I have thought about you too much for the last year, and it's always been in the back of my mind that I might see you if I came over here. We *did* have such good times that crazy spring, like the night you and I stole the butcher's tricycle, and the time we tried to call on the president and you had the old derby rim and the wire cane. Everybody seems so old lately, but I don't feel old a bit. Couldn't we get together some time today for old time's sake? I've got a vile hang-over for the moment, but will be feeling better this afternoon and will look for you about five in the sweatshop at the Ritz.

Always devotedly,
Lorraine.

His first feeling was one of awe that he had actually, in his mature years, stolen a tricycle and pedalled Lorraine all over the Étoile between the small hours and dawn. In retrospect it was a nightmare. Locking out Helen didn't fit in with any other act of his life, but the tricycle incident did—it was one of many. How many weeks or months of dissipation to arrive at that condition of utter irresponsibility?

He tried to picture how Lorraine had appeared to him then—very attractive; Helen was unhappy about it, though she said nothing. Yesterday, in the restaurant, Lorraine had seemed trite, blurred, worn away. He emphatically did not want to see her, and he was glad Alix had not given away his hotel address. It was a relief to think, instead, of Honoria, to think of Sundays spent with her and of saying good morning to her and of knowing she was there in his house at night, drawing her breath in the darkness.

At five he took a taxi and bought presents for all the Peters—a piquant cloth doll, a box of Roman soldiers, flowers for Marion, big linen handkerchiefs for Lincoln.

He saw, when he arrived in the apartment, that Marion had accepted the inevitable. She greeted him now as though he were a recalcitrant member of the family, rather than a menacing outsider. Honoria had been told she was going; Charlie was glad to see that her tact made her conceal her excessive happiness. Only on his lap did she whisper her delight and the question "When?" before she slipped away with the other children.

He and Marion were alone for a minute in the room, and on an impulse he spoke out boldly:

"Family quarrels are bitter things. They don't go according to any rules. They're not like aches or wounds; they're more like splits in the skin that won't heal because there's not enough material. I wish you and I could be on better terms."

"Some things are hard to forget," she answered. "It's a

question of confidence." There was no answer to this and presently she asked, "When do you propose to take her?"

"As soon as I can get a governess. I hoped the day after tomorrow."

"That's impossible. I've got to get her things in shape. Not before Saturday."

He yielded. Coming back into the room, Lincoln offered him a drink.

"I'll take my daily whisky," he said.

It was warm here, it was a home, people together by a fire. The children felt very safe and important; the mother and father were serious, watchful. They had things to do for the children more important than his visit here. A spoonful of medicine was, after all, more important than the strained relations between Marion and himself. They were not dull people, but they were very much in the grip of life and circumstances. He wondered if he couldn't do something to get Lincoln out of his rut at the bank.

A long peal at the door-bell; the *bonne à tout faire* passed through and went down the corridor. The door opened upon another long ring, and then voices, and the three in the salon looked up expectantly; Richard moved to bring the corridor within his range of vision, and Marion rose. Then the maid came back along the corridor, closely followed by the voices, which developed under the light into Duncan Schaeffer and Lorraine Quarles.

They were gay, they were hilarious, they were roaring with laughter. For a moment Charlie was astounded; unable to understand how they had ferreted out the Peters' address.

"Ah-h-h!" Duncan wagged his finger roguishly at Charlie. "Ah-h-h!"

They both slid down another cascade of laughter. Anxious and at a loss, Charlie shook hands with them quickly and presented them to Lincoln and Marion. Marion nodded scarcely speaking. She had drawn back a step toward the fire; her little girl stood beside her, and Marion put an arm about her shoulder.

With growing annoyance at the intrusion, Charlie waited for them to explain themselves. After some concentration Duncan said:

"We came to invite you out to dinner. Lorraine and I insist that all this shishi business 'bout your address got to stop."

Charlie came closer to them, as if to force them backward down the corridor.

"Sorry, but I can't. Tell me where you'll be and I'll phone you in half an hour."

This made no impression. Lorraine sat down suddenly on the side of a chair, and focussing her eyes on Richard, cried, "Oh, what a nice little boy! Come here, little boy." Richard glanced at his mother, but did not move. With a perceptible shrug of her shoulders, Lorraine turned back to Charlie:

"Come and dine. Sure your cousins won' mine. See you so sel'om. Or solemn."

"I can't," said Charlie sharply. "You two have dinner and I'll phone you."

Her voice became suddenly unpleasant. "All right, we'll go. But I remember once when you hammered on my door at four A.M. I was enough of a good sport to give you a drink. Come on, Dunc."

Still in slow motion, with blurred, angry faces, with uncertain feet, they retired along the corridor.

"Good night," Charlie said.

"Good night!" responded Lorraine emphatically.

When he went back into the salon Marion had not moved, only now her son was standing in the circle of her other arm. Lincoln was still swinging Honoria back and forth like a pendulum from side to side.

"What an outrage!" Charlie broke out. "What an absolute outrage!"

Neither of them answered. Charlie dropped into an armchair, picked up his drink, set it down again and said:

"People I haven't seen for two years having the colossal nerve——"

He broke off. Marion had made the sound "Oh!" in one swift, furious breath, turned her body from him with a jerk and left the room.

Lincoln set down Honoria carefully.

"You children go in and start your soup," he said, and when they obeyed, he said to Charlie:

"Marion's not well and she can't stand shocks. That kind of people make her really physically sick."

"I didn't tell them to come here. They wormed your name out of somebody. They deliberately——"

"Well, it's too bad. It doesn't help matters. Excuse me a minute."

Left alone, Charlie sat tense in his chair. In the next room he could hear the children eating, talking in monosyllables, already oblivious to the scene between their elders. He heard a murmur of conversation from a farther room and then the ticking bell of a telephone receiver picked up, and in a panic he moved to the other side of the room and out of earshot.

In a minute Lincoln came back. "Look here, Charlie. I think we'd better call off dinner for tonight. Marion's in bad shape."

"Is she angry with me?"

"Sort of," he said, almost roughly. "She's not strong and——"

"You mean she's changed her mind about Honoria."

"She's pretty bitter right now. I don't know. You phone me at the bank tomorrow."

"I wish you'd explain to her I never dreamed these people would come here. I'm just as sore as you are."

"I couldn't explain anything to her now."

Charlie got up. He took his coat and hat and started down the corridor. Then he opened the door of the dining room and said in a strange voice, "Good night, children."

Honoria rose and ran around the table to hug him.

"Good night, sweetheart," he said vaguely, and then trying to make his voice more tender, trying to conciliate something, "Good night, dear children."

V

Charlie went directly to the Ritz bar with the furious idea of finding Lorraine and Duncan, but they were not there, and he realized that in any case there was nothing he could do. He had not touched his drink at the Peters', and now he ordered a whisky-and-soda. Paul came over to say hello.

"It's a great change," he said sadly. "We do about half the business we did. So many fellows I hear about back in the States lost everything, maybe not in the first crash, but then in the second. Your friend George Hardt lost every cent, I hear. Are you back in the States?"

"No. I'm in business in Prague."

"I heard that you lost a lot in the crash."

"I did," and he added grimly, "but I lost everything I wanted in the boom."

"Selling short?"

"Something like that."

Again the memory of those days swept over him like a nightmare—the people they had met travelling; the people who couldn't add a row of figures or speak a coherent sentence. The little man Helen had consented to dance with at the ship's party, who had insulted her ten feet from the table; the women and girls carried screaming with drink or drugs out of public places . . . the men who locked their wives out in the snow, because the snow of '29 wasn't real snow. If you didn't want it to be snow, you just paid some money.

He went to the phone and called the Peters apartment; Lincoln answered.

"I called up because this thing is on my mind. Has Marion said anything definite?"

"Marion's sick," Lincoln answered shortly. "I know this thing isn't altogether your fault, but I can't have her go to pieces about it. I'm afraid we'll have to let it slide for six months; I can't take the chance of working her up to this state again."

"I see."

"I'm sorry, Charlie."

He went back to his table. His whisky glass was empty, but he shook his head when Alix looked at it questioningly. There wasn't much he could do now except send Honoria some things; he would send her a lot of things tomorrow. He thought rather angrily that this was just money—he had given so many people money. . . .

"No, no more," he said to another waiter. "What do I owe you?"

He would come back some day; they couldn't make him pay forever. But he wanted his child, and nothing was much good now, beside that fact. He wasn't young any more, with a lot of nice thoughts and dreams to have by himself. He was absolutely sure Helen wouldn't have wanted him to be so alone.

The Last Day in the Field

CAROLINE GORDON

Caroline Gordon was born in 1895 at Clarksville, Tennessee, and after several years in New York City and in France she has recently returned to her birthplace, to live with her husband and child on land that has been in her family for generations. The substance of most of her writing has come directly from her Tennessee background and her Virginia ancestry. She attended Bethany College in West Virginia, then did newspaper work in her native state and in New York before beginning her serious work in fiction. Her first novels, *Penhally* (1931), and *Aleck Maury: Sportsman* (1934) are particularly noteworthy for their strong characterization and their rich regional backgrounds. *None Shall Look Back* (1937) is a story of the War between the States, and *The Garden of Adonis* (1937) presents the South as it is today.

THAT was the fall when the leaves stayed green so long. We had a drouth in August and the ponds everywhere were dry and the watercourse shrunken. Then in September heavy rains came. Things greened up. It looked like winter was never coming.

"You aren't going to hunt this year, Aleck," Molly said. "Remember how you stayed awake nights last fall with that pain in your leg."

From *Scribner's Magazine*, March, 1935. Copyright, 1935. Reprinted by permission.

In October light frosts came. In the afternoons when I sat on the back porch going over my fishing tackle I marked their progress on the elderberry bushes that were left standing against the stable fence. The lower, spreading branches had turned yellow and were already sinking to the ground but the leaves in the top clusters still stood up stiff and straight.

"Ah-h, it'll get you yet!" I said, thinking how frost creeps higher and higher out of the ground each night of fall.

The dogs next door felt it and would thrust their noses through the wire fence scenting the wind from the north. When I walked in the back yard they would bound twice their height and whine, for meat scraps Molly said, but it was because they smelled blood on my old hunting coat.

They were almost matched liver-and-white pointers. The big dog had a beautiful, square muzzle and was deep-chested and rangy. The bitch, Judy, had a smaller head and not so good a muzzle but she was springy loined too and had one of the merriest tails I've ever watched.

When Joe Thomas, the boy that owned them, came home from the hardware store he would change his clothes and then come down the back way into the wired enclosure and we would stand there watching the dogs and wondering how they would work. Joe said they were keen as mustard. He was going to take them out the first good Saturday and wanted me to come along.

"I can't make it," I said, "my leg's worse this year than it was last."

The fifteenth of November was clear and so warm that we sat out on the porch till nine o'clock. It was still warm when we went to bed towards eleven. The change must have come in the middle of the night. I woke once, hearing the clock strike two, and felt the air cold on my face and thought before I went back to sleep that the weather had broken at last. When I woke again at dawn the cold air was slapping my face hard. I came wide awake, turned over in bed and looked out of the window.

There was a scaly-bark hickory tree growing on the east side of the house. You could see its upper branches from the bedroom window. The leaves had turned yellow a week ago. But yesterday evening when I walked out there in the yard they had still been flat with green streaks showing in them. Now they were curled up tight and a lot of leaves had fallen on to the ground.

I got out of bed quietly so as not to wake Molly, dressed and went down the back way over to the Thomas house. There was no one stirring but I knew which room Joe's was. The window was open and I could hear him snoring. I went up and stuck my head in.

"Hey," I said, "killing frost."

He opened his eyes and looked at me and then his eyes went shut. I reached my arm through the window and shook him. "Get up," I said, "we got to start right away."

He was awake now and out on the floor stretching. I told him to dress and be over at the house as quick as he could. I'd have breakfast ready for us both.

Aunt Martha had a way of leaving fire in the kitchen stove at night. There were red embers there now. I poked the ashes out and piled kindling on top of them. When the flames came up I put some heavier wood on, filled the coffee pot, and put some grease on in a skillet. By the time Joe got there I had coffee ready and some hoe cakes to go with our fried eggs. Joe had brought a thermos bottle. We put the rest of the coffee in it and I found a ham in the pantry and made some sandwiches.

While I was fixing the lunch Joe went down to the lot to hitch up. He was just driving Old Dick out of the stable when I came down the back steps. The dogs knew what was up, all right. They were whining and surging against the fence and Bob, the big dog, thrust his paw through and into the pocket of my hunting coat as I passed. While Joe was snapping on the leashes I got a few handfuls of straw from the rack and put it in the foot of the buggy. It was twelve miles where we were going; the dogs would need to ride warm coming back late.

Joe said he would drive. We got in the buggy and started out, up Seventh Street and on over to College and out through Scufftown. When we got into the nigger section we could see what a killing frost it had been. A light shimmer over all the ground still and the weeds around the cabins dark and matted the way they are when the frost hits them hard and twists them.

We drove on over the Red River bridge and up into the open country. At Jim Gill's place the cows had come up and were standing waiting to be milked but nobody was stirring yet from the house. I looked back from the top of the hill and saw that the frost mists still hung heavy in the bottom and thought it was a good sign. A day like this when the earth is warmer than the air currents is good for the hunter. Scent particles are borne on the warm air and birds will forage far on such a day.

It took us over an hour to get from Gloversville to Spring Creek. Joe wanted to get out as soon as we hit the big bottom there but I held him down and we drove on to the top of the ridge. We got out there, unhitched Old Dick and turned him into one of Rob Fayerlee's pastures—I thought how surprised Rob would be when he saw him grazing there—put our guns together, and started out, the dogs still on leash.

It was rough, broken ground, scrub oak, with a few gum trees and lots of buckberry bushes. One place a patch of corn ran clear up to the top of the ridge. As we passed along between the rows I could see the frost glistening on the north side of the stalks. I knew it was going to be a good day.

I walked over to the brow of the hill. From here you can see off over the whole valley—I've hunted every foot of it in my time—tobacco land, mostly. One or two patches of corn there on the side of the ridge. I thought we might start there and then I knew that wouldn't do. Quail will linger on the roost a cold day and feed in shelter during the morning. It is only in the afternoon that they will work out to the open.

The dogs were whining. Joe bent down and was about to slip their leashes. "Hey, boy," I said, "don't do that."

I turned around and looked down the other side of the ridge. It was better that way. The corn land of the bottoms ran high up on to the hill in several places there and where the corn stopped there were big patches of ironweed and buckberry. I knocked my pipe out on a stump.

"Let's go that way," I said.

Joe was looking at my old buckhorn whistle that I had slung around my neck. "I forgot to bring mine."

"All right," I said, "I'll handle 'em."

He unfastened their collars and cast off. They broke away, racing for the first hundred yards and barking, then suddenly swerved. The big dog took off to the right along the hillside. The bitch, Judy, skirted a belt of corn along the upper bottomlands. I kept my eye on the big dog. A dog that has bird sense will know cover when he sees it. This big Bob was an independent hunter, all right, I could see him moving fast through the scrub oaks, working his way down toward a patch of ironweed. He caught first scent just on the edge of the weed patch and froze with every indication of class, head up, nose stuck out, and tail straight in air. Judy, meanwhile, had been following the line of the corn field. A hundred yards away she caught sight of Bob's point and backed him.

We went up and flushed the birds. They got up in two bunches. I heard Joe's shot while I was in the act of raising my gun and I saw his bird fall not thirty paces from where I stood. I had covered the middle bird of the larger bunch —that's the one led by the boss cock—the way I usually do. He fell, whirling head over heels, driven a little forward by the impact. A well-centered shot. I could tell by the way the feathers fluffed as he tumbled.

The dogs were off through the grass. They had retrieved both birds. Joe stuck his in his pocket. He laughed. "I thought there for a minute you were going to let him get away."

I looked at him but I didn't say anything. It's a wonderful thing to be twenty years old.

The majority of the singles had flown straight ahead to settle in the rank grass that jutted out from the bottomland. Judy got down to work at once but the big dog broke off to the left, wanting to get footloose to find another covey. I thought of how Trecho, the best dog I ever had— the best dog any man ever had—used always to be wanting to do the same thing and I laughed.

"Naw, you don't," I said, "come back here, you scoundrel, and hunt these singles."

He stopped on the edge of a briar patch, looked at me and heeled up promptly. I clucked him out again. He gave me another look. I thought we were beginning to understand each other better. We got some nice points among those singles but we followed that valley along the creek bed and through two or three more corn fields without finding another covey. Joe was disappointed but I wasn't beginning to worry yet; you always make your bag in the afternoon.

It was twelve o'clock by this time, no sign of frost any-where and the sun beating down steady on the curled-up leaves.

"Come on," I said, "let's go up to Buck's spring and eat."

We walked up the ravine whose bed was still moist with the fall rains and came out at the head of the hollow. They had cleared out some of the trees on the side of the ravine but the spring itself was the same: a deep pool welling up between the roots of an old sycamore. I unwrapped the sandwiches and the piece of cake and laid them on a stump. Joe got the thermos bottle out of his pocket. Something had gone wrong with it and the coffee was stone cold. We were about to drink it that way when Joe saw a good tin can flung down beside the spring. He made a trash fire and we put the coffee in the can and heated it to boiling.

It was warm in the ravine, sheltered from the wind, with the little fire burning. I turned my game leg so that the heat fell full on my knee. Joe had finished his last sandwich and was reaching for the cake.

"Good ham," he said.

"It's John Ferguson's," I told him.

He had got up and was standing over the spring. "Won-der how long this wood'll last, under water this way."

I looked at the sycamore root, green and slick where the thin stream of water poured over it, then my eyes went back to the dogs. They were tired, all right. Judy had gone off to lie down in a cool place at the side of the spring, but the big dog, Bob, lay there, his forepaws stretched out in front of him, never taking his eyes off our faces. I looked at him and thought how different he was from his mate and like some dogs I had known—and men too—who lived only for hunting and could never get enough no matter how long the day. There was something about his head and his markings that reminded one of another dog I used to hunt with a long time ago and I asked the boy who had trained him. He said the old fellow he bought the dogs from had been killed last spring, over in Trigg—Charley Morrison.

Charley Morrison! I remembered how he died, out hunting by himself and the gun had gone off, accidentally they said. Charley had called his dog to him, got blood over him and sent him home. The dog went, all right, but when they got there Charley was dead. Two years ago that was and now I was hunting the last dogs he'd ever trained. . . .

Joe lifted the thermos bottle. "Another cup?"

I held my cup out and he filled it. The coffee was still good and hot. I drank it, standing up, running my eye over the country in front of us. Afternoon is different from morning, more exciting. It isn't only as I say that you'll make your bag in the afternoon, but it takes more figuring. They're fed and rested and when they start out again they'll work in the open and over a wider range.

Joe was stamping out his cigarette: "Let's go."

The dogs were already out of sight but I could see the sedge grass ahead moving and I knew they'd be making for the same thing that took my eye: a spearhead of thicket that ran far out into this open field. We came up over a little rise. There they were, Bob on a point and Judy backing him not fifty feet from the thicket. I saw it was going to be tough shooting. No way to tell whether the birds were between the dog and the thicket or in the thicket itself. Then I saw that the cover was more open along the side of the thicket and I thought that that was the way they'd go if they were in the thicket. But Joe had already broken away to the left. He got too far to the side. The birds flushed to the right and left him standing, flat-footed, without a shot.

He looked sort of foolish and grinned.

I thought I wouldn't say anything and then I found myself speaking: "Trouble with you, you try to out-think the dog."

There was nothing to do about it, though. The chances were that the singles had pitched in the trees below. We went down there. It was hard hunting. The woods were open, the ground everywhere heavily carpeted with leaves. Dead leaves make a tremendous rustle when the dogs surge through them. It takes a good nose to cut scent keenly in such noisy cover. I kept my eye on Bob. He never faltered, getting over the ground in big, springy strides but combing every inch of it. We came to an open place in the woods. Nothing but hickory trees and bramble thickets overhung with trailing vines. Bob passed the first thicket and came to a beautiful point. We went up. He stood perfectly steady but the bird flushed out fifteen or twenty steps ahead of him. I saw it swing to the right, gaining altitude very quickly—woods birds will always cut back to known territory—and it came to me how it would be.

I called to Joe: "Don't shoot yet."

He nodded and raised his gun, following the bird with the barrel. It was directly over the treetops when I gave the word and he shot, scoring a clean kill.

He laughed excitedly as he stuck the bird in his pocket. "My God, man, I didn't know you could take that much time!"

We went on through the open woods. I was thinking about a day I'd had years ago in the woods at Grassdale, with my uncle, James Morris, and his son, Julian. Uncle James had given Julian and me hell for missing just such a shot. I can see him now standing up against a big pine tree, his face red from liquor and his gray hair ruffling in the wind: *"Let him alone! Let him alone!* And establish your lead as he climbs."

Joe was still talking about the shot he'd made. "Lord, I wish I could get another one like that."

"You won't," I said, "we're getting out of the woods now."

We struck a path that led due west and followed it for half a mile. My leg was stiff from the hip down now and every time I brought it over, the pain would start in my knee, Zing! and travel up and settle in the small of my back. I walked with my head down, watching the light catch on the ridges of Joe's brown corduroy trousers and then shift and catch again. Sometimes he would get on ahead and then there would be nothing but the black tree trunks coming up out of the dead leaves.

Joe was talking about some wild land up on the Cumberland. We could get up there on an early train. Have a good day. Might even spend the night. When I didn't answer he turned around: "Man, you're sweating."

I pulled my handkerchief out and wiped my face. "Hot work," I said.

He had stopped and was looking about him. "Used to be a spring somewhere around here."

He had found the path and was off. I sat down on a stump and mopped my face some more. The sun was halfway down through the trees now, the whole west woods ablaze with the light. I sat there and thought that in another hour it would be good and dark and I wished that the day could go on and not end so soon and yet I didn't see how I could make it much farther with my leg the way it was.

Joe was coming up the path with his folding cup full of water. I hadn't thought I was thirsty but the cold water tasted good. We sat there awhile and smoked, then Joe said that we ought to be starting back, that we must be a good piece from the rig by this time.

We set out, working north through the edge of the

woods. It was rough going and I was thinking that it would be all I could do to make it back to the rig when we climbed a fence and came out at one end of a long field that sloped down to a wooded ravine. Broken ground, badly gullied and covered with sedge everywhere except where sumac thickets had sprung up—as birdy a place as ever I saw. I looked it over and knew I had to hunt it, leg or no leg, but it would be close work, for me and the dogs too.

I blew them in a bit and we stood there watching them cut up the cover. The sun was down now; there was just enough light left to see the dogs work. The big dog circled the far wall of the basin and came up wind just off the drain, then stiffened to a point. We walked down to it. The birds had obviously run a bit into the scraggly sumac stalks that bordered the ditch. My mind was so much on the dogs I forgot Joe. He took one step too many. The fullest blown bevy of the day roared up through the tangle. It had to be fast work. I raised my gun and scored with the only barrel I had time to peg. Joe shouted; I knew he had got one too.

We stood there trying to figure out which way the singles had gone but they had fanned out too quick for us, excited as we were, and after beating around awhile we gave up and went on.

We came to the rim of the swale, eased over it, crossed the dry creek bed that was drifted thick with leaves, and started up the other side. I had blown in the dogs, thinking there was no use for them to run their heads off now we'd started home, but they didn't come. I walked on a little farther, then I looked back and saw Bob's white shoulders through a tangle of cinnamon vine.

Joe had turned around too. "They've pinned a single out of that last covey," he said.

I looked over at him quick. "Your shot."

He shook his head. "No, you take it."

I limped back and flushed the bird. It went skimming along the buckberry bushes that covered that side of the swale. In the fading light I could hardly make it out and I shot too quick. It swerved over the thicket and I let go with the second barrel. It staggered, then zoomed up. Up, up, up, over the rim of the hill and above the tallest hickories. It hung there for a second, its wings black against the gold light, before, wings still spread, it came whirling down, like an autumn leaf, like the leaves that were everywhere about us, all over the ground.

Red Coat Day

R. P. HARRISS

Robert P. Harriss was born in 1903 at Fayetteville, North Carolina. After graduation from Duke University and some experience as a seaman in cargo ships to foreign ports, he studied at the Sorbonne and at the École d'Art Animalier, a sculpture atelier in Paris. He did newspaper work for four years in France, and is now an associate editor of the *Baltimore Evening Sun*. His novel *The Foxes* (1936) reflects experiences of his boyhood in North Carolina.

I T WAS about an hour after daybreak and the jaybirds were still making a raucous how-d'ye-do among the trees of the Grove, where squirrel nests hung loosely in the boughs. An old bo-squirrel darted out of a hollow and ran along a limb above the House, chased by three scolding jays, to plump down on the marquee, its paws scraping on the blackened tin. The squirrel sat with twitching tail for an instant and scrambled away again at the sound of voices below and the opening of a door. A tall man in plain riding habit walked into the yard, followed by a boy.

"You tell Giles to watch the road?"

"Yes, father, I told him and he sent Pappy Gola."

Man and boy stared down the tree-bordered drive toward

From *Story*, May, 1935. Part of the novel *The Foxes* (Houghton Mifflin, 1936). Copyright, 1936, by R. P. Harriss. Reprinted by permission of the author, *Story*, and Houghton Mifflin Co.

the highway. From behind the House, and some distance away, came the mellow notes of kennelled hounds, speaking intermittently.

"Old Bluebell," said the man, without shifting his gaze.

"Burly, too," said the staring boy. Then, with animation, "Ain't that a truck? Yep, that's it, all right. I'll go." And as he hurried away the elaborately grotesque figure of an old Negro appeared at the end of the drive, motioning with a stick toward the House. Then came a horseman in a red coat, riding a blaze-faced bay, dazzlingly gay in the October sunshine.

A horse van moved slowly on the uneven road, followed by a van in which rode twenty couples of hounds. More horsemen followed. The horse vans stopped and unloaded by the side of the highway, but the hound van was kept closed. It was large and roomy, with straw bedding on the floor. The boy observed that a rubber hose was attached to the exhaust pipe at the rear, carrying the carbonic fumes up over the roof and away from supersensitive hound noses. A huntsman in top-boots, white breeches, red coat, black velvet cap, mounted on a bright chestnut horse, came up beside the van, accompanied by three scarlet-coated horsemen on grays. A rider of one of the grays took a little brass hunting horn out of his coat and blew a few short notes. *A-eu! a-eu! eu-eu-eu!* Dully from within the hound van came an answering clamor. The other riders dismounted and swung down the door, and the pack tumbled out, massing in the road with waving sterns.

The plain-note of the horn carried along the drive to listeners at the House. A little later, the thud and scrabble of hooves and the *pad-scrit! pad-scrit!* of dogs' feet on gravel. The horseman who had come out of the House was now in the saddle and waiting on the lawn, with several long-eared plantation hounds clustered about his horse's heels. (There were Bluebell and Burly; Drummer—old Drum, whose voice was like the plucked strings of a bass fiddle; Rouster, the quarrelsome; Sheriff, Bugler, Fifer, Bounce, Nimble and Witchcraft.) When the first red-coated rider reached the House, the two horsemen nodded and then rode off together, disappearing into a thicket.

When they were gone the riders on the grays reached the House, bringing up the guest pack. Hounds seemed to flow over the lawn in rolling waves of color: black backs, white chests, white feet, tan ears, tan markings. The horseman on the blaze-faced bay made little caressing sounds, audible whispers, chirrupings, mimicry of the horn notes. He told over their names, softly, for their names were autumnal melody. (Ringwood, Dashwood, Robin, Patrona, Pirate, Gadabout . . . Falstaff, Rockaby, Sweetheart, Tireless, Highlander, Pibroch, Chieftain, Crystal . . . Valkyrie, Beldame, Pickpocket, Tattler, Blackamoor, Dragoon . . . Tipster, Truthful, Hector, Melodious, Lucifer, Strident, Chorister, Lark, Cherokee, Hurricane . . . Phoebe, Fanciful, Juno, Linda.)

As they waited, old Bluebell and Rouster, of the plantation pack, could be heard speaking in the brake, and now and then an encouraging cheer: "Hie-on, rouse him!" The deep-throated music came nearer, the waiting pack grew tense. Suddenly their huntsman, cantering forward, turned in his saddle and shouted, "Hie-on! heu-eu, lads! Go get him!"

The fox had flashed in a russet streak across a lane which skirted the brake. In the thicket the huntsman's velvet cap could be seen bobbing about. Seconds more, and Rouster, Bluebell, Burly and Nimble crashed out of the heavy growth, followed by the fleetest of the guest pack. Then a swirl of hounds springing and tumbling in screaming haste to be clear of the underbrush. The combined packs swept across the lane and over a bramble hedge, the riders followed.

The baying had grown faint and died away and the last horseman disappeared over the low hills when two more riders emerged from the thicket. One was a white boy on a halfbred pony, the other a small Negro riding a mule with an old army saddle. They jogged on slowly, stopping at the top of the rise to listen for hounds. At a place where a scuppernong vine ran from its broken arbor and spread over a sagging rail fence, they waited. The last, sweet grapes, golden and wrinkled, hung in clusters. The little Negro was reaching for a handful of grapes when his mule ceased cropping and stood with pricked ears.

"Hear anything?"

"Naw. But *he* do."

Presently the pony pricked his ears and tugged at the reins; then the cry of hounds became plainly audible. Half a mile away the hunt came into view, moving in a wide semicircle at a steady, swinging gallop. One red-coated rider, possibly deceived by the brambles which hid a wide, deep ditch, went down. The horse struggled up and went on, saddle empty. What became of the rider they could not tell. At the rail fence, which zig-zagged its rambling course away from where the boys were, the hounds' speed was abruptly checked. The baying became doubtful, stopped altogether. A pair of wrens, which dwelt in a bush beside the fence, fluttered up and began an angry chattering. Their curses followed a shadow creeping along the top rail.

"Look!"

"Shut up! Keep still!"

The fox came on without fear for he was moving downwind. He reached the cover of the scuppernong vine, then flattened himself down, head on paws, to rest. At last Old Burly owned that the fox had climbed upon the rails but

the huntsman called the hounds away in the wrong direction along the fence. The fox looked back with evident satisfaction at the pack's futile questing, and the huntsman was
returning again when the boy's pony stamped with an
impatient hoof and blew a loud breath. The fox looked
up and saw. He rose slowly, deliberately, and gazed a long
second before he dropped down from the top rail, looked
back and walked casually away into the brambles.

Burly and Bluebell had gone back alone and were working out the trail together when the huntsman sounded his
horn and called the pack along the fence, this time in the
right direction. At the scuppernong vine, Rouster and
Sheriff recovered the trail and, the rest harking to them,
were away once more on a strong scent. They charged a
tangle of catclaw vines which overgrew a dry ditch, and
again they were running with all their forces, for they were
close upon the fox. Rouster and Nimble had seen him—had
chopped at his disappearing brush. The pack flew over
the ground, catching the scent in the air. He ran in a burst
of speed toward a pasture into which a drove of half-wild
razorbacks had been harbored from the woodlands to fatten
on peanuts before hog-killing time. Hounds saw him again
in the open and ran almost mute in their frenzy to kill.
The leading dogs were springing forward in great strides,
nearly upon him, when his brush flashed under the strong
wire fence of the hog-pasture. He ran through the filth of
the swine lot, which destroyed his trail, and slipped out
at the far side.

The huntsman galloped up on a blown horse, calling the
pack, but ten or twelve hounds had already climbed the
wire fence and were among the squealing, fighting razorbacks. When the pack had been assembled once more, one
of the hounds, Tipster, was left behind. He crawled under
a hedge, licking a wound which ran along flank and belly

and from which protruded a purple fold of entrails, for he had been disemboweled by a boar.

The fox had put a quarter of a mile between his brush and the nose of the closest hound, now slowly puzzling out the trail. He trotted on for many yards in the dust of a cattle path that led to the pinelands, and skulked under a bush. His tongue lolled out. He was thirsty and rank and hot. There he did not stay, for instinct told him he was not yet safe, and if he lay still his legs would become stiff and useless for running. He trotted on again, dodging this way and that, pausing now and again to prick his ears and listen and test the breeze with his nose. At a runnel that flowed over a sandy bed and sparkled into a drain, he stopped, flacking once, twice, with a swollen tongue. He waded in and stood in the feeble current, letting it cleanse his heavily-filthed brush; and having rid himself of the clots of swine dirt in his fell, he waded on several yards, lapping as he went. Even in his haste the fox paused long enough to reach for a frog with a deft paw. It wriggled free and escaped into a bed of moss.

Where the rillet became lost in meadow grasses the fox emerged, sleek and small. He shook the water from him and became larger. After grooming himself briefly, he trotted on. Again he heard hounds speaking on his line, and his trot broke into a swinging lope. As he lolloped through a spinney a partridge hen with her big brood of late chicks, which had been sunning and fluffing themselves in a doodle-dust hole, flapped up and, turning, made as if to run at him, beating her wings angrily. The fox paused in his stride and seized the last of the chicks as they were disappearing with magical suddenness. He ran for four or five yards before dropping the bird.

He crossed two fields, squared by ditch and bramble-hedge, and, trotting again, followed a dim wagon trail leading toward a thicket of pines. Uncle Eli, a Negro wood-chopper, had gone that way, creeping along on his cart drawn by a scrawny little ox. The ox-scent was rank, obliterating that left by the fox. But hounds had followed the line through the hedge of the first field. He heard Burly's voice, Drum's answering bass note, and then the rapid tongue of Rouster in the lead. Again he ran, overtaking the creeping ox-cart. He walked beneath it for a few yards. The sound of the pack, which now had crossed the second square and was clamoring along the road, caused the hair along his back to stand on end. He trembled in his misery, weaving back and forth, darting out from under the cart and in again.

The old Negro saw him at last and, shouting imprecations, whacked at him with a long stick.

"Git, you debbil! Hit de grit!"

The fox snarled, dashed away out of sight, turned, circled, and seeing the bitch Juno, ran back under the cart. This time he was not observed, for the driver was still muttering and waving in the direction he had first taken. Hounds were now panting along on each side of the cart, the wheels of which stirred up a dust. The dry, powdery nimbus made them sneeze, and the strong smell of ox caused them to forget the trail and keep their noses up.

A horseman's head showed beyond the hedge. His laboring horse cleared the ditch and pounded up. Another rider followed. Hounds were baying all around the cart and the fox, seeking shelter, leapt to the feed rack beneath the floor boards, grasping with his paws and swinging himself inside. Meanwhile, the ox—made frantic by so much noise and confusion—humped his back and tried to buck and run, while the old Negro clung on, shouting and pointing with his goad.

The horsemen rode off in the direction he indicated,

calling the dogs. All the pack responded except Rouster, who hung about under the cart. The other rider shouted: "G'on! Get away from there. G'on! 'Ware cart! Heu-heu-heu! hark!" and then swung his whip-lash. Rouster lifted his nose toward the hay-rack in which the fox crouched, peeping out. The hound gazed steadily until the pupils of his eyes became fixed upon a pointed muzzle and flattened ears and fangs. The hound sprang up, snapping at the challenging head, and struck his own head hard against the crossboards. This caused him to break into a storm of baying, at which the ox suddenly jerked the cart forward and ran away, bucking and bellowing: "Baw-aaaaaaah! Bwuah-aaaaaaah!"

Not realizing why Rouster had bayed beneath the cart, and because of the hound's evil reputation, the horseman swore at the hound and whipped him back toward where the rest of the pack quested for a trail now non-existent. Rouster, with tail lowered and back bristling, growled resentment and kept looking away in the direction of the cart disappearing jerkily along the road.

The fox rode until the ox grew tired of running, and then slipped out and away. He had looked into the teeth of his enemy and lived.

The huntsman called the pack and pushed on into a likely thicket, hoping the lost line would be quickly found. "Heu-on! Wind him! Hustle 'm!"

The sounds of horse and hound in the covert waked a large cub that had kennelled there since the dawn. A young fox, never having been hunted before, he trotted back and forth, and in circles, crossing and re-crossing his line in mingled fear and curiosity. When hounds came on the fresh scent, rising thickly, they stormed the covert in a fury. The horn sang *gone away*.

On a stretch of open grassland the pack rolled over the fleeing cub with a throaty rumble. He was chopped in Rouster's jaws, tossed into the air, caught, chewed, pulled, scragged and broken. A warm smell of blood and guts rose and was blown away on the breeze. A horseman approached the boys and dabbed at their cheeks with a bit of bloody fur. "Now," he said, "let's hear you whoop!" The white boy grinned and let out a lusty yell, but the little Negro looked scared and, leaning down, vomited on the grass. When the man turned away the white boy said scornfully, "You fool, that wasn't *our* fox!"

The lights of the late-afternoon sun slanted across the fields, and the fields gave back the light in a glow of goldenrod and burnished sedge. Brightness shone briefly on the returning hunt, as hounds and horsemen moved across an open space in a hedge: on the pied pack, on the glistening, wet coat of a blaze-faced bay; on a silver whip-handle; on the mirroring, smooth-worn surface of saddle leather. Shafts of light ran obliquely on through the pines and were lost in a deepening gloom made audible with the fluttery, bird-piping rumor of night.

Uncurling in the tussock where he had rested, a fox still stiff from running stood up, stretched gratefully, and trotted out into the fields, flairing his nose for scent of cottontail or partridge. A note of the distant horn came faintly, calling a lost hound. The fox cocked an ear, sat back on his haunches and barked; and one last retreating sun-lance was caught and warmed an instant in the color of his coat, before the urgent day sped into darkness.

The Undefeated

ERNEST HEMINGWAY

Ernest Hemingway was born at Oak Park, Illinois, in 1898, the son of a physician. During his boyhood, he took vacations and hunting trips with his father in northern Michigan, and distinguished himself at school in football and boxing. He completed his course at the Oak Park high school, then began to earn his own living as day laborer, farm hand, sparring partner, and later as reporter on the *Kansas City Star*. He volunteered in an American ambulance unit before America entered the war, and later joined the Italian army. He was wounded, and twice decorated by the Italian government. Out of these experiences he drew the background for his novel *A Farewell to Arms*. After the war he returned to newspaper work, in the United States and later in the Near East and at Paris. His first stories, reminiscent of boyhood experience in Michigan, were published in Paris. In *The Sun Also Rises* (1926) he achieved a powerful and sympathetic portrayal of the '20's, particularly of expatriates in Paris. With the publication of this novel and of the short stories collected in *In Our Time* (1925) and *Men Without Women* (1927), Hemingway became one of the most influential writers of his generation. His highly individual style has been widely imitated, never successfully.

Bullfighting, big-game hunting, and deep-sea fishing competed with fiction writing in the field of Hemingway's interest until the outbreak of the Spanish Civil War. His observation of and participation in that conflict find expression in the novel *For Whom the Bell Tolls* (1940).

MANUEL GARCIA climbed the stairs to Don
Miguel Retana's office. He set down his suitcase
and knocked on the door. There was no answer.
Manuel, standing in the hallway, felt there was some one
in the room. He felt it through the door.

"Retana," he said, listening.

There was no answer.

He's there, all right, Manuel thought.

"Retana," he said and banged the door.

"Who's there?" said some one in the office.

"Me, Manolo," Manuel said.

"What do you want?" asked the voice.

"I want to work," Manuel said.

Something in the door clicked several times and it swung
open. Manuel went in, carrying his suitcase.

A little man sat behind a desk at the far side of the room.
Over his head was a bull's head, stuffed by a Madrid taxi-
dermist; on the walls were framed photographs and bullfight posters.

The little man sat looking at Manuel.

"I thought they'd killed you," he said.

Manuel knocked with his knuckles on the desk. The
little man sat looking at him across the desk.

"How many corridas you had this year?" Retana asked.

"One," he answered.

"Just that one?" the little man asked.

"That's all."

"I read about it in the papers," Retana said. He leaned
back in the chair and looked at Manuel.

Manuel looked up at the stuffed bull. He had seen it
often before. He felt a certain family interest in it. It had
killed his brother, the promising one, about nine years ago.

From *Men Without Women,* copyright, 1927, by Charles Scribner's
Sons. Reprinted by permission.

Manuel remembered the day. There was a brass plate on the oak shield the bull's head was mounted on. Manuel could not read it, but he imagined it was in memory of his brother. Well, he had been a good kid.

The plate said: "The Bull 'Mariposa' of the Duke of Veragua, which accepted 9 varas for 7 caballos, and caused the death of Antonio Garcia, Novillero, April 27, 1909."

Retana saw him looking at the stuffed bull's head.

"The lot the Duke sent me for Sunday will make a scandal," he said. "They're all bad in the legs. What do they say about them at the Café?"

"I don't know," Manuel said. "I just got in."

"Yes," Retana said. "You still have your bag."

He looked at Manuel, leaning back behind the big desk.

"Sit down," he said. "Take off your cap."

Manuel sat down; his cap off, his face was changed. He looked pale, and his coleta pinned forward on his head, so that it would not show under the cap, gave him a strange look.

"You don't look well," Retana said.

"I just got out of the hospital," Manuel said.

"I heard they'd cut your leg off," Retana said.

"No," said Manuel. "It got all right."

Retana leaned forward across the desk and pushed a wooden box of cigarettes toward Manuel.

"Have a cigarette," he said.

"Thanks."

Manuel lit it.

"Smoke?" he said, offering the match to Retana.

"No," Retana waved his hand, "I never smoke."

Retana watched him smoking.

"Why don't you get a job and go to work?" he said.

"I don't want to work," Manuel said. "I am a bullfighter."

"There aren't any bullfighters any more," Retana said.

"I'm a bullfighter," Manuel said.

"Yes, while you're in there," Retana said.

Manuel laughed.

Retana sat, saying nothing and looking at Manuel.

"I'll put you in a nocturnal if you want," Retana offered.

"When?" Manuel asked.

"Tomorrow night."

"I don't like to substitute for anybody," Manuel said. That was the way they all got killed. That was the way Salvador got killed. He tapped with his knuckles on the table.

"It's all I've got," Retana said.

"Why don't you put me on next week?" Manuel suggested.

"You wouldn't draw," Retana said. "All they want is Litri and Rubito and La Torre. Those kids are good."

"They'd come to see me get it," Manuel said, hopefully.

"No, they wouldn't. They don't know who you are any more."

"I've got a lot of stuff," Manuel said.

"I'm offering to put you on tomorrow night," Retana said. "You can work with young Hernandez and kill two novillos after the Charlots."

"Whose novillos?" Manuel asked.

"I don't know. Whatever stuff they've got in the corrals. What the veterinaries won't pass in the daytime."

"I don't like to substitute," Manuel said.

"You can take it or leave it," Retana said. He leaned forward over the papers. He was no longer interested. The appeal that Manuel had made to him for a moment when he thought of the old days was gone. He would like to get him to substitute for Larita because he could get him cheaply. He could get others cheaply too. He would like to help him though. Still he had given him the chance. It was up to him.

"How much do I get?" Manuel asked. He was still playing with the idea of refusing. But he knew he could not refuse.

"Two hundred and fifty pesetas," Retana said. He had thought of five hundred, but when he opened his mouth it said two hundred and fifty.

"You pay Villalta seven thousand," Manuel said.

"You're not Villalta," Retana said.

"I know it," Manuel said.

"He draws it, Manolo," Retana said in explanation.

"Sure," said Manuel. He stood up. "Give me three hundred, Retana."

"All right," Retana agreed. He reached in the drawer for a paper.

"Can I have fifty now?" Manuel asked.

"Sure," said Retana. He took a fifty-peseta note out of his pocketbook and laid it, spread out flat, on the table.

Manuel picked it up and put it in his pocket.

"What about a cuadrilla?" he asked.

"There's the boys that always work for me nights," Retana said. "They're all right."

"How about picadors?" Manuel asked.

"They're not much," Retana admitted.

"I've got to have one good pic," Manuel said.

"Get him then," Retana said. "Go and get him."

"Not out of this," Manuel said. "I'm not paying for any cuadrilla out of sixty duros."

Retana said nothing but looked at Manuel across the big desk.

"You know I've got to have one good pic," Manuel said.

Retana said nothing but looked at Manuel from a long way off.

"It isn't right," Manuel said.

Retana was still considering him, leaning back in his chair, considering him from a long way away.

"There're the regular pics," he offered.

"I know," Manuel said. "I know your regular pics."

Retana did not smile. Manuel knew it was over.

"All I want is an even break," Manuel said reasoningly. "When I go out there I want to be able to call my shots on the bull. It only takes one good picador."

He was talking to a man who was no longer listening.

"If you want something extra," Retana said, "go and get it. There will be a regular cuadrilla out there. Bring as many of your own pics as you want. The charlotada is over by 10:30."

"All right," Manuel said. "If that's the way you feel about it."

"That's the way," Retana said.

"I'll see you tomorrow night," Manuel said.

"I'll be out there," Retana said.

Manuel picked up his suitcase and went out.

"Shut the door," Retana called.

Manuel looked back. Retana was sitting forward looking at some papers. Manuel pulled the door tight until it clicked.

He went down the stairs and out of the door into the hot brightness of the street. It was very hot in the street and the light on the white buildings was sudden and hard on his eyes. He walked down the shady side of the steep street toward the Puerta del Sol. The shade felt solid and cool as running water. The heat came suddenly as he crossed the intersecting streets. Manuel saw no one he knew in all the people he passed.

Just before the Puerta del Sol he turned into a café.

It was quiet in the café. There were a few men sitting at tables against the wall. At one table four men played cards. Most of the men sat against the wall smoking, empty coffee cups and liqueur glasses before them on the tables. Manuel went through the long room to a small room in back. A man sat at a table in the corner asleep. Manuel sat down at one of the tables.

A waiter came in and stood beside Manuel's table.

"Have you seen Zurito?" Manuel asked him.

"He was in before lunch," the waiter answered. "He won't be back before five o'clock."

"Bring me some coffee and milk and a shot of the ordinary," Manuel said.

The waiter came back into the room carrying a tray with a big coffee glass and a liqueur glass on it. In his left hand he held a bottle of brandy. He swung these down to the table and a boy who had followed him poured coffee and milk into the glass from two shiny, spouted pots with long handles.

Manuel took off his cap and the waiter noticed his pigtail pinned forward on his head. He winked at the coffee boy as he poured out the brandy into the little glass beside Manuel's coffee. The coffee boy looked at Manuel's pale face curiously.

"You fighting here?" asked the waiter, corking up the bottle.

"Yes," Manuel said. "Tomorrow."

The waiter stood there, holding the bottle on one hip.

"You in the Charlie Chaplins?" he asked.

The coffee boy looked away, embarrassed.

"No. In the ordinary."

"I thought they were going to have Chaves and Hernandez," the waiter said.

"No. Me and another."

"Who? Chaves or Hernandez?"

"Hernandez, I think."

"What's the matter with Chaves?"

"He got hurt."

"Where did you hear that?"

"Retana."

"Hey, Looie," the waiter called to the next room, "Chaves got cogida."

Manuel had taken the wrapper off the lumps of sugar and dropped them into his coffee. He stirred it and drank it down, sweet, hot, and warming in his empty stomach. He drank off the brandy.

"Give me another shot of that," he said to the waiter.

The waiter uncorked the bottle and poured the glass full, slopping another drink into the saucer. Another waiter had come up in front of the table. The coffee boy was gone.

"Is Chaves hurt bad?" the second waiter asked Manuel.

"I don't know," Manuel said, "Retana didn't say."

"A hell of a lot he cares," the tall waiter said. Manuel had not seen him before. He must have just come up.

"If you stand in with Retana in this town, you're a made man," the tall waiter said. "If you aren't in with him, you might just as well go out and shoot yourself."

"You said it," the other waiter who had come in said. "You said it then."

"You're right I said it," said the tall waiter. "I know what I'm talking about when I talk about that bird."

"Look what he's done for Villalta," the first waiter said.

"And that ain't all," the tall waiter said. "Look what he's done for Marcial Lalanda. Look what he's done for Nacional."

"You said it, kid," agreed the short waiter.

Manuel looked at them, standing talking in front of his table. He had drunk his second brandy. They had forgotten about him. They were not interested in him.

"Look at that bunch of camels," the tall waiter went on. "Did you ever see this Nacional II?"

"I seen him last Sunday didn't I?" the original waiter said.

"He's a giraffe," the short waiter said.

"What did I tell you?" the tall waiter said. "Those are Retana's boys."

"Say, give me another shot of that," Manuel said. He had poured the brandy the waiter had slopped over in the saucer into his glass and drunk it while they were talking.

The original waiter poured his glass full mechanically, and the three of them went out of the room talking.

In the far corner the man was still asleep, snoring slightly on the intaking breath, his head back against the wall.

Manuel drank his brandy. He felt sleepy himself. It was too hot to go out into the town. Besides there was nothing to do. He wanted to see Zurito. He would go to sleep while he waited. He kicked his suitcase under the table to be sure it was there. Perhaps it would be better to put it back under the seat, against the wall. He leaned down and shoved it under. Then he leaned forward on the table and went to sleep.

When he woke there was some one sitting across the table from him. It was a big man with a heavy brown face like an Indian. He had been sitting there some time. He had waved the waiter away and sat reading the paper and occasionally looking down at Manuel, asleep, his head on the table. He read the paper laboriously, forming the words with his lips as he read. When it tired him he looked at Manuel. He sat heavily in the chair, his black Cordoba hat tipped forward.

Manuel sat up and looked at him.

"Hello, Zurito," he said.

"Hello, kid," the big man said.

"I've been asleep," Manuel rubbed his forehead with the back of his fist.

"I thought maybe you were."

"How's everything?"

"Good. How is everything with you?"

"Not so good."

They were both silent. Zurito, the picador, looked at Manuel's white face. Manuel looked down at the picador's enormous hands folding the paper to put away in his pocket.

"I got a favor to ask you, Manos," Manuel said.

Manosduros was Zurito's nickname. He never heard it without thinking of his huge hands. He put them forward on the table self-consciously.

"Let's have a drink," he said.

"Sure," said Manuel.

The waiter came and went and came again. He went out of the room looking back at the two men at the table.

"What's the matter, Manola?" Zurito set down his glass.

"Would you pic two bulls for me tomorrow night?" Manuel asked, looking up at Zurito across the table.

"No," said Zurito. "I'm not pic-ing."

Manuel looked down at his glass. He had expected that answer; now he had it. Well, he had it.

"I'm sorry, Manolo, but I'm not pic-ing." Zurito looked at his hands.

"That's all right," Manuel said.

"I'm too old," Zurito said.

"I just asked you," Manuel said.

"Is it the nocturnal tomorrow?"

"That's it. I figured if I had just one good pic, I could get away with it."

"How much are you getting?"

"Three hundred pesetas."

"I get more than that for pic-ing."

"I know," said Manuel. "I didn't have any right to ask you."

"What do you keep on doing it for?" Zurito asked. "Why don't you cut off your coleta, Manolo?"

"I don't know," Manuel said.

"You're pretty near as old as I am," Zurito said.

"I don't know," Manuel said. "I got to do it. If I can fix it so that I get an even break, that's all I want. I got to stick with it, Manos."

"No, you don't."

"Yes, I do. I've tried keeping away from it."

"I know how you feel. But it isn't right. You ought to get out and stay out."

"I can't do it. Besides, I've been going good lately."

Zurito looked at his face.

"You've been in the hospital."

"But I was going great when I got hurt."

Zurito said nothing. He tipped the cognac out of his saucer into his glass.

"The papers said they never saw a better faena," Manuel said.

Zurito looked at him.

"You know when I get going I'm good," Manuel said.

"You're too old," the picador said.

"No," said Manuel. "You're ten years older than I am."

"With me its different."

"I'm not too old," Manuel said.

They sat silent, Manuel watching the picador's face.

"I was going great till I got hurt," Manuel offered. "You ought to have seen me, Manos," Manuel said, reproachfully.

"I don't want to see you," Zurito said. "It makes me nervous."

"You haven't seen me lately."

"I've seen you plenty."

Zurito looked at Manuel, avoiding his eyes.

"You ought to quit it, Manolo."

"I can't," Manuel said. "I'm going good now, I tell you."

Zurito leaned forward, his hands on the table.

"Listen. I'll pic for you and if you don't go big tomorrow night, you'll quit. See? Will you do that?"

"Sure."

Zurito leaned back, relieved.

"You got to quit," he said. "No monkey business. You got to cut the coleta."

"I won't have to quit," Manuel said. "You watch me. I've got the stuff."

Zurito stood up. He felt tired from arguing.

"You got to quit," he said. "I'll cut your coleta myself."

"No, you won't," Manuel said. "You won't have a chance."

Zurito called the waiter.

"Come on," said Zurito. "Come on up to the house."

Manuel reached under the seat for his suitcase. He was happy. He knew Zurito would pic for him. He was the best picador living. It was all simple now.

"Come on up to the house and we'll eat," Zurito said.

Manuel stood in the patio de caballos waiting for the Charlie Chaplins to be over. Zurito stood beside him. Where they stood it was dark. The high door that led into the bull-ring was shut. Above them they heard a shout, then another shout of laughter. Then there was silence. Manuel liked the smell of the stables about the patio de caballos. It smelt good in the dark. There was another roar from the arena and then applause, prolonged applause, going on and on.

"You ever seen these fellows?" Zurito asked, big and looming beside Manuel in the dark.

"No," Manuel said.

"They're pretty funny," Zurito said. He smiled to himself in the dark.

The high, double, tight-fitting door into the bull-ring swung open and Manuel saw the ring in the hard light of the arc lights, the plaza, dark all the way around, rising high; around the edge of the ring were running and bowing two men dressed like tramps, followed by a third in the uniform of a hotel bell-boy who stooped and picked up the hats and canes thrown down onto the sand and tossed them back up into the darkness.

The electric light went on in the patio.

"I'll climb onto one of those ponies while you collect the kids," Zurito said.

Behind them came the jingle of the mules, coming out to go into the arena and be hitched onto the dead bull.

The members of the cuadrilla, who had been watching the burlesque from the runway between the barrera and the seats, came walking back and stood in a group talking, under the electric light in the patio. A good-looking lad in a silver-and-orange suit came up to Manuel and smiled.

"I'm Hernandez," he said and put out his hand.

Manuel shook it.

"They're regular elephants we've got tonight," the boy said cheerfully.

"They're big ones with horns," Manuel agreed.

"You drew the worst lot," the boy said.

"That's all right," Manuel said. "The bigger they are, the more meat for the poor."

"Where did you get that one?" Hernandez grinned.

"That's an old one," Manuel said. "You line up your cuadrilla, so I can see what I've got."

"You've got some good kids," Hernandez said. He was very cheerful. He had been on twice before in nocturnals and was beginning to get a following in Madrid. He was happy the fight would start in a few minutes.

"Where are the pics?" Manuel asked.

"They're back in the corrals fighting about who gets the beautiful horses," Hernandez grinned.

The mules came through the gate in a rush, the whips snapping, bells jangling and the young bull ploughing a furrow of sand.

They formed up for the paseo as soon as the bull had gone through.

Manuel and Hernandez stood in front. The youths of the cuadrillas were behind, their heavy capes furled over their arms. In back, the four picadors, mounted, holding their steel-tipped push-poles erect in the half-dark of the corral.

"It's a wonder Retana wouldn't give us enough light to see the horses by," one picador said.

"He knows we'll be happier if we don't get too good a look at these skins," another pic answered.

"This thing I'm on barely keeps me off the ground," the first picador said.

"Well, they're horses."

"Sure, they're horses."

They talked, sitting their gaunt horses in the dark.

Zurito said nothing. He had the only steady horse of the lot. He had tried him, wheeling him in the corrals, and he responded to the bit and the spurs. He had taken the bandage off his right eye and cut the strings where they had tied his ears tight shut at the base. He was a good, solid horse, solid on his legs. That was all he needed. He intended to ride him all through the corrida. He had already, since he had mounted, sitting in the half-dark in the big, quilted saddle, waiting for the paseo, pic-ed through the whole corrida in his mind. The other picadors went on talking on both sides of him. He did not hear him.

The two matadors stood together in front of their three peones, their capes furled over their left arms in the same fashion. Manuel was thinking about the three lads in back of him. They were all three Madrilenos, like Hernandez, boys about nineteen. One of them, a gypsy, serious, aloof, and dark-faced, he liked the look of. He turned.

"What's your name, kid?" he asked the gypsy.

"Fuentes," the gypsy said.

"That's a good name," Manuel said.

The gypsy smiled, showing his teeth.

"You take the bull and give him a little run when he comes out," Manuel said.

"All right," the gypsy said. His face was serious. He began to think about just what he would do.

"Here she goes," Manuel said to Hernandez.

"All right. We'll go."

Heads up, swinging with the music, their right arms swinging free, they stepped out, crossing the sanded arena under the arc lights, the cuadrillas opening out behind, the picadors riding after; behind came the bull-ring servants and the jingling mules. The crowd applauded Hernandez as they marched across the arena. Arrogant, swinging, they looked straight ahead as they marched.

They bowed before the president, and the procession broke up into its component parts. The bullfighters went over to the barrera and changed their heavy mantles for the light fighting capes. The mules went out. The picadors galloped jerkily around the ring, and two rode out the gate they had come in by. The servants swept the sand smooth.

Manuel drank a glass of water poured for him by one of Retana's deputies, who was acting as his manager and sword-handler. Hernandez came over from speaking with his own manager.

"You got a good hand, kid," Manuel complimented him.

"They like me," Hernandez said happily.

"How did the paseo go?" Manuel asked Retana's man.

"Like a wedding," said the handler. "Fine. You came out like Joselito and Belmonte."

Zurito rode by, a bulky equestrian statue. He wheeled his horse and faced him toward the toril on the far side of the ring where the bull would come out. It was strange under the arc light. He pic-ed in the hot afternoon sun for big money. He didn't like this arc-light business. He wished they would get started.

Manuel went up to him.

"Pic him, Manos," he said. "Cut him down to size for me."

"I'll pic him, kid," Zurito said. "What's holding it up?"

"He's coming now," Manuel said.

Zurito sat there, his feet in the box-stirrups, his great legs in the buckskin-covered armor gripping the horse, the reins in his left hand, the long pic held in his right hand, his broad hat well down over his eyes to shade them from the lights, watching the distant door of the toril. His horse's ears quivered. Zurito patted him with his left hand.

The red door of the toril swung back and for a moment Zurito looked into the empty passageway far across the arena. Then the bull came out in a rush, skidding on his four legs as he came out under the lights, then charging in a gallop, moving softly in a fast gallop, silent except as he woofed through wide nostrils as he charged, glad to be free after the dark pen.

In the first row of seats, slightly bored, leaning forward to write on the cement wall in front of his knees, the substitute bullfight critic of *El Heraldo* scribbled: "Campagnero, Negro, 42, came out at 90 miles an hour with plenty of gas——"

Manuel, leaning against the barrera, watching the bull,

waved his hand and the gypsy ran out, trailing his cape. The bull, in full gallop, pivoted and charged the cape, his head down, his tail rising. The gypsy moved in a zigzag, and as he passed, the bull caught sight of him and abandoned the cape to charge the man. The gypsy sprinted and vaulted the red fence of the barrera as the bull struck it with his horns. He tossed into it twice with his horns, banging into the wood blindly.

The critic of *El Heraldo* lit a cigarette and tossed the match at the bull, then wrote in his notebook, "large and with enough horns to satisfy the cash customers, Campagnero showed a tendency to cut into the terrain of the bull-fighters."

Manuel stepped out on the hard sand as the bull banged into the fence. Out of the corner of his eye he saw Zurito sitting the white horse close to the barrera, about a quarter of the way around the ring to the left. Manuel held the cape close in front of him, a fold in each hand, and shouted at the bull. "Huh! Huh!" The bull turned, seemed to brace against the fence as he charged in a scramble, driving into the cape as Manuel side-stepped, pivoted on his heels with the charge of the bull, and swung the cape just ahead of the horns. At the end of the swing he was facing the bull again and held the cape in the same position close in front of his body, and pivoted again as the bull recharged. Each time, as he swung, the crowd shouted.

Four times he swung with the bull, lifting the cape so it billowed full, and each time bringing the bull around to charge again. Then, at the end of the fifth swing, he held the cape against his hip and pivoted, so the cape swung out like a ballet dancer's skirt and wound the bull around himself like a belt, to step clear, leaving the bull facing Zurito on the white horse, come up and planted firm, the horse facing the bull, its ears forward, its lips nervous, Zurito, his hat over his eyes, leaning forward, the long pole sticking out before and behind in a sharp angle under his right arm, held halfway down, the triangular iron point facing the bull.

El Heraldo's second-string critic, drawing on his cigarette, his eyes on the bull, wrote: "the veteran Manolo designed a series of acceptable veronicas, ending in a very Belmontistic recorte that earned applause from the regulars, and we entered the tercio of the cavalry."

Zurito sat his horse, measuring the distance between the bull and the end of the pic. As he looked, the bull gathered himself together and charged, his eyes on the horse's chest. As he lowered his head to hook, Zurito sunk the point of the pic in the swelling bump of muscle above the bull's shoulder, leaned all his weight on the shaft, and with his left hand pulled the white horse into the air, front hoofs pawing, and swung him to the right as he pushed the bull under and through so the horns passed safely under the horse's belly and the horse came down, quivering, the bull's tail brushing his chest as he charged the cape Hernandez offered him.

Hernandez ran sideways, taking the bull out and away with the cape, toward the other picador. He fixed him with a swing of the cape, squarely facing the horse and rider, and stepped back. As the bull saw the horse he charged. The picador's lance slid along his back, and as the shock of the charge lifted the horse, the picador was already halfway out of the saddle, lifting his right leg clear as he missed with the lance and falling to the left side to keep the horse between him and the bull. The horse, lifted and gored, crashed over with the bull driving into him, the picador gave a shove with his boots against the horse and lay clear, waiting to be lifted and hauled away and put on his feet.

Manuel let the bull drive into the fallen horse; he was in no hurry, the picador was safe; besides, it did a picador like that good to worry. He'd stay on longer next time. Lousy pics! He looked across the sand at Zurito a little way out from the barrera, his horse rigid, waiting.

"Huh!" he called to the bull, "Tomar!" holding the cape in both hands so it would catch his eye. The bull detached himself from the horse and charged the cape, and Manuel, running sideways and holding the cape spread wide, stopped, swung on his heels, and brought the bull sharply around facing Zurito.

"Campagnero accepted a pair of varas for the death of one rosinante, with Hernandez and Manolo at the quites," *El Heraldo's* critic wrote. "He pressed on the iron and clearly showed he was no horse-lover. The veteran Zurito resurrected some of his old stuff with the pike-pole, notably the suerte——"

"Ole! Ole!" the man sitting beside him shouted. The shout was lost in the roar of the crowd, and he slapped the critic on the back. The critic looked up to see Zurito, directly below him, leaning far out over his horse, the length of the pic rising in a sharp angle under his armpit, holding the pic almost by the point, bearing down with all his weight, holding the bull off, the bull pushing and driving to get at the horse, and Zurito, far out, on top of him, holding him, holding him, and slowly pivoting the horse against the pressure, so that at last he was clear. Zurito felt the moment when the horse was clear and the bull could come past, and relaxed the absolute steel lock of his resistance, and the triangular steel point of the pic ripped in the bull's hump of shoulder muscle as he tore loose to find Hernandez's cape before his muzzle. He charged blindly into the cape and the boy took him out into the open arena.

Zurito sat patting his horse and looking at the bull charging the cape that Hernandez swung for him out under the bright light while the crowd shouted.

"You see that one?" he said to Manuel.

"It was a wonder," Manuel said.

"I got him that time," Zurito said. "Look at him now."

At the conclusion of a closely turned pass of the cape the bull slid to his knees. He was up at once, but far out across the sand Manuel and Zurito saw the shine of the pumping flow of blood, smooth against the black of the bull's shoulder.

"I got him that time," Zurito said.

"He's a good bull," Manuel said.

"If they gave me another shot at him, I'd kill him," Zurito said.

"They'll change the thirds on us," Manuel said.

"Look at him now," Zurito said.

"I got to go over there," Manuel said, and started on a run for the other side of the ring, where the monos were leading a horse out by the bridle toward the bull, whacking him on the legs with rods and all, in a procession, trying to get him toward the bull, who stood, dropping his head, pawing, unable to make up his mind to charge.

Zurito, sitting his horse, walking him toward the scene, not missing any detail, scowled.

Finally the bull charged, the horse leaders ran for the barrera, the picador hit too far back, and the bull got under the horse, lifted him, threw him onto his back.

Zurito watched. The monos, in their red shirts, running out to drag the picador clear. The picador, now on his feet, swearing and flopping his arms. Manuel and Hernandez standing ready with their capes. And the bull, the great, black bull, with a horse on his back, hooves dangling, the bridle caught in the horns. Black bull with a horse on his back, staggering short-legged, then arching his neck and lifting, thrusting, charging to slide the horse off, horse sliding down. Then the bull into a lunging charge at the cape Manuel spread for him.

The bull was slower now, Manuel felt. He was bleeding badly. There was a sheen of blood all down his flank.

Manuel offered him the cape again. There he came, eyes open, ugly, watching the cape. Manuel stepped to the side and raised his arms, tightening the cape ahead of the bull for the veronica.

Now he was facing the bull. Yes, his head was going down a little. He was carrying it lower. That was Zurito.

Manuel flopped the cape; there he comes; he side-stepped and swung in another veronica. He's shooting awfully accurately, he thought. He's had enough fight, so he's watching now. He's hunting now. Got his eye on me. But I always give him the cape.

He shook the cape at the bull; there he comes; he side-stepped. Awful close that time. I don't want to work that close to him.

The edge of the cape was wet with blood where it had swept along the bull's back as he went by.

All right, here's the last one.

Manuel, facing the bull, having turned with him each charge, offered the cape with his two hands. The bull looked at him. Eyes watching, horns straight forward, the bull looked at him, watching.

"Huh!" Manuel said, "Toro!" and leaning back, swung the cape forward. Here he comes. He side-stepped, swung the cape in back of him, and pivoted, so the bull followed a swirl of cape and then was left with nothing, fixed by the pass, dominated by the cape. Manuel swung the cape under his muzzle with one hand, to show the bull was fixed, and walked away.

There was no applause.

Manuel walked across the sand toward the barrera, while Zurito rode out of the ring. The trumpet had blown to change the act to the planting of the banderillos while

Manuel had been working with the bull. He had not consciously noticed it. The monos were spreading canvas over the two dead horses and sprinkling sawdust around them.

Manuel came up to the barrera for a drink of water. Retana's man handed him the heavy porous jug.

Fuentes, the tall gypsy, was standing, holding a pair of banderillos, holding them together, slim, red sticks, fishhook points out. He looked at Manuel.

"Go on out there," Manuel said.

The gypsy trotted out. Manuel set down the jug and watched. He wiped his face with his handkerchief.

The critic of *El Heraldo* reached for the bottle of warm champagne that stood between his feet, took a drink, and finished his paragraph: "—the aged Manolo rated no applause for a vulgar series of lances with the cape and we entered the third of the palings."

Alone in the center of the ring the bull stood, still fixed. Fuentes, tall, flat-backed, walking toward him arrogantly, his arms spread out, the two slim, red sticks, one in each hand, held by the fingers, points straight forward. Fuentes walked forward. Back of him and to one side was a peon with a cape. The bull looked at him and was no longer fixed.

His eyes watched Fuentes, now standing still. Now he leaned back, calling to him. Fuentes twitched the two banderillos and the light on the steel points caught the bull's eye.

His tail went up and he charged.

He came straight, his eyes on the man. Fuentes stood still, leaning back, the banderillos pointing forward. As the bull lowered his head to hook, Fuentes leaned backward, his arms came together and rose, his two hands touching, the banderillos two descending red lines, and leaning forward drove the points into the bull's shoulder, leaning far in over the bull's horns and pivoting on the two upright sticks, his legs tight together, his body curving to one side to let the bull pass.

"Ole!" from the crowd.

The bull was hooking wildly, jumping like a trout, all four feet off the ground. The red shaft of the banderillos tossed as he jumped.

Manuel, standing at the barrera, noticed that he looked always to the right.

"Tell him to drop the next pair on the right," he said to the kid who started to run out to Fuentes with the new banderillos.

A heavy hand fell on his shoulder. It was Zurito.

"How do you feel, kid?" he asked. Manuel was watching the bull.

Zurito leaned forward on the barrera, leaning the weight of his body on his arms. Manuel turned to him.

"You're going good," Zurito said.

Manuel shook his head. He had nothing to do now until the next third. The gypsy was very good with the banderillos. The bull would come to him in the next third in good shape. He was a good bull. It had all been easy up to now. The final stuff with the sword was all he worried over. He did not really worry. He did not even think about it. But standing there he had a heavy sense of apprehension. He looked out at the bull, planning his faena, his work with the red cloth that was to reduce the bull, to make him manageable.

The gypsy was walking out toward the bull again, walking heel-and-toe, insultingly, like a ballroom dancer, the red shafts of the banderillos twitching with his walk. The bull watched him, not fixed now, hunting him, but waiting to get close enough so he could be sure of getting him, getting the horns into him.

As Fuentes walked forward the bull charged. Fuentes ran

across the quarter of a circle as the bull charged and, as he passed running backward, stopped, swung forward, rose on his toes, arm straight out, and sunk the banderillos straight down into the tight of the big shoulder muscles as the bull missed him.

The crowd were wild about it.

"That kid won't stay in this night stuff long," Retana's man said to Zurito.

"He's good," Zurito said.

"Watch him now."

They watched.

Fuentes was standing with his back against the barrera. Two of the cuadrilla were back of him, with their capes ready to flop over the fence to distract the bull.

The bull, with his tongue out, his barrel heaving, was watching the gypsy. He thought he had him now. Back against the red planks. Only a short charge away. The bull watched him.

The gypsy bent back, drew back his arms, the banderillos pointing at the bull. He called to the bull, stamped one foot. The bull was suspicious. He wanted the man. No more barbs in the shoulder.

Fuentes walked a little closer to the bull. Bent back. Called again. Somebody in the crowd shouted a warning.

"He's too damn close," Zurito said.

"Watch him," Retana's man said.

Leaning back, inciting the bull with the banderillos, Fuentes jumped, both feet off the ground. As he jumped the bull's tail rose and he charged. Fuentes came down on his toes, arms straight out, whole body arching forward, and drove the shafts straight down as he swung his body clear of the right horn.

The bull crashed into the barrera where the flopping capes had attracted his eye as he lost the man.

The gypsy came running along the barrera toward Manuel, taking the applause of the crowd. His vest was ripped where he had not quite cleared the point of the horn. He was happy about it, showing it to the spectators. He made the tour of the ring. Zurito saw him go by, smiling, pointing at his vest. He smiled.

Somebody else was planting the last pair of banderillos. Nobody was paying any attention.

Retana's man tucked a baton inside the red cloth of a muleta, folded the cloth over it, and handed it over the barrera to Manuel. He reached in the leather sword-case, took out a sword, and holding it by its leather scabbard, reached it over the fence to Manuel. Manuel pulled the blade out by the red hilt and the scabbard fell limp.

He looked at Zurito. The big man saw he was sweating.

"Now you get him, kid," Zurito said.

Manuel nodded.

"He's in good shape," Zurito said.

"Just like you want him," Retana's man assured him.

Manuel nodded.

The trumpeter, up under the roof, blew for the final act, and Manuel walked across the arena toward where, up in the dark boxes, the president must be.

In the front row of seats the substitute bullfight critic of *El Heraldo* took a long drink of the warm champagne. He had decided it was not worth while to write a running story and he would write up the corrida back in the office. What the hell was it anyway? Only a nocturnal. If he missed anything he would get it out of the morning papers. He took another drink of the champagne. He had a date at Maxim's at twelve. Who were these bullfighters anyway? Kids and bums. A bunch of bums. He put his pad of paper in his pocket and looked over toward Manuel, standing very much alone in the ring, gesturing with his hat in a salute toward a box he could not see high up in the dark plaza. Out in the ring the bull stood quiet, looking at nothing.

"I dedicate this bull to you, Mr. President, and to the public of Madrid, the most intelligent and generous of the world," was what Manuel was saying. It was a formula. He said it all. It was a little long for nocturnal use.

He bowed at the dark, straightened, tossed his hat over his shoulder, and, carrying the muleta in his left hand and the sword in his right, walked out toward the bull.

Manuel walked toward the bull. The bull looked at him; his eyes were quick. Manuel noticed the way the banderillos hung down on his left shoulder and the steady sheen of blood from Zurito's pic-ing. He noticed the way the bull's feet were. As he walked forward, holding the muleta in his left hand and the sword in his right, he watched the bull's feet. The bull could not charge without gathering his feet together. Now he stood square on them, dully.

Manuel walked toward him, watching his feet. This was all right. He could do this. He must work to get the bull's head down, so he could go in past the horns and kill him. He did not think about the sword, not about killing the bull. He thought about one thing at a time. The coming things oppressed him, though. Walking forward, watching the bull's feet, he saw successively his eyes, his wet muzzle, and the wide, forward-pointing spread of his horns. The bull had light circles about his eyes. His eyes watched Manuel. He felt he was going to get this little one with the white face.

Standing still now and spreading the red cloth of the muleta with the sword, pricking the point into the cloth so that the sword, now held in his left hand, spread the red flannel like the jib of a boat, Manuel noticed the points of the bull's horns. One of them was splintered from banging against the barrera. The other was sharp as a porcupine quill.

Manuel noticed while spreading the muleta that the white base of the horn was stained red. While he noticed these things he did not lose sight of the bull's feet. The bull watched Manuel steadily.

He's on the defensive now, Manuel thought. He's reserving himself. I've got to bring him out of that and get his head down. Always get his head down. Zurito had his head down once, but he's come back. He'll bleed when I start him going and that will bring it down.

Holding the muleta, with the sword in his left hand widening it in front of him, he called to the bull.

The bull looked at him.

He leaned back insultingly and shook the wide-spread flannel.

The bull saw the muleta. It was a bright scarlet under the arc light. The bull's legs tightened.

Here he comes. Whoosh! Manuel turned as the bull came and raised the muleta so that it passed over the bull's horns and swept down his broad back from head to tail. The bull had gone clean up in the air with the charge. Manuel had not moved.

At the end of the pass the bull turned like a cat coming around a corner and faced Manuel.

He was on the offensive again. His heaviness was gone. Manuel noted the fresh blood shining down the black shoulder and dripping down the bull's leg. He drew the sword out of the muleta and held it in his right hand. The muleta held low down in his left hand, leaning toward the left, he called to the bull. The bull's legs tightened, his eyes on the muleta. Here he comes, Manuel thought. Yuh!

He swung with the charge, sweeping the muleta ahead of the bull, his feet firm, the sword following the curve, a point of light under the arcs.

The bull recharged as the pass natural finished and Manuel

raised the muleta for a pase de pecho. Firmly planted, the bull came by his chest under the raised muleta. Manuel leaned his head back to avoid the clattering banderillo shafts. The hot, black bull body touched his chest as it passed.

Too damn close, Manuel thought. Zurito, leaning on the barrera, spoke rapidly to the gypsy, who trotted out toward Manuel with a cape. Zurito pulled his hat down low and looked out across the arena at Manuel.

Manuel was facing the bull again, the muleta held low and to the left. The bull's head was down as he watched the muleta.

"If it was Belmonte doing that stuff, they'd go crazy," Retana's man said.

Zurito said nothing. He was watching Manuel out in the center of the arena.

"Where did the boss dig this fellow up?" Retana's man asked.

"Out of the hospital," Zurito said.

"That's where he's going damn quick," Retana's man said.

Zurito turned on him.

"Knock on that," he said, pointing to the barrera.

"I was just kidding, man," Retana's man said.

"Knock on the wood."

Retana's man leaned forward and knocked three times on the barrera.

"Watch the faena," Zurito said.

Out in the center of the ring, under the lights, Manuel was kneeling, facing the bull, and as he raised the muleta in both hands the bull charged, tail up.

Manuel swung his body clear and, as the bull recharged, brought around the muleta in a half-circle that pulled the bull to his knees.

"Why that one's a great bullfighter," Retana's man said.

"No, he's not," said Zurito.

Manuel stood up and, the muleta in his left hand, the sword in his right, acknowledged the applause from the dark plaza.

The bull had humped himself up from his knees and stood waiting, his head hung low.

Zurito spoke to two of the other lads of the cuadrilla and they ran out to stand back of Manuel with their capes. There were four men back of him now. Hernandez had followed him since he first came with the muleta. Fuentes stood watching, his cape held against his body, tall, in repose, watching lazy-eyed. Now the two came up. Hernandez motioned them to stand one at each side. Manuel stood alone, facing the bull.

Manuel waved back the men with capes. Stepping back cautiously, they saw his face was white and sweating.

Didn't they know enough to keep back? Did they want to catch the bull's eye with the capes after he was fixed and ready? He had enough to worry about without that kind of thing.

The bull was standing, his four feet square, looking at the muleta. Manuel furled the muleta in his left hand. The bull's eyes watched it. His body was heavy on his feet. He carried his head low, but not too low.

Manuel lifted the muleta at him. The bull did not move. Only his eyes watched.

He's all lead, Manuel thought. He's all square. He's framed right. He'll take it.

He thought in bullfight terms. Sometimes he had a thought and the particular piece of slang would not come into his mind and he could not realize the thought. His instincts and his knowledge worked automatically, and his brain worked slowly and in words. He knew all about bulls. He did not have to think about them. He just did the right thing. His eyes noted things and his body performed the necessary measures without thought. If he thought about it, he would be gone.

Now, facing the bull, he was conscious of many things at the same time. There were the horns, the one splintered, the other smoothly sharp, the need to profile himself toward the left horn, lance himself short and straight, lower the muleta so the bull would follow it, and, going in over the horns, put the sword all the way into a little spot about as big as a five-peseta piece straight in back of the neck, between the sharp pitch of the bull's shoulders. He must do all this and must then come out from between the horns. He was conscious he must do all this, but his only thought was in words: "Corto y derecho."

"Corto y derecho," he thought, furling the muleta. Short and straight. Corto y derecho, he drew the sword out of the muleta, profiled on the splintered left horn, dropped the muleta across his body, so his right hand with the sword on the level with his eye made the sign of the cross, and, rising on his toes, sighted along the dipping blade of the sword at the spot high up between the bull's shoulders.

Corto y derecho he launched himself on the bull.

There was a shock, and he felt himself go up in the air. He pushed on the sword as he went up and over, and it flew out of his hand. He hit the ground and the bull was on him. Manuel, lying on the ground, kicked at the bull's muzzle with his slippered feet. Kicking, kicking, the bull after him, missing him in his excitement, bumping him with his head, driving the horns into the sand. Kicking like a man keeping a ball in the air, Manuel kept the bull from getting a clean thrust at him.

Manuel felt the wind on his back from the capes flopping at the bull, and then the bull was gone, gone over him in a rush. Dark, as his belly went over. Not even stepped on.

Manuel stood up and picked up the muleta. Fuentes handed him the sword. It was bent where it had struck the shoulder blade. Manuel straightened it on his knee and ran toward the bull, standing now beside one of the dead horses. As he ran, his jacket flopped where it had been ripped under his armpit.

"Get him out of there," Manuel shouted to the gypsy. The bull had smelled the blood of the dead horse and ripped into the canvas cover with his horns. He charged Fuentes's cape, with the canvas hanging from his splintered horn, and the crowd laughed. Out in the ring, he tossed his head to rid himself of the canvas. Hernandez, running up from behind him, grabbed the end of the canvas and neatly lifted it off the horn.

The bull followed it in a half-charge and stopped still. He was on the defensive again. Manuel was walking toward him with the sword and muleta. Manuel swung the muleta before him. The bull would not charge.

Manuel profiled toward the bull, sighting along the dipping blade of the sword. The bull was motionless, seemingly dead on his feet, incapable of another charge.

Manuel rose to his toes, sighting along the steel, and charged.

Again there was the shock and he felt himself being borne back in a rush, to strike hard on the sand. There was no chance of kicking this time. The bull was on top of him. Manuel lay as though dead, his head on his arms, and the bull bumped him. Bumped his back, bumped his face in the sand. He felt the horn go into the sand between his folded arms. The bull hit him in the small of the back. His face drove into the sand. The horn drove through one of his sleeves and the bull ripped it off. Manuel was tossed clear and the bull followed the capes.

Manuel got up, found the sword and muleta, tried the

point of the sword with his thumb, and then ran toward the barrera for a new sword.

Retana's man handed him the sword over the edge of the barrera.

"Wipe off your face," he said.

Manuel, running again toward the bull, wiped his bloody face with his handkerchief. He had not seen Zurito. Where was Zurito?

The cuadrilla had stepped away from the bull and waited with their capes. The bull stood, heavy and dull again after the action.

Manuel walked toward him with the muleta. He stopped and shook it. The bull did not respond. He passed it right and left, left and right before the bull's muzzle. The bull's eyes watched it and turned with the swing, but he would not charge. He was waiting for Manuel.

Manuel was worried. There was nothing to do but go in. Corto y derecho. He profiled close to the bull, crossed the muleta in front of his body and charged. As he pushed in the sword, he jerked his body to the left to clear the horn. The bull passed him and the sword shot up in the air, twinkling under the arc lights, to fall red-hilted on the sand.

Manuel ran over and picked it up. It was bent and he straightened it over his knee.

As he came running toward the bull, fixed again now, he passed Hernandez standing with his cape.

"He's all bone," the boy said encouragingly.

Manuel nodded, wiping his face. He put the bloody handkerchief in his pocket.

There was the bull. He was close to the barrera now. Damn him. Maybe he was all bone. Maybe there was not any place for the sword to go in. The hell there wasn't! He'd show them.

He tried a pass with the muleta and the bull did not

move. Manuel chopped the muleta back and forth in front of the bull. Nothing doing.

He furled the muleta, drew the sword out, profiled and drove in on the bull. He felt the sword buckle as he shoved it in, leaning his weight on it, and then it shot high in the air, end-over-ending into the crowd. Manuel had jerked clear as the sword jumped.

The first cushions thrown down out of the dark missed him. Then one hit him in the face, his bloody face looking toward the crowd. They were coming down fast. Spotting the sand. Somebody threw an empty champagne bottle from close range. It hit Manuel on the foot. He stood there watching the dark, where the things were coming from. Then something whished through the air and struck by him. Manuel leaned over and picked it up. It was his sword. He straightened it over his knee and gestured with it to the crowd.

"Thank you," he said. "Thank you."

Oh, the dirty bastards! Dirty bastards! Oh, the lousy, dirty bastards! He kicked into a cushion as he ran.

There was the bull. The same as ever. All right, you dirty, lousy bastard!

Manuel passed the muleta in front of the bull's black muzzle.

Nothing doing.

You won't! All right. He stepped close and jammed the sharp peak of the muleta into the bull's damp muzzle.

The bull was on him as he jumped back and as he tripped on a cushion he felt the horn go into him, into his side. He grabbed the horn with his two hands and rode backward, holding tight onto the place. The bull tossed him and he was clear. He lay still. It was all right. The bull was gone.

He got up coughing and feeling broken and gone. The dirty bastards!

"Give me the sword," he shouted. "Give me the stuff."

Fuentes came up with the muleta and the sword.

Hernandez put his arm around him.

"Go on to the infirmary, man," he said. "Don't be a damn fool."

"Get away from me," Manuel said. "Get to hell away from me."

He twisted free. Hernandez shrugged his shoulders. Manuel ran toward the bull.

There was the bull standing, heavy, firmly planted.

All right, you bastard! Manuel drew the sword out of the muleta, sighted with the same movement, and flung himself onto the bull. He felt the sword go in all the way. Right up to the guard. Four fingers and his thumb into the bull. The blood was hot on his knuckles, and he was on top of the bull.

The bull lurched with him as he lay on, and seemed to sink; then he was standing clear. He looked at the bull going down slowly over on his side, then suddenly four feet in the air.

Then he gestured at the crowd, his hand warm from the bull blood.

All right, you bastards! He wanted to say something, but he started to cough. It was hot and choking. He looked down for the muleta. He must go over and salute the president. President hell! He was sitting down looking at something. It was the bull. His four feet up. Thick tongue out. Things crawling around on his belly and under his legs. Crawling where the hair was thin. Dead bull. To hell with the bull! To hell with them all! He started to get to his feet and commenced to cough. He sat down again, coughing. Somebody came and pushed him up.

They carried him across the ring to the infirmary, running with him across the sand, standing blocked at the gate

as the mules came in, then around under the dark passageway, men grunting as they took him up the stairway, and
then laid him down.

The doctor and two men in white were waiting for him.
They laid him out on the table. They were cutting away his
shirt. Manuel felt tired. His whole chest felt scalding inside.
He started to cough and they held something to his mouth.
Everybody was very busy.

There was an electric light in his eyes. He shut his eyes.

He heard some one coming very heavily up the stairs.
Then he did not hear it. Then he heard it. Then he heard a
noise far off. That was the crowd. Well, somebody would
have to kill his other bull. They had cut away all his shirt.
The doctor smiled at him. There was Retana.

"Hello, Retana!" Manuel said. He could not hear his voice.

Retana smiled at him and said something. Manuel could
not hear it.

Zurito stood beside the table, bending over where the
doctor was working. He was in his picador clothes, without
his hat.

Zurito said something to him. Manuel could not hear it.

Zurito was speaking to Retana. One of the men in white
smiled and handed Retana a pair of scissors. Retana gave
them to Zurito. Zurito said something to Manuel. He could
not hear it.

To hell with this operating table. He'd been on plenty of
operating tables before. He was not going to die. There
would be a priest if he was going to die.

Zurito was saying something to him. Holding up the
scissors.

That was it. They were going to cut off his coleta. They
were going to cut off his pigtail.

Manuel sat up on the operating table. The doctor stepped
back, angry. Some one grabbed him and held him.

"You couldn't do a thing like that, Manos," he said.

He heard suddenly, clearly, Zurito's voice.

"That's all right," Zurito said. "I won't do it. I was joking."

"I was going good," Manuel said. "I didn't have any luck. That was all."

Manuel lay back. They had put something over his face. It was all familiar. He inhaled deeply. He felt very tired. He was very, very tired. They took the thing away from his face.

"I was going good," Manuel said weakly. "I was going great."

Retana looked at Zurito and started for the door.

"I'll stay here with him," Zurito said.

Retana shrugged his shoulders.

Manuel opened his eyes and looked at Zurito.

"Wasn't I going good, Manos?" he asked, for confirmation.

"Sure," said Zurito. "You were going great."

The doctor's assistant put the cone over Manuel's face and he inhaled deeply. Zurito stood awkwardly, watching.

Eveline

JAMES JOYCE

James Joyce was born in Dublin in 1882, and spent his boyhood and youth there, attending Belvidere College and University College. In 1904 he left Ireland permanently, except for brief intervals, and lived in Italy, Switzerland, and France. In his early twenties Joyce wrote the stories of his native city which make up the volume *Dubliners,* completed in 1905 but not published until 1914—stories noteworthy for their frank portrayal of a wide range of Dublin life, their psychological penetration, and their vivid, poetic style. In 1916 he published the autobiographical novel *Portrait of the Artist as a Young Man. Ulysses,* published in Paris in 1922 but in America not until 1934, has had a profound influence on modern literature. *Finnegan's Wake* was published in 1939. Joyce died in Zurich, Switzerland, on January 13, 1941.

SHE sat at the window watching the evening invade the avenue. Her head was leaned against the window curtains and in her nostrils was the odor of dusty cretonne. She was tired.

Few people passed. The man out of the last house passed on his way home; she heard his footsteps clacking along

From *Dubliners,* by James Joyce. Reprinted by permission of The Viking Press, Inc., New York.

the concrete pavement and afterwards crunching on the cinder path before the new red houses. One time there used to be a field there in which they used to play every evening with other people's children. Then a man from Belfast bought the field and built houses in it—not like their little brown houses but bright brick houses with shining roofs. The children of the avenue used to play together in that field—the Devines, the Waters, the Dunns, little Keogh the cripple, she and her brothers and sisters. Ernest, however, never played: he was too grown up. Her father used often to hunt them in out of the field with his blackthorn stick; but usually little Keogh used to keep *nix* and call out when he saw her father coming. Still they seemed to have been rather happy then; and besides, her mother was alive. That was a long time ago; she and her brothers and sisters were all grown up; her mother was dead. Tizzie Dunn was dead, too, and the Waters had gone back to England. Everything changes. Now she was going to go away like the others, to leave her home.

Home! She looked round the room, reviewing all its familiar objects which she had dusted once a week for so many years, wondering where on earth the dust came from. Perhaps she would never see again those familiar objects from which she had never dreamed of being divided. And yet during all those years she had never found out the name of the priest whose yellowing photograph hung on the wall above the broken harmonium beside the colored print of the promises made to Blessed Margaret Mary Alacoque. He had been a school friend of her father. Whenever he showed the photograph to a visitor her father used to pass it with a casual word:

"He is in Melbourne now."

She had consented to go away, to leave her home. Was that wise? She tried to weigh each side of the question. In her home anyway she had shelter and food; she had those whom she had known all her life about her. Of course she had to work hard, both in the house and at business. What would they say of her in the Stores when they found out that she had run away with a fellow? Say she was a fool, perhaps; and her place would be filled up by advertisement. Miss Gavan would be glad. She had always had an edge on her, especially whenever there were people listening.

"Miss Hill, don't you see these ladies are waiting?"

"Look lively, Miss Hill, please."

She would not cry many tears at leaving the Stores.

But in her new home, in a distant unknown country, it would not be like that. Then she would be married— she, Eveline. People would treat her with respect then. She would not be treated as her mother had been. Even now, though she was over nineteen, she sometimes felt herself in danger of her father's violence. She knew it was that that had given her the palpitations. When they were growing up he had never gone for her, like he used to go for Harry and Ernest, because she was a girl; but latterly he had begun to threaten her and say what he would do to her only for her dead mother's sake. And now she had nobody to protect her. Ernest was dead, and Harry, who was in the church decorating business, was nearly always down somewhere in the country. Besides, the invariable squabble for money on Saturday nights had begun to weary her unspeakably. She always gave her entire wages—seven shillings—and Harry always sent up what he could but the trouble was to get any money from her father. He said she used to squander the money, that she had no head, that he wasn't going to give her his hard-earned money to throw about the streets, and much more, for he was usually fairly bad on Saturday night. In the end he would give her the money and ask her had she any intention of buying Sunday's dinner. Then she had to rush out as quickly as she could and do her marketing, holding her black leather purse tightly in her hand as she elbowed her way through the crowds and returning home late under her load of provisions. She had hard work to keep the house together and to see that the two young children who had been left to her charge went to school regularly and got their meals regularly. It was hard work—a hard life—but now that she was about to leave it she did not find it a wholly undesirable life.

She was about to explore another life with Frank. Frank was very kind, manly, open-hearted. She was to go away with him by the night boat to be his wife and to live with him in Buenos Aires where he had a home waiting for her. How well she remembered the first time she had seen him; he was lodging in a house on the main road where she used to visit. It seemed a few weeks ago. He was standing at the gate, his peaked cap pushed back on his head and his hair tumbled forward over a face of bronze. Then they had come to know each other. He used to meet her outside the Stores every evening and see her home. He took her to see *The Bohemian Girl* and she felt elated as she sat in an unaccustomed part of the theatre with him. He was awfully fond of music and sang a little. People knew that they were courting and, when he sang about the lass that loves a sailor, she always felt pleasantly confused. He used to call her Poppens out of fun. First of all it had been an excitement for her to have a fellow and then she had begun to like him. He had tales of distant countries. He had started as a deck boy at a pound a month on a ship of the Allan Line going out to Canada. He told her the names of the ships he had been on and the names of the different services. He had sailed through the Straits of Magellan and he told her stories of the terrible Patagonians. He had fallen on his feet in Buenos Aires, he said, and had come over to the old country just for a holiday. Of course, her father had found out the affair and had forbidden her to have anything to say to him.

"I know these sailor chaps," he said.

One day he had quarrelled with Frank and after that she had to meet her lover secretly.

The evening deepened in the avenue. The white of two letters in her lap grew indistinct. One was to Harry; the other was to her father. Ernest had been her favorite but she liked Harry too. Her father was becoming old lately, she noticed; he would miss her. Sometimes he could be very nice. Not long before, when she had been laid up for a day, he had read her out a ghost story and made toast for her at the fire. Another day, when their mother was alive, they had all gone for a picnic to the Hill of Howth. She remembered her father putting on her mother's bonnet to make the children laugh.

Her time was running out but she continued to sit by the window, leaning her head against the window curtain, inhaling the odor of dusty cretonne. Down far in the avenue she could hear a street organ playing. She knew the air. Strange that it should come that very night to remind her of the promise to her mother, her promise to keep the home together as long as she could. She remembered the last night of her mother's illness; she was again in the close dark room at the other side of the hall and outside she heard a melancholy air of Italy. The organ player had been ordered to go away and given sixpence. She remembered her father strutting back into the sickroom saying:

"Damned Italians! coming over here!"

As she mused the pitiful vision of her mother's life laid its spell on the very quick of her being—that life of commonplace sacrifices closing in final craziness. She trembled as she heard again her mother's voice saying constantly with foolish insistence:

"Derevaun Seraun! Derevaun Seraun!"

She stood up in a sudden impulse of terror. Escape! She must escape! Frank would save her. He would give her life, perhaps love, too. But she wanted to live. Why should she be unhappy? She had a right to happiness. Frank would take her in his arms, fold her in his arms. He would save her.

She stood among the swaying crowd in the station at the North Wall. He held her hand and she knew that he was speaking to her, saying something about the passage, over and over again. The station was full of soldiers with brown baggage. Through the wide doors of the sheds she caught a glimpse of the black mass of the boat, lying in beside the quay wall, with illumined portholes. She answered nothing. She felt her cheek pale and cold and, out of a maze of distress, she prayed to God to direct her, to show her what was her duty. The boat blew a long mournful whistle into the mist. If she went, tomorrow she would be on the sea with Frank, steaming towards Buenos Aires. Their passage had been booked. Could she still draw back after all he had done for her? Her distress awoke a nausea in her body and she kept moving her lips in silent fervent prayer.

A bell clanged upon her heart. She felt him seize her hand:

"Come!"

All the seas of the world tumbled about her heart. He was drawing her into them: he would drown her. She gripped with both hands at the iron railing.

"Come!"

No! No! No! It was impossible. Her hands clutched the

iron in frenzy. Amid the seas she sent a cry of anguish!

"Eveline! Evvy!"

He rushed beyond the barrier and called to her to follow. He was shouted at to go on but he still called to her. She set her white face to him, passive, like a helpless animal. Her eyes gave him no sign of love or farewell or recognition.

There Are Smiles

RING LARDNER

Ringgold W. Lardner was born in 1885 at Niles, Michigan, and died in 1933. He attended the Niles high school and studied engineering at the Armour Institute of Technology, but left at the end of two years to become a reporter on the South Bend, Indiana, *Tribune*. He continued as a sports writer in St. Louis, Boston, Chicago, and New York until his death. Lardner's first book of fiction, the sketches of baseball players in *You Know Me, Al* (1916), came directly out of his work as a reporter. Later his writing broadened to include Americans of widely varied type and background, but he treated them all with the trained reporter's alert recognition of significant detail, and with a particularly accurate ear for the rhythms of American speech. His forceful, sometimes coldly dispassionate analysis of characters and motives gave way at times to a warm though restrained recognition of beauty and goodness. His stories are collected in *Round Up* (1929).

AT THE busy corner of Fifth Avenue and Forty-sixth Street there was, last summer, a traffic policeman who made you feel that he didn't have such a terrible job after all. Lots of traffic policemen seem to enjoy abusing you, sadistic complex induced by exposure to bad weather and worse drivers, and, possibly, brutal wives. But Ben Collins just naturally appeared to be having a good time whether he was scolding you or not; his large freckled face fairly beamed with joviality and refused to cloud up even under the most trying conditions.

It heartened you to look at him. It amused you to hear him talk. If what he said wasn't always so bright, the way he said it was.

Ben was around thirty years old. He was six feet four inches tall and weighed two hundred and eighteen pounds. This describes about eighty per cent of all the traffic officers between Thirty-second Street and the Park. But Ben was distinguished from the rest by his habitual good humor and—well, I guess you'd have to call it his subtlety.

For example, where Noonan or Wurtz or Carmody was content with the stock "Hey! Get over where you belong!" or "Where the hell do you think you're going?" Ben was wont to finesse.

"How are you, Barney?" he would say to a victim halted at the curb.

"My name isn't Barney."

"I beg your pardon. The way you was stepping along, I figured you must be Barney Oldfield."

Or, "I suppose you didn't see that red light."

"No."

"Well, what did you think the other cars was stopped for? Did you think they'd all ran out of gas at once?"

Or, "What business are you in?"

"I'm a contractor."

"Well, that's a good, honorable business, and, if I was you, I wouldn't be ashamed of it. I'd quit trying to make people believe I was in the fire department."

Or, "How do you like London?"

"Me? I've never been there."

"I thought that's where you got the habit of driving on the wrong side of the street."

Transgressions at Ben's corner, unless they resulted seriously, were seldom punished beyond these sly rebukes, which were delivered in such a nice way that you were kind of glad you had done wrong.

Off duty he was "a big good-natured boy," willing to take Grace to a picture, or go over to the Arnolds' and play cards, or just stay at home and do nothing.

And then one morning in September, a dazzlingly new Cadillac roadster, blue with yellow trimmings, flashed down from the north, violating all the laws of common sense and the State and City of New York. Shouts and whistles from Carmody and Noonan, at Forty-eighth and Forty-seventh, failed to check its crazy career, but Ben, first planting his huge bulk directly in its path, giving the driver the choice of slackening speed or running into him, and then, with an alertness surprising in one so massive, sidestepping and jumping onto the running board, succeeded in forcing a surrender at the curb halfway between his post and Forty-fifth Street.

He was almost mad and about to speak his mind in words beginning with capitals when he got his first look at the miscreant's impudent, ill-timed, irresistible smile, a smile that spoiled other smiles for you once for all.

"Well—" Ben began falteringly; then recovering something of his stage presence: "Where's your helmet?"

She made no reply, but continued to smile.

"If you're in the fire department," said Ben, "you ought to wear a helmet and a badge. Or paint your car red and get a sireen."

Still no reply.

"Maybe I look like a bobby. Maybe you thought you was in London where they drive on the left side of the street."

"You're cute," she said, and her voice was as thrilling as her smile. "I could stay here all morning and listen to you. That is I could, but I can't. I've got a date down on Eighth Street and I'm late for it now. And I know you're busy, too. So we mustn't keep each other any longer now. But I'd like to hear your whole line some day."

"Oh, you would!"

"Where do you live?"

"At home."

"That isn't very polite, is it? I was thinking you might live in the Bronx——"

"I do."

"—and that's on the way to Rye, where I live, so I might drive you."

"Thanks. When I die, I want to die of old age."

"Oh, I'm not a bad driver, really. I do like to go fast, but I'm careful. In Buffalo, where we lived before, the policemen all knew I was careful and they generally let me go as fast as I wanted to."

"This ain't Buffalo. And this ain't no speedway. If you want to go fast, stay off Fifth Avenue."

The girl looked him right in the eye. "Would you like that?"

"No," said Ben.

She smiled at him again. "What time are you through?"

"Four o'clock," said Ben.

"Well," said the girl, "some afternoon I may be going home about then——"

"I told you I wasn't ready to die."

"I'd be extra careful."

Ben suddenly realized that they were playing to a large staring audience and that, for once, he was not the star.

"Drive on!" he said in his gruffest tone. "I'm letting you go because you're a stranger, but you won't get off so easy next time."

"I'm very, very grateful," said the girl. "Just the same I don't like being a stranger and I hope you won't excuse me on that ground again."

Which remark, accompanied by her radiant smile, caused Mr. Collins, hitherto only a bathroom singer, to hum quite loudly all the rest of his working day snatches of a gay Ohman and Arden record that his wife had played over and over the night before.

His relief, Tim Martin, appeared promptly at four, but Ben seemed in no hurry to go home. He pretended to listen to two new ones Tim had heard on the way in from Flushing, one about a Scotchman and some hotel towels and one about two Heebs in a night club. He managed to laugh in the right place, but his attention was on the northbound traffic, which was now none of his business.

At twenty minutes past four he said good-by to Martin and walked slowly south on the east side of the street. He walked as far as Thirty-sixth, in vain. Usually he caught a ride home with some Bronx or north suburban motorist, but now he was late and had to pay for his folly by hurrying to Grand Central and standing up in a subway express.

"I was a sucker!" he thought. "She probably drove up some other street on purpose to miss me. Or she might have came in on one of them cross streets after I'd walked past it. I ought to stuck at Forty-fourth a while longer. Or maybe some other fella done his duty and had her locked up. Not if she smiled at him, though."

But she wouldn't smile like that at everybody. She had smiled at him because she liked him, because she really thought he was cute. Yes, she did! That was her regular line. That was how she had worked on them Buffalo fellas. "Cute!" A fine word to use on a human Woolworth Building. She was kidding. No, she wasn't; not entirely. She'd liked his looks as plenty other gals had, and maybe that stuff about the fire department and London had tickled her.

Anyway, he had seen the most wonderful smile in the world and he still felt warm from it when he got home, so warm that he kissed his wife with a fervor that surprised her.

When Ben was on the day shift, he sometimes entertained Grace at supper with an amusing incident or two of his work. Sometimes his stories were pure fiction and she suspected as much, but what difference did it make? They were things that ought to have happened even if they hadn't.

On this occasion he was wild to talk about the girl from Rye, but he had learned that his wife did not care much for anecdotes concerning pretty women. So he recounted one-sided arguments with bungling drivers of his own sex which had very little foundation in fact.

"There was a fella coming south in a 1922 Buick and the light changed and when it was time to go again, he thought he was starting in second, and it was reverse instead, and he backed into a big Pierce from Greenwich. He didn't do no damage to the Pierce and only bent himself a little. But they'd have held up the parade ten minutes talking it over if I hadn't bore down.

"I got the Buick fella over to the curb and I said to him, 'What's the matter? Are you homesick?' So he said what did I mean, homesick, and I said, 'Well, you was so anxious to get back to wherever you come from that you couldn't even wait to turn around.'

"Then he tried to explain what was the matter, just like I didn't know. He said this was his first trip in a Buick and he was used to a regular gear shift.

"I said, 'That's fine, but this ain't no training-camp. The place to practice driving is four blocks farther down, at Forty-second. You'll find more automobiles there and twicet as many pedestrians and policemen, and besides, they've got street-cars and a tower to back into.'

"I said, 'You won't never learn nothing in a desert like this.' You ought to heard the people laugh."

"I can imagine!" said Grace.

"Then there was a Jordan, an old guy with a gray beard. He was going to park right in front of Kaskel's. He said he wouldn't be more than half an hour. I said, 'Oh, that's too bad! I wished you could spend the weekend.' I said, 'If you'd let us know you was coming, we'd have arranged some parties for you.' So he said, 'I've got a notion to report you for being too fresh.'

"So I said, 'If you do that, I'll have you arrested for driving without your parents' consent.' You ought to have heard them laugh. I said, 'Roll, Jordan, roll!' You ought to havᵉ heard them."

"I'll bet!" said Grace.

Ben fell into a long, unaccustomed silence.

"What are you thinking about?"

It came out against his better judgment. "There was a gal in a blue Cadillac."

"Oh! There was! What about her?"

"Nothing. Only she acted like it was her Avenue and I give her hell."

"What did you say to her?"

"I forget."

"Was she pretty?"

"I didn't notice. I was sore."

"You!"

"She all but knocked me for a corpse."

"And you probably just smiled at her."

"No. She done the smiling. She smiled—" He broke off and rose from the table. "Come on, babe. Let's go to the Franklin. Joe Frisco's there. And a Chaplin picture."

Ben saw nothing of the blue Cadillac or its mistress the rest of that week, but in all his polemics he was rehearsing lines aimed to strengthen her belief in his "cuteness." When she suddenly appeared, however, late on the following Tuesday afternoon, he was too excited to do anything but stare, and he would have lost an opportunity of hearing her enchanting voice if she hadn't taken the initiative. Northbound, she stopped at the curb a few feet above his corner and beckoned to him.

"It's after four," she said. "Can't I drive you home?"

What a break! It was his week on the late shift.

"I just come to work. I won't be off till midnight."

"You're mean! You didn't tell me you were going to change."

"I change every week. Last week, eight to four; this week, four to twelve."

"And next week eight to four?"

"Yes'm."

"Well, I'll just have to wait."

He couldn't say a word.

"Next Monday?"

He made an effort. "If you live."

She smiled that smile. "I'll live," she said. "There's an incentive."

She was on her way and Ben returned to his station, dizzy.

"Incentive, incentive, incentive," he repeated to himself, memorizing it, but when he got home at half past one, he couldn't find it in Grace's abridged Webster; he thought it was spelled with an *s*.

The longest week in history ended. A little before noon on Monday the Cadillac whizzed past him going south and he caught the word "later." At quitting time, while

Tim Martin was still in the midst of his first new one about two or more Heebs, Ben was all at once aware that she had stopped right beside him, was blocking the traffic, waiting for him.

Then he was in her car, constricting his huge bulk to fit it and laughing like a child at Tim's indelicate ejaculation of surprise.

"What are you laughing at?"

"Nothing. I just feel good."

"Are you glad to be through?"

"Yes. Today."

"Not always?"

"I don't generally care much."

"I don't believe you do. I believe you enjoy your job. And I don't see how you can because it seems to me such a hard job. I'm going to make you tell me all about it as soon as we get out of this jam."

A red light stopped them at Fifty-first Street and she turned and looked at him amusedly.

"It's a good thing the top is down," she said. "You'd have been hideously uncomfortable in one more fold."

"When I get a car of my own," said Ben, "it'll have to be a Mack, and even then I'll have to hire a man to drive it."

"Why a man?"

"Men ain't all crazy."

"Honestly, I'm not crazy. Have I come near hitting anything?"

"You've just missed everything. You drive too fast and you take too many chances. But I knew it before I got in, so I can't kick."

"There isn't room for you to, anyway. Do you want to get out?"

"No."

"I doubt if you could. Where do you live?"

"Hundred and sixty-fourth, near the Concourse," said Ben.

"How do you usually go home?"

"Like this."

"And I thought I was saving you from a tiresome subway ride or something. I ought to have known you'd never lack invitations. Do you?"

"Hardly ever."

"Do the people ask you all kinds of questions?"

"Yes."

"I'm sorry. Because I wanted to and now I can't."

"Why not?"

"You must be tired of answering."

"I don't always answer the same."

"Do you mean you lie to people, to amuse yourself?"

"Sometimes."

"Oh, that's grand! Come on, lie to me. I'll ask you questions, probably the same questions they all ask, and you answer them as if I were a fool. Will you?"

"I'll try."

"Well, let's see. What shall I ask you first? Oh, yes. Don't you get terribly cold in winter?"

He repeated a reply he had first made to an elderly lady, obviously a visitor in the city, whose curiosity had prompted her to cross-examine him for over twenty minutes on one of the busiest days he had ever known.

"No. When I feel chilly, I stop a car and lean against the radiator."

His present interviewer rewarded him with more laughter than was deserved.

"That's wonderful!" she said. "And I suppose when your ears are cold, you stop another car and borrow its hood."

"I'll remember that one."

"Now what next? Do you ever get hit?"

"Right along, but only glancing blows. I very seldom get knocked down and run over."

"Doesn't it almost kill you, standing on your feet all day?"

"It ain't near as bad as if it was my hands. Seriously, Madam, I get so used to it that I sleep that way nights."

"Don't the gasoline fumes make you sick?"

"They did at first, but now I can't live without them. I have an apartment near a public garage so I can run over there any time and re-fume myself."

"How tall are you?"

"Six feet ten."

"Not really!"

"You know better, don't you? I'm six feet four, but when women ask me, I tell them anything from six feet eight to seven feet two. And they always say, 'Heavens!'"

"Which do you have the most trouble with, men drivers or women drivers?"

"Men drivers."

"Honestly?"

"Sure. There's fifty times as many of them."

"Do lots of people ask you questions?"

"No. You're the first one."

"Were you mad at me for calling you cute the other day?"

"I couldn't be mad at you."

A silence of many blocks followed. The girl certainly did drive fast and Ben might have been more nervous if he had looked ahead, but mostly his eyes were on her profile which was only a little less alluring than her smile.

"Look where we are!" she exclaimed as they approached Fordham Road. "And you live at a Hundred and sixty-fourth! Why didn't you tell me?"

"I didn't notice."

"Don't get out. I'll drive you back."

"No, you won't. I'll catch a ride. There's a fella up this way I v'ant to see."

"You were nice to take a chance with me and not to act scared. Will you do it again?"

"Whenever you say."

"I drive in once a week. I go down to Greenwich Village to visit my sister. Generally on Mondays."

"Next Monday I'll be on the late shift."

"Let's make it the Monday after."

"That's a long ways off."

"The time will pass. It always does."

It did, but so haltingly! And the day arrived with such a threat of rain that Ben was afraid she wouldn't come in. Later on, when the threat was fulfilled and the perils of motoring trebled by a steady drizzle and slippery pavements, he was afraid she would. Prudence, he knew, was not in her make-up and if she had an engagement with her sister, nothing short of a flood would prevent her keeping it.

Just before his luncheon time, the Cadillac passed, going south. Its top was up and its squeegee flying back and forth across the front glass.

Through the rain he saw the girl smile and wave at him briefly. Traffic was thick and treacherous and both must keep their minds on it.

It was still drizzling when she reappeared and stopped for him at four.

"Isn't this a terrible day?" she said.

"Not now!"

She smiled, and in an instant he forgot all the annoyance and discomfort of the preceding hours.

"If we leave the top up, you'll get stoop-shouldered, and if we take it down, we'll be drowned."

"Leave it up. I'm all right."

"Do you mind if we don't talk much? I feel quiet."

He didn't answer and nothing more was said until they turned east at Mount Morris Park. Then:

"I could find out your name," she said, "by remembering your number and having somebody look it up. But you can save me the trouble by telling me."

"My name is Ben Collins. And I could learn yours by demanding to see your driver's license."

"Heavens! Don't do that! I haven't any. But my name is Edith Dole."

"Edith Dole. Edith Dole," said Ben.

"Do you like it?"

"It's pretty."

"It's a funny combination. Edith means happiness and Dole means grief."

"Well," said Ben, "you'll have plenty of grief if you drive without a license. You'll have it anyway if you drive fast on these kind of streets. There's nothing skiddier than car tracks when it's raining."

They were on upper Madison, and the going was dangerous. But that was not the only reason he wanted her to slow down.

Silence again until they were on the Concourse.

"Are you married?" she asked him suddenly.

"No," he lied. "Are you?"

"I will be soon."

"Who to?"

"A man in Buffalo."

"Are you stuck on him?"

"I don't know. But he wants me and my father wants him to have me."

"Will you live in Buffalo?"

"No. He's coming here to be my father's partner."

"And yours."

"Yes. Oh, dear! Here's a Hundred and sixty-fourth and I mustn't take you past it today, not in this weather. Do you think you can extricate yourself?"

He managed it with some difficulty.

"I don't suppose I'll see you again for two weeks."

"I'm afraid not," she said.

He choked down the words that wanted to come out. "Miss Dole," he said, "take my advice and don't try for no records getting home. Just loaf along and you'll be there an hour before your supper's ready. Will you? For that guy's sake in Buffalo?"

"Yes."

"And my sake, too."

Gosh! What a smile to remember!

He must walk slow and give himself a chance to calm down before he saw Grace. Why had he told the girl he wasn't married? What did she care?

Grace's greeting was a sharp command. "Take a hot bath right away! And wear your bathrobe afterwards. We won't be going anywhere tonight."

She and Mary Arnold had been in Mount Vernon at a card party. They had got soaked coming home. She talked about it all through supper, thank the Lord!

After supper he tried to read, but couldn't! He listened awhile to the Ohman and Arden record which his wife couldn't get enough of. He went to bed, wishing he could sleep and dream, wishing he could sleep two weeks.

He was up early, early enough to look at the paper before breakfast. "Woman Motorist Killed By Street-Car in Bronx." His eyes felt funny as he read: "Miss Edith Dole, twenty-two, of Rye, was instantly killed when the automobile she was driving skidded and struck a street-car at the corner of Fordham Road and Webster Avenue, the Bronx, shortly after four-thirty yesterday afternoon."

"Grace," he said in a voice that was not his own. "I forgot. I'm supposed to be on the job at seven this morning. There's some kind of a parade."

Out of the house, alone, he talked aloud to himself for the first time since he was a kid.

"I can't feel as bad as I think I do. I only seen her four or five times. I can't really feel this bad."

Well, on an afternoon two or three weeks later, a man named Hughes from White Plains, driving a Studebaker, started across Forty-sixth Street out of turn and obeyed a stern order to pull over to the curb.

"What's your hurry?" demanded the grim-faced traffic policeman. "Where the hell do you think you're going? What's the matter with you, you so-and-so?"

"I forgot myself for a minute. I'm sorry," said Mr. Hughes. "If you'll overlook it, I'll pick you up on my way home and take you to the Bronx. Remember, I give you a ride home last month? Remember? That is, it was a fella that looked like you. That is, he looked something like you. I can see now it wasn't you. It was a different fella."

The Doll's House

KATHERINE MANSFIELD

Kathleen Beauchamp was born at Wellington, New Zealand, in 1888, the daughter of a banker. She spent five years at Queen's College in London, and later lived in London on a small allowance from her father, studying music and writing. Her first stories to find publication, collected in 1911 as *In a German Pension* by "Katherine Mansfield," were written while she was convalescing in Germany after a physical breakdown the effects of which persisted throughout her life. She died in 1923 of tuberculosis. She admired the stories of Chekhov, and like him she realized in her writing the dramatic value and emotional significance of seemingly trivial events in the lives of ordinary people. She was always sharply self-critical, never satisfied with her achievement. She has had a wide influence on contemporary literature, not only through her stories—three volumes of which were published during her lifetime and four after her death —but also through her *Journals* and *Letters* edited by her husband, J. Middleton Murry.

WHEN dear old Mrs. Hay went back to town after staying with the Burnells she sent the children a doll's house. It was so big that the carter and Pat carried it into the courtyard, and there it stayed, propped up on two wooden boxes beside the feed-

From *The Dove's Nest,* by Katherine Mansfield (Knopf, 1923). Copyright, 1923, by Alfred A. Knopf, Inc. Reprinted by permission of and special arrangement with Alfred A. Knopf, Inc., authorized publishers.

room door. No harm could come of it; it was summer. And perhaps the smell of paint would have gone off by the time it had to be taken in. For, really, the smell of paint coming from that doll's house ("Sweet of old Mrs. Hay, of course; most sweet and generous!")—but the smell of paint was quite enough to make any one seriously ill, in Aunt Beryl's opinion. Even before the sacking was taken off. And when it was. . . .

There stood the doll's house, a dark, oily, spinach green, picked out with bright yellow. Its two solid little chimneys, glued on to the roof, were painted red and white, and the door, gleaming with yellow varnish, was like a little slab of toffee. Four windows, real windows, were divided into panes by a broad streak of green. There was actually a tiny porch, too, painted yellow, with big lumps of congealed paint hanging along the edge.

But perfect, perfect little house! Who could possibly mind the smell? It was part of the joy, part of the newness.

"Open it quickly, some one!"

The hook at the side was stuck fast. Pat pried it open with his penknife, and the whole house front swung back, and—there you were, gazing at one and the same moment into the drawing room and dining room, the kitchen and two bedrooms. That is the way for a house to open! Why don't all houses open like that? How much more exciting than peering through the slit of a door into a mean little hall with a hatstand and two umbrellas! That is—isn't it?—what you long to know about a house when you put your hand on the knocker. Perhaps it is the way God opens houses at dead of night when He is taking a quiet turn with an angel. . . .

"O-oh!" The Burnell children sounded as though they were in despair. It was too marvellous; it was too much for them. They had never seen anything like it in their lives. All the rooms were papered. There were pictures on the walls, painted on the paper, with gold frames complete. Red carpet covered all the floors except the kitchen; red plush chairs in the drawing room, green in the dining room; tables, beds with real bedclothes, a cradle, a stove, a dresser with tiny plates and one big jug. But what Kezia liked more than anything, what she liked frightfully, was the lamp. It stood in the middle of the dining-room table, an exquisite little amber lamp with a white globe. It was even filled all ready for lighting, though, of course, you couldn't light it. But there was something inside that looked like oil, and that moved when you shook it.

The father and mother dolls, who sprawled very stiff as though they had fainted in the drawing room, and their two little children asleep upstairs, were really too big for the doll's house. They didn't look as though they belonged. But the lamp was perfect. It seemed to smile at Kezia, to say, "I live here." The lamp was real.

The Burnell children could hardly walk to school fast enough the next morning. They burned to tell everybody, to describe, to—well—to boast about their doll's house before the school-bell rang.

"I'm to tell," said Isabel, "because I'm the eldest. And you two can join in after. But I'm to tell first."

There was nothing to answer. Isabel was bossy, but she was always right, and Lottie and Kezia knew too well the powers that went with being eldest. They brushed through the thick buttercups at the road edge and said nothing.

"And I'm to choose who's to come and see it first. Mother said I might."

For it had been arranged that while the doll's house stood in the courtyard they might ask the girls at school, two at a time, to come and look. Not to stay to tea, of course, or to come traipsing through the house. But just to stand quietly in the courtyard while Isabel pointed out the beauties, and Lottie and Kezia looked pleased. . . .

But hurry as they might, by the time they had reached the tarred palings of the boys' playground the bell had begun to jangle. They only just had time to whip off their hats and fall into line before the roll was called. Never mind. Isabel tried to make up for it by looking very important and mysterious and by whispering behind her hand to the girls near her, "Got something to tell you at playtime."

Playtime came and Isabel was surrounded. The girls of her class nearly fought to put their arms round her, to walk away with her, to beam flatteringly, to be her special friend. She held quite a court under the huge pine trees at the side of the playground. Nudging, giggling together, the little girls pressed up close. And the only two who stayed outside the ring were the two who were always outside, the little Kelveys. They knew better than to come anywhere near the Burnells.

For the fact was, the school the Burnell children went to was not at all the kind of place their parents would have chosen if there had been any choice. But there was none. It was the only school for miles. And the consequence was all the children in the neighborhood, the Judge's little girls, the doctor's daughters, the storekeeper's children, the milkman's, were forced to mix together. Not to speak of there being an equal number of rude, rough little boys as well. But the line had to be drawn somewhere. It was drawn at the Kelveys. Many of the children, including the Burnells, were not allowed even to speak to them. They walked past the Kelveys with their heads in the air, and as they set the fashion in all matters of behavior, the Kelveys were shunned by everybody. Even the teacher had a special voice for them, and a special smile for the other children when Lil Kelvey came up to her desk with a bunch of dreadfully common-looking flowers.

They were the daughters of a spry, hardworking little washerwoman, who went about from house to house by the day. This was awful enough. But where was Mr. Kelvey? Nobody knew for certain. But everybody said he was in prison. So they were the daughters of a washerwoman and a gaolbird. Very nice company for other people's children! And they looked it. Why Mrs. Kelvey made them so conspicuous was hard to understand. The truth was they were dressed in "bits" given to her by the people for whom she worked. Lil, for instance, who was a stout, plain child, with big freckles, came to school in a dress made from a green art-serge tablecloth of the Burnells', with red' plush sleeves from the Logans' curtains. Her hat, perched on top of her high forehead, was a grown-up woman's hat, once the property of Miss Lecky, the postmistress. It was turned up at the back and trimmed with a large scarlet quill. What a little guy she looked! It was impossible not to laugh. And her little sister, our Else, wore a long white dress, rather like a nightgown, and a pair of little boy's boots. But whatever our Else wore she would have looked strange. She was a tiny wishbone of a child, with cropped hair and enormous solemn eyes—a little white owl. Nobody had ever seen her smile; she scarcely ever spoke. She went through life holding on to Lil, with a piece of Lil's skirt screwed up in her hand. Where Lil went our Else followed. In the playground, on the road going to and from school, there was Lil marching in front and our Else holding on behind. Only when she wanted anything, or when she was out of breath, our Else gave Lil a tug, a twitch, and Lil stopped and turned round. The Kelveys never failed to understand each other.

Now they hovered at the edge; you couldn't stop them

listening. When the little girls turned round and sneered, Lil, as usual, gave her silly, shamefaced smile, but our Else only looked.

And Isabel's voice, so very proud, went on telling. The carpet made a great sensation, but so did the beds with real bedclothes, and the stove with an oven door.

When she finished Kezia broke in. "You've forgotten the lamp, Isabel."

"Oh, yes," said Isabel, "and there's a teeny little lamp, all made of yellow glass, with a white globe that stands on the dining-room table. You couldn't tell it from a real one."

"The lamp's best of all," cried Kezia. She thought Isabel wasn't making half enough of the little lamp. But nobody paid any attention. Isabel was choosing the two who were to come back with them that afternoon and see it. She chose Emmie Cole and Lena Logan. But when the others knew they were all to have a chance, they couldn't be nice enough to Isabel. One by one they put their arms round Isabel's waist and walked her off. They had something to whisper to her, a secret. "Isabel's *my* friend."

Only the little Kelveys moved away forgotten; there was nothing more for them to hear.

Days passed, and as more children saw the doll's house, the fame of it spread. It became the one subject, the rage. The one question was, "Have you seen Burnells' doll's house? Oh, ain't it lovely!" "Haven't you seen it? Oh, I say!"

Even the dinner hour was given up to talking about it. The little girls sat under the pines eating their thick mutton sandwiches and big slabs of johnnycake spread with butter. While always, as near as they could get, sat the Kelveys, our Else holding on to Lil, listening too, while they chewed their jam sandwiches out of a newspaper soaked with large red blobs. . . .

"Mother," said Kezia, "can't I ask the Kelveys just once?"

"Certainly not, Kezia."

"But why not?"

"Run away, Kezia; you know quite well why not."

At last everybody had seen it except them. On that day the subject rather flagged. It was the dinner hour. The children stood together under the pine trees, and suddenly, as they looked at the Kelveys eating out of their paper, always by themselves, always listening, they wanted to be horrid to them. Emmie Cole started the whisper.

"Lil Kelvey's going to be a servant when she grows up."

"O-oh, how awful!" said Isabel Burnell, and she made eyes at Emmie.

Emmie swallowed in a very meaning way and nodded to Isabel as she'd seen her mother do on those occasions.

"It's true—it's true—it's true," she said.

Then Lena Logan's little eyes snapped. "Shall I ask her?" she whispered.

"Bet you don't," said Jessie May.

"Pooh, I'm not frightened," said Lena. Suddenly she gave a little squeal and danced in front of the other girls. "Watch! Watch me! Watch me now!" said Lena. And sliding, gliding, dragging one foot, giggling behind her hand, Lena went over to the Kelveys.

Lil looked up from her dinner. She wrapped the rest quickly away. Our Else stopped chewing. What was coming now?

"Is it true you're going to be a servant when you grow up, Lil Kelvey?" shrilled Lena.

Dead silence. But instead of answering, Lil only gave her silly, shamefaced smile. She didn't seem to mind the question at all. What a sell for Lena! The girls began to titter.

Lena couldn't stand that. She put her hands on her hips; she shot forward. "Yah, yer father's in prison!" she hissed, spitefully.

This was such a marvellous thing to have said that the little girls rushed away in a body, deeply, deeply excited, wild with joy. Some one found a long rope, and they began skipping. And never did they skip so high, run in and out so fast, or do such daring things as on that morning.

In the afternoon Pat called for the Burnell children with the buggy and they drove home. There were visitors. Isabel and Lottie, who liked visitors, went upstairs to change their pinafores. But Kezia thieved out at the back. Nobody was about; she began to swing on the big white gates of the courtyard. Presently, looking along the road, she saw two little dots. They grew bigger, they were coming towards her. Now she could see that one was in front and one close behind. Now she could see that they were the Kelveys. Kezia stopped swinging. She slipped off the gate as if she was going to run away. Then she hesitated. The Kelveys came nearer, and beside them walked their shadows, very long, stretching right across the road with their heads in the buttercups. Kezia clambered back on the gate; she had made up her mind; she swung out.

"Hullo," she said to the passing Kelveys.

They were so astounded that they stopped. Lil gave her silly smile. Our Else stared.

"You can come and see our doll's house if you want to," said Kezia, and she dragged one toe on the ground. But at that Lil turned red and shook her head quickly.

"Why not?" asked Kezia.

Lil gasped, then she said, "Your ma told our ma you wasn't to speak to us."

"Oh, well," said Kezia. She didn't know what to reply. "It doesn't matter. You can come and see our doll's house all the same. Come on. Nobody's looking."

But Lil shook her head still harder.

"Don't you want to?" asked Kezia.

Suddenly there was a twitch, a tug at Lil's skirt. She turned round. Our Else was looking at her with big, imploring eyes; she was frowning; she wanted to go. For a moment Lil looked at our Else very doubtfully. But then our Else twitched her skirt again. She started forward. Kezia led the way. Like two little stray cats they followed across the courtyard to where the doll's house stood.

"There it is," said Kezia.

There was a pause. Lil breathed loudly, almost snorted; our Else was still as a stone.

"I'll open it for you," said Kezia kindly. She undid the hook and they looked inside.

"There's the drawing room and the dining room, and that's the——"

"Kezia!"

Oh, what a start they gave!

"Kezia!"

It was Aunt Beryl's voice. They turned round. At the back door stood Aunt Beryl, staring as if she couldn't believe what she saw.

"How dare you ask the little Kelveys into the courtyard?" said her cold, furious voice. "You know as well as I do, you're not allowed to talk to them. Run away, children, run away at once. And don't come back again," said Aunt Beryl. And she stepped into the yard and shooed them out as if they were chickens.

"Off you go immediately!" she called, cold and proud.

They did not need telling twice. Burning with shame, shrinking together, Lil huddling along like her mother, our Else dazed, somehow they crossed the big courtyard and squeezed through the white gate.

"Wicked, disobedient little girl!" said Aunt Beryl bitterly to Kezia, and she slammed the doll's house to.

The afternoon had been awful. A letter had come from Willie Brent, a terrifying, threatening letter, saying if she did not meet him that evening in Pulman's Bush, he'd come to the front door and ask the reason why! But now that she had frightened those little rats of Kelveys and given Kezia a good scolding, her heart felt lighter. That ghastly pressure was gone. She went back to the house humming.

When the Kelveys were well out of sight of Burnells', they sat down to rest on a big red drainpipe by the side of the road. Lil's cheeks were still burning; she took off the hat with the quill and held it on her knee. Dreamily they looked over the hay paddocks, past the creek, to the group of wattles where Logan's cows stood waiting to be milked. What were their thoughts?

Presently our Else nudged up close to her sister. But now she had forgotten the cross lady. She put out a finger and stroked her sister's quill; she smiled her rare smile.

"I seen the little lamp," she said, softly.

Then both were silent once more.

The Little Wife

WILLIAM MARCH

William March Campbell was born at Mobile, Alabama, in 1896. He spent most of his boyhood in the South, but has lived in many parts of the United States. He attended Valparaiso University in Indiana and studied law at the University of Alabama. He served in France with the American Marine Corps, and was severely wounded and gassed. From this experience came materials for some of his short stories and for the novel *Company K* (1934). He has written also the novels *Come In At the Door* (1934) and *The Tallons* (1936), and short stories collected in *The Little Wife* (1935) and *Some Like Them Short* (1939).

JOE HINCKLEY selected a seat on the shady side of the train and carefully stowed away his travelling bag and his heavy, black catalogue case. It was unusually hot for early June. Outside, the heat waves shimmered and danced above the hot slag roadbed, and the muddy river that ran by the station was low between its red banks. "If it's as hot as this in June, it sure will be awful in August," he thought. He looked at his watch: two twenty-eight—the train was five minutes late in getting out. If he had known

From *The Little Wife and Other Stories*. Copyright, 1935, by William March. Reprinted by permission of the author and of Random House, Inc.

the two twenty-three was going to be late he might have had time to pack his sample trunk and get it to the station, but he couldn't have anticipated that, of course. He had had so little time after getting that telegram from Mrs. Thompkins—barely time to pack his bag and check out of the hotel. Joe loosened his belt and swabbed his neck with a limp handkerchief. "It don't matter so much about the trunk," he thought. "One of the boys at the hotel can express it to me, or I can pick it up on my way back."

Joe noticed that one end of his catalogue case protruded slightly. With his foot he shoved it farther under the seat. It was a battered black case, made strongly to withstand constant travelling and reinforced at its corners with heavy copper cleats. One of the handles had been broken and mended with newer leather. On the front of the case there had once been stamped in gilt the firm name of "Boykin & Rosen, Wholesale Hardware, Chattanooga, Tenn.," but time had long since worn away the gold lettering.

The telegram had upset Joe: it had come so suddenly, so unexpectedly. He felt vaguely that somebody was playing a joke on him. He felt confused and helpless. It was difficult to believe that Bessie was so desperately sick. He sat for a time staring at his fingernails. Suddenly he remembered an appointment for four o'clock with the buyer for Snowdoun and Sims, and he rose quickly from his seat with some vague idea of telephoning or sending a message to explain his absence. Then he realized that the train was in motion. "I'll write him a letter when I get to Mobile," said Joe to himself; "he'll understand all right when I explain the circumstances. He won't blame me for breaking that date when I tell him about my wife being so sick." Joe sat down heavily in his seat and again looked at his hands.

Ahead of him two young girls were leaning out of the window and waving to their friends. Their eyes were shining and their cheeks were flushed and they were laughing with excitement at the prospect of going away.

Across the aisle sat a gaunt farm-woman. Her red-veined eyes protruded. Her neck was swollen with a goitre. In her arms she held a bouquet of red crêpe-myrtle, which was already wilting in the heat. Beside her she had placed her straw suitcase and several bulky paper-wrapped parcels. She gazed steadily out of the window as if afraid that someone would catch her eye and try to talk to her.

It was very hot in the coach. The small electric fan at the end of the car droned and wheezed sleepily, but succeeded only in stirring up the hot air.

Joe took from his pocket the telegram that he had received from his mother-in-law and read it again: "J. G. Hinckley, American Hotel, Montgomery, Ala. Come home at once. Doctor says Bessie not expected live through day. Will wire again if necessary. It was a boy. Mother."

Joe's hands clenched suddenly and then relaxed. It had all happened so suddenly; he couldn't quite get it through his head, even yet. He had taken a buyer to lunch that day and they had laughed and talked and told each other stories. Then at two o'clock he had gone back to the hotel to freshen up and the clerk had reached into his box and taken out the key to his room and the telegram. The telegram had been waiting for him for two hours, the clerk said. Joe read it through twice and then looked at the address to make sure that the message was really for him. He hadn't understood: Bessie was getting along so nicely—she had had no trouble at all—and the baby was not expected for a month. He had arranged his itinerary so that he would be with her when the baby was born. They had gone over all that and had arranged everything. And now everything was upset. . . . Then he thought: "I was out talking and laughing with that buyer and the telegram was waiting here all the time."

That thought hurt him. He stood repeating stupidly: "I was out laughing and telling smutty stories and that telegram was here all the time."

Joe leaned his head against the red plush of the seat. He felt numb and very tired. At first the signature "Mother" had puzzled him. He couldn't understand what his mother would be doing in Mobile with Bessie; then he realized that it was Bessie's mother who had sent the telegram. He had never thought of Bessie's mother by any name except Mrs. Thompkins.

When he had married Bessie her mother had come to live with them as a matter of course. He was rather glad of that arrangement: he was really fond of the old lady in an impersonal sort of way. Then, too, it was pleasant for Bessie to have some one with her while he was on the road. His work made it impossible for him to get home oftener than every other week end; and many times it was difficult for him to get home that often, but he had always managed to make it, one way or another. He couldn't disappoint Bessie, no matter what happened. Their year of married life had been the happiest that he had ever known. And Bessie had been happy too. . . . Suddenly he had a clear picture of her lying on their bed, her face white with suffering, and a quick panic gripped his heart. To reassure himself he whispered: "Those damned doctors don't know everything. She'll be all right. Mrs. Thompkins was just excited and frightened. Everything's going to be all right!"

Ahead of him a white-haired old gentleman opened his bag and took out a travelling cap. He had some difficulty in fastening the catch while holding his straw hat in his hand; but his wife, sitting with him, took the bag and fastened it at once. Then she took his hat and held it on her lap. The wife was reading a magazine. She did not look up from the magazine when she fastened the bag.

Down the aisle came the Negro porter. He had a telegram in his hand. When he reached the center of the coach he stopped and called out: "Telegram for Mr. J. G. Hinckley!" Joe let him call the name three times before he claimed the message. The porter explained that the telegram had been delivered to the train by a messenger from the American Hotel just as the train was getting under way. Joe gave the porter twenty-five cents for a tip and went back to his seat.

The country woman looked up for an instant and then turned her eyes away. The young girls giggled and whispered and looked boldly at Joe; and the old gentleman, after settling his cap firmly on his head, took a cigar from his case and went to the smoking room.

Joe's throat felt tight, and he noticed that his hands were shaking. He wanted to put his head on the window sill, but he was afraid that people would think him sick and try to talk to him. He placed the unopened telegram on the seat beside him and stared at it for a long time. Then he re-read the first telegram very slowly. "It must be from Mrs. Thompkins, all right," he thought; "she said she'd wire again if—" Then he thought: "It may be from somebody else; it may be from Boykin and Rosen about that cancellation in Meridian. That's who it's from: it's from the House; it's not from Mrs. Thompkins at all!" He looked up quickly and saw that the two young girls had turned around and were watching him, making laughing remarks to each other behind their hands.

He arose from his seat feeling weak and slightly nauseated, the unopened telegram in his hand. He passed through several coaches until he reached the end of the train, and went out on the rear vestibule. He had a sudden wish to jump from the end of the train and run off into the woods, but a brakeman was there tinkering with a red lantern and Joe realized that such an act would look very strange. When the brakeman looked up and saw Joe's face, he put down his lantern and asked: "Are you feeling all right, mister?" Joe said, "Yes, I'm feeling all right; but it's a little hot, though." Finally the brakeman finished his job and left, and Joe was very glad of that. He wanted to be alone. He didn't want anybody around him.

The rails clicked rhythmically and the wilted country-side flew past. A little Negro girl . . . in a patched pink dress . . . ran down to the track . . . and waved her hand. A lame old country man . . . ploughing in his stumpy field . . . pulled up his lazy mule . . . to stare at the passing train. The rails clattered and clicked and the train flew over the hot slag roadbed. "There's no need of going so fast," thought Joe, "we've got all the time in the world." He felt sick. In the polished metal of the car he caught a distorted glimpse of his face. It was white and terrified. He thought: "No wonder that brakeman asked me how I was feeling." Then he thought: "Do I look so bad that people can tell it?" That worried him. He didn't want people to notice him or to talk to him. There was nothing that anybody could say, after all.

He kept turning the telegram over in his hand, thinking: "I've got to open it now; I've got to open it and read it." Finally he said aloud: "It's not true! I don't believe it! It's from the House about that cancellation in Meridian—it isn't from Mrs. Thompkins at all." Then he tore the unopened telegram into tiny bits and threw the pieces from the end of the train. A wind fluttered and shimmered the yellow fragments before they settled down lightly on the hard hot roadbed. He thought: "They look like a cloud of yellow butterflies dancing and settling that way." Immediately he felt better. He drew back his shoulders and sucked in lungsful of the country air. "Everything's all right!" he said. "I'm going home to see the little wife and everything's all right!"

He laughed happily. He felt like a man who has just escaped some terrible calamity. When he could no longer see the scraps of paper on the track he went back to his seat humming a tune. He felt very gay and immensely relieved.

Joe reached his seat just as the conductor came through the train. He nodded pleasantly as he gave up his ticket.

"Don't let anybody talk you out of a free ride," he said.

"No chance of that, Cap'," said the conductor.

Joe laughed with ringing heartiness and the conductor looked at him in surprise. Then he laughed a little himself. "You sure are in a good humor, considering how hot it is," he said.

"And why shouldn't I be in a good humor?" asked Joe. "I'm going home to see the little wife." Then he whispered, as if it were a great secret. "It's a boy!"

"That's fine; that's simply fine!" said the conductor. He put his papers and his tickets on the seat and shook Joe's hand heartily. Joe blushed and laughed again. Then, as the conductor moved off, he nudged Joe's ribs and said: "Give my regards to the madam."

"I sure will," said Joe happily.

Joe was sorry that the conductor couldn't stay longer. He felt an imperative need of talking to someone. He felt that he must talk about Bessie to someone. He looked around the car to see if there was any one whom he knew. The two young girls smiled at him. Joe understood perfectly; they were just two nice kids going on a trip. Either one, alone, would never think of smiling at a strange man, but being together changed things entirely. That made it an exciting adventure—something to be laughed over and discussed later with their friends. Joe decided that he would go over and talk to them. He walked over casually and seated himself.

"Where are you girls going?" he asked.

"Don't you think that you have a great deal of nerve?" asked the black-eyed girl.

"Sure I have. I wouldn't be the best hardware salesman on the road if I didn't have lots of nerve," said Joe pleasantly.

Both of the girls laughed at that and Joe knew that everything was all right. He decided that the blue-eyed girl was the prettier of the two, but the black-eyed girl had more snap.

"We're getting off at Flomaton," said the blue-eyed girl.

"We've been in school in Montgomery," said the black-eyed girl.

"We're going home for the summer vacation."

"And we want the cock-eyed world to know we're glad of it!"

Joe looked at them gravely. "Don't make a mistake, young ladies; get all the education you can—you'll regret it later on if you don't."

Both the girls started laughing. They put their arms around each other and laughed until tears came into their eyes. Joe laughed too, although he wondered what the joke was. After awhile the girls stopped laughing, but a sudden giggle from the blue-eyed girl set them off again, worse than before.

"This is awfully silly," said the black-eyed girl.

"What's the joke?" asked Joe, who was really laughing as much as either of the girls.

"You sounded so—so—" explained the blue-eyed girl.

"So damned *fatherly!*" finished the black-eyed girl.

Then they went off into another whirlwind of mirth, laughing and hugging each other. The old lady across the aisle put down her magazine and started laughing too, but the woman with the goitre held her bouquet of crêpe-myrtle rigidly and stared out of the window.

Joe waited until the girls had exhausted themselves. Finally

they wiped their eyes and opened their vanity cases to look
at themselves in their mirrors and to re-powder their noses.
Then he said:

"Well, I guess I ought to sound fatherly: I just got a telegram saying that I was a proud parent."

That interested the young girls and they crowded him
with questions; they wanted to know all about it. Joe felt
very happy. As he started to talk he noticed that the old
lady had been listening and that she had moved over in her
seat in order to hear better. Joe felt friendly toward everybody. "Won't you come over and join us?" he asked.

"Yes, indeed," said the nice old lady, and Joe moved over
and made a place for her.

"Now tell us all about it!" demanded the blue-eyed girl.

"You must be very happy," said the nice old lady.

"I sure am happy," said Joe. Then he added: "There's
not a whole lot to tell except that I got a telegram from Mrs.
Thompkins—Mrs. Thompkins is my mother-in-law—saying
that Bessie had given birth to a fine boy and that both of
them were doing splendidly; the doctor said that he'd never
seen anybody so well before, but of course my wife wanted
me to be with her, and so I just dropped everything and
here I am. You see Bessie and I have only been married for
a year. We've been very happy. The only bad thing is that I
don't get home very often; but it wouldn't do to have everything perfect in the world, would it? She sure is the finest
little wife a man ever had. She don't complain at all about
my being away so much. But some day we hope to have
things different."

"There isn't anything nicer than a baby," said the blue-
eyed girl.

"What are you going to name him?" asked the nice old
lady.

"Well, Bessie wants to name him for me, but I can't see

much sense in that. My first name's Joe and I think that's a little common, don't you? But I'll leave the naming part up to Bessie. She can name him anything she wants to. She sure has been a fine little wife to me."

Then Joe started talking rapidly. He told in detail of the first time he had met Bessie: it had been in the home of Jack Barnes, one of the boys whom he had met on the road, and he had been invited over for dinner and a little stud poker later. Mrs. Barnes didn't play poker, so Bessie, who lived across the street, had been invited over to keep Mrs. Barnes company while the men played. He had liked Bessie at once, and the boys had kidded him about not keeping his mind on the game. He had never told anybody this before, but when the boys started kidding him he made up his mind not to look at Bessie again, as he didn't want her to think that he was fresh; but he couldn't stop looking at her, and every time he caught her eye she would smile in a sweet, friendly sort of way. Finally everybody noticed it and they started joking Bessie too, but she hadn't minded at all. He had lost fourteen dollars and fifty cents that night, but he had met Bessie. You couldn't call Bessie exactly beautiful but she was sweet and nice. Bessie was the sort of girl that any man would want to marry.

He told of their courtship. He quoted whole paragraphs from letters that she had written, to prove a particular point which he had brought up. Bessie hadn't liked him especially, not right at first, at any rate; of course she had liked him as a friend from the first but not in any serious way. There were one or two other fellows hanging around, too. Bessie had a great deal of attention; she could have gone out every night with a different man if she had wanted to. Being on the road all the time had been pretty much of a disadvantage. He didn't have an opportunity to see her often. Or maybe that was an advantage—anyway, he wrote her every day.

Then, finally, they had become engaged. She hadn't even let him kiss her until then. He knew from the first that she would make a wonderful little wife, but he was still puzzled why a girl as superior as Bessie would want to marry him.

He talked on and on, rapidly—feverishly. He told how he had once determined not to get married at all, but that was before he had met Bessie. She had changed all that. . . . Two hours passed before he knew it. His audience was getting bored, but Joe didn't realize it.

Finally the old gentleman with the cap came back from the smoking room; and his wife, glad of a chance to get away, made her excuses and went over to sit with him. Joe smiled and nodded, but paused only a moment in his story. He was in the midst of a long description of Mrs. Thompkins. Mrs. Thompkins wasn't at all like the comic supplement mother-in-law. Quite the contrary. He didn't see how he and Bessie would get along without her. To show you the sort of woman she really was, she always took his side in any dispute—not that he and Bessie ever quarreled! Oh, no! But occasionally they had little friendly discussions, like all other married couples, and Mrs. Thompkins always took his side of the argument. That was unusual, wasn't it? Joe talked and talked, totally unconscious of the passing of time.

Finally the train reached Flomaton, and the porter came to help the girls off with their bags. They were very glad to get away. They were getting a little nervous. There was something about Joe they couldn't understand. At first they had thought him just jolly and high spirited, but after a time they came to the conclusion that he must be a little drunk or, possibly, slightly demented. For the past hour they had been nudging each other significantly.

Joe helped them off the train and onto the station platform. Just as the train pulled out, the black-eyed girl waved her hand and said: "Give my love to Bessie and the son and heir," and the blue-eyed girl said: "Be sure and kiss the baby for me."

"I sure will," said Joe.

Joe went back to the coach. "Just a couple of nice kids," he thought to himself. He looked at his watch. It was five twenty-five. He was surprised. The time had passed very quickly. "It won't be long now before I'm in Mobile," he thought.

He went back to his seat, but he was restless. He decided that he would have a cigarette. He found three men in the smoker. One of them was an old man with a tuft of gray whiskers. His face was yellow and sunken, and blue veins stood out on his hands. He was chewing tobacco gravely and spitting into the brass cuspidor. The second man was large and flabby. When he laughed, his eyes disappeared entirely and his fat belly shook. His fingernails were swollen and his underlip hung down in a petulant droop. The third man was dark and nervous looking. He had on his little finger a ring with a diamond much too large.

They were telling jokes and laughing when Joe came in. Joe wanted to talk to them about Bessie, but he couldn't bring her name up in such an atmosphere. Suddenly he thought: "I was laughing and telling smutty stories with that buyer in Montgomery, and the telegram was there all the time." His face contracted with pain. He crushed the thought from his mind. Quickly he threw away his cigarette and went back to his seat.

A bright-skinned waiter came through the train announcing the first call to dinner. At first Joe thought that he would have his dinner on the train, as that would break the monotony of the trip and help pass the time; but immediately he remembered that Mrs. Thompkins would have dinner for him at home—a specially prepared dinner with all of the things that he liked. "I'll wait till I get home," thought Joe. "I wouldn't disappoint Mrs. Thompkins and the little wife for the world after they went to all that trouble for me."

Again he felt that curious, compulsive need of talking about Bessie to someone. He had a feeling that as long as he talked about her, she would remain safe. He saw the old lady and her husband in their seat eating a lunch which they had brought with them and he decided to go over and talk with them. "Can I come over and talk to you folks?" asked Joe.

"Certainly, sir," said the old gentleman with the cap. Then, in order to make conversation he said: "My wife has been telling me that you are going home to see your new son."

"That's right," said Joe, "that's right." He started talking rapidly, hardly pausing for breath. The old lady looked at her husband reproachfully. "Now see what you started!" her glance seemed to say.

Joe talked of his wedding. It had been very quiet: Bessie was the sort of girl who didn't go in for a lot of show. There had been present only a few members of the family and one or two close friends. George Orcutt, who travelled with a line of rugs out of New York, had been his best man. Bessie was afraid that someone would try to play a joke on them: something like tying tin cans to the automobile that was to take them to the station, or marking their luggage with chalk. But everything had gone off smoothly. The Barneses had been at the wedding, of course; he had met Bessie in their home and they were such close neighbors that they couldn't overlook them; but almost nobody else, outside the family, was there.

Then he told of the honeymoon they had spent in New Orleans—all the places they had visited there and just what Bessie had thought and said about each one. He talked on and on and on. He told of the first weeks of their married life and how happy they were. He told what a splendid cook Bessie was and what an excellent housekeeper, how much she had loved the home he had bought for her, and her delight when she knew that she was going to have a baby.

The old gentleman was staring at Joe in a puzzled manner. He was wondering if he hadn't better call the conductor, as it was his private opinion that Joe had a shot of cocaine in him. The old lady had folded her hands like a martyr. She continued to look at her husband with an I-told-you-so expression.

Joe had lost all idea of time. He talked on and on—rapidly, excitedly. He had gotten as far as Bessie's plans for the child's education when the porter touched him on the arm and told him that they were pulling into the station at Mobile. He came to himself with a start and looked at his watch: seven thirty-five! He didn't believe it possible that two hours had passed so quickly.

"It sure has been a pleasure talking to you folks," said Joe.

"Oh, that's all right," said the man with the cap.

Joe gave the porter a tip and stepped off the train jauntily. As he turned to pick up his bag, he saw that the woman with the goitre was staring at him. He walked over to the window that framed her gaunt face. "Goodbye, lady; I hope you have a nice trip." The woman answered: "The doctors said it wasn't no use operating on me: I waited too late." "Well, that's fine!—That sure is fine!" said Joe. He laughed gaily and waved his hand. Then he picked up his bag and his catalogue case and followed the people through the gate. The woman with the goitre stared at him until he was out of sight.

On the other side of the iron fence Joe saw Mrs. Thompkins. She was dressed all in black and she wore a black veil. Joe went over to her briskly, and Mrs. Thompkins put her arms around him and kissed him twice. "Poor Joe!" she said. Then she looked at his smiling, excited face with amazement. Joe noticed that her eyes were red and swollen.

"Didn't you get my telegram?" she asked. Joe wrinkled his brow in an effort to remember. Finally he said: "Oh, yes, I got it at the hotel."

"Did you get my second telegram?" insisted Mrs. Thompkins.

She looked steadily into Joe's eyes. A feeling of terror swept over him. He knew that he could no longer lie to himself. He could no longer keep Bessie alive by talking about her. His face was suddenly twisted with pain and his jaw trembled like a child's. He leaned against the iron fence for support, and Mrs. Thompkins held his hand and said: "You can't give in. You got to be a man; you can't give in like that, Joe!"

Finally he said: "I didn't read your telegram. I didn't want to know that she was dead. I wanted to keep her alive a little longer." He sat down suddenly on an empty baggage truck and hid his face in his hands. He sat there for a long time while Mrs. Thompkins stood guard over him, her black veil trailing across his shoulder. Finally he asked: "What time did Bessie die?" His voice was tight and hard. It seemed to come from behind his teeth. Mrs. Thompkins answered: "She died at three minutes past two."

A man in a dirty uniform came up. "I'm sorry, mister, but you'll have to move. We got to use that truck."

Joe picked up his catalogue case and his bag and followed Mrs. Thompkins out of the station.

Lord Mountdrago

W. SOMERSET MAUGHAM

W. Somerset Maugham was born in Paris in 1874, the son of a prominent British lawyer. He attended a public school in England and the University of Heidelberg, and studied medicine at St. Thomas's Hospital in London. Although he never practiced medicine, his experience as a medical student provided much of the material for his first novel, *Liza of Lambeth* (1897) and for his masterpiece, *Of Human Bondage* (1915). He has travelled widely in the Orient and has lived for most of his later years in France. He has been widely popular as playwright, novelist, and short story writer. His work is uniformly brilliant in craftsmanship, but varies in spirit and intention from the frankly commercial to the wholly sincere. He has commented significantly on his own life and work as a writer in *The Summing Up* (1938).

DOCTOR AUDLIN looked at the clock on his desk. It was twenty minutes to six. He was surprised that his patient was late, for Lord Mountdrago prided himself on his punctuality; he had a sententious way of expressing himself which gave the air of an epigram to a commonplace remark, and he was in the habit of saying that punctuality is a compliment you pay to the intelligent and a

From *The Mixture as Before,* by W. Somerset Maugham (Doubleday, Doran, 1940). Copyright, 1933, 1940. Reprinted by permission of Doubleday, Doran and Company, Inc.

rebuke you administer to the stupid. Lord Mountdrago's appointment was for five-thirty.

There was in Doctor Audlin's appearance nothing to attract attention. He was tall and spare, with narrow shoulders and something of a stoop; his hair was gray and thin, his long, sallow face deeply lined. He was not more than fifty, but he looked older. His eyes, pale blue and rather large, were weary. When you had been with him for a while you noticed that they moved very little; they remained fixed on your face, but so empty of expression were they that it was no discomfort. They seldom lit up. They gave no clue to his thoughts nor changed with the words he spoke. If you were of an observant turn it might have struck you that he blinked much less often than most of us. His hands were on the large side, with long, tapering fingers; they were soft but firm, cool but not clammy. You could never have said what Doctor Audlin wore unless you had made a point of looking. His clothes were dark. His tie was black. His dress made his sallow lined face paler and his pale eyes more wan. He gave you the impression of a very sick man.

Doctor Audlin was a psychoanalyst. He had adopted the profession by accident and practised it with misgiving. When the war broke out he had not been long qualified and was getting experience at various hospitals; he offered his services to the authorities, and after a time was sent out to France. It was then that he discovered his singular gift. He could allay certain pains by the touch of his cool, firm hands, and by talking to them often induce sleep in men who were suffering from sleeplessness. He spoke slowly. His voice had no particular color, and its tone did not alter with the words he uttered, but it was musical, soft and lulling. He told the men that they must rest, that they mustn't worry, that they must sleep; and rest stole into their jaded bones, tranquillity pushed their anxieties away, like a man finding a place for himself on a crowded bench, and slumber fell on their tired eyelids like the light rain of spring upon the fresh-turned earth. Doctor Audlin found that by speaking to men with that low, monotonous voice of his, by looking at them with his pale, quiet eyes, by stroking their weary foreheads with his long firm hands, he could soothe their perturbations, resolve the conflicts that distracted them and banish the phobias that made their lives a torment. Sometimes he effected cures that seemed miraculous. He restored speech to a man who, after being buried under the earth by a bursting shell, had been struck dumb, and he gave back the use of his limbs to another who had been paralyzed after a crash in a plane. He could not understand his powers; he was of a sceptical turn, and though they say that in circumstances of this kind the first thing is to believe in yourself, he never quite succeeded in doing that; and it was only the outcome of his activities, patent to the most incredulous observer, that obliged him to admit that he had some faculty, coming from he knew not where, obscure and uncertain, that enabled him to do things for which he could offer no explanation. When the war was over he went to Vienna and studied there, and afterwards to Zurich; and then settled down in London to practise the art he had so strangely acquired. He had been practising now for fifteen years, and had attained, in the speciality he followed, a distinguished reputation. People told one another of the amazing things he had done, and though his fees were high, he had as many patients as he had time to see. Doctor Audlin knew that he had achieved some very extraordinary results; he had saved men from suicide, others from the lunatic asylum, he had assuaged griefs that embittered useful lives, he had turned unhappy marriages into happy ones, he had eradicated abnormal instincts and thus delivered not a few from a hateful bondage, he had given health to the sick in spirit; he had done all this, and yet at the back of his mind remained the suspicion that he was little more than a quack.

It went against his grain to exercise a power that he could not understand, and it offended his honesty to trade on the faith of the people he treated when he had no faith in himself. He was rich enough now to live without working, and the work exhausted him; a dozen times he had been on the point of giving up practice. He knew all that Freud and Jung and the rest of them had written. He was not satisfied; he had an intimate conviction that all their theory was hocus-pocus, and yet there the results were, incomprehensible, but manifest. And what had he not seen of human nature during the fifteen years that patients had been coming to his dingy back room in Wimpole Street? The revelations that had been poured into his ears, sometimes only too willingly, sometimes with shame, with reservations, with anger, had long ceased to surprise him. Nothing could shock him any longer. He knew by now that men were liars, he knew how extravagant was their vanity; he knew far worse than that about them; but he knew that it was not for him to judge or to condemn. But year by year as these terrible confidences were imparted to him his face grew a little grayer, its lines a little more marked and his pale eyes more weary. He seldom laughed, but now and again when for relaxation he read a novel he smiled. Did their authors really think the men and women they wrote of were like that? If they only knew how much more complicated they were, how much more unexpected, what irreconcilable elements coexisted within their souls and what dark and sinister contentions afflicted them!

It was a quarter to six. Of all the strange cases he had been called upon to deal with, Doctor Audlin could remember none stranger than that of Lord Mountdrago. For one thing the personality of his patient made it singular.

Lord Mountdrago was an able and a distinguished man. Appointed Secretary for Foreign Affairs when still under forty, now after three years in office he had seen his policy prevail. It was generally acknowledged that he was the ablest politician in the Conservative Party, and only the fact that his father was a peer, on whose death he would no longer be able to sit in the House of Commons, made it impossible for him to aim at the premiership. But if in these democratic times it is out of the question for a Prime Minister of England to be in the House of Lords, there was nothing to prevent Lord Mountdrago from continuing to be Secretary for Foreign Affairs in successive Conservative administrations and so for long directing the foreign policy of his country.

Lord Mountdrago had many good qualities. He had intelligence and industry. He was widely travelled and spoke several languages fluently. From early youth he had specialized in foreign affairs and had conscientiously made himself acquainted with the political and economic circumstances of other countries. He had courage, insight and determination. He was a good speaker, both on the platform and in the House, clear, precise and often witty. He was a brilliant debater and his gift of repartee was celebrated. He had a fine presence: he was a tall, handsome man, rather bald and somewhat too stout, but this gave him solidity and an air of maturity that were of service to him. As a young man he had been something of an athlete and had rowed in the Oxford boat, and he was known to be one of the best shots in England. At twenty-four he had married a girl of eighteen whose father was a duke and her mother a great American heiress, so that she had both position and wealth, and by her he had had two sons. For several years they had lived privately apart, but in public united, so that appearances were saved, and no other at-

tachment on either side had given the gossips occasion
to whisper. Lord Mountdrago indeed was too ambitious,
too hardworking, and it must be added too patriotic, to
be tempted by any pleasures that might interfere with his
career. He had in short a great deal to make him a popular
and successful figure. He had unfortunately great defects.

He was a fearful snob. You would not have been surprised at this if his father had been the first holder of the
title. That the son of an ennobled lawyer, manufacturer
or distiller should attach an inordinate importance to his
rank is understandable. The earldom held by Lord Mountdrago's father was created by Charles II, and the barony
held by the first earl dated from the Wars of the Roses. For
three hundred years the successive holders of the title had
allied themselves with the noblest families of England. But
Lord Mountdrago was as conscious of his birth as a nouveau
riche is conscious of his money. He never missed an opportunity of impressing it upon others. He had beautiful manners when he chose to display them, but this he did only
with people whom he regarded as his equals. He was coldly
insolent to those whom he looked upon as his social in-
feriors. He was rude to his servants and insulting to his
secretaries. The subordinate officials in the government offices to which he had been successively attached feared
and hated him. His arrogance was horrible. He knew that
he was a great deal cleverer than most of the persons he
had to do with, and never hesitated to apprise them of the
fact. He had no patience with the infirmities of human
nature. He felt himself born to command and was irritated
with people who expected him to listen to their arguments
or wished to hear the reasons for his decisions. He was
immeasurably selfish. He looked upon any service that was
rendered him as a right due to his rank and intelligence
and therefore deserving of no gratitude. It never entered

his head that he was called upon to do anything for others. He had many enemies: he despised them. He knew no one who merited his assistance, his sympathy or his compassion. He had no friends. He was distrusted by his chiefs because they doubted his loyalty; he was unpopular with his party, because he was overbearing and discourteous; and yet his merit was so great, his patriotism so evident, his intelligence so solid and his management of affairs so brilliant, that they had to put up with him. And what made it possible to do this was that on occasion he could be enchanting: when he was with persons whom he considered his equals, or whom he wished to captivate, in the company of foreign dignitaries or women of distinction, he could be gay, witty and debonair; his manners then reminded you that in his veins ran the same blood as had run in the veins of Lord Chesterfield; he could tell a story with point, he could be natural, sensible and even profound. You were surprised at the extent of his knowledge and the sensitiveness of his taste. You thought him the best company in the world; you forgot that he had insulted you the day before and was quite capable of cutting you dead the next.

Lord Mountdrago almost failed to become Doctor Audlin's patient. A secretary rang up the doctor and told him that his lordship, wishing to consult him, would be glad if he would come to his house at ten o'clock on the following morning. Doctor Audlin answered that he was unable to go to Lord Mountdrago's house, but would be pleased to give him an appointment at his consulting room at five o'clock on the next day but one. The secretary took the message and presently rang back to say that Lord Mountdrago insisted on seeing Doctor Audlin in his own house and the doctor could fix his own fee. Doctor Audlin replied that he saw patients only in his consulting room and expressed his regret that unless Lord Mountdrago was prepared to come to him he could not give him his attention. In a quarter of an hour a brief message was delivered to him that his lordship would come not next day but one, but next day, at five.

When Lord Mountdrago was then shown in he did not come forward, but stood at the door and insolently looked the doctor up and down. Doctor Audlin perceived that he was in a rage; he gazed at him, silently, with still eyes. He saw a big heavy man, with graying hair, receding on the forehead so that it gave nobility to his brow, a puffy face with bold regular features and an expression of haughtiness. He had somewhat the look of one of the Bourbon sovereigns of the eighteenth century.

"It seems that it is as difficult to see you as a Prime Minister, Doctor Audlin. I'm an extremely busy man."

"Won't you sit down?" said the doctor.

His face showed no sign that Lord Mountdrago's speech in any way affected him. Doctor Audlin sat in his chair at the desk. Lord Mountdrago still stood, and his frown darkened.

"I think I should tell you that I am His Majesty's Secretary for Foreign Affairs," he said acidly.

"Won't you sit down?" the doctor repeated.

Lord Mountdrago made a gesture, which might have suggested that he was about to turn on his heel and stalk out of the room; but if that was his intention he apparently thought better of it. He seated himself. Doctor Audlin opened a large book and took up his pen. He wrote without looking at his patient.

"How old are you?"

"Forty-two."

"Are you married?"

"Yes."

"How long have you been married?"

"Eighteen years."

"Have you any children?"

"I have two sons."

Doctor Audlin noted down the facts as Lord Mountdrago abruptly answered his questions. Then he leaned back in his chair and looked at him. He did not speak; he just looked, gravely, with pale eyes that did not move.

"Why have you come to see me?" he asked at length.

"I've heard about you. Lady Chanute is a patient of yours, I understand. She tells me you've done her a certain amount of good."

Doctor Audlin did not reply. His eyes remained fixed on the other's face, but they were so empty of expression that you might have thought he did not even see him.

"I can't do miracles," he said at length. Not a smile, but the shadow of a smile flickered in his eyes. "The Royal College of Physicians would not approve of it if I did."

Lord Mountdrago gave a brief chuckle. It seemed to lessen his hostility. He spoke more amiably.

"You have a very remarkable reputation. People seem to believe in you."

"Why have you come to me?" repeated Doctor Audlin. Now it was Lord Mountdrago's turn to be silent. It looked as though he found it hard to answer. Doctor Audlin waited. At last Lord Mountdrago seemed to make an effort. He spoke.

"I'm in perfect health. Just as a matter of routine I had myself examined by my own doctor the other day, Sir Augustus Fitzherbert, I daresay you've heard of him, and he tells me I have the physique of a man of thirty. I work hard, but I'm never tired, and I enjoy my work. I smoke very little and I'm an extremely moderate drinker. I take a sufficiency of exercise and I lead a regular life. I am a perfectly sound, normal, healthy man. I quite expect you to think it very silly and childish of me to consult you."

Doctor Audlin saw that he must help him.

"I don't know if I can do anything to help you. I'll try. You're distressed?"

Lord Mountdrago frowned.

"The work that I'm engaged in is important. The decisions I am called upon to make can easily affect the welfare of the country and even the peace of the world. It is essential that my judgment should be balanced and my brain clear. I look upon it as my duty to eliminate any cause of worry that may interfere with my usefulness."

Doctor Audlin had never taken his eyes off him. He saw a great deal. He saw behind his patient's pompous manner and arrogant pride an anxiety that he could not dispel.

"I asked you to be good enough to come here because I know by experience that it's easier for some one to speak openly in the dingy surroundings of a doctor's consulting room than in his accustomed environment."

"They're certainly dingy," said Lord Mountdrago acidly. He paused. It was evident that this man who had so much self-assurance, so quick and decided a mind that he was never at a loss, at this moment was embarrassed. He smiled in order to show the doctor that he was at his ease, but his eyes betrayed his disquiet. When he spoke again it was with unnatural heartiness.

"The whole thing's so trivial that I can hardly bring myself to bother you with it. I'm afraid you'll just tell me not to be a fool and waste your valuable time."

"Even things that seem very trivial may have their importance. They can be a symptom of a deep-seated derangement. And my time is entirely at your disposal."

Doctor Audlin's voice was low and grave. The monotone in which he spoke was strangely soothing. Lord Mountdrago at length made up his mind to be frank.

"The fact is I've been having some very tiresome dreams lately. I know it's silly to pay any attention to them, but—well, the honest truth is that I'm afraid they've got on my nerves."

"Can you describe any of them to me?"

Lord Mountdrago smiled, but the smile that tried to be careless was only rueful.

"They're so idiotic, I can hardly bring myself to narrate them."

"Never mind."

"Well, the first I had was about a month ago. I dreamt that I was at a party at Connemara House. It was an official party. The King and Queen were to be there, and of course decorations were worn. I was wearing my ribbon and my star. I went into a sort of cloakroom they have to take off my coat. There was a little man there called Owen Griffiths, who's a Welsh member of Parliament, and to tell you the truth, I was surprised to see him. He's very common, and I said to myself: 'Really, Lydia Connemara is going too far, whom will she ask next?' I thought he looked at me rather curiously, but I didn't take any notice of him; in fact I cut the little bounder and walked upstairs. I suppose you've never been there?"

"Never."

"No, it's not the sort of house you'd ever be likely to go to. It's a rather vulgar house, but it's got a very fine marble staircase, and the Connemaras were at the top receiving their guests. Lady Connemara gave me a look of surprise when I shook hands with her, and began to giggle; I didn't pay much attention—she's a very silly, ill-bred woman, and her manners are no better than those of her ancestress whom King Charles II made a duchess. I must say the reception rooms at Connemara House are stately. I walked through, nodding to a number of people and shaking hands;

then I saw the German Ambassador talking with one of the Austrian archdukes. I particularly wanted to have a word with him, so I went up and held out my hand. The moment the Archduke saw me he burst into a roar of laughter. I was deeply affronted. I looked him up and down sternly, but he only laughed the more. I was about to speak to him rather sharply, when there was a sudden hush, and I realized that the King and Queen had come. Turning my back on the Archduke, I stepped forward, and then, quite suddenly, I noticed that I hadn't got any trousers on. I was in short silk drawers, and I wore scarlet sock suspenders. No wonder Lady Connemara had giggled; no wonder the Archduke had laughed! I can't tell you what that moment was. An agony of shame. I awoke in a cold sweat. Oh, you don't know the relief I felt to find it was only a dream."

"It's the kind of dream that's not so very uncommon," said Doctor Audlin.

"I daresay not. But an odd thing happened next day. I was in the lobby of the House of Commons, when that fellow Griffiths walked slowly past me. He deliberately looked down at my legs, and then he looked me full in the face, and I was almost certain he winked. A ridiculous thought came to me. He'd been there the night before and seen me make that ghastly exhibition of myself and was enjoying the joke. But of course I knew that was impossible because it was only a dream. I gave him an icy glare, and he walked on. But he was grinning his head off."

Lord Mountdrago took his handkerchief out of his pocket and wiped the palms of his hands. He was making no attempt now to conceal his perturbation. Doctor Audlin never took his eyes off him.

"Tell me another dream."

"It was the night after, and it was even more absurd than

the first one. I dreamt that I was in the House. There was a debate on foreign affairs which not only the country, but the world, had been looking forward to with the gravest concern. The government had decided on a change in their policy which vitally affected the future of the Empire. The occasion was historic. Of course the House was crowded. All the ambassadors were there. The galleries were packed. It fell to me to make the important speech of the evening. I had prepared it carefully. A man like me has enemies— there are a lot of people who resent my having achieved the position I have at an age when even the cleverest men are content with situations of relative obscurity—and I was determined that my speech should not only be worthy of the occasion, but should silence my detractors. It excited me to think that the whole world was hanging on my lips. I rose to my feet. If you've ever been in the House you'll know how members chat to one another during a debate, rustle papers and turn over reports. The silence was the silence of the grave when I began to speak. Suddenly I caught sight of that odious little bounder on one of the benches opposite, Griffiths, the Welsh member; he put out his tongue at me. I don't know if you've ever heard a vulgar music-hall song called 'A Bicycle Made For Two.' It was very popular a great many years ago. To show Griffiths how completely I despised him I began to sing it. I sang the first verse right through. There was a moment's surprise, and when I finished they cried 'Hear, hear,' on the opposite benches. I put up my hand to silence them and sang the second verse. The House listened to me in stony silence and I felt the song wasn't going down very well. I was vexed, for I have a good baritone voice, and I was determined that they should do me justice. When I started the third verse the members began to laugh; in an instant the laughter spread; the ambassadors, the strangers in the

Distinguished Strangers' Gallery, the ladies in the Ladies' Gallery, the reporters, they shook, they bellowed, they held their sides, they rolled in their seats; every one was overcome with laughter except the ministers on the Front Bench immediately behind me. In that incredible, in that unprecedented, uproar they sat petrified. I gave them a glance, and suddenly the enormity of what I had done fell upon me. I had made myself the laughingstock of the whole world. With misery I realized that I should have to resign. I woke and knew it was only a dream."

Lord Mountdrago's grand manner had deserted him as he narrated this, and now having finished he was pale and trembling. But with an effort he pulled himself together. He forced a laugh to his shaking lips.

"The whole thing was so fantastic that I couldn't help being amused. I didn't give it another thought, and when I went into the House on the following afternoon I was feeling in very good form. The debate was dull, but I had to be there, and I read some documents that required my attention. For some reason I chanced to look up, and I saw that Griffiths was speaking. He has an unpleasant Welsh accent and an unprepossessing appearance. I couldn't imagine that he had anything to say that it was worth my while to listen to, and I was about to return to my papers when he quoted two lines from 'A Bicycle Made For Two.' I couldn't help glancing at him, and I saw that his eyes were fixed on me with a grin of bitter mockery. I faintly shrugged my shoulders. It was comic that a scrubby little Welsh member should look at me like that. It was an odd coincidence that he should quote two lines from that disastrous song that I'd sung all through in my dream. I began to read my papers again, but I don't mind telling you that I found it difficult to concentrate on them. I was a little puzzled. Owen Griffiths had been in my first dream, the one at Connemara House, and I'd received a very definite impression afterwards that he knew the sorry figure I'd cut. Was it a mere coincidence that he had just quoted those two lines? I asked myself if it was possible that he was dreaming the same dreams as I was. But of course the idea was preposterous, and I determined not to give it a second thought."

There was a silence. Doctor Audlin looked at Lord Mountdrago and Lord Mountdrago looked at Doctor Audlin.

"Other people's dreams are very boring. My wife used to dream occasionally and insist on telling me her dreams next day with circumstantial detail. I found it maddening."

Doctor Audlin faintly smiled.

"You're not boring me."

"I'll tell you one more dream I had a few days later. I dreamt that I went into a public house at Limehouse. I've never been to Limehouse in my life and I don't think I've ever been in a public house since I was at Oxford, and yet I saw the street and the place I went into as exactly as if I were at home there. I went into a room—I don't know whether they call it the saloon bar or the private bar; there was a fireplace and a large leather armchair on one side of it, and on the other a small sofa; a bar ran the whole length of the room, and over it you could see into the public bar. Near the door was a round marble-topped table and two armchairs beside it. It was a Saturday night, and the place was packed. It was brightly lit, but the smoke was so thick that it made my eyes smart. I was dressed like a rough, with a cap on my head and a handkerchief round my neck. It seemed to me that most of the people there were drunk. I thought it rather amusing. There was a gramophone going, or the radio, I don't know which, and in front of the fireplace two women were doing a grotesque dance. There was a little crowd round them, laughing, cheering and singing. I went up to have a look, and some man said to me: 'Ave a drink, Bill.' There were glasses on the table full of a dark liquid which I understand is called brown ale. He gave me a glass, and not wishing to be conspicuous I drank it. One of the women who were dancing broke away from the other and took hold of the glass.

"'Ere, what's the idea?' she said. 'That's my beer you're putting away.' 'Oh, I'm so sorry,' I said, 'this gentleman offered it me, and I very naturally thought it was his to offer.' 'All right, mate,' she said, 'I don't mind. You come an' 'ave a dance with me.' Before I could protest she'd caught hold of me and we were dancing together. And then I found myself sitting in the armchair with the woman on my lap and we were sharing a glass of beer. I should tell you that sex has never played any great part in my life. I married young because in my position it was desirable that I should marry, but also in order to settle once for all the question of sex. I had the two sons I had made up my mind to have, and then I put the whole matter on one side. I've always been too busy to give much thought to that kind of thing, and living so much in the public eye as I do, it would have been madness to do anything that might give rise to scandal. The greatest asset a politician can have is a blameless record as far as women are concerned. I have no patience with the men who smash up their careers for women. I only despise them. The woman I had on my knees was drunk; she wasn't pretty and she wasn't young: in fact, she was just a blowsy old prostitute. She filled me with disgust, and yet when she put her mouth to mine and kissed me, though her breath stank of beer and her teeth were decayed, though I loathed myself, I wanted her—I wanted her with all my soul. Suddenly I heard a voice: 'That's right, old boy, have a good time.' I looked up, and there was Owen Griffiths. I tried to spring out of the chair, but that horrible woman wouldn't let me. 'Don't you pay no attention to 'im,' she said, ''e's only one of them nosy parkers.' 'You go to it,' he said. 'I know Moll. She'll give you your money's worth all right.' You know, I wasn't so much annoyed at his seeing me in that absurd situation as angry that he should address me as old boy. I pushed the woman aside and stood up and faced him. 'I don't know you, and I don't want to know you,' I said. 'I know you all right,' he said. 'And my advice to you, Molly, is, see that you get your money, he'll bilk you if he can.' There was a bottle of beer standing on the table close by. Without a word I seized it by the neck and hit him over the head with it as hard as I could. I made such a violent gesture that it woke me up."

"A dream of that sort is not incomprehensible," said Doctor Audlin. "It is the revenge nature takes on persons of unimpeachable character."

"The story's idiotic. I haven't told it you for its own sake. I've told it you for what happened next day. I wanted to look up something in a hurry, and I went into the library of the House. I got the book and began reading. I hadn't noticed when I sat down that Griffiths was sitting in a chair close by me. Another of the Labor Members came in and went up to him. 'Hullo, Owen,' he said to him, 'you're looking pretty dicky today.' 'I've got an awful headache,' he answered, 'I feel as if I'd been cracked over the head with a bottle.' "

Now Lord Mountdrago's face was gray with anguish.

"I knew then that the idea I'd had and dismissed as preposterous was true. I knew that Griffiths was dreaming my dreams and that he remembered them as well as I did."

"It may also have been a coincidence."

"When he spoke he didn't speak to his friend, he deliberately spoke to me. He looked at me with sullen resentment."

"Can you offer any suggestion why this same man should come into your dreams?"

"None."

Doctor Audlin's eyes had not left his patient's face and he saw that he lied. He had a pencil in his hand, and he drew a straggling line or two on his blotting paper. It often took a long time to get people to tell the truth, and yet they knew that unless they told it he could do nothing for them.

"The dream you've just described to me took place just over three weeks ago. Have you had any since?"

"Every night."

"And does this man Griffiths come into them all?"

"Yes."

The doctor drew more lines on his blotting paper. He wanted the silence, the drabness, the dull light of that little room to have its effect on Lord Mountdrago's sensibility. Lord Mountdrago threw himself back in his chair and turned his head away so that he should not see the other's grave eyes.

"Doctor Audlin, you must do something for me. I'm at the end of my tether. I shall go mad if this goes on. I'm afraid to go to sleep. Two or three nights I haven't. I've sat up reading and when I felt drowsy put on my coat and walked till I was exhausted. But I must have sleep. With all the work I have to do I must be at concert pitch; I must be in complete control of all my faculties. I need rest; sleep brings me none. I no sooner fall asleep than my dreams begin, and he's always there, that vulgar little cad, grinning at me, mocking me, despising me. It's a monstrous persecution. I tell you, Doctor, I'm not the man of my dreams; it's not fair to judge me by them. Ask any one you like. I'm an honest, upright, decent man. No one can say anything against my moral character either private or public. My whole ambition is to serve my country and maintain its greatness. I have money, I have rank, I'm not exposed to many of the temptations of lesser men, so that it's no credit to me to be incorruptible; but this I can claim, that no honor, no personal advantage, no thought of self would induce me to swerve by a hairsbreadth from my duty. I've sacrificed everything to become the man I am. Greatness is my aim. Greatness is within my reach, and I'm losing my nerve. I'm not that mean, despicable, cowardly, lewd creature that horrible little man sees. I've told you three of my dreams; they're nothing; that man has seen me do things that are so beastly, so horrible, so shameful, that even if my life depended on it I wouldn't tell them. And he remembers them. I can hardly meet the derision and disgust I see in his eyes, and I even hesitate to speak because I know my words can seem to him nothing but utter humbug. He's seen me do things that no man with any self-respect would do, things for which men are driven out of the society of their fellows and sentenced to long terms of imprisonment; he's heard the foulness of my speech; he's seen me not only ridiculous, but revolting. He despises me and he no longer pretends to conceal it. I tell you that if you can't do something to help me I shall either kill myself or kill him."

"I wouldn't kill him if I were you," said Doctor Audlin coolly, in that soothing voice of his. "In this country the consequences of killing a fellow creature are awkward."

"I shouldn't be hanged for it, if that's what you mean. Who would know that I'd killed him? That dream of mine has shown me how. I told you, the day after I'd hit him over the head with a beer bottle he had such a headache that he couldn't see straight. He said so himself. That shows that he can feel with his waking body what happens to his body asleep. It's not with a bottle I shall hit him next time. One night, when I'm dreaming, I shall find myself with a knife in my hand or a revolver in my pocket—I must because I want to so intensely—and then I shall seize my opportunity. I'll stick him like a pig; I'll shoot him like a dog. In the heart. And then I shall be free of this fiendish persecution."

Some people might have thought that Lord Mountdrago was mad; after all the years during which Doctor Audlin had been treating the diseased souls of men he knew how thin a line divides those whom we call sane from those whom we call insane. He knew how often in men who to all appearance were healthy and normal, who were seemingly devoid of imagination, and who fulfilled the duties of common life with credit to themselves and with benefit to their fellows, when you gained their confidence, when you tore away the mask they wore to the world, you found not only hideous abnormality, but kinks so strange, mental extravagances so fantastic, that in that respect you could only call them lunatic. If you put them in an asylum, not all the asylums in the world would be large enough. Anyhow, a man was not certifiable because he had strange dreams and they had shattered his nerve. The case was singular, but it was only an exaggeration of others that had come under Doctor Audlin's observation; he was doubtful, however, whether the methods of treatment that he had so often found efficacious would here avail.

"Have you consulted any other member of my profession?" he asked.

"Only Sir Augustus. I merely told him that I suffered from nightmares. He said I was overworked and recommended me to go for a cruise. That's absurd. I can't leave the Foreign Office just now when the international situation needs constant attention. I'm indispensable, and I know it. On my conduct at the present juncture my whole future depends. He gave me sedatives. They had no effect. He gave me tonics. They were worse than useless. He's an old fool."

"Can you give any reason why it should be this particular man who persists in coming into your dreams?"

"You asked me that question before. I answered it."

That was true. But Doctor Audlin had not been satisfied with the answer.

"Just now you talked of persecution. Why should Owen Griffiths want to persecute you?"

"I don't know."

Lord Mountdrago's eyes shifted a little. Doctor Audlin was sure that he was not speaking the truth.

"Have you ever done him an injury?"

"Never."

Lord Mountdrago made no movement, but Doctor Audlin had a queer feeling that he shrank into his skin. He saw before him a large, proud man who gave the impression that the questions put to him were an insolence, and yet for all that, behind the façade was something shifting and startled that made you think of a frightened animal in a trap. Doctor Audlin leaned forward and by the power of his eyes forced Lord Mountdrago to meet them.

"Are you quite sure?"

"Quite sure. You don't seem to understand that our ways lead along different paths. I don't wish to harp on it, but I must remind you that I am a Minister of the Crown and Griffiths is an obscure member of the Labor Party. Naturally there's no social connection between us; he's a man of very humble origin, he's not the sort of person I should be likely to meet at any of the houses I go to; and politically our respective stations are so far separated that we could not possibly have anything in common."

"I can do nothing for you unless you tell me the complete truth."

Lord Mountdrago raised his eyebrows. His voice was rasping.

"I'm not accustomed to having my word doubted, Doctor Audlin. If you're going to do that, I think to take up any more of your time can only be a waste of mine. If you will kindly let my secretary know what your fee is, he will see that a check is sent to you."

For all the expression that was to be seen on Doctor Audlin's face you might have thought that he simply had not heard what Lord Mountdrago said. He continued to look steadily into his eyes, and his voice was grave and low.

"Have you done anything to this man that he might look upon as an injury?"

Lord Mountdrago hesitated. He looked away, and then, as though there were in Doctor Audlin's eyes a compelling force that he could not resist, looked back. He answered sulkily:

"Only if he was a dirty, second-rate little cad."

"But that is exactly what you've described him to be."

Lord Mountdrago sighed. He was beaten. Doctor Audlin knew that the sigh meant he was going at last to say what he had till then held back. Now he had no longer to insist. He dropped his eyes and began again drawing vague geometrical figures on his blotting paper. The silence lasted two or three minutes.

"I'm anxious to tell you everything that can be of any use to you. If I didn't mention this before, it's only because it was so unimportant that I didn't see how it could possibly have anything to do with the case. Griffiths won a seat at the last election, and he began to make a nuisance of himself almost at once. His father's a miner, and he worked in a mine himself when he was a boy; he's been a schoolmaster in the board schools and a journalist. He's that half-baked, conceited intellectual, with inadequate knowledge, ill-considered ideas and impractical plans, that compulsory education has brought forth from the working classes. He's a scrawny, gray-faced man who looks half starved, and he's always very slovenly in appearance; heaven knows members nowadays don't bother much about their dress, but his clothes are an outrage to the dignity of the House. They're ostentatiously shabby, his collar's never clean, and his tie's never tied properly; he looks as if he hadn't had a bath for a month, and his hands are filthy. The Labor Party have two or three fellows on the Front Bench who've got a certain ability, but the rest of them don't amount to much. In the kingdom of the blind the one-eyed man is king: because Griffiths is glib and has a lot of superficial information on a number of subjects, the Whips on his side began to put him up to speak whenever there was a chance. It appeared that he fancied himself on foreign affairs, and he was continually asking me silly, tiresome questions. I don't mind telling you that I made a point of snubbing him as soundly as I thought he deserved. From the beginning I hated the way he talked, his whining voice and his vulgar accent; he had nervous mannerisms that intensely irritated me. He talked rather shyly, hesitatingly, as though it were torture to him to speak and yet he was forced to by some inner passion, and often he used to say some very disconcerting things. I'll admit that now and again he had a sort of tub-thumping eloquence. It had a certain influence over the ill-regulated minds of the members of his party. They were impressed by his earnestness, and they weren't, as I was, nauseated by his sentimentality. A certain sentimentality is the common coin of political debate. Nations are governed by self-interest, but they prefer to believe that their aims are altruistic, and the politician is justified if with fair words and fine phrases he can persuade the electorate that the hard bargain he is driving for his country's advantage tends to the good of humanity. The mistake people like Griffiths make is to take these fair words and fine phrases at their face value. He's a crank, and a noxious crank. He calls himself an idealist. He has at his tongue's end all the tedious blather that the intelligentsia have been boring us with for years. Nonresistance. The brotherhood of man. You know the hopeless rubbish. The worst of it was that it impressed not only his own party, it even shook some of the sillier, more sloppy-minded members of ours. I heard rumors that Griffiths was likely to get office when a Labor Government came in; I even heard it suggested that he might get the Foreign Office. The notion was grotesque but not impossible. One day I had occasion to wind up a debate on foreign affairs which Griffiths had opened. He'd spoken for an hour. I thought it a very good opportunity to cook his goose, and by God, sir, I cooked it. I tore his speech to pieces. I pointed out the faultiness of his reasoning and emphasized the deficiency of his knowledge. In the House of Commons the most devastating weapon is ridicule: I mocked him; I bantered him; I was in good form that day and the House rocked with laughter. The Opposition sat glum and silent, but even some of them couldn't help laughing once or twice; it's not intolerable, you know, to see a colleague, perhaps a rival, made a fool of. And if ever a man was made a fool of, I made a fool of Griffiths. He shrank down in his seat; I saw his face go white, and presently he buried it in his hands. When I sat down I'd killed him. I'd destroyed his prestige for ever; he had no more chance of getting office when a Labor Government came in than the policeman at the door. I heard afterwards that his father, the old miner, and his mother had come up from Wales, with various supporters of his in the constituency, to watch the triumph they expected him to have. They had seen only his utter humiliation. He'd won the constituency by the narrowest margin. An incident like that might very easily lose him his seat. But that was no business of mine."

"Should I be putting it too strongly if I said you had ruined his career?" asked Doctor Audlin.

"I don't suppose you would."

"That is a very serious injury you've done him."

"He brought it on himself."

"Have you never felt any qualms about it?"

"I think perhaps if I'd known that his father and mother were there I might have let him down a little more gently."

There was nothing further for Doctor Audlin to say, and he set about treating his patient in such a manner as he thought might avail. He sought by suggestion to make him forget his dreams when he awoke; he sought to make his sleep so deep that he would not dream. He found Lord Mountdrago's resistance impossible to break down. At the end of an hour he dismissed him.

Since then he had seen Lord Mountdrago half a dozen times. He had done him no good. The frightful dreams continued every night to harass the unfortunate man, and it was clear that his general condition was growing rapidly worse. He was worn out. His irritability was uncontrollable. Lord Mountdrago was angry because he received no benefit from his treatment, and yet continued it, not only because it seemed his only hope, but because it was a relief to him to have some one with whom he could talk openly. Doctor Audlin came to the conclusion at last that there was only one way in which Lord Mountdrago could achieve deliverance, but he knew him well enough to be assured that of his own free will he would never, never take it. If Lord

Mountdrago was to be saved from the breakdown that was threatening, he must be induced to take a step that must be abhorrent to his pride of birth and his self-complacency. Doctor Audlin was convinced that to delay was impossible. He was treating his patient by suggestion, and after several visits found him more susceptible to it. At length he managed to get him into a condition of somnolence. With his low, soft, monotonous voice he soothed his tortured nerves. He repeated the same words over and over again. Lord Mountdrago lay quite still, his eyes closed; his breathing was regular, and his limbs were relaxed. Then Doctor Audlin in the same quiet tone spoke the words he had prepared.

"You will go to Owen Griffiths and say that you are sorry that you caused him that great injury. You will say that you will do whatever lies in your power to undo the harm that you have done him."

The words acted on Lord Mountdrago like the blow of a whip across his face. He shook himself out of his hypnotic state and sprang to his feet. His eyes blazed with passion, and he poured forth upon Doctor Audlin a stream of angry vituperation such as even he had never heard. He swore at him. He cursed him. He used language of such obscenity that Doctor Audlin, who had heard every sort of foul word, sometimes from the lips of chaste and distinguished women, was surprised that he knew it.

"Apologize to that filthy little Welshman? I'd rather kill myself."

"I believe it to be the only way in which you can regain your balance."

Doctor Audlin had not often seen a man presumably sane in such a condition of uncontrollable fury. Lord Mountdrago grew red in the face, and his eyes bulged out of his head. He did really foam at the mouth. Doctor Audlin watched him coolly, waiting for the storm to wear itself out, and presently he saw that Lord Mountdrago, weakened by the strain to which he had been subjected for so many weeks, was exhausted.

"Sit down," he said then, sharply.

Lord Mountdrago crumpled up into a chair.

"Christ, I feel all in. I must rest a minute and then I'll go."

For five minutes perhaps they sat in complete silence. Lord Mountdrago was a gross, blustering bully, but he was also a gentleman. When he broke the silence he had recovered his self-control.

"I'm afraid I've been very rude to you. I'm ashamed of the things I've said to you, and I can only say you'd be justified if you refused to have anything more to do with me. I hope you won't do that. I feel that my visits to you do help me. I think you're my only chance."

"You mustn't give another thought to what you said. It was of no consequence."

"But there's one thing you mustn't ask me to do, and that is to make excuses to Griffiths."

"I've thought a great deal about your case. I don't pretend to understand it, but I believe that your only chance of release is to do what I proposed. I have a notion that we're none of us one self, but many, and one of the selves in you has risen up against the injury you did Griffiths and has taken on the form of Griffiths in your mind and is punishing you for what you cruelly did. If I were a priest I should tell you that it is your conscience that has adopted the shape and lineaments of this man to scourge you to repentance and persuade you to reparation."

"My conscience is clear. It's not my fault if I smashed the man's career. I crushed him like a slug in my garden. I regret nothing."

It was on these words that Lord Mountdrago had left him. Reading through his notes, while he waited, Doctor

Audlin considered how best he could bring his patient to the state of mind that, now that his usual methods of treatment had failed, he thought alone could help him. He glanced at his clock. It was six. It was strange that Lord Mountdrago did not come. He knew he had intended to because a secretary had rung up that morning to say that he would be with him at the usual hour. He must have been detained by pressing work. This notion gave Doctor Audlin something else to think of: Lord Mountdrago was quite unfit to work and in no condition to deal with important matters of state. Doctor Audlin wondered whether it behooved him to get in touch with some one in authority, the Prime Minister or the Permanent Undersecretary for Foreign Affairs, and impart to him his conviction that Lord Mountdrago's mind was so unbalanced that it was dangerous to leave affairs of moment in his hands. It was a ticklish thing to do. He might cause needless trouble and get roundly snubbed for his pains. He shrugged his shoulders.

"After all," he reflected, "the politicians have made such a mess of the world during the last five-and-twenty years, I don't suppose it makes much odds if they're mad or sane."

He rang the bell.

"If Lord Mountdrago comes now, will you tell him that I have another appointment at six-fifteen and so I'm afraid I can't see him."

"Very good, sir."

"Has the evening paper come yet?"

"I'll go and see."

In a moment the servant brought it in. A huge headline ran across the front page: Tragic Death of Foreign Minister.

"My God!" cried Doctor Audlin.

For once he was wrenched out of his wonted calm. He was shocked, horribly shocked, and yet he was not altogether surprised. The possibility that Lord Mountdrago might commit suicide had occurred to him several times, for that it was suicide he could not doubt. The paper said that Lord Mountdrago had been waiting in a tube station, standing on the edge of the platform, and as the train came in was seen to fall on the rail. It was supposed that he had had a sudden attack of faintness. The paper went on to say that Lord Mountdrago had been suffering for some weeks from the effects of overwork, but had felt it impossible to absent himself while the foreign situation demanded his unremitting attention. Lord Mountdrago was another victim of the strain that modern politics placed upon those who played the more important parts in it. There was a neat little piece about the talents and industry, the patriotism and vision, of the deceased statesman, followed by various surmises upon the Prime Minister's choice of his successor. Doctor Audlin read all this. He had not liked Lord Mountdrago. The chief emotion that his death caused in him was dissatisfaction with himself because he had been able to do nothing for him.

Perhaps he had done wrong in not getting into touch with Lord Mountdrago's doctor. He was discouraged, as always when failure frustrated his conscientious efforts, and repulsion seized him for the theory and practice of this empiric doctrine by which he earned his living. He was dealing with dark and mysterious forces that were perhaps beyond the powers of the human mind to understand. He was like a man blindfold trying to feel his way to he knew not whither. Listlessly he turned the pages of the paper. Suddenly he gave a great start, and an exclamation once more was forced from his lips. His eyes had fallen on a small paragraph near the bottom of a column. Sudden Death of an M.P., he read. Mr. Owen Griffiths, member for so-and-so, had been taken ill in Fleet Street that afternoon and when he was brought to Charing Cross Hospital life was found to be extinct. It was supposed that death was due to natural causes, but an inquest would be held. Doctor Audlin could hardly believe his eyes. Was it possible that the night before Lord Mountdrago had at last in his dream found himself possessed of the weapon, knife or gun, that he had wanted, and had killed his tormentor, and had that ghostly murder, in the same way as the blow with the bottle had given him a racking headache on the following day, taken effect a certain number of hours later on the waking man? Or was it, more mysterious and more frightful, that when Lord Mountdrago sought relief in death, the enemy he had so cruelly wronged, unappeased, escaping from his own mortality, had pursued him to some other sphere, there to torment him still? It was strange. The sensible thing was to look upon it merely as an odd coincidence. Doctor Audlin rang the bell.

"Tell Mrs. Milton that I'm sorry I can't see her this evening, I'm not well."

It was true; he shivered as though of an ague. With some kind of spiritual sense he seemed to envisage a bleak, a horrible void. The dark night of the soul engulfed him, and he felt a strange, primeval terror of he knew not what.

The Man with the Good Face

FRANK LUTHER MOTT

Frank Luther Mott was born in Iowa in 1886. He attended Simpson College and later taught there. Graduate study at Columbia University and editorship of rural newspapers for several years helped to prepare him for his present position as Director of the School of Journalism of the State University of Iowa. He received the Pulitzer award in history in 1939 for his *History of American Magazines.*

A SUBWAY express train roared into the Fourteenth Street Station and came to a full stop, and the doors slid open. It was just at the lull of traffic before the rush of the late afternoon, and the cars were only comfortably filled. As the train stopped, a small, unobtrusive man, sitting near one end of the third car, quickly rose from his seat on the side of the car facing the station platform, and peered through the opposite windows. All the way up from Wall Street this little man had sat quietly observing through his deepset gray eyes every man or woman who had entered or left the car. His figure was slight, and the office pallor that overspread his serious face seemed to give to his eyes a singular intensity of gaze. Now he peered intently out at the people on the Fourteenth Street platform.

From *The Midland,* December, 1920. Reprinted by permission of the author.

Suddenly his eyes dilated; he leaned toward the window, and raised both hands as if to shade his eyes. Then he turned and ran toward the door, which was sliding shut. The little man's face was white as chalk; his eyes were round and blazing with excitement. Against the protests of the guard, he squeezed through the door and made his escape just as the train was beginning to move. Heedless of the commotion he caused, the man dodged wildly across the platform toward a local which stood there, gongs ringing and doors closing. For all his haste, the little man was too late to enter. He pounded on the glass of one of the closed doors imperiously.

"Next train," said the guard shortly.

"Let me on!" demanded the little man, waving his arms wildly. "Let me on! You have time!"

"Next train," repeated the guard.

The train began to move swiftly. The little man ran alongside, peering in through the windows at something or somebody inside.

"Look out!" called the guard, watching him.

The man, however, paid no attention to the warning. It was strange that he was not hurt as he ran blindly alongside the train. Perilously near the end of the platform he stopped short and put his hand to his head. The train thundered away, its colored rear-lights vanishing far off in the black tunnel. Oblivious to the interest of the spectators, oblivious to all the hurrying and running and crowding as other trains roared into the underground station, the little man leaned limply against a pillar.

"He's gone!" he muttered to himself. "He's gone!"

For upward of twenty years Mr. James Neal had been a clerk in the offices of Fields, Jones & Houseman on Lower Broadway. Every day of these twenty-odd years, if we except Sundays and holidays, Mr. Neal had spent an hour and a half on Subway trains. An hour and a half every day for more than twenty years he had spent in the great underground system of the Interborough. Its ceaseless roar benumbed his senses as he was hurtled from the Bronx, where he had a room, to the Imperial Building, where he worked, and back again. This, as he had often computed, amounted to fifty-eight and a half working days each year, or about two months' time. Such was the fee he paid to Time for the privilege of using other hours for working and living. It had seemed a cruel loss at first—this hour and a half from every working day—but that was in the early days of his experience in the city. Then he had been driven by boundless energy and hope—the same energy and the same hope that had brought him here from his little mid-western community in the first place. Year by year, however, as custom calloused him to the only part in life he seemed fit to play, he forgot about the waste of time in the Interborough cars. Destiny, he said to himself, had hollowed out the Subway as the rut in which his life was ordained to travel; destiny had condemned him inescapably to an underground roar.

He never confessed to any one that he held the Subway as the sign and symbol of the rut into which his life had grown. There was, indeed, nobody to whom he might impart such thoughts as he had about the deeper meanings of life. When Mr. Neal first came to Fields, Jones & Houseman's, timid and green from the country, he had been repelled by the lack of interest in his new problems on the part of his fellow clerks, and he had then put on for the first time that armor of indifference which now clung to him with the familiarity of an accustomed garment. Nor did he feel a greater kinship with the family in the Bronx with which he lodged. They were at pains not to annoy him; he kept apart from them.

Perhaps the pallid little clerk with the large gray eyes

would have become very lonesome if he had not eventually found a real interest in life. This, then, was the manner and substance of his finding.

As he travelled back and forth on the Subway morning and evening, day in and day out, week after week, he wasted the hours much more completely than most of his fellow-travellers. The average Subway passenger reads his newspaper and forgets the world; he knows by some sixth sense when the train has arrived at his station, and only then does he look up from his reading. Mr. Neal seldom read newspapers. The blatancy, the crassness, of the daily prints revolted him. Perhaps there was another reason, too, which Mr. Neal himself did not realize: perhaps the settled selfishness which his manner of life had fixed upon him had destroyed a natural craving for the so-called "human interest" that is spread over the pages of the journals of the metropolis. He despised the little brawls aired in the papers, the bickerings of politics, the fights and strikes and broils of all humanity reflected in daily mirrors.

Self-deprived of the newspaper, it was natural that he should fall to watching the people on the cars. He got to studying faces. At first he did it unconsciously, and he had probably been analyzing features idly for years before he discovered and fully realized how extremely interesting this occupation was becoming. One half-holiday he went up to the Library and read a book on physiognomy, and after that he laid out his course of study carefully, classifying and laying away in his memory the various types of faces that he saw. He pursued his investigations in the detached, careful spirit of the scientist, but as time passed he was absorbingly interested. Every morning and every evening he worked in his laboratory—the Subway trains.

He never had to stand up in the cars, for he boarded them, whether at one end of his trip or the other, before they were crowded; but as soon as crowds began to fill up the aisles he always gave up his seat. This naturally gained him repeated credit for courtesy, but the real reason for his apparent gallantry was that he could not see people's faces when he was sitting while others stood in the aisles. But when he hung to a strap and looked at the window in front of him, the blackness outside combined with the bright light of the car to make the glass of the window an excellent mirror to reflect the faces of those who stood near him.

To classify faces according to nationality was not easy in the polyglot crowds of this East Side line. But Mr. Neal devised many schemes to help him. He watched the papers they read: everybody read papers! He even ventured when greatly curious to ask a question of the object of his interest, so that the man might reveal his origin. Usually he was rebuffed, but sometimes he was successful. He read all the books on immigrants he could get his hands on. More than once he even followed a rare specimen—shadowed him to his work and there made guarded inquiries. Such investigations had several times made him late to work, so that his chief had made sarcastic remarks. The chief clerk at Fields, Jones & Houseman's was a tall, gaunt, old-young man with a hawk-like nose that carried eyeglasses perched perilously astride it, and he had a tongue that spit caustic. But the chief clerk's ugly words did not annoy Mr. Neal if his inquiry had been successful.

At length he became so skillful that he could separate the Slavic types into their various nationalities, and he could tell Polish, Lithuanian and Roumanian Jews apart. He could name the provinces from which Italians and Germans came with few errors.

But the most interesting set of categories according to which he filed away the various faces he saw was that of their ruling passions. There was the scholar, the sport, the miser, the courtesan, the little shopkeeper, the clerk, the housewife, the artist, the brute, the hypocrite, the clergyman, the barhound, the gambler. The charm of this classification was that the categories were not mutually exclusive, and permitted infinite variation.

Mr. Neal became as devoted to this fascinating game as ever any enthusiast has been to billiards, golf, baseball or poker. He looked forward all day, while in the midst of the ancient grind of Fields, Jones & Houseman, to the moment when he could establish himself in a position of vantage on a Subway car, and get back to his study of faces. All night long he dreamed of faces—faces wise and foolish, good and evil.

Yet more and more the ugliness in the Subway faces oppressed Mr. Neal. Sometimes he looked into faces loosened by liquor and saw such a foulness looking out at him that he was heartstick. Then he would look at all the faces about him and see sin in manifold guise marking all of them. The sodden eyes of disillusion, the protruding underlip of lust, the flabby wrinkles of dissipation, the vacuous faces of women: it was a heart-breaking picture gallery.

Every face was stamped with the little passion peculiar to it—the mark of its peculiar spirit. The mouths, especially, betrayed the souls within. Somewhere Mr. Neal had once read weird stories of souls seen to escape from the bodies of dying persons, and always they had been seen to issue from the open mouths of the corpses. There was a singular appropriateness in this phenomenon, it seemed to Mr. Neal, for the soul stamped the mouth even before it marked the eyes. Lewd mouths, and cunning mouths, and hateful mouths there were aplenty. Even the mouths of children were old in evil.

"I'm sorry I've learned it," breathed Mr. Neal one day. "Now I must always look into a man's soul when I look into his face."

It was true. Men who could hide secret sins from bosom friends—even from their wives—were defenseless against this little clerk hanging to a strap—this man with the serious pale face and the large gray eyes who had learned by years of systematic observation to pierce every barrier of reserve.

His study and classification went on for several years before it occurred to him that there was one kind of face that he never saw—one type that he never found in all the Manhattan crowds. When he had first discovered that this face was missing he had called it "the good face"; and though he realized the insufficiency of this designation he could not think of a better, and the term stuck. It was not that he never saw faces with good qualities stamped upon them: he sometimes saw faces marked with benevolence, honesty and resolution, for example, and these were all good faces in a way. But they were not what Mr. Neal was looking for—what he searched for more intently with the passing months. He remembered the face of his own mother dimly through the years; it was a little like what he wanted to see here in the Subway. He searched for simplicity, for transparent truth, for depth of spirituality, for meek strength and gentle power. But simplicity in the Subway? Guileless transparency of any sort? Spirituality? Mockery!

The face he never saw became an obsession with Mr. Neal. He hunted for it in various parts of the city. He tried the Broadway line of the Subway, where the faces are notably pleasanter, more prosperous, and smugger. But neither there nor about the Universities on Morningside Heights and on the banks of the Harlem, nor in Brooklyn, nor anywhere he looked, did he find the face he sought. He could always see it when he closed his eyes. At night he dreamed of it continuously—of meeting it on the Subway and looking into eyes of ineffable kindness.

It came finally to affect his life—this search for the unseen face. It gradually altered his attitude toward all his Subway folk. He came to have a great pity for the ignorant, and
pain filled his heart at all the marks of Cain he saw. He
came to have an inexpressible hunger for the sight of spiritual
quality lighting the faces of the people of the Subway crowds.
He did not express his hunger in words, as people do when
they want to make a thing definite and tangible. It was
perfectly clear and distinct to him when he closed his eyes:
then he saw the Face.

The time came when Mr. Neal could not sleep of nights
for the evil faces that leered at him from every side out of
the darkness. It was only when he slept that he could see,
in his dreams, the "good face." Finally, he was driven to
make a resolution. He would consciously seek for the good
faces; the evil ones he would pass over quickly. Thencefor-
ward he was happier. As his train roared through the tunnels
of night under New York, his eyes dwelt most upon the
faces that were marked, however, lightly, with the qualities
that reached their united culmination in the "good face." He
found his old faith in the perfectibility of man renewed, and
often he would keep his eyes closed for many minutes together, so that he could see the face of his dreams.

So months went on, and joined together into years.

Then, one day in the Subway, with his eyes full open,
James Neal suddenly saw the Face! He had been going home
from work in the evening quite as usual. The express train
on which he was riding was about to leave Fourteenth Street
Station when a tall man who was about to enter the local
train standing at the other side of the station platform turned
and looked directly at him. Mr. Neal's heart almost stopped
beating. His eyes were blinded, and yet he saw the Face so
distinctly that he could never forget it. It was just as he
had known it would be, and yet gentler and stronger. A mo-

ment Mr. Neal stood spellbound. The door of his own car was sliding shut; he leaped toward it, and, as we have already seen, squeezed through and ran toward the other train. Though he was too late to get in, still he could see the Face within the moving car. Thinking about it later, as he did very, very often, he realized that he could not tell how the man with the "good face" was dressed; he could see only his face, and that for a moment only, as the local moved swiftly out of the station. Suddenly he found himself alone and disconsolate.

He went home sick in spirit. As he lay in his bed that night, trying to go to sleep, he said to himself that if ever he should see the Face again—and he prayed that he might— no merely physical barriers should keep him from seeking out the rare spirit that animated such features. Ah, but it had been much even to have seen that Face; even that had been worth living for. At last he fell asleep peacefully.

The next morning Mr. Neal entered upon a new life. He had seen the Face; it had not been a dream after all. He felt young again—not young with the ambition he had once felt so strongly, but glad and cleansed and strengthened by a sure faith in the supremacy of truth and goodness in the world. A happy smile lighted his serious face that morning; a faint flush touched the pallor of his cheeks; and his deep gray eyes were unusually luminous.

Even the roar of the Subway did not pull his spirits down, and when he briskly entered the office of Fields, Jones & Houseman, the old-fashioned high desks and stools and all the worn, dingy furniture of the room seemed to the little clerk with the shining face to be strangely new. The chief clerk, sitting at a dusty old roll-top desk in the corner, looked up at Mr. Neal sharply as he entered. The chief clerk always looked up sharply. There was a preternatural leanness about the chief clerk which was accentuated by his sharp hawk's nose, and when he looked up quickly from his position hunched over his desk, his sharp little eyes pierced his subordinate through and through, and his glasses, perched halfway down his nose, trembled from the quickness of his movements.

"Morning!" he said briefly, and dived down again into his work, with his shoulders humped.

But Mr. Neal was more expansive.

"Good morning!" he called, so cheerily that the whole office felt the effect of his good humor.

A young man with a very blond pompadour was just slipping into a worn office coat.

"Well, Mr. Neal!" he exclaimed. "I swear you're getting younger every day!"

Mr. Neal laughed happily as he changed his own coat and climbed upon his familiar stool. His desk neighbor turned and regarded him good-naturedly.

"He'll be running off and getting married pretty soon," prophesied the neighbor, for the benefit of the whole office force.

Mr. Neal laughed again.

"You're judging me by your own case, Bob," he rejoined. Then in a lower tone, "That romance of yours, now—how is it coming?"

That was enough to cause the young man to pour into Mr. Neal's willing ear all the latest developments of Bob's acquaintance with the only girl in the world.

For a long time Mr. Neal lived in the daily hope of seeing the Face again. He got into the habit of changing to a local at Fourteenth Street because it was at that station he had seen the Face before, but he caught not a glimpse of any face resembling the one that he could see at any time he closed his eyes. Yet he was not discouraged. He was happy, because he felt that something big and noble had come into his life—

that now he had something to live for. It was only a question of time, he told himself, until he should find the Face. It was but a question of time—and he could wait.

So the weeks and months passed by. Mr. Neal never relaxed his search for the Face; it had become a part of his life. There was no monotony in his great game. He always found new faces interesting to classify, some unusual combination, some degree of emotional development he had not seen before. But the Face never.

Until one Saturday half-holiday in December. This is the way it happened.

Mr. Neal employed this particular half-holiday at Columbus Park. Long ago he had found this park, adjoining Chatham Square and near Chinatown, Mulberry Bend and the Bowery, a great gathering place for the lower types of humanity, and such half-holidays as he did not spend at the Library studying Lombroso, Darwin, Piderit, Lavater, and other physiognomists, he usually employed at Columbus Park. Sometimes he wandered over to Hester Street, or up Orchard or some other Ghetto street off Delancey, or sometimes he spent a few hours in Battery Park or in the tenement district of the lower West Side. On this particular Saturday he found Columbus Park less populous than it had been on his last visit a month before, for many of its habitués had sought warmer climes. The weather was seasonably cold, and Mr. Neal felt really sorry for some of the old, broken-down men and women he saw.

Toward the end of the short December afternoon, he found an old man, shaking with the cold, huddled up on one of the benches of the park. The haggard, unshaven face told the usual story of the derelict, but something in the face—perhaps the abject fear that glowered in the eyes—sounded before he knew it the depths of pity in the little clerk's heart. Mr. Neal tried to talk to him, but there was no ready beggar's tale to be poured into the ears of benevolence; there was only fear of the cold, and of misery, and of death. Yielding suddenly to an impulse so strong that it bore down all thoughts of prudence, Mr. Neal slipped out of his own overcoat and put it about the man's threadbare shoulders, and then hurried off toward the Worth Street Station of the Subway.

The wintry breeze chilled him as he hastened along, a slight figure in a worn business suit, leaning against the wind, but his heart was warm and light within him. Down he hurried into the Subway station, and dropped his tithe of tribute into the multiple maw of the Interborough. The train was thundering in, its colored lights growing momentarily brighter as they came down the black tunnel. The train was crammed to the doors, for it was the rush hour and even down here the trains were crowded. Mr. Neal edged into the nearest door and then squirmed over to a place against the opposite door in the vestibule, where he could see people as they came out.

The train shot again into the dark tunnels. A thousand men and women were being hurtled at terrific thundering speed, by some strange power but half understood, through the black corridors of the Night that reigned under old Manhattan, to some unseen goal. It was magnificent; it was colossal; but it was uncanny. Mr. Neal had always been moved by the romance of the Subway, but tonight, in his elevation of spirit, it seemed something of epic quality, full of a strange, unreal grandeur. Faint red lights here and there revealed nothing of the tunnel; they but lent mystery to dimly seen arches and darkling bastions, fleeting by the roaring train.

They stopped a minute at Canal Street, and more people pushed into the overcrowded car, and then the train was off again. The man pushing against Mr. Neal was heavy-jowled as a prize fighter, but if ever he had followed the ring his fighting days were over now. Good feeding had done for him; he breathed heavily in the fetid atmosphere of the car. He was almost squeezing the breath out of the little man with a heavy red mustache who stood just behind him. The red mustache made the little man's face seem out of proportion; there was not enough of chin to make a proper balance.

At Spring Street two women struggled to get off.

"Let 'em off!" came the familiar admonition of the guard.

Those about the women made every effort to give them room, but at the best they had a hard fight to make their way out. Both the women were modishly dressed, and their complexions were correctly made. There was, too, that hardness about the mouths of both of them that Mr. Neal found in the faces of most of the women he saw—a hardness that even the stress of their effort to get out of the car could not disturb. When they finally got out, others crowded in.

Mr. Neal was happy, and he looked about him to find other happy faces. But they were nowhere to be seen; the faces were stolid, or indifferent, or intent, or vacuous. None of them were glad. If their mouths would only turn up at the corners! Well, it was the same old story. Mouths that turned up at the corners were seldom met with in Mr. Neal's book of Subway faces.

Bleecker Street, and a worse jam than ever, but there was encouragement in the thought that Fourteenth Street would soon relieve the pressure. Two girls crowded on at Bleecker, amid shrill laughter and many smothered exclamations. Their lips were carmined and their eyes bold. Every swerve of the train brought giggles or stifled screams from them.

As the train was slowing down for Astor Place Station, an express train passed it, speeding for Fourteenth Street. Mr. Neal turned with an effort (for he was wedged in tightly) and looked through the glass door at the brightly lighted cars as they passed, and then slowly gained upon, his own train. The express was crowded too, with people standing in the aisles, hanging to straps. The faces were very clearly distinguishable in the bright light; and Mr. Neal, strangely excited at this rapid panorama of faces, saw each one distinctly. Suddenly he leaned forward, close to the glass. He saw it! The Face! It was there! But it was gone in a moment. It had been like a flash in the dark tunnel. His own train had come to a jarring stop, and the express was only thunder in the distance.

Mr. Neal felt that he must rush out of the car, must get out into the open. But the big prize fighter still pressed against him, and in a moment they were rushing on again into the darkness.

Now the clerk had no eyes for the occupants of his car. His face was pressed against the glass door. He saw, out there in the darkness, that serenely beautiful Face, beatific, transcendent. And even as he looked he saw again the rear lights of the express. They were going to overtake it—to pass it again! It had been halted by the block signals of the train ahead, perhaps; at any rate, it was now moving very slowly. As the local shot by, the panorama of faces was unfolded much more rapidly than it had been before, but Mr. Neal caught a glimpse of the Face once more. It looked directly at him, as it had before, and he thought it smiled upon him a little.

The little clerk was greatly excited. As soon as the local had come to a stop at the Fourteenth Street Station and the doors had been opened, he darted out and hurried to the other side of the platform. There he stood leaning out to watch for the approach of the express. In a moment it came, rumbling in quite as usual, mechanically and regularly, and the doors slid open to allow the flood of people to pour out. Mr. Neal squirmed through the crowd, looking in at the windows and watching the people coming out; but he did not see the Face, and, frantic lest he should lose it once more, he crowded into one of the cars again at the last minute. He tried at first to pass through the train searching for the man with the "good face," but the guards rebuffed him, and the usually good-natured crowd was provoked to impatience by his squirming efforts; and he himself soon became so exhausted in his attempt that he gave it up. At Grand Central Station he again hurried out upon the platform to watch the crowds getting off. The gong had begun to ring again when he caught sight of a tall figure mounting a short flight of stairs toward the upper platform, and he immediately knew that there was the man he sought. The Face was turned away, but he thought he could not be mistaken. He rushed toward the stairway, bumping into others so many times in his haste that he really made little speed. When he reached the top of the stairs he looked about. For one heartsick moment he thought he had lost the man after all. Then, away across the station, near one of the exits, he saw the tall figure again. The man was leaving the station, and as he passed out, for a moment he turned his Face toward the crowd within; and Mr. Neal knew then that he had not been mistaken.

To the little clerk it seemed an age before he could reach the exit through which the tall figure had passed. He ran around people and dodged and ducked, oblivious of the curious watching of the crowd. At last he gained the exit. The tall man was nowhere to be seen.

Mr. Neal found himself on Forty-second Street, east of Park Avenue. It was night, and the December wind pierced his clothing and cut to his very bones like a knife. He buttoned his sackcoat up tightly and turned up the collar. He decided to walk east down Forty-second Street, in the hope of seeing the Face again. He walked very rapidly, impelled both by the desire to keep as warm as possible, and the thought that whatever chance he had of finding the man would be lost if he did not hurry.

As he stood for a moment on the curb before crossing Lexington Avenue, halted by a long string of passing automobiles, he thought he saw the tall man at about the middle of the next block. Taking his life in his hands, he scurried across the street, dodging in and out among the vehicles with the curses of drivers in his ears. But he got across safely, and now he was certain that he had been right; there was the tall figure he could not mistake. Now he gained on the man, who turned south into Third Avenue. As Mr. Neal breathlessly turned the corner he saw the tall man mounting the stoop of a shabby four-story apartment house a little way down the street. About to enter, he turned his Face toward the running clerk, and even by the dim light at the entrance to the dingy house, Mr. Neal could see how ineffably spiritual and strong the Face was. Joy filled the little clerk's heart so full that tears came to his eyes. At last he was to meet the man with the "good face"—after so long! He managed to find breath to call out.

"I say!" he shouted.

But he was too late, for the door had closed almost before the words left his mouth.

Leaping up the steps, he found that the door was not locked, and he entered a dark hallway. He heard a step on the landing above, and called out again, but there was no answer. He hurried up the creaking stairs, but he was just in time to see the first door on his left closed silently but firmly.

Mr. Neal hesitated. He took off his hat and wiped his forehead. Then he rang the bell.

The hallway was dimly lighted with one small gas jet over against the discolored wall. Mr. Neal waited. Presently he heard footsteps. Then the door was opened and a flood of warm light poured into the dim little hall. A short, white-bearded old man stood in the doorway. He seemed the very personification of serene happiness, and over his shoulder peered an old lady whose face was lighted by the same kindly joy. There was an atmosphere of quiet goodness about them both; it flooded out into the hallway as sensibly as the glow of light itself. The old couple looked questioningly at Mr. Neal. The little clerk was somewhat embarrassed.

"I—I wanted to see the gentleman who just came in here," he said.

The white-bearded old man seemed surprised.

"Why, nobody has come in here," he said in a gentle voice. "Not since I came home over an hour ago."

"Oh, the tall man, with—with——"

"But nobody has come in, Sir," reiterated the old man.

"Just now, you know," insisted Mr. Neal. "A tall man——"

A shadow crossed the old man's face—a shade of alarm. The woman withdrew a little. Some of the happiness seemed to leave their faces, allowing the wrinkles of age to show themselves.

"I don't know what you mean, Sir," the old man said slowly, "but we two are alone here. There is no tall man here, I assure you. Please——"

"But haven't you a lodger?" asked Mr. Neal hopefully. "This was a very tall man; that was the reason I could see him so well in the Subway. He has a good Face—a really wonderful Face——"

Mr. Neal hesitated a moment, realizing that he had been led to reveal his secret to one who might not understand.

Pity came into the old gentleman's eyes.

"Ah," he said, and nodded. "If I could be of any help to you—would you come in?"

"Didn't he come in here, really? Hasn't a tall man been here?"

"Nobody is here, Sir, but us. But if I can do anything for you, I'd be glad to."

Mr. Neal saw that the old gentleman thought he was dealing with a demented man; he saw too that the denial was an honest one.

"Thank you," said Mr. Neal. "No. I must be going. I am very sorry I troubled you."

The old man bade him a cheery good night, but he looked after Mr. Neal in solicitude as the clerk went slowly down the steps.

The air was bitter cold outside, and Mr. Neal realized for the first time that he did not have his overcoat. He shivered.

Hunching his shoulders up against the blast, he hurried back to the Subway.

Heartbreaking though his disappointment was, Mr. Neal was not embittered. . . . There was one thing that he knew now beyond all cavil or doubt: he knew that he should find the man with the good face. He knew that he should eventually meet him somewhere, sometime, and come to know him. How Mr. Neal longed for that time words cannot describe, but his settled faith that his desire would one day be fulfilled kept him tranquil and happy. Why should he be impatient? Perhaps today or tomorrow—perhaps in this car he was entering, perhaps just around the next corner—he would see the Face.

"It will be soon," he would say to himself. "I know it will be soon."

The beggars in front of the Imperial Building came to

know the little clerk and thank him in advance for his
alms. The elevator men and the newsies came to watch for
him. Mr. Neal himself took an interest in everybody. He
formed the habit of watching crowds wherever they were
greatest, partly because thereby his chance of discovering
the Face was enhanced, and partly because crowds thrilled
him. What a tremendous mass of emotions—hopes, fears,
ambitions, joys, sorrows—were in these thousand faces
swirling about him in ceaseless tide! They were all individuals; that was the wonder of it! All were individuals;
with personalities of their own, with their own lives to live
and their own problems to think out. He would like to
help them all.

Mr. Neal at last formed the acquaintance of the members
of the family with whom he had lodged so long. One evening just outside his room he met a red-cheeked boy whom
he supposed to be the son of his landlord, and it came to
him with a shock that he scarcely knew these people under
whose roof he had lived for many years. The boy seemed
surprised and a little frightened when Mr. Neal tried to
talk to him, and the clerk resolved there and then to make
amends for past neglect. The very next evening he made
an excuse to visit the father of the household. A fine hearty
fellow he found him, sitting in the kitchen with his stock-
inged feet up on a chair, smoking an old clay pipe and
reading the evening paper. Mr. Neal learned he was a hardworking teamster. The man seemed pleased with his
lodger's attentions, and invited him to come again, and Mr.
Neal did come again and often, for he liked his landlord
from the start. There were three children, two of them
pictures of health, but the third thin and pale and unable
to romp about because of a twisted leg.

Mr. Neal became a veritable member of the household,
and when he discovered from a chance remark of the father

that they were saving money penny by penny to buy a brace for the crooked leg, he insisted on "loaning" the money to make up the balance still lacking.

"Funny thing," commented the teamster one evening. "We used to think you wasn't human exactly." He laughed heartily. "Gotta get acquainted with a guy, ain't you?"

Then his wife, a thin, washed-out little woman, embarrassed the little clerk greatly by saying gravely,

"Mr. Neal, you're a good man."

Her eyes were on the little cripple.

In the same vein was the comment of the office force at Fields, Jones & Houseman's on the occasion of Arnold's injury in the elevator accident, when Mr. Neal took up a collection for the injured man, heading the subscription himself.

"Funny thing," exclaimed the chief clerk to a stenographer as they were leaving the office that afternoon. "Funny thing: when I first came here James Neal was close as a clam; never a word out of him. Paid no attention to anybody; all gloom. Now look at him helping everybody! Best old scout in the office!"

As he nodded his head in emphasis, his eyeglasses trembled on his nose—but they stuck.

"I've not got a better friend in the whole town than James Neal, and I know it," he added, "and I guess that's true of everybody in the office!"

It was true that Mr. Neal and the chief clerk had become fast friends. They had come to spend their Sundays together, and even to share confidences, and so it was natural that when Mr. Neal saw the Face for the third time he should be moved to tell his friend about it. This telling of his secret was epochal in Mr. Neal's life.

The two men sat on a bench in a more or less secluded part of Bronx Park. Mr. Neal looked off among the trees as he told the story of the Face hesitatingly, often in difficulty for the right word, the light of the mystic in his glowing eyes. The chief clerk listened attentively, his cane across his knees, his lean face serious. His eyes bored into the very mind of his friend with their keen gaze. When Mr. Neal told of his failure to find the man with the good face in the house on Third Avenue, his friend shook his head definitely.

"No!" he said. "No! I'll tell you what it is; it is what they call a hallucination."

"Oh, no," replied Mr. Neal calmly. "It is real, John. There's no doubt it's real."

The chief clerk shook his head sharply again, and there was a pause.

"I felt I must tell you," resumed Mr. Neal at length, "because I saw him again last night."

His friend looked quickly at the little clerk, who gazed away among the trees, his eyes luminous.

"I saw him in the Pennsylvania Subway Station, and I followed him out. There was no doubt about it: I saw his face. He went down Eighth Avenue, and I saw him turn in at a door. I wasn't far behind him. The door was right next to a pawnshop. It was unlatched, and I went in. I found myself in a dark hallway, but toward the other end there was light coming from a half-opened door. I was excited, John. Tremendously. You see, John, it was the great experience of my life—no wonder I was trembling.

"I stepped quietly back to where the light was, and looked into the room that it came from. What do you think I saw, John? There was a young mother and two fresh-cheeked boys; one of the boys was reading at the table, and the other one sat in a low chair at his mother's knee and she was talking to him—telling him stories, I think. The room was poor, John, but the mother's face! It was wonderful! It reminded me of my own mother's. There is just one word to describe it, John: it was a Madonna's face—a Madonna of Eighth Avenue!"

Mr. Neal paused and glanced at his friend. The chief clerk said nothing, but dug at the turf with his stick.

"But the tall man was not there," resumed Mr. Neal. "I knocked at the door and asked about him. The woman didn't know; no man was in their rooms, she said. She was a poor widow. She wanted to know how I got in. I could see I was frightening her, so I left, and I could hear the door locked behind me."

The little clerk sighed, and passed his hand over his eyes.

His friend rose suddenly.

"Come," he said. "Let's walk—and talk about something else."

This was but the first of many talks the two clerks had about the Face. Mr. Neal's friend became more and more sympathetic toward the quest. One afternoon Mr. Neal detained the chief clerk as he was leaving the office after work. The little clerk's eyes were very serious, and his voice was low as he said,

"John, I know that I am going to find him very soon. I know it."

"How do you know it?" asked the chief clerk. "Something—well—psychic?"

"Oh, no. It's not mysterious. It's just a—a certainty, John. I know I shall find him very, very soon."

"Well, you know—" and the chief clerk looked at Mr. Neal steadily, "you know that I—I should like to know him, too."

Mr. Neal wrung his friend's hand. They went down together in the elevator, and parted. Mr. Neal hurried down into his Subway station. There were not many waiting on the platforms. Far down the black tunnels in either direction the little white lights glimmered. The echoing silence of a great cave was in the station. Then suddenly the red and green lights of a train appeared far away; then a rumble and a roar, the doors of the train slid open and Mr. Neal stepped in. All the way home he kept his eyes shut. The hurtling roar, the crush of people growing greater as they approached the great business sections, the calls of the guards, did not disturb Mr. Neal. He kept his eyes closed so he might see the Face.

It was about one o'clock of the next day that the accident occurred of which James Neal was the victim. He had been trying to cross the street in defiance of traffic regulations, and had been struck by a heavily loaded truck and knocked down, with some injury to his skull. He had been taken, unconscious, to St. Cecilia's Hospital.

Little work was done by the clerks of Fields, Jones & Houseman that afternoon. One of the clerks had seen the accident; indeed he had been talking to Mr. Neal just before the latter had rushed into the street. He had seen the little clerk suddenly raise his hand and point across the street.

"I see it! There he is!" Mr. Neal had said in a voice exultant with joy, and then he had dodged recklessly into the traffic.

The chief clerk was greatly distressed. He could not work. He would sit with his lank form huddled up in his office chair, gazing fixedly over his eyeglasses at nothing in particular. About two o'clock he bethought himself to look up in the telephone directory the family with which Mr. Neal lodged and to inform them of the accident. The whole office force listened to the conversation over the telephone, and heard the chief's voice break as he told of the seriousness of the injury. Then the chief clerk shut his books sharply, clapped on his street coat and rusty straw hat, and set out for the hospital.

Long before the chief clerk arrived at the hospital, a white-coated doctor, standing momentarily in a doorway of the ward in which Mr. James Neal lay, met a nurse coming out. The doctor's face was such a one as would have delighted Mr. Neal if he had been able to see it. It was a benevolent face. A profound knowledge of the problems of humanity had marked it with depth of understanding, and withal, a kindliness and sympathy that made it worthy a second and a third glance in any company, however distinguished.

"How about the skull fracture?" asked the doctor in a low voice, as the nurse was passing out.

"He is dead," said the nurse.

"When?" asked the doctor.

"Just now. I just left him."

"There was no chance," said the doctor.

The nurse was about to pass on when the doctor detained her.

"That tall man," he said, "who was with him: where has he gone?"

The nurse looked at the doctor in surprise.

"There was no one with him but me," she said.

"Oh, yes," said the doctor. "I saw a man bending over the bed—a very tall man with a remarkable face. I wondered who he could be."

The nurse turned, and with the doctor looked over toward the bed where the body of James Neal lay.

"That is strange," said the nurse.

"I saw him there," said the doctor, "just as you were leaving the patient; now he is gone."

"Queer! I saw no one," said the nurse, and moved away to attend to other duties.

The doctor walked over to the bed where the body of the little clerk lay.

"It is strange," he mused. "I surely saw him . . . the most beautiful face I ever saw."

Then he looked down at what had been James Neal.

"He was very fortunate," said the doctor in a low tone, "to die with a face like that looking into his."

There was a smile on the death-white lips of the little clerk.

The Prairie

WALTER J. MUILENBURG

Walter J. Muilenburg was born at Orange City, Iowa, in 1893. After his graduation from the State University of Iowa in 1915, he edited a country newspaper, then turned to the teaching of English at the high school in Manistee, Michigan; the State University of Iowa; and Michigan State College. His novel *Prairie* (1925) was the first novel published by the Viking Press. He has contributed stories and articles to various magazines. He lives at present on his farm at Glennie, Alcona County, Michigan.

THE prairie lay dreaming in the warmth of early summer. Level, monotonous, it stretched away until its green became drab in the far distance. It was alive, and yet lifeless; full of color, yet colorless; intangible mystery lurked in its contrast, a mystery of light and shadow and tints. Strange, dreaming, lovely, it lay beneath the intense blue sky. Underfoot the ground was bright with young grass and flowers, through which the light wind rippled soundlessly. It was only when earth and sky met and their colors merged that one caught the hint of the wild power of the prairie, its sweep, its changelessness, its passive cruelty and callousness.

But John Barrett and his wife, newly-married and filled

From *The Midland,* August, 1915. Reprinted by permission of the author.

with the sense of dominant power which animate life feels over inanimate life, had thrown the challenge to the prairie. Even now, on that summer morning, their sod house stood out bravely in the silent sunshine. About it lay a wide circle of vivid green, half-grown crops of grain which were to supply the necessities of their pioneer life.

They had come from the East. The village where they were born had early labelled Barrett a "ne'er-do-well" and when he married Lizzie Delton it had passed final and irrevocable judgment on both. He was shiftless, a rolling stone, while she—oh, she was only one of the Deltons—a colorless, undersized woman with lackluster eyes.

After his sudden marriage, Barrett was seized again with the desire of change. His wife agreed, unquestioning, devoted as a faithful dog. Married life seemed stimulating to Barrett. They would emigrate into the prairie and win an easy life from the unplowed soil. His eyes glowed.

"Why, Lizzie, it'll be fine! Us, alone, out there together, a nice little house, farming on the side, we can raise some stock—it'll be great! And then, if we want to, we can always go to town and stock up."

"I guess it's all right, John—anything you say." Her face remained blank, but her hands clasped and unclasped almost eagerly.

Barrett was uplifted by her dependence, and an injured pride came into his voice, "We'll leave this little burg for good. They talk too dam' much about us. If we make good, they'd hate us; if we lose out, they'd laugh."

A week later they were on the way in an old, canvas-covered wagon. As they went out of civilization, the woman's face changed; a hint of color came into her cheeks and an occasional smile touched her face with a twisted beauty. •

They reached the prairie in early spring. It invited them

in its soft, wandering colors. The woman, as she breathed the mellow air, heavy with the odor of earth, grew more alive; sometimes she laughed at her husband's dry humor. The prairie lay before them, unscarred by trails, and they rambled leisurely over the soft grass, finding a pleasant excitement in the fact that their home might be just past the next swell of ground. To wander about the prairie was mysterious, romantic. The days were dreamily warm, the sky deep-blue, the meadow lark's song quivered continually; and beyond this was the lure of the tinted horizon, most mysterious when night came on. It came slowly always; the air dimmed and the immensity of the earth gained emphasis by sweeping breeze and twinkling vastness of the dark sky.

Late one afternoon they came to a small river. After camping there, they decided to make a home on its banks. A few days' hard work, the woman helping, and the sod house was complete. Next, they turned up the black prairie soil and sowed their grain. Everything promised success. Some impulse of life seemed to come to them from the depths of the earth. It was a paradise for the man and the woman.

"If it'll only last," she said hesitatingly, one evening at supper.

The man laughed.

Then over the prairie two months passed. The softness of spring widened into the fiercer heat of summer. Not a drop of rain had fallen for two weeks; the man's face shadowed as he watched his crops. And slowly the heat became more intense. The man began to curse under his breath. Then, as the heat of midsummer grew, the iron soul of the prairie bared itself to them. Grim, silent, it seemed waiting, with torturing patience, to achieve some master-stroke of tragedy. The man, longing for rain to save his crops, became morose with helpless anger. The crops withered slowly, drooping for the water which the soil could not give. Beauty brooded over the prairie. The sky was blue in the early morning, white at noon, and brilliant at sunset. But no clouds.

As time passed, a change came in the man and woman. They began to give themselves up to sudden, heavy silences, their talk was listless: when they smiled there was no spontaneity. The grip of the prairie seemed to close upon their souls. During the day, the man worked with sullen determination. The woman remained indoors, hands often idle, eyes vacantly on the horizon. In the evening, and after supper, they sat in front of the shack, facing the West, and watched the sun go down under the level line at the end of the world. It was then that the menace of the prairie stood out strongest. The last light was never a benediction, but always something ominous. Its beauty was savage, overpowering. There was nothing to hide the fierce, red light. The earth stretched, level and unmarked except for a single, twisted scrub oak by the dry creek bed—an empty horror of unobstructed space that grew indistinct in the red dimness of approaching darkness.

On one such night they had stayed outside longer than usual. The man sat, chin in hand, looking heavily at the ground. His wife, narrow shoulders drooping, inexpressibly weary, watched the dusk growing in the sky. Finally he rose as though to enter the house. She got up silently. He caught her outline against the pale light. How frail she was! Never strong, she seemed more delicate now than before. He stepped to her.

"Say, Lizzie, ain't you gettin' tired of this? Le's go back?"

She did not answer for a moment. He could see her hands open and close slowly. Then she said, "No, not yet."

A moment of silence and she flamed in sudden fierceness, "I don't see why everything's against us so. Back East, people looked down on us. We wasn't respectable—I don't know why. Ever since I can remember, I had to work, work, work—from morning till night. What did I ever get for it? People thought there was something wrong with me because I never dressed up like they did. Even my folks called me 'poor Lizzie.' An' when you come along last spring, it was the only good time I ever had. But we'll never go back. We'll stay right here."

Barrett's face was grim at her unexpected outburst.

"It ain't right," he broke out suddenly, "it's dam' unfair!" His groan ended in a half-cry. The woman looked up at him, a look so full of tortured confidence that he cursed again. She shivered. The evening breeze struck them coldly; they went inside.

In spite of his determination to remain, Barrett knew that they were in a desperate condition. Already he had to dig deep in the dry creek bed for water and they had exhausted half of their second load of provisions. The horses, too, grew lean on the scant burned grass of the prairie. But they would have to face something worse than this before giving up!

The hot, dry weather continued. The sky was always bright. The crops lay dead on the fevered soil. All animal life, too, had vanished from the plains. One morning, the woman saw a crow flapping heavily toward the shack. She watched in hope to see the bird alight—there had been so many birds in the spring—but it wavered only a moment above her and then swept its low flight on toward the East. She looked at the gray universe about her, and her face, also gray, hardened into quivering defiance. It seemed as if eternity lay about them; the past was dead, the future did not exist. They were living in an eternal present, a void that would endure forever. And always the heat, the quivering heat, and the gray menace of the horizon.

Summer merged into early autumn. The nights grew chilly, though the noon sun still burned. All the green life of the spring was yellow and dry as tinder. From sun-rising to sun-setting, the man and the woman hardly spoke. Helpless in the midst of a power before which their strength was nothing, they waited. Yet, dulled as they were, body and soul, they defied the prairie, passive, yet unconquered.

But they were approaching desperation. Days of heavy idleness, few words spoken, a silent sky and a silent earth were corroding their souls like poison. Perhaps the lack of speech was hardest to endure. But what was there to say in the face of that wide, empty horror? Still they refused to yield.

As time passed, he saw that her strength was failing. A strangeness brooded about her from which her husband recoiled with a feeling of being haunted; he was unaware that the same haggard spirit looked out of his own eyes. He wished that they might talk as in the careless days of spring—his heart swelled as he thought of those days. But it was impossible; the grip of the silent plains was on his throat. Why, he thought dumbly, did they need to be doomed? He tried prayer, but found that he was praying and cursing only to the power of the prairie.

One night, as they sat at supper, the man burst out with the bitterness of his heart. The woman listened, immovable. Her stolid silence and her brooding calmness filled him with sudden rage and he swore at her. His fingers gripped the edge of the table as though to keep him from striking her. She said nothing, but the wild anger of something at bay flashed in her eyes. When the tension relaxed, both felt a horror of the primitive animal each had seen in the other.

Next morning, as the man stood in the doorway, he noticed a haze at the north. Then he sniffed at the sharp morning air. Turning, he spoke to his wife and went out.

A little later, the horses were plowing furrows around the little shack. Toward the north, a deeper haze was growing. The horizon had a white, transparent color, as though a film of cloud were being drawn across the blue. The cloud-film grew rapidly. Then came the faint odor of smoke. The woman stopped a cry in her throat and stood, white-faced, hair awry in the morning wind. Had they not suffered enough? Then she started after her husband. He did not stop plowing or even look up at her.

The cloud in the north thickened. It became veined with streaks of dull red. As it climbed in the sky, its outline broke into ragged, grotesque peaks, standing black and tempestuous against the pale blue sky. Then the wind strengthened and the acrid heat swept toward them.

The man stopped his work and put his team in the stable. He stroked their necks for a moment. The bitterness had gone from him and he spoke gently to the woman. She tried to answer him with a smile, but could not. He awkwardly tried to comfort her.

From the north came a vibrating hum; the man looked up. Then his hands clenched slowly. Sweeping toward them, a distant wall of fire shone red through the growing smoke, its flames darting in pointed, wavering spires. It was moving with incredible swiftness toward the shack.

Then the fire caught them. Burning bits of grass, carried over the plowed strip, started small fires in the thatch roof of the shack. The two fought the flames with wet sacks, their faces showing hard and wild through the eddies of smoke. The thin, blank face of the woman was transformed; the cheeks, drawn into taut lines, were livid with hate.

Several times the flames caught the shack, but each time they were beaten out. The barn caught and the man unloosed the horses. A shrill scream as they bolted directly into the wall of fire, and then the flames hid them. There, with the fire roaring above, in the vortex of a blind, insensate force, the naked force of the prairie, they still fought, beating out the flames upon the shack. The woman fell several times. At last she lay quiet on the hot ground, and the man fought the fire alone. It seemed to eat into his lungs, his head roared with it. Then he, too, gave up. He drew the woman close to him and putting a wet sack over her face, he crouched close to the ground, breathing in big, rasping gasps.

It seemed an eternity. When it was over, the man got up. Far to the south the fire still retreated. All around lay the blackened face of the prairie, with the mockery of the blue sky crouching above. The man stooped to uncover the face of his wife. She lay unconscious. He carried her into the shack. When she opened her eyes, they were so bright and hard that the man shrank from them.

But, as he saw the thin, white cheeks and the swollen veins on her forehead, he knew that the remnant of life would not last long. And for this he was glad. A few hours later, with the fierce heat of noon beating in at the door, she died. She had not the harsh strength to live. Life had not played fair with her. Dry-eyed and staring, the man sat beside the bed. All that afternoon he sat there. His face had fallen into long, hard lines, and was grim yet with defiance. Outside, the prairie smoked in the hazy afternoon.

That night, as the sun painted the west, he buried her. Then, staring across the blackened land, he watched the dimming sky. The glow grew fainter in the west. The angry red burned down to softer orange and yellow. Gray light closed over it. The man stood there a long time, watching the night deepen, the only living creature in all the blackened waste.

The next morning was gray with rain. The sky hovered near the earth and bound it in. The man came out of the shack with a bundle on his shoulders. Head bent, eyes to the ground, he walked away into the west, into the mysterious part of the horizon. His figure became vague as the mists hemmed him in. The rain ceased for a moment. In the distance his figure stood black against the bank of fog on the horizon. Then the rain commenced again and he was lost behind the gray clouds. All about, the prairie stretched away—cold, dreary, lifeless.

Are We Leaving Tomorrow?

JOHN O'HARA

John O'Hara, born January 31, 1905, came to the writing of fiction from an experience of ten years in work for newspapers and magazines, including *The New York Herald Tribune, The Daily Mirror, Time,* and *The New Yorker.* He carried a newsman's feeling for significant action and concise, objective writing into his brief, almost colloquial novels of everyday American life, *Appointment in Samarra* (1934); *Butterfield 8* (1935); and *Hope of Heaven* (1938). His short stories in the collections *The Doctor's Son* (1935) and *Files on Parade* (1940) are noteworthy for economy and acute observation.

I T WAS cool, quite cool, the way the weather is likely to be at an in-between resort when the Florida season is over but the Northern summer season has not yet begun. Every morning the tall young man and his young wife would come down the steps of the porch and go for their walk. They would go to the mounting block where the riders would start for the trails. The tall young man and his wife would stand not too close to the block, not speaking to any one; just watching. But there might have been a little in his attitude, in his manner, of a man who felt that he was starting the riders, as though his presence there made their start official. He would stand there, hatless and tanned, chin down almost to his chest, his hands dug deep in the pockets of his handsome tweed topcoat. His wife would stand beside him with her arm in his, and when she would speak to him she would put her face in front of him and look up. Almost always his answer would be a smile and a nod, or perhaps a single word that expressed all he wanted to put into words. They would watch the riders for a while, and then they would stroll over to the first tee of the men's golf course to watch the golfers start off. There it would be the same: not much talk, and the slightly superior manner or attitude. After they had watched their quota of golfers they would go back to the porch and she would go up to their rooms and a Negro bellboy would bring him his papers, *The Montreal Star* and *The New York Times.* He would sit there lazily looking at the papers, never so interested in a news item that he would not look up at every person who came in or went out of the hotel, or passed his chair on the porch. He watched every car come up the short, winding drive, watched the people get in and out, watched the car drive away; then when there was no human activity he would return to his paper, holding it rather far away, and on his face and in his eyes behind the gold-rimmed spectacles there was always the same suspicion of a smile.

He would go to his room before lunch, and they would come down together. After lunch, like almost every one else, they would retire, apparently for a nap, not to appear until the cocktail hour. They would be the first, usually, in the small, cheery bar, and until it was time to change for dinner he would have a highball glass, constantly refilled, in his hand. He drank slowly, sipping teaspoonfuls at a time. In that time she might drink two light highballs while he was drinking eight. She always seemed to have one of the magazines of large format in her lap, but at these times it was she who would look up, while he hardly turned his head.

Not long after they came she began to speak to people; to bow and pass the time of day. She was a pleasant, friendly little woman, not yet thirty. Her eyes were too pretty for the rest of her face; in sleep she must have been very plain indeed, and her skin was sensitive to the sun. She had good bones—lovely hands and feet—and when she was in sweater and skirt her figure always got a second look from the golfers and riders.

Their name was Campbell—Douglas Campbell, and Sheila. They were the youngest people over fifteen in the hotel. There were a few children, but most of the guests were forty or thereabouts. One afternoon when the Campbells were in the bar a woman came in; after hesitating at the entrance she said, "Good afternoon, Mrs. Campbell. You didn't happen to see my husband?"

"No, I didn't," said Mrs. Campbell.

The woman came closer slowly and put her hand on the back of a chair near them. "I was afraid I'd missed him," she said to no one; then suddenly she said, "Do you mind if I sit with you while he comes?"

"No, not at all," said Mrs. Campbell.

"Please do," said Campbell. He got to his feet and stood very erect. He set his glass on the little table and put his hands behind his back.

"I'm sorry I don't remember your name," said Mrs. Campbell.

"Mrs. Loomis."

Mrs. Campbell introduced her husband, who said, "Wouldn't you like a cocktail meanwhile?"

Mrs. Loomis thought a moment and said she would—a

dry Daiquiri. Then Campbell sat down, picking up his drink and beginning to sip.

"I think we were the first here, as usual," said Mrs. Campbell, "so we couldn't have missed Mr. Loomis."

"Oh, it's all right. One of us is always late, but it isn't important. That's why I like it here. The general air of informality." She smiled. "I've never seen you here before. Is this your first year?"

"Our first year," said Mrs. Campbell.

"From New York?"

"Montreal," said Mrs. Campbell.

"Oh, Canadians. I met some awfully nice Canadians in Palm Beach this winter," said Mrs. Loomis. She named them off, and Mrs. Campbell said they knew them, and he smiled and nodded. Then Mrs. Loomis tried to remember the names of some other people she knew in Montreal (they turned out to have been Toronto people), and Mr. Loomis arrived.

A white-haired man, a trifle heavy and about fifty, Mr. Loomis wore young men's clothes. He was brown and heavy-lidded. He had good manners. It was he who corrected his wife about the people from Montreal who actually were from Toronto. That was the first time the Loomises and the Campbells had done more than speak in passing, and Mrs. Campbell was almost gay that afternoon.

The Campbells did not come down to dinner that evening, but they were out for their stroll the next morning. Mr. Loomis waved to them at the first tee, and they waved—*she* waved, Campbell nodded. They did not appear for cocktails that afternoon. For the next few days they took their stroll, but they had their meals in their room. The next time they came to the cocktail lounge they took a small table at the side of the bar, where there was room only for the table and two chairs. No one spoke to them, but that

night was one of the nights when the hotel showed movies
in the ballroom, and after the movie the Loomises fell in
with them and insisted on buying them a drink, just a
nightcap. That was the way it was.

Mr. Loomis brought out his cigar case and offered Mr.
Campbell a cigar, which was declined, and gave the orders
for drinks, "Scotch, Scotch, Scotch, and a Cuba Libre."
Mrs. Loomis was having the Cuba Libre. As the waiter
took the order Mr. Campbell said, "And bring the bottle."

There was a fraction of a second's incredulity in Mr.
Loomis's face; incredulity, or more likely doubt that he
had heard his own ears. But he said, "Yes, bring the bottle."
Then they talked about the picture. It had been a terrible
picture, they all agreed. The Loomises said it was too bad,
too, because they had crossed with the star two years ago
and she had seemed awfully nice, not at all what you'd
expect a movie star to be like. They all agreed that the
Mickey Mouse was good, although Mr. Loomis said he was
getting a little tired of Mickey Mouse. Their drinks came,
and Mrs. Loomis was somewhat apologetic about her drink,
but ever since she had been in Cuba she'd developed a taste
for rum, always rum. "And before that, gin," said Mr.
Loomis. Mr. Campbell's glass was empty and he called the
waiter to bring some more ice and another Cuba Libre,
and he replenished the highball glasses from the bottle of
Scotch on the table.

"Now this was my idea," said Mr. Loomis.

"Only the first one," said Mr. Campbell. They let it go
at that, and the ladies returned to the subject of the star
of the picture, and soon Mr. Loomis joined in. They got
all mixed up in the star's matrimonial record, which in-
evitably brought up the names of other movie stars and
their matrimonial records. Mr. and Mrs. Loomis provided
the statistics, and Mrs. Campbell would say yes or no as

the statement of opinion required. Mr. Campbell sipped his
drink wordlessly until the Loomises, who had been married
a long time, became simultaneously aware of Mr. Campbell's silence, and they began directing their remarks at
him. The Loomises were not satisfied with Mrs. Campbell's
ready assents. They would address the first few words of
a remark to the young wife, because she had been such a
polite listener, but then they would turn to Mr. Campbell
and most of what they had to say was said to him.

For a while he would smile and murmur "Mm—hmm,"
more or less into his glass. Then it seemed after a few
minutes that he could hardly wait for them to end an item
or an anecdote. He began to nod before it was time to nod,
and he would keep nodding, and he would say, "Yes, yes,
yes," very rapidly. Presently, in the middle of an anecdote,
his eyes, which had been growing brighter, became very
bright. He put down his drink and leaned forward, one
hand clasping and unclasping the other. "And—yes—and—
yes," he kept saying, until Mrs. Loomis had finished her
story. Then he leaned farther forward and stared at Mrs.
Loomis, with that bright smile and with his breathing becoming short and fast.

"Can I tell you a story?" he said.

Mrs. Loomis beamed. "Why, of course."

Then Campbell told a story. It had in it a priest, female
anatomy, improbable situations, a cuckold, unprintable
words, and no point.

Long before Campbell finished his story Loomis was
frowning, glancing at his wife and at Campbell's wife,
seeming to listen to Campbell but always glancing at the
two women. Mrs. Loomis could not look away; Campbell
was telling her the story, and he looked at no one else.
While Mrs. Campbell, the moment the story was begun,
picked up her drink, took a sip, and put the glass on the

table and kept her eyes on it until Campbell signalled by his chuckling that the story was at an end.

He kept chuckling and looking at Mrs. Loomis after he had finished, and then he smiled at Loomis. "Huh" came from Loomis, and on his face a muscular smile. "Well, dear," he said. "Think it's about time——"

"Yes," said Mrs. Loomis. "Thank you so much. Good night, Mrs. Campbell, and good night." Campbell stood up, erect, bowing.

When they were entirely out of the room he sat down and crossed his legs. He lit a cigarette and resumed his drinking and stared at the opposite wall. She watched him. His eyes did not even move when he raised his glass to his mouth.

"Oh," she said suddenly. "I wonder if the man is still there at the travel desk. I forgot all about the tickets for tomorrow."

"Tomorrow? Are we leaving tomorrow?"

"Yes."

He stood up and pulled the table out of her way, and when she had left he sat down to wait for her.

The Waltz

DOROTHY PARKER

Dorothy (Rothschild) Parker was born in New Jersey in 1893. She attended Miss Dana's School at Morristown, New Jersey, and Blessed Sacrament Convent in New York City. She has worked on the editorial staffs of *Vogue, Vanity Fair,* and *The New Yorker.* Her first book, of light verse, *Enough Rope* (1927), was a best seller. Her short stories, chiefly satirical in purpose and dealing with sophisticated metropolitan life, are collected in the volume *Here Lies* (1939).

W*HY, thank you so much. I'd adore to.*
I don't want to dance with him. I don't want to dance with anybody. And even if I did, it wouldn't be him. He'd be well down among the last ten. I've seen the way he dances; it looks like something you do on St. Walpurgis Night. Just think, not a quarter of an hour ago, here I was sitting, feeling so sorry for the poor girl he was dancing with. And now *I'm* going to be the poor girl. Well, well. Isn't it a small world?

And a peach of a world, too. A true little corker. Its events are so fascinatingly unpredictable, are not they? Here I was, minding my own business, not doing a stitch of harm to any living soul. And then he comes into my life, all smiles and city manners, to sue me for the favor of one memorable mazurka. Why, he scarcely knows my name, let alone what it stands for. It stands for Despair, Bewilderment, Futility, Degradation, and Premeditated Murder, but little does he wot. I don't wot his name, either; I haven't any idea what it is. Jukes, would be my guess from the look in his eyes. How do you do, Mr. Jukes? And how is that dear little brother of yours, with the two heads?

Ah, now why did he have to come around me, with his low requests? Why can't he let me lead my own life? I ask so little—just to be left alone in my quiet corner of the table, to do my evening brooding over all my sorrows. And he must come, with his bows and his scrapes and his may-I-have-this-ones. And I had to go and tell him that I'd adore to dance with him. I cannot understand why I wasn't struck right down dead. Yes, and being struck dead would look like a day in the country, compared to struggling out a dance with this boy. But what could I do? Every one else at the table had got up to dance, except him and me. There I was, trapped. Trapped like a trap in a trap.

What can you say, when a man asks you to dance with him? I most certainly will *not* dance with you, I'll see you in hell first. Why, thank you, I'd like to awfully, but I'm having labor pains. Oh, yes, *do* let's dance together—it's so nice to meet a man who isn't a scaredy-cat about catching my beriberi. No. There was nothing for me to do but say I'd adore to. Well, we might as well get it over with. All right, Cannonball, let's run out on the field. You won the toss; you can lead.

Why, I think it's more of a waltz, really. Isn't it? We might just listen to the music a second. Shall we? Oh, yes, it's a waltz. Mind? Why, I'm simply thrilled. I'd love to waltz with you.

I'd love to waltz with you. I'd love to waltz with you,

I'd love to have my tonsils out, I'd love to be in a midnight fire at sea. Well, it's too late now. We're getting under way. *Oh.* Oh, dear. Oh, dear, dear, dear. Oh, this is even worse than I thought it would be. I suppose that's the one dependable law of life—everything is always worse than you thought it was going to be. Oh, if I had had any real grasp of what this dance would be like, I'd have held out for sitting it out. Well, it will probably amount to the same thing in the end. We'll be sitting it out on the floor in a minute, if he keeps this up.

I'm so glad I brought it to his attention that this is a waltz they're playing. Heaven knows what might have happened, if he had thought it was something fast; we'd have blown the sides right out of the building. Why does he always want to be somewhere that he isn't? Why can't we stay in one place just long enough to get acclimated? It's this constant rush, rush, rush, that's the curse of American life. That's the reason that we're all of us so—*Ow!* For God's sake, don't *kick,* you idiot; this is only second down. Oh, my shin. My poor, poor shin, that I've had ever since I was a little girl!

Oh, no, no, no. Goodness, no. It didn't hurt the least little bit. And anyway it was my fault. Really it was. Truly. Well, you're sweet to say that. It really was all my fault.

I wonder what I'd better do—kill him this instant, with my naked hands, or wait and let him drop in his traces. Maybe it's best not to make a scene. I guess I'll just lie low, and watch the pace get him. He can't keep this up indefinitely—he's only flesh and blood. Die he must, and die he shall, for what he did to me. I don't want to be of the oversensitive type, but you can't tell me that kick was unpremeditated. Freud says there are no accidents. I've led no cloistered life, I've known dancing partners who have spoiled my slippers and torn my dress; but when it comes to kicking, I am Outraged Womanhood. When you kick me in the shin, *smile*.

Maybe he didn't do it maliciously. Maybe it's just his way of showing his high spirits. I suppose I ought to be glad that one of us is having such a good time. I suppose I ought to think myself lucky if he brings me back alive. Maybe it's captious to demand of a practically strange man that he leave your shins as he found them. After all, the poor boy's doing the best he can. Probably he grew up in the hill country, and never had no larnin'. I bet they had to throw him on his back to get shoes on him.

Yes, it's lovely, isn't it? It's simply lovely. It's the loveliest waltz. Isn't it? Oh, I think it's lovely, too.

Why, I'm getting positively drawn to the Triple Threat here. He's my hero. He has the heart of a lion, and the sinews of a buffalo. Look at him—never a thought of the consequences, never afraid of his face, hurling himself into every scrimmage, eyes shining, cheeks ablaze. And shall it be said that I hung back? No, a thousand times no. What's it to me if I have to spend the next couple of years in a plaster cast? Come on, Butch, right through them! Who wants to live forever?

Oh. Oh, dear. Oh, he's all right, thank goodness. For a while I thought they'd have to carry him off the field. Ah, I couldn't bear to have anything happen to him. I love him. I love him better than anybody in the world. Look at the spirit he gets into a dreary, commonplace waltz; how effete the other dancers seem, beside him. He is youth and vigor and courage, he is strength and gayety and—*Ow!* Get off my instep, you hulking peasant! What do you think I am, anyway—a gangplank? *Ow!*

No, of course it didn't hurt. Why, it didn't a bit. Honestly. And it was all my fault. You see, that little step of yours —well, it's perfectly lovely, but it's just a tiny bit tricky to follow at first. Oh, did you work it up yourself? You really did? Well, aren't you amazing! Oh, now I think I've got it. Oh, I think it's lovely. I was watching when you were dancing before. It's awfully effective when you look at it.

It's awfully effective when you look at it. I bet I'm awfully effective when you look at me. My hair is hanging along my cheeks, my skirt is swaddled about me, I can feel the cold damp of my brow. I must look like something out of the Fall of the House of Usher. This sort of thing takes a fearful toll of a woman my age. And he worked up his little step himself, he with his degenerate cunning. And it was just a tiny bit tricky at first, but now I think I've got it. Two stumbles, slip, and a twenty-yard dash; yes, I've got it. I've got several other things, too, including a split shin and a bitter heart. I hate this creature I'm chained to. I hated him the moment I saw his leering, bestial face. And here I've been locked in his noxious embrace for the thirty-five years this waltz has lasted. Is that orchestra never going to stop playing? Or must this obscene travesty of a dance go on until hell burns out?

Oh, they're going to play another encore. Oh, goody. Oh, that's lovely. Tired? I should say I'm not tired. I'd like to go on like this forever.

I should say I'm not tired. I'm dead, that's all I am. Dead, and in what a cause! And the music is never going to stop playing, and we're going on like this, Double-Time Charlie and I, throughout eternity. I suppose I won't care any more, after the first hundred thousand years. I suppose nothing will matter then, not heat nor pain nor broken heart nor cruel, aching weariness. Well. It can't come too soon for me.

I wonder why I didn't tell him I was tired. I wonder why I didn't suggest going back to the table. I could have said let's just listen to the music. Yes, and if he would, that would be the first bit of attention he has given it all evening. George Jean Nathan said that the lovely rhythms of the waltz should be listened to in stillness and not be accompanied by strange gyrations of the human body. I think that's what he said. I think it was George Jean Nathan. Anyhow, whatever he said and whoever he was and whatever he's doing now, he's better off than I am. That's safe. Anybody who isn't waltzing with this Mrs. O'Leary's cow I've got here is having a good time.

Still, if we were back at the table, I'd probably have to talk to him. Look at him—what could you say to a thing like that! Did you go to the circus this year, what's your favorite kind of ice cream, how do you spell cat? I guess I'm well off here. As well off as if I were in a cement mixer in full action.

I'm past all feeling now. The only way I can tell when he steps on me is that I can hear the splintering of bones. And all the events of my life are passing before my eyes. There was the time I was in a hurricane in the West Indies, there was the day I got my head cut open in the taxi smash, there was the night the drunken lady threw a bronze ashtray at her own true love and got me instead, there was that summer that the sailboat kept capsizing. Ah, what an easy, peaceful time was mine, until I fell in with Swifty, here. I didn't know what trouble was, before I got drawn into this *danse macabre*. I think my mind is beginning to wander. It almost seems to me as if the orchestra were stopping. It couldn't be, of course; it could never, never be. And yet in my ears there is a silence like the sound of angel voices. . . .

Oh, they've stopped, the mean things. They're not going to play any more. Oh, darn. Oh, do you think they would? Do you really think so, if you gave them fifty dollars? Oh, that would be lovely. And look, do tell them to play this same thing. I'd simply adore to go on waltzing.

A Crop of Beans

MARJORIE KINNAN RAWLINGS

Marjorie Kinnan Rawlings did not come to know the Florida hammock country which she has made her own as a writer until 1928. She was born in 1896 at Washington, D. C., and spent her girlhood in Maryland on her father's farm. She attended the University of Wisconsin, and for the next ten years did journalistic writing of various sorts in Louisville, New York City, and Rochester, New York. In 1928 she moved to a farm in a thinly populated part of Florida, unfrequented by tourists but possessed of great natural interest and charm. Mrs. Rawlings' novels of her adopted region, *South Moon Under* (1933) and *The Yearling* (1938), and the short stories collected in *When the Whippoorwill* (1940), reveal unusual breadth of creative vision. She recognizes and reveals elements of humor, heroism, and spiritual integrity in lives in which less sympathetic observers see only the limiting effects of ignorance and poverty.

A TILLIE-HAWK swooped into the top of a dead cypress. The mockingbirds and redbirds that had scurried like wind-buffeted leaves ahead of him stirred uneasily in the live oaks and palmettos where they had concealed themselves. The sky had emptied itself for him of living things. Against the blinding blue of the

Florida afternoon hung indolent masses of white cloud. The hawk shifted from one claw to the other, hitching his shoulders like a cripple. There ran a road—a fat chicken snake—a man——

The young man swung his shotgun from his waist to his shoulder in a quick semi-circle. The tillie-hawk exploded into a mass of buff feathers and tumbled to the edge of the road. The girl caught her breath.

"Lige," she reproached him. "You hadn't orter wasted a shell on a ol' tillie-hawk."

A horn sounded behind them and a truck loaded with bean hampers lurched by in the deep ruts of the sand road. Old man Tainter and his Negro driver passed without the customary "Hey!" or lift of the hand. The young woman crowded back into the dry dog-fennel. The man no more than stepped aside, unbreaching his gun. He kicked a cloud of sand after the truck.

"His beans ain't a mite better'n mine. Parts of 'em is plumb sorry-lookin'."

"They're earlier, ain't they?"

"Jest a week. He ain't no more likely to miss frost than me. Ary time, now it's a'most November, we're like to git us one o' them piddlin' leetle ol' frosts don't mean nothin'. Tonight, mebbe."

They turned between chinaberries into the Widow Sellers' gate. Her sharp tongue clicked at them from the porch.

"You Lige Gentry, you, how'll I ever git my cane cut? I ain't payin' you by the week reg'lar to traipse around with your wife."

He rose to the familiar bait.

"Dog take it, ol' woman, Drenna's been a-cuttin' cane with me all evenin'. An' who'll pay for it? Not you. I'll be hornswoggled if you ain't the meanest white woman in the county."

He stamped across the porch. Drenna dropped down on the top step, draping her gray-percale skirt across her worn shoes. The widow hunched herself on the cowhide seat of her hickory rocker, drawing her shawl around her shoulders against the chill air from the northwest.

"Ain't you sick o' keepin' Drenna hangin' around where you kin look at her all the day? I ain't done laughin', the way you begun a-courtin' her, like you was huntin' a squirrel goin' acrost a oak thicket an' you tryin' to keep sight of it. How many years ago was it? Two, three? Anyways, long enough to git you a couple o' young uns. An' you ain't sick o' lookin' at her yit!"

Lige towered over her. He shook back the curly sun-bleached hair from his sweaty forehead like an infuriated bull. He plunged roaring into her trap.

"Dog take you! You ain't fitten to fish the same creek 'long-side of her! Drenna, move offen the stoop away from her! You'd orter study on sayin', is she sick o' lookin' at me! A pore sorry thing like me to git a woman——"

The Widow Sellers rocked violently in sheer delight. Her little black chinquapin eyes danced. She scratched her white head excitedly with a piece of the okra she was cutting. She shrilled above him.

"Now you said it! Now you and me agrees for onct, Mister Gentry! A pore sorry thing like you. Now you're talkin'!"

He stopped short.

"Oh, go to the devil," he said good-naturedly.

Drenna smiled uneasily. The ribald quarreling of this pair still disturbed her. It was scandalous for two people so dependent on each other to talk so. No other man, black or white, would work so hard for the old woman, at the low wages of six dollars a week. Certainly no other employer would allow Lige time off every afternoon to work his own few acres. They threw these facts at each other at every encounter.

The Widow Sellers was admitting now, "Shore you works hard. Bless Katy, all you know is to work. You don't know nothin' else. You got you no sense."

"You wait 'til my beans gits top price next week. You'll say I got sense."

"You got Davis wax, eh? Them newfangled ones. They're pretty, but they ain't got the good flavor. Sellers always planted Wardwell's. You won't never make you no crop," she said comfortably. "Here," she reached behind her rocker and pushed a pair of worn child's shoes in his hands. "I had me a box from Janey, in Alabamy. Git along to your sorry bean-patch."

He hurled the shoes past her head.

"Give your dogged shoes to a nigger young un."

He spat over the edge of the porch and strode off fiercely.

"Fust crop o' beans I make," he called back over his shoulder, "you've seed the last o' me, ol' woman."

"You'll be white-headed as me," she mocked after him, "an' still proud to be takin' my rations money!"

"No need to holler," he soothed from the gate. "You got you a voice like a limpkin."

"A limpkin?" she puzzled. "That brownified crane screeches like a wild-cat?"

"Now you said it!" he whooped.

His teeth flashed in his tanned face. He was off at a violent trot for his two acres of beans. The old woman grinned.

"Ain't he the biggetty thing!"

"Hain't biggetty," the young woman said gently. "Jest turrible prideful. . . . He shot him a tillie-hawk a ways back, jest account o' ol' man Tainter was drivin' up behind us. He figgers he's as good as ary man to shoot his shells reckless."

The old woman nodded and chuckled. She put down her pan of okra and picked up the child shoes, dusting them with her apron. Drenna put them under her arm.

"Thank you, ma'am. They'll fit one o' the chappies, shore."

They walked together to the road. The widow shivered.

"That scamp knows as good as I do we'll git heavy frost tonight. We cain't skip it. The whole State o' Texas is a-breathin' cold in on us. Floridy don't make none o' her own troubles," she grumbled. "They all comes in from some'eres else. Wind from the south an' cold from Texas. He better say good ·bye to them beans today whilst they're ·purty."

She laid a hand on the girl's arm.

"I was jest a-baitin' Lige about you. Leave me tell you, when he got you, he got him a saint."

The chinaberry cast a lacelike shadow across the translucence of the young sharp-chiselled face.

"There's no harm to neither one of you," the girl said quietly. "I don't pay no mind when either one or t'other of you gits to rarin'."

The three-room rough-pine dwelling a mile from the village was bare and shabby. Drenna's father, prospering one year in hogs, had given her a small melodeon. It was the sole ornament of the main room. When Lige was not so tired that he tumbled, sometimes in his underwear, sometimes fully dressed, into their bed in the adjoining room, he coaxed her at night to play on it. She sat stiffly upright on the seat and picked out awkward, quavering hymns.

Tonight he sat teetering in his pine-slab chair, smoking his pipe, his blue eyes staring into space. Drenna put the drowsy children, the baby and a boy of three, between clean unbleached muslin sheets over a corn-husk mattress on the handmade bed opposite the fireplace. When Lige did not make the usual sign, she went hesitantly to the melodeon. He relaxed a little as the notes of "Rock of Ages" wheezed sweetly from it.

"Dog take it, Drenna, that's purty."

His voice, with her, was gentle. Men who had grown up with him, gone their few scattered seasons with him to the village school, were still astonished at the taming of his exuberance. Passing the small house at night, they reported, through fire-lit windows, the sight of wild Lige smoking peacefully by the hearth, his eyes wide and hungry on the woman pedalling and playing. Tonight the spell did not hold. Suddenly he stood up and knocked out his pipe into the knot fire.

"I cain't set here an' let my beans freeze," he burst out. "Tainter's firin'. He's got him smudges all over his field. I don't figger it'll do a mite o' good to burn wood, but I got to try it."

"What wood you got to use, Lige?"

He ran his big hand across his head.

"I aim to give your winter woodpile the devil, ma'am."

He went whistling to the field. The full moon had risen, coldly silver, on a night so still he heard the gray fox in the hammock on dry magnolia leaves. The young beans hung thickly on the bushes, slim and faintly yellow in the moonlight. The dark, tangled hammock pressed in on three sides of the clearing. The field was ordered and beautiful. He cursed out loud.

"Jesus! Only three days more'd o' made them beans——"

He had no hope of his fatwood fires, but building them, he felt better. A line of them blazed along the westerly, higher end. Thick black smoke drifted across the patch to settle in the lower corner. Drenna joined him toward midnight with a paper of cornbread. The cold was tangible. In the stillness it moved in perceptibly, a chill white ghost from Texas. Under the ineffectual blanket of smoke, it closed stiff hands tight about the succulent plants.

At daybreak, a breeze stirred from the southeast. The day, and the days following, would be warm. There would perhaps not be frost again until the next full moon. The frosted leaves were curling. White spots appeared on the beans. Then they turned translucent like pale yellow icicles. By night they would be mush; the leaves black and shrivelled.

Walking around the wilting field, Lige saw that he had saved the lower end. The smudge had lain across the last few rows. The east line of the hammock protected them from the sun, as deadly on the injured plants as the frost itself. He made a quick estimate. Fifteen or twenty hampers saved——

He was late at the Widow Sellers', shivering in his thin blue shirt and pin-checked pants. She greeted him amiably. Her own crops of okra, squash, peanuts, corn and sweet potatoes were safely harvested.

"Thermometer went to forty at day," she told him.

"No need to tell me," he answered wearily. "I been settin' up nussin' them forty degrees. I fired. I figger I jest about saved my seed an' fertilizer. I'm clearin' more o' the hammock. Next time I plant late, I'm goin' to have four acres inst'd o' two, all at the lower end. Then if frost ketches me, I got more'll come thu."

She stared at him.

"The bigger fool, you. You'd do best to leave off beans an' work for me full time. I could mebbe pay ten dollars a week," she said slyly.

"You mind your own business, ol' woman. I'll make me a crop o' beans'll git me shut o' you an' your ten dollars, an' your six."

She eyed him dubiously.

"What did you fire with?"

He walked away carelessly.

"A damn good woodpile an' a damn good woman."

II

When a stranger—a Georgia truck driver or a platform buyer—asked Lige his business, he answered with a mustered defiance:

"I'm a bean man!"

It was true. The long hours he gave to the Widow Sellers' rich farms had no meaning beyond their moment. In mid-afternoon he hurried off to his own field, sweaty and excited, to turn furrows, to plant, to cultivate, to hoe, to harvest.

The quick growth of the crop stirred him. One week, the sandy loam lay golden, its expanse passive for the reception of the seed. The next week, the clearing in the hammock was covered with cotyledons, pale-green and pushing, like twin sails dotting a tawny sea. In forty-eight days the first crop was ready for picking. The emerald bushes crowded one another in the straight rows. The long beans hung like pendants, butter-yellow if they were wax, jade-green if Giant Stringless or Red Valentine.

The earth responded to him. When he and the soil were not interfered with, they made beans as fine as old man Tainter's, who kept a wagonload of Negroes and bought fertilizer by the carload.

He was betrayed constantly by elements beyond his control. He fared no worse than the other growers, but the common misfortunes struck more implacably. Men who could borrow money for seed and fertilizer and rations, who were free to do other farming or stock raising, made out more or less comfortably until the inevitable time when a good crop sold on a high market. There was a finality about his loss of a crop.

He lost beans from cold or rain or blight three seasons in succession. The fourth season, the second autumn, he made a fair crop. The market dropped so low it scarcely paid to ship. In October he quarreled violently with the Widow Sellers. The old woman, in a growing security that he would never shake free of her, taunted him.

"You jest as good to say you're done. You jest as good to say you got no sense for bean-makin'. Drenna's like to go naked, and you piddlin' away with beans. Your young uns'd be stark-naked if 'tan't for Janey's things from Alabamy. You know it. You take me up on steady work at ten dollars, afore I studies you ain't wuth nothin'."

If Drenna had been with him, he would not have touched her. He shook the old woman by the shoulders until she screeched for her neighbors. He shouted her down.

"Damn your gizzard! If I figgered like niggers, you'd put a cunjur on my bean-field! 'Twon't be too long 'til you sees the last o' me. Dogged if I wouldn't ruther do without rations than take your talk."

They sputtered fiercely at each other. It did not occur to her to fire him, nor to him to quit.

He was excited when he came home to supper that night. He had forgotten his anger at the widow. He had forgotten his unprofitable season. He was eager with his plans for spring beans. His lunch bucket had contained the usual meal of soda biscuits and syrup, but he sat at the table, scarcely eating. Drenna listened with her grave smile.

"We got to make out on four dollars a week this winter an' save two. I kin make me a crop o' beans on that hammock land and I know it. I aim to have six acres ready, come spring. Does the rains come on me to drownd 'em, I'll ditch. Does frost come, I'll lay me a smudge. And dog take it, Drenna, if they ain't no rain at all, an' them beans goes to swivvellin', I kin water 'em a gourdful at a time."

The three-year-old nodded gravely.

"I kin water 'em."

Drenna smiled at him.

"Tell your Daddy the whole lot of us kin tote water for him."

"Tainter don't always make a crop," he went on, "and I cain't always lose."

"Shore cain't," she agreed placidly.

Lige and Drenna planted when the red-bud came in bloom. All the signs were of warmth. Robins and bluebirds were moving north. The cautious chinaberry had put out young leaves. The last of the jasmine perfumed the road-side. Lige strode steadily up and down the long furrows, seeing nothing but the white seed dropping against the golden earth. Drenna stopped now and then to straighten her back. Her gray eyes rested on the rosy flush across the hammock. They picked out the swaying palms, precise and formal against a turquoise sky. When she bent to her work again, the half-smile habitual to her was brighter.

Lige sent her to the house when the end of the planting was in sight.

"Go git me my rations, woman," he told her. He turned her away from the field. "Git!" He took his hands from her shoulders. "Now shame to me. My hands has smuttied your clean dress."

"Soap an' water's plentiful."

His eyes followed her across the clearing and into the house.

The March night was chilly. When supper was eaten, he piled the fireplace with blocks of magnolia. The cream-colored wood gave out a sweet odor, like a mild thin spice.

As the fire dulled, he threw on pine. He took off his high boots and stretched his bare sandy toes to the fire.

"Wisht I'd takened my boots off in the dark. Look at them feet. Now I got to git up an' wash 'em afore I goes to bed."

From the kitchen Drenna brought him a basin of warm water and a towel of flour sacking.

"Whooey, ain't that fine!"

He dabbled luxuriously, drying his feet with the warm towel.

"Now, you been a-waitin' on me, leave me do somethin' for you. Leave me play for you."

They both laughed. His playing was limited to two tunes on the mouth organ.

"I'll blow 'The Tall Pine Tree.' "

She sat on a three-legged stool by the fireplace, her smooth head resting against the gray clay, her eyes closed. Lige played his tunes over and over, patting his bare right foot on the pine floor. The children stirred in their low bed, sighing in deep sleep. The magnolia burned into soft gray checks. Drenna nodded.

"Go on to bed, Sugar. I'll set up a whiles. I've wore you out, plantin' them beans. But Drenna—I got no question. We'll make us a crop, shore as dogs runs rabbits."

"Shore will," she agreed sleepily.

He sat by the fire an hour after she had gone, blowing softly into the harmonica, patting his foot.

Lige saved his beans two weeks later by a scanty margin. He had planted dangerously early, and as the crooks came through, it was plain that heavy frost was moving in. Two nights in succession were increasingly colder. All the beans in the region were slightly nipped. The third night would bring real damage. A smudge would be useless over the young juicy plants.

In the crisp morning he said to Drenna, "Ain't a reason in the world why I cain't cover them leetle bean plants with dirt today."

But when he drove the mule and cultivator between the rows, the earth he turned did not quite cover them.

Drenna, come out to watch him, said, "Kin do it by hand, Lige."

"Six acres?"

"Well, what we kin git covered is better'n nothin.'"

The work went surprisingly fast. Except for the increasing ache of their backs, it was satisfying to move rapidly down the straight lines, swinging and stooping, ape-fashion, and cup the soft yellow dirt over the tops of the plants with their two hands. The three-year-old was fascinated. He followed like a young monkey, and in his clumsy way, throwing sand with too great enthusiasm, imitated them on adjacent rows.

"I can rest tomorrow," Drenna thought, and after dinner went at it again.

They worked until the night blended plants and earth and hammock and sky into a nothingness as deep and black as a 'gator cave. Drenna brought out kerosene lanterns. They were toiling slowly. The extra labor of moving the lights seemed insupportable. The beans were covered down to a last half-acre at the lower end. They went, stooped, for they could not quite straighten their backs, to their cold bed. They could do nothing more.

The night's frost wiped out the entire section, including Tainter. Those who had the money were planting again. Those who did not were done for the season. Lige waited two days for the cold to pass. Under a benign March sun, with a neighbor boy hired in the light of his hopes, he carefully fingered the sandy loam away from his beans. The plants emerged a little yellowed, wilted and leathery, but none the worse for their warm burying.

The town was aghast at news of the saving.

The Widow Sellers said to Lige, "Nobody but you'd be fool enough to scratch dirt over six acres o' beans—and then scratch 'em out again!"

He was generous in his good fortune. He pinched her wrinkled cheek and jumped away before her quick hand fell.

"Ol' woman, don't you wisht you'd had you a real man like me, to make you crops when nobody else couldn't make 'em?"

It became apparent that Lige would have almost the earliest beans in the State. Other sections had been drowned out on the first planting, and he would come in at least two weeks ahead of his neighbors. He ordered fancy hampers, with green and red bands. The small crate factory trusted him for them. His beans were perfection. The bushes were loaded.

His first picking was small. He and Drenna and the neighbor boy managed it without help. The beans ripened rapidly, inexorably. The storekeeper, interested, loaned him money to hire pickers. He brought in a truckload of hands for the second picking. Drenna culled, sorted and packed. The Widow Sellers came over. Other neighbor women dropped in to look at the big crop, and stayed to help with the packing. Drenna cooked a generous dinner of ham and grits and cornbread; made a great kettle of coffee and chicory; opened Mason jars of the past summer's blueberries and peaches and figs.

In the field, white and Negro pickers worked alternate rows. The white children squatted on their haunches, sliding along from bush to bush. The Negroes for the most part bent to their picking, their black arms gathering the beans like swift sickles. The six acres were alive.

Lige worked desperately in and out of the field. The sorting and packing proceeded steadily under Drenna's quiet authority. The volunteer neighbor help chattered and gossiped, but the work was familiar, and they did it carefully. A Negro asked "Captain Gentry" for buckets of drinking water to take to the pickers. The Widow Sellers' tongue flashed like hail across the work. Her small black eyes watched uneasily the growing spread of finished hampers, stacked up to go to the express office. The picking totalled a hundred and thirty hampers. The neighbors divided up the cull beans and went home.

The third picking ran to nearly two hundred crates. It was the most ample yield the section had produced in seasons. The checks began to arrive. A telegram from the New York commission house preceded the first. Lige's initial shipment had brought the record price of nine dollars a hamper.

The market price dropped rapidly as other sections came in. Yet his returns were consistently good. The last three checks reached him on one mail. His net for the crop was over fifteen hundred dollars.

He went a little crazy.

III

Lige began his celebration at four o'clock in the afternoon. He hurled himself into the house; changed into Sunday clothes without washing or shaving. He slapped into Drenna's hand the accumulation of bean checks, keeping out one for fifty dollars. His stiff store collar was already wet with sweat. Tousled hair hung damp in his eyes.

"Drenna, if I ain't fitten tomorrow, you git the ice-truck to take you to Pondland and go to the bank and put these in it. It's what they call openin' a account."

"You don't want I should git the cash-money an' fetch it back and hide it?"

"Now, Drenna, you do like I tell you. That's the ol'-timey way. Don't nobody hide their money these days."

He was bounding down the low steps.

"Lige, what you fixin' to do?"

"Sugar, I'm fixin' to git so drunk you'll be 'shamed for me all year, but I got it to do an' you got it to put up with."

He waved a long arm and was gone at his loping trot down the road toward the village, where the Brinley boys waited in their old Ford. The earth swayed from under her. She dropped trembling on the rickety stoop. She wanted to run after him, to call him back, but numbness held her. Lige had been so good; with her, so gentle. Year after year, with his bean-crops failing him, he had been patient. Yet violence simmered in him. He had been always like a great kettle of cane juice, ready, at a little too much heat, to boil over. With her, he had been like a wild animal tamed; a 'coon or 'possum or young panther, that had come to enjoy captivity. Now, in his prosperity, he had broken out of the cage and was gone, dangling his ropes behind him. For a moment, he did not seem to belong to her. It was as though a stranger had gone galloping down the road to meet the Brinley boys and get drunk.

She rose from the stoop, told the children to stay in the house, and went to the Widow Sellers.

"Yes," the old woman said before she could speak, "the grand rascal's been here an' gone. Th'owed over his job an' gone to raise some hell."

Drenna stiffened. She lifted her chin.

"If he's took the notion to git drunk, I reckon he's got the right to do it."

The widow gaped. When the young woman turned defiantly for home again, she scurried through town telling that Drenna didn't give a rap whether Lige got drunk or no. The town buzzed with it.

"I ain't surprised at Lige, but who'd a-figgered Drenna'd turn out plumb shameless!"

No one came near her that evening. The village was busy waiting for news of Lige's hilarity to come in piece by piece. Drenna sat in her low rocker, holding the baby. The older child played in and out of the house and at last gave up asking questions. Twilight came, and still she sat, rocking and staring. She put the children to bed and went back to her rocker. The kerosene lamps went unlit. She wrapped a patchwork quilt around her. A hoot-owl startled her in the pine tree by the window. In the hammock, the first whippoorwill gave his yearning cry.

"When the whippoorwill calls, it's time for the corn to be in the ground."

Would Lige bother to plant corn this spring? Would he get drunk every once and again, now he had money? They had planned to repair the leaking shingled roof; to buy hogs and raise peanuts and chufas; there was money in stock, if you could get a start; to have a real mattress for the bed, some more chairs and a new cook-stove; to take a trip to Alabama to visit Drenna's folks; to be done once and for all with the Widow Sellers; and of course, to lay by money for an increasing acreage of beans.

She listened intently at every sound. A car went by, a nigger riding a mule and singing. A pair of hounds bayed past, trailing 'coon. She was drowsing in her chair when a clatter sounded on the porch and Lige was home.

" 'Lo, Sugar. I shore done the job."

She was trembling again. To keep from looking at him, she did not light a lamp. He was knocking into everything. She took his arm and led him into the bedroom.

"Lay down, Lige, an' leave me take off your shoes an' breeches."

He was asleep, puffing and moaning, before she could undress him. She got off his shoes and threw a cover over him. Lying between the babies, she dozed the two or three hours until daylight.

She roused him at breakfast-time to offer a cup of coffee. He took a few swallows and was suddenly sick. He turned over on his side, groaning, and went to sleep again. She shut the door of the room when she saw two women coming up the walk.

People came all morning; women to bring her juicy bits about the drunken night, with Lige and the Brinleys and the Twillers and Tom Parker driving all over the county shouting and treating everybody. Men came to ask, grinning, if she needed any help with Lige; curious, to see how she was taking it; and men and women grabbing for the bean money.

The owner of the crate factory came for his pay. She gave him one of the checks endorsed in Lige's uneven hand. The storekeeper came for the picking money. The Widow Lykes came whining to borrow whatever she could get. Drenna was bewildered; then resentful.

She was dressed to go to Pondland to the bank when the preacher arrived. It startled her. He had never been in the house before, although she had slipped in and out of church almost every preaching Sunday. He spoke severely on the sin of drunkenness. She braced herself to it. He spoke at last of the desirability, under the shocking circumstances, of tithing the fortune they were squandering, and giving to the Lord. She caught her breath. The parson was after the bean money, too.

Fury took possession of her, like a moccasin swallowing a small gray rabbit. She hated everybody; Lige, crying out now and then behind the closed doors in his drunken sickness; the town, with its intruding eyes and waggling tongues;

the Widow Sellers; the Parson; above everything else, the bean money. She stamped her foot.

"What's a-goin' on ain't nobody's business. I'll settle with God when I git straightened out. I got no money for you now, maybe never. I've give what I could for missions, an' I always will. But I need what we got now for the chappies an' things you know nothin' about. You go on now."

She drove him from the house, locked the door and plodded furiously down the road to hail the ice-truck. In Pondland, she opened the account at the bank with a boldness foreign to her.

"I want fifty dollars o' that back in cash money," she said belligerently.

Her lips moved.

"Jest what Lige takened," she said to herself.

On the streets of the city again, she found herself dazed. The bills were clutched in her fist. She knew only that she intended to spend them, recklessly, foolishly, wickedly. In the shop windows were dresses for summer; hats and shoes. She smoothed back her soft hair. She had come off without any hat at all. A red-chiffon dress caught her eye. She walked in a dream into the shop and pointed out the frock. The saleswomen lifted their eyebrows at one another. They helped her take off her calico dress and put on the red chiffon over her white-muslin slip.

"Of course now, with a silk slip, and nice shoes——"

In the long mirror were reflected a white frightened face with gray eyes, pale tight lips, and bare arms and throat above a flaming pile of soft fabric. She nodded. The saleswoman folded the dress in tissue paper and laid it carefully in a box.

"Forty-five dollars."

She held out the bills.

Bean money. Lige's fine crop of beans. She saw the six

acres, green with gold pendants hung over them. She remembered the pickers moving in with the tall hampers on their shoulders, swaying and singing. The field was empty now, waiting for fall beans. The new bills crackled in her fingers. This was all they had to show for the crop. The rest was in Lige's tormented belly; and in a strange, impersonal bank, dropped from sight like a stone in a pound.

The bean money had been queer stuff. Checks in writing that everybody scrambled to get at. . . . Lige acting scandalously. . . . Her impudence to the preacher. . . . Now a red dress tempting her to go about like a lewd woman. She shivered.

"I cain't do it."

She put the money behind her back.

"I cain't do it."

Outside the shop she stuffed the bills inside her blouse. She rode home on the loaded ice-truck.

She walked from the heart of the village out to the house, running the last of the way. The children were playing with chicken feathers in the sandy yard. Lige was lying awake in bed, smoking his pipe. He put his arm over his face in mock shame.

"Say it, Drenna," he grinned. "I got it comin'. Your ol' man's disgraced you, like I tol' you. But dog take it,"— she sat on the bed, and he reached out his arms for her—"it was fine! Jest to turn that ol' quart bottle topside down an' let 'er drip!"

She had to laugh at him. They wouldn't say any more about it. She had very nearly done as wrong as he. She had been wilder, crazier.

She was cooking dinner when the ice-truck lumbered up to the gate. Tim ran up the walk and into the house.

"Drenna! The Pondland bank's closed down! No more'n

a good hour after you-all put your money in. Tainter jest brought the word. Everybody's caught."

He mopped his face and started away again.

"I got to go out back o' the Creek and tell the Philbins."

At the gate he waved his hand to her and called:

"Tell Lige ever'body says they bet he'll wish he'd got twicet as drunk!"

He rattled off.

She watched the truck out of sight. She was not astonished. She had not been brought up to consider a bank the place for money.

Her father had always said, "Nothin' ain't safe nor sartin excusin' a iron pot o' gold or siller, put deep in a place where nobody cain't find hit."

She went into the bedroom to Lige. He was getting his wracked body into clean clothes.

"I heerd him! Oh my God, Drenna!"

Sweat rolled into his bloodshot eyes.

"I'll kill somebody for this——"

He was unsteady on his feet. He picked up his shotgun from behind the head of the bed.

"Philbins 'll go. Buckshot's too good for that bank president."

"Lige," she said gently.

He stopped. His eyes softened.

"No need to take on so. Banks closes and you cain't blame nobody special."

She drew out the fifty dollars from her blouse. The stiff paper was warm from the skin of her breast. He stared. The money was real and tangible.

"Reckon I was jest led to keep it out in cash-money. It'll git us seed for fall."

"But, Drenna—all that other gone like as if 'twas stole——"

"Don't study that-a-way. I figger, we jest lost another bean-crop."

He replaced the shotgun slowly. He sat down on the side of the bed, his muscular hands closing and unclosing. He pondered. At last he nodded gravely.

"Jest done lost us another crop o' beans."

Mr. Kaplan and the Magi

LEONARD Q. ROSS

Leo C. Rosten, born in Poland in 1908, was brought to the U. S. at the age of two years. After varied experience as delivery boy, drugstore clerk, rent collector, and newspaper reporter, he entered the University of Chicago and obtained a degree in 1930. For a time he taught in a night school for adults. He has contributed stories and articles to *The New Yorker, Harper's Magazine,* and other periodicals.

W HEN Mr. Parkhill saw that Miss Mitnick, Mr. Bloom, and Mr. Hyman Kaplan were absent, and that a strange excitement pervaded the beginners' grade, he realized that it was indeed the last night before the holidays and that Christmas was only a few days off. Each Christmas the classes in the American Night Preparatory School for Adults gave presents to their respective teachers. Mr. Parkhill, a veteran of many sentimental Yuletides, had come to know the procedure. That night, before the class session had begun, there must have been a hurried collection; a Gift Committee of three had been chosen; at this moment the Committee was probably in

From *The Education of Hyman Kaplan,* by Leonard Q. Ross (Harcourt, Brace & Co., 1937). Copyright, 1937, by Harcourt, Brace & Co., Inc. Reprinted by permission of the publishers.

Mickey Goldstein's Arcade, bargaining feverishly, arguing about the appropriateness of a pair of pajamas or the color of a dozen linen handkerchiefs, debating whether Mr. Parkhill would prefer a pair of fleece-lined slippers to a set of mother-of-pearl cuff links.

"We shall concentrate on—er—spelling drill tonight," Mr. Parkhill announced.

The students smiled wisely, glanced at the three empty seats, exchanged knowing nods, and prepared for spelling drill. Miss Rochelle Goldberg giggled, then looked ashamed as Mrs. Rodriguez shot her a glare of reproof.

Mr. Parkhill always chose a spelling drill for the night before the Christmas vacation: it kept all the students busy simultaneously; it dampened the excitement of the occasion; above all, it kept him from the necessity of resorting to elaborate pedagogical efforts in order to hide his own embarrassment.

Mr. Parkhill called off the first words. Pens and pencils scratched, smiles died away, eyes grew serious, preoccupied, as the beginners' grade assaulted the spelling of "banana . . . romance . . . groaning." Mr. Parkhill sighed. The class seemed incomplete without its star student, Miss Mitnick, and barren without its most remarkable one, Mr. Hyman Kaplan. Mr. Kaplan's most recent linguistic triumph had been a fervent speech extolling the D'Oyly Carte Company's performance of an operetta by two English gentlemen referred to as "Goldberg and Solomon."

"Charming . . . horses . . . float," Mr. Parkhill called off.

Mr. Parkhill's mind was not really on "charming . . . horses . . . float." He could not help thinking of the momentous event which would take place that night. After the recess the students would come in with flushed faces and shining eyes. The Committee would be with them, and one member of the Committee, carrying an elaborately bound

Christmas package, would be surrounded by several of the largest students in the class, who would try to hide the parcel from Mr. Parkhill's eyes. The class would come to order with uncommon rapidity. Then, just as Mr. Parkhill resumed the lesson, one member of the Committee would rise, apologize nervously for interrupting, place the package on Mr. Parkhill's desk, utter a few half-swallowed words, and rush back to his or her seat. Mr. Parkhill would say a few halting phrases of gratitude and surprise, everyone would smile and fidget uneasily, and the lesson would drag on, somehow, to the final and distant bell.

"Accept . . . except . . . cucumber."

And as the students filed out after the final bell, they would cry "Merry Christmas, Happy New Year!" in joyous voices. The Committee would crowd around Mr. Parkhill with tremendous smiles to say that if the present wasn't just right in size or color (if it was something to wear) or in design (if it was something to use), Mr. Parkhill could exchange it. He didn't have to abide by the Committee's choice. He could exchange the present for anything. They would have arranged all that carefully with Mr. Mickey Goldstein himself.

That was the ritual, fixed and unchanging, of the last night of school before Christmas.

"Nervous . . . goose . . . violets."

The hand on the clock crawled around to eight. Mr. Parkhill could not keep his eyes off the three seats, so eloquent in their vacancy, which Miss Mitnick, Mr. Bloom, and Mr. Kaplan ordinarily graced with their presences. He could almost see these three in the last throes of decision in Mickey Goldstein's Arcade, harassed by the competitive attractions of gloves, neckties, an electric clock, a cane, spats, a "lifetime" fountain pen. Mr. Parkhill grew cold as he thought of a fountain pen. Three times already he had been presented with "lifetime" fountain pens, twice with "lifetime" pencils to match. Mr. Parkhill had exchanged these gifts: he had a fountain pen. Once he had chosen a woollen vest instead; once a pair of mittens and a watch chain. Mr. Parkhill hoped it wouldn't be a fountain pen. Or a smoking jacket. He had never been able to understand how the Committee in '32 had decided upon a smoking jacket. Mr. Parkhill did not smoke. He had exchanged it for fur-lined gloves.

Just as Mr. Parkhill called off "Sardine . . . exquisite . . . palace," the recess bell rang. The heads of the students bobbed up as if propelled by a single spring. There was a rush to the door, Mr. Sam Pinsky well in the lead. Then, from the corridor, their voices rose. Mr. Parkhill began to print "banana" on the blackboard, so that the students could correct their own papers after recess. He tried not to listen, but the voices in the corridor were like the chatter of a flock of sparrows.

"Hollo, Mitnick!"

"Bloom, Bloom, vat is it?"

"So vat did you gat, Keplen? Tell!"

Mr. Parkhill could hear Miss Mitnick's shy "We bought—" interrupted by Mr. Kaplan's stern cry, "Mitnick! Don' say! Plizz, faller-students! Come don mit de voices! Titcher vill awreddy hearink, you hollerink so lod! Still! Order! Plizz!" There was no question about it: Mr. Kaplan was born to command.

"Did you bought a Tsheaffer's Fontain Pan Sat, guarantee for de whole life, like I said?" one voice came through the door. A Sheaffer Fountain Pen Set, Guaranteed. That was Mrs. Moskowitz. Poor Mrs. Moskowitz, she showed so little imagination, even in her homework. "Moskovitz! Mein Gott!" the stentorian whisper of Mr. Kaplan soared through the air. "Vy you don' open op de door Ticher should positivel hear? Ha! Let's goink to odder and fromm de hall!"

The voices of the beginners' grade died away as they moved to the "odder and" of the corridor, like the chorus of "Aida" vanishing into Egyptian wings.

Mr. Parkhill printed "charming" and "horses" on the board. For a moment he thought he heard Mrs. Moskowitz's voice repeating stubbornly, "Did-you-bought-a-Tsheaffer-Fountain-Pan-Sat-Guarantee?"

Mr. Parkhill began to say to himself, "Thank you, all of you. It's just what I wanted," again and again. One Christmas he hadn't said "It's just what I wanted" and poor Mrs. Oppenheimer, chairman of the Committee that year, had been hounded by the student's recriminations for a month.

It seemed an eternity before the recess bell rang again. The class came in en masse, and hastened to the seats from which they would view the impending spectacle. The air hummed with silence.

Mr. Parkhill was printing "cucumber." He did not turn his face from the board as he said, "Er—please begin correcting your own spelling. I have printed most of the words on the board."

There was a low and heated whispering. "Stend op, Mitnick!" he heard Mr. Kaplan hiss. "You should stend op too!"

"The whole Committee," Mr. Bloom whispered. "Stand op!"

Apparently Miss Mitnick, a gazelle choked with embarrassment, did not have the fortitude to "stend op" with her colleagues.

"A fine raprezantitif you'll gonna make!" Mr. Kaplan hissed scornfully. "Isn't for mine self I'm eskink, Mitnick. Plizz stend op!"

There was a confused, half-muted murmur, and the anguished voice of Miss Mitnick saying, "I can't." Mr. Parkhill printed "violets" on the board. Then there was a tense silence. And then the voice of Mr. Kaplan rose, firmly, clearly, with a decision and dignity which left no doubt as to its purpose.

"Podden me, Mr. Pockheel!"

It had come.

"Er—yes?" Mr. Parkhill turned to face the class.

Messrs. Bloom and Kaplan were standing side by side in front of Miss Mitnick's chair, holding between them a large, long package, wrapped in cellophane and tied with huge red ribbons. A pair of small hands touched the bottom of the box, listlessly. The owner of the hands, seated in the front row, was hidden by the box.

"De hends is Mitnick," Mr. Kaplan said apologetically.

Mr. Parkhill gazed at the tableau. It was touching.

"Er—yes?" he said again feebly, as if he had forgotten his lines and was repeating his cue.

"Hau Kay!" Mr. Kaplan whispered to his confreres. The hands disappeared behind the package. Mr. Kaplan and Mr. Bloom strode to the platform with the box. Mr. Kaplan was beaming, his smile rapturous, exalted. They placed the package on Mr. Parkhill's desk, Mr. Bloom dropped back a pace, and Mr. Kaplan said, "Mr. Pockheel! Is mine beeg honor, becawss I'm Chairman fromm de Buyink an' Deliverink to You a Prazent Committee, to givink to you dis fine peckitch."

Mr. Parkhill was about to stammer, "Oh, thank you," when Mr. Kaplan added hastily, "Also I'll sayink a few voids."

Mr. Kaplan took an envelope out of his pocket. He whispered loudly, "Mitnick, you still got time to comm op mit de Committee," but Miss Mitnick only blushed furiously and lowered her eyes. Mr. Kaplan sighed, straightened the envelope, smiled proudly at Mr. Parkhill, and read.

"Dear Titcher—dat's de beginnink. Ve stendink on de adge fromm a beeg holiday." He cleared his throat. "Ufcawss is all kinds holidays in U. S. A. Holidays for politic, for religious, an' plain holidays. In Fabrary, ve got Judge Vashington's boitday, a fine holiday. Also Abram Lincohen's. In May ve got Memorable Day, for dad soldiers. In July comms, netcheral, Fort July. Also ve have Labor Day, Denksgivink, for de Peelgrims, an' for de feenish fromm de Voild Var, Armistress Day."

Mr. Parkhill played with a piece of chalk nervously.

"But arond dis time year ve have a difference kind holiday, a spacial, movvellous time. Dat's called—Chrissmas."

Mr. Parkhill put the chalk down.

"All hover de voild," Mr. Kaplan mused, "is pipple celebraking dis vunderful time. Becawss for som pipple is Christmas like for odder pipple is Passover. Or Chanukah, batter. De most fine, de most beauriful, de most secret holiday fromm de whole bunch!"

("'Sacred,' Mr. Kaplan, 'sacred,'" Mr. Parkhill thought, ever the pedagogue.)

"Ven ve valkink don de stritt an' is snow on de floor an' all kinds tarrible cold!" Mr. Kaplan's hand leaped up dramatically, like a flame. "Ven ve see in de vindows trees mit rad an' grin laktric lights boinink! Ven is de time for tellink de fancy-tales abot Sandy Claws commink fromm Naut Pole on rainenimals, an' climbink don de jiminies mit stockings for all de leetle kits! Ven ve hearink abot de beauriful toughts of de Tree Vise Guys who vere follerink a star fromm de dasert! Ven pipple sayink, 'Oh, Mary Chrissmas! Oh, Heppy Noo Yiss! Oh, bast regott!' Den ve all got a varm fillink in de heart for all humanity vhich should be brodders!"

Mr. Feigenbaum nodded philosophically at this profound thought; Mr. Kaplan, pleased, nodded back.

"You got de fillink, Mr. Pockheel. I got de fillink, dat's no qvastion abot! Bloom, Pinsky, Caravello, Schneiderman, even Mitnick"—Mr. Kaplan was punishing Miss Mitnick tenfold for her perfidy—"got de fillink! An' vat is it?" There was a momentous pause. "De Chrissmas Spirits!"

("'Spirit,' Mr. Kaplan, 'spirit,'" the voice of Mr. Parkhill's conscience said.)

"Now I'll givink de prazent," Mr. Kaplan announced subtly. Mr. Bloom shifted his weight. "Becawss you a foistcless titcher, Mr. Pockheel, an' learn abot gremmer an' spallink an' de hoddest pots pernonciation—ve know is a planty hod jop mit soch students—so ve fill you should havink a sample fromm our—fromm our—" Mr. Kaplan turned the envelope over hastily—"aha! Fromm our santimental!"

Mr. Parkhill stared at the long package and the huge red ribbons.

"Fromm de cless, to our lovely Mr. Pockheel!"

Mr. Parkhill started. "Er—?" he asked involuntarily.

"Fromm de cless, to our lovely Mr. Pockheel!" Mr. Kaplan repeated with pride.

("'Beloved,' Mr. Kaplan, 'beloved.'")

A hush had fallen over the room. Mr. Kaplan, his eyes bright with joy, waited for Mr. Parkhill to take up the ritual. Mr. Parkhill tried to say, "Thank you, Mr. Kaplan," but the phrase seemed meaningless, so big, so ungainly, that it could not get through his throat. Without a word Mr. Parkhill began to open the package. He slid the big red ribbons off. He broke the tissue paper inside. For some reason his vision was blurred and it took him a moment to identify the present. It was a smoking jacket. It was black and gold, and a green dragon was embroidered on the breast pocket.

"Horyantal style," Mr. Kaplan whispered delicately.

Mr. Parkhill nodded. The air trembled with the tension. Miss Mitnick looked as if she were ready to cry. Mr. Bloom peered intently over Mr. Kaplan's shoulder. Mrs. Moskowitz sat entranced, sighing with behemothian gasps. She looked as if she were at her daughter's wedding.

"Thank you," Mr. Parkhill stammered at last. "Thank you, all of you."

Mr. Bloom said, "Hold it op everyone should see."

Mr. Kaplan turned on Mr. Bloom with an icy look. "I'm de chairman!" he hissed.

"I—er—I can't tell you how much I appreciate your kindness," Mr. Parkhill said without lifting his eyes.

Mr. Kaplan smiled. "So now you'll plizz hold op de prazent. Plizz."

Mr. Parkhill took the smoking jacket out of the box and held it up for all to see. There were gasps—"Oh's" and "Ah's!" and Mr. Kaplan's own ecstatic "My! Is beauriful!" The green tongue on the dragon seemed alive.

"Maybe ve made a mistake," Mr. Kaplan said hastily. "Maybe you don' smoke—dat's how Mitnick thought." The scorn dripped. "But I said, 'Ufcawss is Titcher smokink! Not in de cless, netcheral! At home! At least a pipe!'"

"No, no, you didn't make a mistake. It's—it's just what I wanted!"

The great smile on Mr. Kaplan's face became dazzling. "Hooray! Vear in de bast fromm helt!" he cried impetuously. "Mary Chrissmas! Heppy Noo Yiss! You should have a hondert more!"

This was the signal for a chorus of acclaim. "Mary Chrissman!" "Wear in best of health!" "Happy New Year!" Miss Schneiferman burst into applause, followed by Mr. Scymzak and Mrs. Weinstein. Miss Caravello, carried away by all the excitement, uttered some felicitations in rapid Italian. Mrs. Moskowitz sighed once more and said, "Soch a sveet ceremonia." Miss Mitnick smiled feebly, blushing, and twisted her handkerchief.

The ceremony was over. Mr. Parkhill began to put the smoking jacket back into the box with fumbling hands. Mr. Bloom marched back to his seat. But Mr. Kaplan stepped a little closer to the desk. The smile had congealed on Mr. Kaplan's face. It was poignant and profoundly earnest.

"Er—thank you, Mr. Kaplan," Mr. Parkhill said gently.

Mr. Kaplan shuffled his feet, looking at the floor. For the first time since Mr. Parkhill had known him, Mr. Kaplan seemed to be embarrassed. Then, just as he turned to rush back to his seat, Mr. Kaplan whispered, so softly that no ears but Mr. Parkhill's heard it, "Maybe de spitch I rad vas too formmal. But avery void I said—it came from below mine heart!"

Mr. Parkhill felt that, for all his weird, unorthodox English, Mr. Kaplan had spoken with the tongues of the Magi.

The Lumber-Room

SAKI

Hector Hugh Munro was born in Burma in 1870. His father was an officer in the British Army. He spent most of his childhood in England, in the care of his grandmother and two aunts. Later he travelled with his father in Europe, and served for a year in the Burma Military Police. Bad health caused his return to England and led to his undertaking to earn a living by writing for London periodicals. His political and social satires, published under the pen name of "Saki," were immediately successful because of their sharp and witty characterization, whimsicality, and brilliantly clever style. He enlisted at the opening of the World War, and was killed in action in 1916.

THE children were to be driven, as a special treat, to the sands at Jagborough. Nicholas was not to be of the party; he was in disgrace. Only that morning he had refused to eat his wholesome bread-and-milk on the seemingly frivolous ground that there was a frog in it. Older and wiser and better people had told him that there could not possibly be a frog in his bread-and-milk and that he was not to talk nonsense; he continued, nevertheless, to talk what seemed the veriest nonsense, and described with much detail the coloration and markings of the alleged frog. The dramatic part of the incident was that there really was a frog in Nicholas' basin of bread-and-milk; he had put it there himself, so he felt entitled to know something about it. The sin of taking a frog from the garden and putting it into a bowl of wholesome bread-and-milk was enlarged on at great length, but the fact that stood out clearest in the whole affair, as it presented itself to the mind of Nicholas, was that the older, wiser, and better people had been proved to be profoundly in error in matters about which they had expressed the utmost assurance.

"You said there couldn't possibly be a frog in my bread-and-milk; there *was* a frog in my bread-and-milk," he repeated, with the insistence of a skilled tactician who does not intend to shift from favorable ground.

So his boy-cousin and girl-cousin and his quite uninteresting younger brother were to be taken to Jagborough sands that afternoon and he was to stay at home. His cousins' aunt, who insisted, by an unwarranted stretch of imagination, in styling herself his aunt also, had hastily invented the Jagborough expedition in order to impress on Nicholas the delights that he had justly forfeited by his disgraceful conduct at the breakfast-table. It was her habit, whenever one of the children fell from grace, to improvise something of a festival nature from which the offender would be rigorously debarred; if all the children sinned collectively they were suddenly informed of a circus in a neighboring town, a circus of unrivalled merit and uncounted elephants, to which, but for their depravity, they would have been taken that very day.

A few decent tears were looked for on the part of Nicholas when the moment for the departure of the expedition arrived. As a matter of fact, however, all the crying was done by his girl-cousin, who scraped her knee rather painfully against the step of the carriage as she was scrambling in.

"How she did howl," said Nicholas cheerfully, as the party drove off without any of the elation of high spirits that should have characterized it.

"She'll soon get over that," said the *soi-disant* aunt; "it will be a glorious afternoon for racing about over those beautiful sands. How they will enjoy themselves!"

"Bobby won't enjoy himself much, and he won't race much either," said Nicholas with a grim chuckle; "his boots are hurting him. They're too tight."

"Why didn't he tell me they were hurting?" asked the aunt with some asperity.

"He told you twice, but you weren't listening. You often don't listen when we tell you important things."

"You are not to go into the gooseberry garden," said the aunt, changing the subject.

"Why not?" demanded Nicholas.

"Because you are in disgrace," said the aunt loftily.

Nicholas did not admit the flawlessness of the reasoning; he felt perfectly capable of being in disgrace and in a gooseberry garden at the same moment. His face took on an expression of considerable obstinacy. It was clear to his aunt that he was determined to get into the gooseberry garden, 'only," as she remarked to herself, "because I have told him he is not to."

Now the gooseberry garden had two doors by which it might be entered, and once a small person like Nicholas could slip in there he could effectually disappear from view amid the masking growth of artichokes, raspberry canes, and fruit bushes. The aunt had many other things to do that afternoon, but she spent an hour or two in trivial gardening operations among flower beds and shrubberies, whence she could keep a watchful eye on the two doors that led to the forbidden paradise. She was a woman of few ideas, with immense powers of concentration.

Nicholas made one or two sorties into the front garden, wriggling his way with obvious stealth of purpose towards one or the other of the doors, but never able for a moment to evade the aunt's watchful eye. As a matter of fact, he had no intention of trying to get into the gooseberry garden, but it was extremely convenient for him that his aunt should believe that he had; it was a belief that would keep her on self-imposed sentry-duty for the greater part of the afternoon. Having thoroughly confirmed and fortified her suspicions, Nicholas slipped back into the house and rapidly put into execution a plan of action that had long germinated in his brain. By standing on a chair in the library one could reach a shelf on which reposed a fat, important-looking key. The key was as important as it looked; it was the instrument which kept the mysteries of the lumber-room secure from unauthorized intrusion, which opened a way only for aunts and such-like privileged persons. Nicholas had not had much experience of the art of fitting keys into keyholes and turning locks, but for some days past he had practiced with the key of the schoolroom door; he did not believe in trusting too much to luck and accident. The key turned stiffly in the lock, but it turned. The door opened, and Nicholas was in an unknown land, compared with which the gooseberry garden was a stale delight, a mere material pleasure.

Often and often Nicholas had pictured to himself what the lumber-room might be like, that region that was so carefully sealed from youthful eyes and concerning which no questions were ever answered. It came up to his expectations. In the first place it was large and dimly lit, one high window opening on to the forbidden garden being its only source of illumination. In the second place it was a storehouse of unimagined treasures. The aunt-by-assertion was one of those people who think that things spoil by use and consign them to dust and damp by way of preserving them. Such parts of the house as Nicholas knew best were rather bare and cheerless, but here there were wonderful things for the eye to feast on. First and foremost there was a piece of framed tapestry that was evidently meant to be a fire screen. To Nicholas it was a living, breathing story; he sat down on a roll of Indian hangings, glowing in wonderful colors beneath a layer of dust, and took in all the details of the tapestry picture. A man, dressed in the hunting costume of some remote period, had just transfixed a stag with an arrow; it could not have been a difficult shot because the stag was only one or two paces away from him; in the thickly growing vegetation that the picture suggested it would not have been difficult to creep up to a feeding stag, and the two spotted dogs that were springing forward to join in the chase had evidently been trained to keep to heel till the arrow was discharged. That part of the picture was simple, if interesting, but did the huntsman see, what Nicholas saw, that four galloping wolves were coming in his direction through the wood? There might be more than four of them hidden behind the trees, and in any case would the man and his dogs be able to cope with the four wolves if they made an attack? The man had only two arrows left in his quiver, and he might miss with one or both of them; all one knew about his skill in shooting was that he could hit a large stag at a ridiculously short range. Nicholas sat for many golden minutes revolving the possibilities of the scene; he was inclined to think that there were more than four wolves and that the man and his dogs were in a tight corner.

But there were other objects of delight and interest claiming his instant attention: there were quaint twisted candle-

sticks in the shape of snakes, and a teapot fashioned like
a china duck, out of whose open beak the tea was supposed
to come. How dull and shapeless the nursery teapot seemed
in comparison! And there was a carved sandalwood box
packed tight with aromatic cotton-wool, and between the
layers of cotton-wool were little brass figures, hump-necked
bulls, and peacocks and goblins, delightful to see and to
handle. Less promising in appearance was a large square
book with plain black covers; Nicholas peeped into it, and,
behold, it was full of colored pictures of birds. And such
birds! In the garden, and in the lanes when he went for
a walk, Nicholas came across a few birds, of which the
largest were an occasional magpie or wood-pigeon; here
were herons and bustards, kites, toucans, tiger-bitterns, brush
turkeys, ibises, golden pheasants, a whole portrait gallery
of undreamed-of creatures. And as he was admiring the
coloring of the mandarin duck and assigning a life-history
to it, the voice of his aunt in shrill vociferation of his name
came from the gooseberry garden without. She had grown
suspicious at his long disappearance, and had leapt to the
conclusion that he had climbed over the wall behind the
sheltering screen of the lilac bushes; she was now engaged
in energetic and rather hopeless search for him among the
artichokes and raspberry canes.

"Nicholas, Nicholas!" she screamed, "you are to come
out of this at once. It's no use trying to hide there, I can
see you all the time."

It was probably the first time for twenty years that any
one had smiled in that lumber-room.

Presently the angry repetitions of Nicholas' name gave
way to a shriek, and a cry for somebody to come quickly.
Nicholas shut the book, restored it carefully to its place in
a corner, and shook some dust from a neighboring pile of
newspapers over it. Then he crept from the room, locked

the door, and replaced the key exactly where he had found it. His aunt was still calling his name when he sauntered into the front garden.

"Who's calling?" he asked.

"Me," came the answer from the other side of the wall; "didn't you hear me? I've been looking for you in the gooseberry garden, and I've slipped into the rain-water tank. Luckily there's no water in it, but the sides are slippery and I can't get out. Fetch the little ladder from under the cherry tree——"

"I was told I wasn't to go into the gooseberry garden," said Nicholas promptly.

"I told you not to, and now I tell you that you may," came the voice from the rain-water tank, rather impatiently.

"Your voice doesn't sound like aunt's," objected Nicholas; "you may be the Evil One tempting me to be disobedient. Aunt often tells me that the Evil One tempts me and that I always yield. This time I'm not going to yield."

"Don't talk nonsense," said the prisoner in the tank; "go and fetch the ladder."

"Will there be strawberry jam for tea?" asked Nicholas innocently.

"Certainly there will be," said the aunt, privately resolving that Nicholas should have none of it.

"Now I know that you are the Evil One and not aunt," shouted Nicholas gleefully; "when we asked aunt for strawberry jam yesterday she said there wasn't any. I know there are four jars of it in the store cupboard, because I looked, and of course you know it's there, but *she* doesn't, because she said there wasn't any. Oh, Devil, you *have* sold yourself!"

There was an unusual sense of luxury in being able to talk to an aunt as though one was talking to the Evil One, but Nicholas knew, with childish discernment, that such luxuries were not to be overindulged in. He walked noisily away, and it was a kitchenmaid, in search of parsley, who eventually rescued the aunt from the rain-water tank.

Tea that evening was partaken of in a fearsome silence. The tide had been at its highest when the children had arrived at Jagborough Cove, so there had been no sands to play on—a circumstance that the aunt had overlooked in the haste of organizing her punitive expedition. The tightness of Bobby's boots had had disastrous effect on his temper the whole of the afternoon, and altogether the children could not have been said to have enjoyed themselves. The aunt maintained the frozen muteness of one who had suffered undignified and unmerited detention in a rain-water tank for thirty-five minutes. As for Nicholas, he, too, was silent, in the absorption of one who has much to think about; it was just possible, he considered, that the huntsman would escape with his hounds while the wolves feasted on the stricken stag.

Water

ROSS SANTEE

Ross Santee was born in Iowa, attended high school at
Moline, Illinois, then studied at the Chicago Art Institute.
Years of work on cattle ranches in Arizona provided material for drawings of horses, cattle, and cowboys, and later
for stories, published in many magazines and in several
books including *Horses* (1933). Since 1935 he has been
Director of the Arizona Writers' Project of WPA.

SMITH dug out the spring while I fought the cattle
back with a shovel. They were crazy for water. They
had upset the trough. It was as dry as a bone and they
had tramped the pipe into the mud. There was a big steer
in the bunch that had showed his hocks to my pony several
times on Mescal Mountain. He was as wild as a blacktailed
buck. Now his sunken eyes burned like live coals. I had
to bat him twice with the shovel.

We set the trough in place and Smith cleaned out the
pipe with a wire. There was only a trickle of water. He
ran the wire through the pipe again—there was only a
little trickle. Smith went kind of crazy then. He picked

From *Collier's: The National Weekly,* April 27, 1935. Copyright,
1935. Reprinted by permisssion of the author and of the editors of
Collier's.

up a shovel and throwed it as far as he could. He said he hoped to God it never rained. He laughed and he cursed.

Then he went an' got on his pony. He didn't speak all the way into the ranch. I didn't say anything either. There wasn't anything to say with Mud Springs dry; it was all over. The outfit was blowed up and broke.

It was tough on Smith. It was tough on his wife, too. I was thinking of her as we rode to the ranch. Only the day before I'd come ahead of Smith and found her kneeling on the ranch-house porch. "God give us rain," she says.

I don't know how she stood it as long as she did with the cattle bawling for water. They bawled all day. They bawled all night. It was a never-ending sound. It was getting on me so I dreaded to come in nights. Even in the ranch house it was always in your ears.

Supper was waiting when Smith and me got in that night. His wife was pleasant as usual. And Smith was apparently over that spell of his at the spring. It was when she fetched the coffee that I noticed how old and tired she was. Then I looked at Smith. He had aged ten years that day.

I noticed she didn't touch her food nor take a sip of coffee. Once way back when it started she had said it was all she could do to get it down when she thought of the thirsty cattle.

Nobody spoke. Outside the cattle bawled for water. Her eyes were on Smith's face. He wasn't eating either. Finally he pushed his plate aside. "I guess you know," he says.

She nodded her head. When she spoke her voice was firm. "I know," she says. "Mud Springs went dry today."

Something pinched me in the throat when the woman smiled, an' I walked outside the house. I knew they wanted to be alone.

Some thunderheads were hanging low over Mescal Rim.

Once in the long ago that had been a sign of rain. But with tomorrow's blazing sun they would disappear again. A new moon was rising over Turnbull Peak. I had watched the new moon rise two years ago from the same place on the ranch-house porch the night I came to work for Smith.

It was a regular cow spread then, with fat ponies to ride and fat cattle. There had been good rains the year I came. There was plenty of feed and water. The big flats were covered with filaree where the cattle grazed knee-deep. There was grama on the hills. There wasn't an outfit in Arizona any better fixed for water.

I had often heard the woman speak of how they started out over twenty years before. She was teaching school. She had met Smith at a dance one night when he was a wild young puncher breaking horses at the Circles. Smith started to save his wages then an' he kept away from town. It was four years later that she put her money in with his and they bought a little remnant of cattle.

Smith had built the little house himself and he had put in all the corrals. Often she had held the lantern when he worked on them at night. There had been her little garden and an orchard.

Like all cow folks in Arizona they had had their ups and downs. There had been wet years and dry. They had owed the bank at different times but they always had paid out. They had watched the little remnant grow until they owned five thousand head. Then the drought. Now there wasn't half that many.

With rain the outfit could pull through even now. The cattle could live on browse and buckbrush if only they had water. Even now there was plenty of feed way back in the hills if it rained an' put out water.

Thinking back, it was hard to remember when Smith or I had used a rope or branding iron. We rode with picks and shovels digging out the springs an' water holes. For weeks and months the thunderheads had come each day to mock us. But somehow there was always hope until Mud Springs went dry.

Their light still showed when I unrolled my bedroll on the porch. It didn't seem as if I'd been asleep. But it was the patter on the roof that woke me at daybreak. The sky was dark an' overcast. Mescal Rim was hid. The patter stopped an' then it came, it came in driving torrents.

I could hear the folks inside as I pulled on my boots. I guess I acted funny. I didn't remember that I yelled. Later Smith said that was the first time he ever saw a puncher drunk on nothing except water.

But I remember the woman kneeling in the rain an' Smith, his head thrown back, the water streaming from his face, both hands stretching toward the sky.

And still it came. It was noon when we thought of breakfast. We laughed an' talked all through the meal. We ate with the rain still pounding on the roof without any sign of a letup.

The three of us sat late that night, it was pleasant on the porch. We sat and listened to the rain. And for the first time in the long, cruel months the bawling cattle was quiet.

It was just before they went inside Smith turned to me an' spoke. "Yesterday at the spring," he said, "I didn't mean it—what I said about it never raining."

The Leader of the People

J O H N   S T E I N B E C K

John Steinbeck was born in California in 1902, attended high school at Salinas and Stanford University, and now lives on a farm in central California. Wide experience in varied employments—on a freighter, as reporter, bricklayer, watchman, and farm hand—gave him the understanding of homeless men which he has expressed to such powerful and varied effect in *Tortilla Flat* (1935), *Of Mice and Men* (1937), and *The Grapes of Wrath* (1939). *In Dubious Battle* (1936) is especially noteworthy for the impartial and broadly sympathetic quality of its portrayal of the conflict between employers and migratory workers in the fruit orchards of California. Steinbeck's sureness in detail, his integrity of literary purpose, and his extraordinary understanding of childhood and of old age characterize the stories collected in *The Red Pony* (1937) and *The Long Valley* (1938).

O N SATURDAY afternoon Billy Buck, the ranch-hand, raked together the last of the old year's haystack and pitched small forkfuls over the wire fence to a few mildly interested cattle. High in the air small clouds like puffs of cannon smoke were driven eastward by the March wind. The wind could be heard whishing in the brush on the ridge crests, but no breath of it penetrated down into the ranch-cup.

The little boy, Jody, emerged from the house eating a thick piece of buttered bread. He saw Billy working on the last of the haystack. Jody tramped down scuffing his shoes in a way he had been told was destructive to good shoe leather. A flock of white pigeons flew out of the black cypress tree as Jody passed, and circled the tree and landed again. A half-grown tortoise-shell cat leaped from the bunk-house porch, galloped on stiff legs across the road, whirled and galloped back again. Jody picked up a stone to help the game along, but he was too late, for the cat was under the porch before the stone could be discharged. He threw the stone into the cypress tree and started the white pigeons on another whirling flight.

Arriving at the used-up haystack, the boy leaned against the barbed-wire fence. "Will that be all of it, do you think?" he asked.

The middle-aged ranch-hand stopped his careful raking and stuck his fork into the ground. He took off his black hat and smoothed down his hair. "Nothing left of it that isn't soggy from ground moisture," he said. He replaced his hat and rubbed his dry leathery hands together.

"Ought to be plenty mice," Jody suggested.

"Lousy with them," said Billy. "Just crawling with mice."

"Well, maybe, when you get all through, I could call the dogs and hunt the mice."

"Sure, I guess you could," said Billy Buck. He lifted a forkful of the damp ground-hay and threw it into the air. Instantly three mice leaped out and burrowed frantically under the hay again.

Jody sighed with satisfaction. Those plump, sleek, arro-gant mice were doomed. For eight months they had lived and multiplied in the haystack. They had been immune from cats, from traps, from poison and from Jody. They had grown smug in their security, overbearing and fat. Now the time of disaster had come; they would not survive another day.

Billy looked up at the top of the hills that surrounded the ranch. "Maybe you better ask your father before you do it," he suggested.

"Well, where is he? I'll ask him now."

"He rode up to the ridge ranch after dinner. He'll be back pretty soon."

Jody slumped against the fence post. "I don't think he'd care."

As Billy went back to his work he said ominously, "You'd better ask him anyway. You know how he is."

Jody did know. His father, Carl Tiflin, insisted upon giving permission for anything that was done on the ranch, whether it was important or not. Jody sagged farther against the post until he was sitting on the ground. He looked up at the little puffs of wind-driven cloud. "Is it like to rain, Billy?"

"It might. The wind's good for it, but not strong enough."

"Well, I hope it don't rain until after I kill those damn mice." He looked over his shoulder to see whether Billy had noticed his mature profanity. Billy worked on without comment.

Jody turned back and looked at the side-hill where the road from the outside world came down. The hill was washed with lean March sunshine. Silver thistles, blue lupins and a few poppies bloomed among the sage bushes. Halfway up the hill Jody could see Doubletree Mutt, the black dog, digging in a squirrel hole. He paddled for a while and then paused to kick bursts of dirt out between his hind legs, and he dug with an earnestness which belied the knowledge he must have had that no dog had ever caught a squirrel by digging in a hole.

Suddenly, while Jody watched, the black dog stiffened, and backed out of the hole and looked up the hill toward the cleft in the ridge where the road came through. Jody looked up too. For a moment Carl Tiflin on horseback stood out against the pale sky and then he moved down the road toward the house. He carried something white in his hand.

The boy started to his feet. "He's got a letter," Jody cried. He trotted away toward the ranch house, for the letter would probably be read aloud and he wanted to be there. He reached the house before his father did, and ran in. He heard Carl Tiflin dismount from his creaking saddle and slap the horse on the side to send it to the barn where Billy would unsaddle it and turn it out.

Jody ran into the kitchen. "We got a letter!" he cried.

His mother looked up from a pan of beans. "Who has?"

"Father has, I saw it in his hand."

Carl strode into the kitchen then, and Jody's mother asked, "Who's the letter from, Carl?"

He frowned quickly. "How did you know there was a letter?"

She nodded her head in the boy's direction. "Big-Britches Jody told me."

Jody was embarrassed.

His father looked down at him contemptuously. "He is getting to be a Big-Britches," Carl said. "He's minding everybody's business but his own. Got his big nose into everything."

Mrs. Tiflin relented a little. "Well, he hasn't enough to keep him busy. Who's the letter from?"

Carl still frowned on Jody. "I'll keep him busy if he isn't careful." He held out a sealed letter. "I guess it's from your father."

Mrs. Tiflin took a hairpin from her head and slit open the flap. Her lips pursed judiciously. Jody saw her eyes snap back and forth over the lines. "He says," she translated, "he's going to drive out Saturday to stay for a little while. Why, this is Saturday. The letter must have been delayed." She looked at the postmark. "This was mailed day before yesterday. It should have been here yesterday." She looked up questioningly at her husband, and then her face darkened angrily. "Now what have you got that look on your face for? He doesn't come often."

Carl turned his eyes away from her anger. He could be stern with her most of the time, but when occasionally her temper arose, he could not combat it.

"What's the matter with you?" she demanded again.

In his explanation there was a tone of apology Jody himself might have used. "It's just that he talks," Carl said lamely, "Just talks."

"Well, what of it? You talk yourself."

"Sure I do. But your father only talks about one thing."

"Indians!" Jody broke in excitedly. "Indians and crossing the plains!"

Carl turned fiercely on him. "You get out, Mr. Big-Britches! Go on, now! Get out!"

Jody went miserably out the back door and closed the screen with elaborate quietness. Under the kitchen window his shamed, downcast eyes fell upon a curiously shaped stone, a stone of such fascination that he squatted down and picked it up and turned it over in his hands.

The voices came clearly to him through the open kitchen window. "Jody's damn well right," he heard his father say. "Just Indians and crossing the plains. I've heard that story about how the horses got driven off about a thousand times. He just goes on and on, and he never changes a word in the things he tells."

When Mrs. Tiflin answered, her tone was so changed that Jody, outside the window, looked up from his study of the stone. Her voice had become soft and explanatory. Jody knew how her face would have changed to match the tone. She said quietly, "Look at it this way, Carl. That was the big thing in my father's life. He led a wagon train clear across the plains to the coast, and when it was finished, his life was done. It was a big thing to do, but it didn't last long enough. Look!" she continued, "it's as though he were born to do that, and after he finished it, there wasn't anything more for him to do but think about it and talk about it. If there'd been any farther west to go, he'd have gone. He's told me so himself. But at last there was the ocean. He lives right by the ocean where he had to stop."

She had caught Carl, caught him and entangled him in her soft tone.

"I've seen him," he agreed quietly. "He goes down and stares off west over the ocean." His voice sharpened a little. "And then he goes up to the Horseshoe Club in Pacific Grove, and he tells people how the Indians drove off the horses."

She tried to catch him again. "Well, it's everything to him. You might be patient with him and pretend to listen."

Carl turned impatiently away. "Well, if it gets too bad, I can always go down to the bunkhouse and sit with Billy," he said irritably. He walked through the house and slammed the front door after him.

Jody ran to his chores. He dumped the grain to the chickens without chasing any of them. He gathered the eggs from the nests. He trotted into the house with the wood and interlaced it so carefully in the wood-box that two armloads seemed to fill it to overflowing.

His mother had finished the beans by now. She stirred up the fire and brushed off the stove-top with a turkey wing. Jody peered cautiously at her to see whether any rancor toward him remained. "Is he coming today?" Jody asked.

"That's what his letter said."

"Maybe I better walk up the road to meet him."

Mrs. Tiflin clanged the stove-lid shut. "That would be nice," she said. "He'd probably like to be met."

"I guess I'll just do it then."

Outside, Jody whistled shrilly to the dogs. "Come on up the hill," he commanded. The two dogs waved their tails and ran ahead. Along the roadside the sage had tender new tips. Jody tore off some pieces and rubbed them on his hands until the air was filled with the sharp wild smell. With a rush the dogs leaped from the road and yapped into the brush after a rabbit. That was the last Jody saw of them, for when they failed to catch the rabbit, they went back home.

Jody plodded on up the hill toward the ridge top. When he reached the little cleft where the road came through, the afternoon wind struck him and blew up his hair and ruffled his shirt. He looked down on the little hills and ridges below and then out at the huge green Salinas Valley. He could see the white town of Salinas far out in the flat and the flash of its windows under the waning sun. Directly below him, in an oak tree, a crow congress had convened. The tree was black with crows all cawing at once.

Then Jody's eyes followed the wagon road down from the ridge where he stood, and lost it behind a hill, and picked it up again on the other side. On that distant stretch he saw a cart slowly pulled by a bay horse. It disappeared behind the hill. Jody sat down on the ground and watched the place where the cart would reappear again. The wind sang on the hilltops and the puff-ball clouds hurried eastward.

Then the cart came into sight and stopped. A man dressed in black dismounted from the seat and walked to the horse's head. Although it was so far away, Jody knew he had unhooked the check-rein, for the horse's head dropped forward. The horse moved on, and the man walked slowly up the hill beside it. Jody gave a glad cry and ran down the road toward them. The squirrels bumped along off the road, and a road-runner flirted its tail and raced over the edge of the hill and sailed out like a glider.

Jody tried to leap into the middle of his shadow at every step. A stone rolled under his foot and he went down. Around a little bend he raced, and there, a short distance ahead, were his grandfather and the cart. The boy dropped from his unseemly running and approached at a dignified walk.

The horse plodded stumble-footedly up the hill and the old man walked beside it. In the lowering sun their giant shadows flickered darkly behind them. The grandfather was dressed in a black broadcloth suit and he wore kid congress gaiters and a black tie on a short, hard collar. He carried his black slouch hat in his hand. His white beard was cropped close and his white eyebrows overhung his eyes like moustaches. The blue eyes were sternly merry. About the whole face and figure there was a granite dignity, so that every motion seemed an impossible thing. Once at rest, it seemed the old man would be stone, would never move again. His steps were slow and certain. Once made, no step could ever be retraced; once headed in a direction, the path would never bend nor the pace increase nor slow.

When Jody appeared around the bend, Grandfather waved his hat slowly in welcome, and he called, "Why, Jody! Come down to meet me, have you?"

Jody sidled near and turned and matched his step to the

old man's step and stiffened his body and dragged his heels a little. "Yes, sir," he said. "We got your letter only today."

"Should have been yesterday," said Grandfather. "It certainly should. How are all the folks?"

"They're fine, sir." He hesitated and then suggested shyly, "Would you like to come on a mouse hunt tomorrow, sir?"

"Mouse hunt, Jody?" Grandfather chuckled. "Have the people of this generation come down to hunting mice? They aren't very strong, the new people, but I hardly thought mice would be game for them."

"No, sir. It's just play. The haystack's gone. I'm going to drive out the mice to the dogs. And you can watch, or even beat the hay a little."

The stern, merry eyes turned down on him. "I see. You don't eat them, then. You haven't come to that yet."

Jody explained. "The dogs eat them, sir. It wouldn't be much like hunting Indians, I guess."

"No, not much—but then later, when the troops were hunting Indians and shooting children and burning teepees, it wasn't much different from your mouse hunt."

They topped the rise and started down into the ranch cup, and they lost the sun from their shoulders. "You've grown," Grandfather said. "Nearly an inch, I should say."

"More," Jody boasted. "Where they mark me on the door, I'm up more than an inch since Thanksgiving even."

Grandfather's rich throaty voice said, "Maybe you're getting too much water and turning to pith and stalk. Wait until you head out, and then we'll see."

Jody looked quickly into the old man's face to see whether his feelings should be hurt, but there was no will to injure, no punishing nor putting-in-your-place light in the keen blue eyes. "We might kill a pig," Jody suggested.

"Oh, no! I couldn't let you do that. You're just humoring me. It isn't the time and you know it."

"You know Riley, the big boar, sir?"

"Yes, I remember Riley well."

"Well, Riley ate a hole into that same haystack, and it fell down on him and smothered him."

"Pigs do that when they can," said Grandfather.

"Riley was a nice pig, for a boar, sir. I rode him sometimes, and he didn't mind."

A door slammed at the house below them, and they saw Jody's mother standing on the porch waving her apron in welcome. And they saw Carl Tiflin walking up from the barn to be at the house for the arrival.

The sun had disappeared from the hills by now. The blue smoke from the house chimney hung in flat layers in the purpling ranch cup. The puff-ball clouds, dropped by the falling wind, hung listlessly in the sky.

Billy Buck came out of the bunkhouse and flung a washbasin of soapy water on the ground. He had been shaving in mid-week, for Billy held Grandfather in reverence, and Grandfather said that Billy was one of the few men of the new generation who had not gone soft. Although Billy was in middle age, Grandfather considered him a boy. Now Billy was hurrying toward the house too.

When Jody and Grandfather arrived, the three were waiting for them in front of the yard gate.

Carl said, "Hello, sir. We've been looking for you."

Mrs. Tiflin kissed Grandfather on the side of his beard, and stood still while his big hand patted her shoulder. Billy shook hands solemnly, grinning under his straw moustache. "I'll put up your horse," said Billy, and he led the rig away.

Grandfather watched him go, and then, turning back to the group, he said as he had said a hundred times before, "There's a good boy. I knew his father, old Mule-tail Buck. I never knew why they called him Mule-tail except he packed mules."

Mrs. Tiflin turned and led the way into the house. "How

long are you going to stay, Father? Your letter didn't say."

"Well, I don't know, I thought I'd stay about two weeks. But I never stay as long as I think I'm going to."

In a short while they were sitting at the white oilcloth table eating their supper. The lamp with the tin reflector hung over the table. Outside the dining-room windows the big moths battered softly against the glass.

Grandfather cut his steak into tiny pieces and chewed slowly. "I'm hungry," he said. "Driving out here got my appetite up. It's like when we were crossing. We all got so hungry every night we could hardly wait to let the meat get done. I could eat about five pounds of buffalo meat every night."

"It's moving around does it," said Billy. "My father was a government packer. I helped him when I was a kid. Just the two of us could about clean up a deer's ham."

"I knew your father, Billy," said Grandfather. "A fine man he was. They called him Mule-tail Buck. I don't know why except he packed mules."

"That was it," Billy agreed. "He packed mules."

Grandfather put down his knife and fork and looked around the table. "I remember one time we ran out of meat—" his voice dropped to a curious low singsong, dropped into a tonal groove the story had worn for itself. "There was no buffalo, no antelope, not even rabbits. The hunters couldn't even shoot a coyote. That was the time for the leader to be on the watch. I was the leader, and I kept my eyes open. Know why? Well, just the minute the people began to get hungry they'd start slaughtering the team oxen. Do you believe that? I've heard of parties that ate up their draft cattle. Started from the middle and worked toward the ends. Finally they'd eat the lead pair, and then the wheelers. The leader of a party had to keep them from doing that."

In some manner a big moth got into the room and circled the hanging kerosene lamp. Billy got up and tried to clap it between his hands. Carl struck with a cupped palm and caught the moth and broke it. He walked to the window and dropped it out.

"As I was saying," Grandfather began again, but Carl interrupted him. "You'd better eat some more meat. All the rest of us are ready for our pudding."

Jody saw a flash of anger in his mother's eyes. Grandfather picked up his knife and fork. "I'm pretty hungry, all right," he said. "I'll tell you about that later."

When supper was over, when the family and Billy Buck sat in front of the fireplace in the other room, Jody anxiously watched Grandfather. He saw the signs he knew. The bearded head leaned forward, the eyes lost their sternness and looked wonderingly into the fire; the big lean fingers laced themselves on the black knees. "I wonder," he began, "I just wonder whether I ever told you how those thieving Piutes drove off thirty-five of our horses."

"I think you did," Carl interrupted. "Wasn't it just before you went up into the Tahoe country?"

Grandfather turned quickly toward his son-in-law. "That's right, I guess I must have told you that story."

"Lots of times," Carl said cruelly, and he avoided his wife's eyes. But he felt the angry eyes on him, and he said, " 'Course I'd like to hear it again."

Grandfather looked back at the fire. His fingers unlaced and laced again. Jody knew how he felt, how his insides were collapsed and empty. Hadn't Jody been called a Big-Britches that very afternoon? He arose to heroism and opened himself to the term Big-Britches again. "Tell about Indians," he said softly.

Grandfather's eyes grew stern again. "Boys always want to hear about Indians. It was a job for men, but boys want to hear about it. Well, let's see. Did I ever tell you how I wanted each wagon to carry a long iron plate?"

Everyone but Jody remained silent. Jody said, "No. You didn't."

"Well, when the Indians attacked, we always put the wagons in a circle and fought from between the wheels. I thought that if every wagon carried a long plate with rifle holes, the men could stand the plates on the outside of the wheels when the wagons were in the circle and they would be protected. It would save lives and that would make up for the extra weight of the iron. But of course the party wouldn't do it. No party had done it before and they couldn't see why they should go to the expense. They lived to regret it, too."

Jody looked at his mother, and knew from her expression that she was not listening at all. Carl picked at a callus on his thumb and Billy Buck watched a spider crawling up the wall.

Grandfather's tone dropped into its narrative groove again. Jody knew in advance exactly what words would fall. The story droned on, speeded up for the attack, grew sad over the wounds, struck a dirge at the burials on the great plains. Jody sat quietly watching Grandfather. The stern blue eyes were detached. He looked as though he were not very interested in the story himself.

When it was finished, when the pause had been politely respected as the frontier of the story, Billy Buck stood up and stretched and hitched his trousers. "I guess I'll turn in," he said. Then he faced Grandfather. "I've got an old powder horn and a cap and ball pistol down to the bunkhouse. Did I ever show them to you?"

Grandfather nodded slowly. "Yes, I think you did, Billy. Reminds me of a pistol I had when I was leading the people across." Billy stood politely until the little story was done, and then he said, "Good night," and went out of the house.

Carl Tiflin tried to turn the conversation then. "How's the country between here and Monterey? I've heard it's pretty dry."

"It is dry," said Grandfather. "There's not a drop of water in the Laguna Seca. But it's a long pull from '87. The whole country was powder then, and in '61 I believe all the coyotes starved to death. We had fifteen inches of rain this year."

"Yes, but it all came too early. We could do with some now." Carl's eye fell on Jody. "Hadn't you better be getting to bed?"

Jody stood up obediently. "Can I kill the mice in the old haystack, sir?"

"Mice? Oh! Sure, kill them all off. Billy said there isn't any good hay left."

Jody exchanged a secret and satisfying look with Grandfather. "I'll kill every one tomorrow," he promised.

Jody lay in his bed and thought of the impossible world of Indians and buffaloes, a world that had ceased to be forever. He wished he could have been living in the heroic time, but he knew he was not of heroic timber. No one living now, save possibly Billy Buck, was worthy to do the things that had been done. A race of giants had lived then, fearless men, men of a staunchness unknown in his day. Jody thought of the wide plains and of the wagons moving across like centipedes. He thought of Grandfather on a huge white horse, marshaling the people. Across his mind marched the great phantoms, and they marched off the earth and were gone.

He came back to the ranch for a moment, then. He heard the dull rushing sound that space and silence make. He heard one of the dogs, out in the doghouse, scratching a flea and bumping his elbow against the floor with every stroke. Then the wind arose again and the black cypress groaned and Jody went to sleep.

He was up half an hour before the triangle sounded for breakfast. His mother was rattling the stove to make the flames roar when Jody went through the kitchen. "You're up early," she said. "Where are you going?"

"Out to get a good stick. We're going to kill the mice today."

"Who is 'we'?"

"Why, Grandfather and I."

"So you've got him in it. You always like to have some one in with you in case there's blame to share."

"I'll be right back," said Jody. "I just want to have a good stick ready for after breakfast."

He closed the screen door after him and went into the cool blue morning. The birds were noisy in the dawn and the ranch cats came down from the hill like blunt snakes. They had been hunting gophers in the dark, and although the four cats were full of gopher meat, they sat in a semi-circle at the back door and mewed piteously for milk. Doubletree Mutt and Smasher moved sniffing along the edge of the brush, performing the duty with rigid cere-mony, but when Jody whistled, their heads jerked up and their tails waved. They plunged down to him, wrig-gling their skins and yawning. Jody patted their heads seri-ously, and moved on to the weathered scrap pile. He selected an old broom handle and a short piece of inch-square scrap wood. From his pocket he took a shoelace and tied the ends of the sticks loosely together to make a flail. He whistled his new weapon through the air and struck the ground experimentally, while the dogs leaped aside and whined with apprehension.

Jody turned and started down past the house toward the old haystack ground to look over the field of slaughter, but Billy Buck, sitting patiently on the back steps, called to him, "You better come back. It's time for breakfast."

Jody changed his course and moved toward the house. He leaned his flail against the steps. "That's to drive the mice out," he said. "I'll bet they're fat. I'll bet they don't know what's going to happen to them today."

"No, nor you either," Billy remarked philosophically, "nor me, nor any one."

Jody was staggered by this thought. He knew it was true. His imagination twitched away from the mouse hunt. Then his mother came out on the back porch and struck the triangle, and all thoughts fell in a heap.

Grandfather hadn't appeared at the table when they sat down. Billy nodded at the empty chair. "He's all right? He isn't sick?"

"He takes a long time to dress," said Mrs. Tiflin. "He combs his whiskers and rubs up his shoes and brushes his clothes."

Carl scattered sugar on his mush. "A man that's led a wagon train across the plains has got to be pretty careful how he dresses."

Mrs. Tiflin turned on him. "Don't do that, Carl! Please don't!" There was more of threat than of request in her tone. And the threat irritated Carl.

"Well, how many times do I have to listen to the story of the iron plates, and the thirty-five horses? That time's done. Why can't he forget it, now it's done?" He grew angrier while he talked, and his voice rose. "Why does he have to tell them over and over? He came across the plains. All right! Now it's finished. Nobody wants to hear about it over and over."

The door of the kitchen closed softly. The four at the table sat frozen. Carl laid his mush spoon on the table and touched his chin with his fingers.

Then the kitchen door opened and Grandfather walked in. His mouth smiled tightly and his eyes were squinted. "Good morning," he said, and he sat down and looked at his mush dish.

Carl could not leave it there. "Did—did you hear what I said?"

Grandfather jerked a little nod.

"I don't know what got into me, sir. I didn't mean it. I was just being funny."

Jody glanced in shame at his mother, and he saw that she was looking at Carl, and that she wasn't breathing. It was an awful thing that he was doing. He was tearing himself to pieces to talk like that. It was a terrible thing to him to retract a word, but to retract it in shame was infinitely worse.

Grandfather looked sidewise. "I'm trying to get right side up," he said gently. "I'm not being mad. I don't mind what you said, but it might be true, and I would mind that."

"It isn't true," said Carl. "I'm not feeling well this morning, I'm sorry I said it."

"Don't be sorry, Carl. An old man doesn't see things sometimes. Maybe you're right. The crossing is finished. Maybe it should be forgotten, now it's done."

Carl got up from the table. "I've had enough to eat. I'm going to work. Take your time, Billy!" He walked quickly out of the dining room. Billy gulped the rest of his food and followed soon after. But Jody could not leave his chair.

"Won't you tell any more stories?" Jody asked.

"Why, sure I'll tell them, but only when—I'm sure people want to hear them."

"I like to hear them, sir."

"Oh! Of course you do, but you're a little boy. It was a job for men, but only little boys like to hear about it."

Jody got up from his place. "I'll wait outside for you, sir, I've got a good stick for those mice."

He waited by the gate until the old man came out on the porch. "Let's go down and kill the mice now," Jody called.

"I think I'll just sit down in the sun, Jody. You go kill the mice."

"You can use my stick if you like."

"No, I'll just sit here awhile."

Jody turned disconsolately away, and walked down toward the haystack. He tried to whip up his enthusiasm with thoughts of the fat juicy mice. He beat the ground with his flail. The dogs coaxed and whined about him, but he could not go. Back at the house he could see Grandfather sitting on the porch, looking small and thin and black.

Jody gave up and went to sit on the steps at the old man's feet.

"Back already? Did you kill the mice?"

"No, sir. I'll kill them some other day."

The morning flies buzzed close to the ground and the ants dashed about in front of the steps. The heavy smell of sage slipped down the hill. The porch boards grew warm in the sunshine.

Jody hardly knew when Grandfather started to talk. "I shouldn't stay here, feeling the way I do." He examined his strong old hands. "I feel as though the crossing wasn't worth doing." His eyes moved up the side-hill and stopped on a motionless hawk perched on a dead limb. "I tell those old stories, but they're not what I want to tell. I only know how I want people to feel when I tell them.

"It wasn't Indians that were important, nor adventures, nor even getting out here. It was a whole bunch of people made into one big crawling beast. And I was the head. It was westering and westering. Every man wanted something for himself, but the big beast that was all of them wanted only westering. I was the leader, but if I hadn't been there, some one else would have been the head. The thing had to have a head.

"Under the little bushes the shadows were black at white noonday. When we saw the mountains at last, we cried—all of us. But it wasn't getting here that mattered, it was movement and westering.

"We carried life out here and set it down the way those ants carry eggs. And I was the leader. The westering was as big as God, and the slow steps that made the movement piled up and piled up until the continent was crossed.

"Then we came down to the sea, and it was done." He stopped and wiped his eyes until the rims were red. "That's what I should be telling instead of stories."

When Jody spoke, Grandfather started and looked down at him. "Maybe I could lead the people some day," Jody said.

The old man smiled. "There's no place to go. There's the ocean to stop you. There's a line of old men along the shore hating the ocean because it stopped them."

"In boats I might, sir."

"No place to go, Jody. Every place is taken. But that's not the worst—no, not the worst. Westering has died out of the people. Westering isn't a hunger any more. It's all done. Your father is right. It is finished." He laced his fingers on his knee and looked at them.

Jody felt very sad. "If you'd like a glass of lemonade I could make it for you."

Grandfather was about to refuse, and then he saw Jody's face. "That would be nice," he said. "Yes, it would be nice to drink a lemonade."

Jody ran into the kitchen where his mother was wiping the last of the breakfast dishes. "Can I have a lemon to make a lemonade for Grandfather?"

His mother mimicked—"And another lemon to make a lemonade for you."

"No, ma'am. I don't want one."

"Jody! You're sick!" Then she stopped suddenly. "Take a lemon out of the cooler," she said softly. "Here, I'll reach the squeezer down to you."

Uprooted

RUTH SUCKOW

Ruth Suckow (pronounced "Soo-koe") was born in 1892 at Hawarden, Iowa, the daughter of a Congregational minister, and spent her girlhood in the several Iowa towns and villages of her father's changing pastorates. She attended Grinnell College, the Boston School of Expression, and the University of Denver. For six years she owned and managed an apiary at Earlville, Iowa. After a few years in New York City she returned to Iowa and now lives at Cedar Falls. In 1929 she married Ferner Nuhn. Her novels and short stories are unequalled in the accuracy and insight of their portrayal of American life on the farms and in the towns and villages of the Middle West. Among her books are the novels *Country People* (1924), *The Odyssey of a Nice Girl* (1925), and *The Folks* (1934); and the collections of short stories, *Iowa Interiors* (1926) and *Children and Older People* (1931).

H AT had brought "the relationship" together at the old home this summer. She had written that the old folks were getting pretty feeble, especially ma, ever since that fall she had had in the winter, and that it was time something was being done. Every one had felt that it could not be put off much longer.

They were all in the parlor now. They had come there with one accord after dinner, as if there had been a secret compact among them. There was a general conviction that the time had come to "settle something." The sense of conspiracy that attends family conclaves lay heavy upon them. The air was thick with undercurrents of feeling, schemes, secret alliances and antipathies. They had all eaten too much and they sat with the discomfort of middle age in the stiff old-fashioned chairs. The three men were making a pretense that the whole affair amounted to nothing. They refused to meet the meaning glances, full of dire warning and portent, which their wives cast at them from time to time. Whenever, in a pause of the furious squeaking of Jen's rocking chair, the clatter of dishes and shrill children's voices sounded loud from the kitchen, they were suddenly stricken, condemned with an obscure sense of guilt.

This was their chance. The old people and the children, who were "not supposed to know," were out of the way. Ma had been persuaded to lie down in her bedroom. Pa had been sent to show the chickens and the cow to Hat's little Benny. Jen's Margaret and Hat's Allie had been bribed and commanded to wash the dinner dishes. Jen's Herbert had been the worst to dispose of. Just when they thought they were rid of him, he would be discovered in the doorway, staring at them through the big tortoise-shell spectacles that he had just begun to wear, solemn and uncannily disconcerting. Finally Sam had sent him downtown with fifty cents to consume chocolate sodas in Vielle's Ice Cream Parlor.

But it was hard to make use of the chance they had tried so long to get. The little parlor was suddenly and overwhelmingly eloquent of the life that had been in it. The close musty air, thick with the smell of the carpet, told that it had not been opened for months. It had a dank chill, even in the clear warmth of the September afternoon. The enlarged pictures on the walls looked as if they had frozen into their silver frames. The closed organ, with its insertions of faded silk, was a tomb of wheezy melodies. The big illustrated Bible with its steel clasp lay beside the *Life of Abraham Lincoln*— which Art had peddled once—on the knitted lace doily of the stand. Knitted tidies were fastened with ribbons to the backs of chairs. A black memorial card on one of the little balconies of the organ stated in gold that John Luther Shafer had died at the age of thirty-two—"The Lord giveth, and the Lord taketh away." A large pink shell lay beside the door. A bunch of withered pampas grass stuck up from a blue-painted vase in the corner.

The women had entered into a discussion of operations— the one neutral spot on which they could still meet. The men let out a conscientious word from time to time. They crossed and recrossed their knees.

Sam tried to make Lou look at him. He wanted to get back to the hotel. He could not get settled on the bumpy springs of the great orange-plush chair where he was sitting. Sam had grown used to easy chairs.

". . . Oh, yes, it was an awful thing," Lou was saying. "They had to cut away one whole side of the breast."

Tch-tch, went the women's tongues.

"Well, it's a miracle what they can do these days," said Jen after a pause.

Sam gave a bounce in the orange chair. "Well, folkses, isn't it about time we were getting down to business?" he asked, with a heavy assumption of cheerfulness.

A sudden solemn quiet fell upon them all. They cleared their throats and changed positions. The magnificent pretense of a pleasant family gathering which they had been instinctively keeping up was shattered. Sam twisted in his chair with the sense that he had made a social blunder. Lou, who should have backed him up, put on an air of elaborate unconcern. The other women had a hungry look of suppressed excitement. Little Henry, Hat's husband, who was the poorest and had the least to say, gazed with a mild boredom at his swinging foot.

Sam refused to give up his air of cheerful briskness. He was convicted, but his riches made him bold. When it came right down to it, he had the say-so, and they all knew it.

"Now, let's just talk this thing over quietly among us and come to some decision that will satisfy every one," he said blandly. He had put that neatly, he thought.

Jen shot a triumphant glance at Art. They had talked it over in the night, subduing Herbert, who had a bed on the floor of their room, and who kept whimpering that they wouldn't let a fellow sleep, by proclaming that they had matters to discuss which he could know nothing about. But when Margaret, who was in the next room with her Aunt Hat, had come bouncing in and announced that they had better shut up if they did not want Aunt Hat to hear every single word they were saying about her, they had been subdued themselves. So they had not got much farther than Jen's deciding that "Sams" ought to take the old folks if any one did, for they were certainly best able to afford it. "But they'll get out of it some way, you just see if they don't," she had prophesied bitterly.

"Now, don't let them make you agree to anything you don't want," she had warned Art. "I guess we've got something to say in this matter. It concerns us just as much as it does them, and I think the whole relationship ought *all* to decide it equally."

But it was hard to be firm in the sight of Lou's elaborate silver coiffure. Both Jen and Hat—between whom, as those most likely to be "put upon," there was a defensive alliance—had agreed that it would be all right if they had to deal with Sam alone, but that Lou was sure to be at the

bottom of the whole thing. Whatever was done would be
Her Doings. There she sat, with her large hard bosom
plastered with silver and beading, and her maddening air
of being only remotely, and by virtue of her own gracious-
ness, connected with the affairs of the Shafer family. Jen
raged inwardly. Lou hadn't always been so much. It was
Sam who had made the money, not Lou, but of course he
would do whatever *she* said.

"Well—suppose we get started," repeated Sam. "Art,
you ought to have something to suggest. You preachers
usually have something to say," he added with ponderous
jocularity.

Art ran his hand slowly over the wrinkles of his waistcoat. He felt Jen's eyes burn into him. She was sitting rigid.

"Well—of course we want to do what's best for the
old people," he began, in his ministerial tone, for which
he hated himself.

"Oh, of course, certainly," Sam agreed hastily.

"Yes, but just what *is* best for Mother and Father Shafer?
That's what we all want to know," Lou put in sweetly.

Jen gave a jerk. "I'm sure that Arthur and I are willing
to do anything," she cried touchily, with her air of putting
them all in wrong. "I'm sure that no one has been a better
son than Arthur, whether any one realizes it or not."

Lou smiled inscrutably. They all knew that Sam was
Mother Shafer's favorite child.

Art flushed. "It's a delicate thing to decide," he murmured.

"Yes, of course," said Sam soothingly. "We're all willing
to do whatever is—of course."

Now that the thing was started, he felt at ease. If it
wasn't for the way that confounded chair kept sticking
into him! He sat, large and amenable, but prosperous. He
had the look of hotels and Pullman cars that made them

acknowledge his leadership. He had white hair thinning on a rosy skull, and a neat gray moustache.

"Now, as I've figured it out," he went on smoothly, "it's practically impossible for mother and father to spend another winter here alone. Isn't that about the size of it, Hat?"

"I guess so," Hat muttered.

"Yes, of course. We all see that. The place is in frightful condition. They can't keep it up——"

"They can't be expected to," Lou interrupted.

"No, of course they can't. And they really can't take care of themselves much longer—" Sam paused for confirmation.

Jen rocked, her lips tightly pursed together. It was as she had expected. "Sams" were running the whole thing. Art had given right in to them. Sam was doing the talking, but Lou had put him up to it. She was acting so sweet, but Jen knew there was something back of it.

"Well, then," Sam remarked pleasantly, with an air of putting it all impartially before them, "what shall we do?"

Jen broke violently out of her offended silence. "I think those who are best able to take them, ought to," she cried. "I'm sure Arthur and I are willing enough—no one's more willing—but no one realizes the exactions of a minister's life. I just escaped being in the hospital this spring. I couldn't stand one thing more. It's just go, go, go from morning to night. I'm just ready to break down now. No one realizes——"

"No, no. Now, we haven't said anything about any one's taking the old people," Sam interrupted. "All that remains to be decided."

Jen began to rock again, with her lips tighter, Lou smiled.

Art's face grew red. He felt guiltily that he ought to offer his home. He was ashamed of Jen, and of himself as seeming to agree with her. He would have put his refusal on a moral basis. It was not that he was not glad and willing to have the old people—but there would be so much confusion, it would mean that he would have to ask his people for an addition to the parsonage, and that would be difficult just now. New London was his first parish of any size, and certain things were expected of him. His father and mother would not fit in. They would not be happy there——

"Perhaps it won't be necessary for them to leave," Sam suggested pacifically. "Perhaps we can make some arrangement here."

"Have you thought of doing this?" Lou observed, smiling. "Of getting some responsible person to stay here and care for Mother and Father Shafer?"

Jen broke out again. "We thought of it, but I'm sure that even if they aren't my own parents I would never consent to leave them to the care of strangers!"

"Oh, I didn't say strangers, I didn't mention strangers," Lou replied with dignity. "You may be sure that Sam would never, never agree to anything of that kind."

Sam cleared his throat deprecatingly. He was thinking that he wished the women would keep out of this thing and let the men settle it. They could do it reasonably and in half the time. The women were always making a fuss and getting stirred up about every little thing. It was time he was taking the thing into his own hands.

"Now, let's—let's——"

He glared at Lou. Why didn't she speak out and not leave the whole thing to him? She had been concerned enough about it last night. It was so confoundedly hard to make suggestions to this bunch, with Hat never opening her mouth and Jen sitting there just ready to fly off the handle if any one winked. He couldn't do it all and he wasn't going to. If she couldn't help him, she could take the consequences.

Lou rose smilingly to the rescue. "I think we must all appreciate what Hattie has done," she observed with a majestic sweetness that created an instant atmosphere of suspicion. "She has come here to Lenaville every little while and relieved others of us who are more tied by responsibilities. I think we all ought to thank Hattie."

There was a murmur of polite approval. Jen smiled sardonically. She wanted to ask what responsibilities *Lou* had! With her clubs and her dressmakers probably. Whatever they were, they didn' keep her from gadding all over the country—everywhere but to Lenaville.

Hattie moved uncomfortably. She was a bulkily built woman who seemed to overflow the small cane-seated rocking chair which she had hitched into an inconspicuous corner. She had always been considered "not like the rest of them," although in some respects she resembled Art. She was said to have his hair and skin, heavy black hair and skin of a thick dark pallor, but the face which she now turned, with a faint instinct of defensiveness, toward Lou, wore a look of protesting stupidity.

Little Henry, who had been summoned from his feed store in Hobart for the conference, still swung his foot and examined the cracks in his finger tips. No one needed to consider him. He made just enough to get along on. But his air of detachment gave him a pale distinction. It convinced, where Lou's elaborately smiling unconcern aroused distrust.

Lou had not finished. She reached up to adjust a pearl earring that was half sunk in a fold of loose white flesh.

"But we must agree," she continued, "that we simply cannot expect Hattie to keep on coming to Lenaville every month or so. We cannot expect that of any one."

"I ain't going to do it any more. That's all," said Hattie sullenly.

"Of course not. We wouldn't think of asking it of you. Besides, even such excellent care isn't enough now. Father and Mother Shafer need some one with them *all* the time." Lou beamed upon Hattie, whose dull black eyes stared back at her uncomprehendingly. "Now, it just occurs to me—why couldn't Hattie and—Henry arrange to spend all their time here?"

"Yes, yes, certainly, why not?" exclaimed Art with an instinctive breath of relief. Then his satisfaction withered under the look of contemptuous triumph that Jen shot at him. So that was what *she* had been hatching up! They might have known that a desire to give no trouble to the old folks was not the only reason why "Sams" had stayed at the hotel!

Every one looked questioningly at Hattie. It was evident that she did not quite take it in. But her look of protest deepened. She glanced hesitatingly at Henry, who was sucking in his lips to the tune of "Marching through Georgia" in a kind of inverted whistle. "Well—I dunno—do you mean live here?" she asked weakly.

Sam plunged briskly in. Now that the thing was out, he was himself again. "Yes, that's the idea—live here. Stay right here with them. If the house isn't big enough, why—I'll see to that."

"You mean—move away from Hobart?" said Hat slowly.

"What about Henry's business?" demanded Art. "Would that have to be given up?"

Hat's mouth opened slightly.

"Oh, no, not necessarily," Sam said hastily. "You see, Hobart and Lenaville are only a few miles apart——"

"Forty miles!" ejaculated Art.

Sam waved his hand. "Oh—forty miles! What's forty

miles these days? Henry could easily run that business at forty miles. Let that boy of his—what's his name? John, Joe?—stay with the business. Be the making of him. Besides, this place is full of possibilities if some one will take hold and make it go. Pa's let it run to seed the last few years. There's a good living for somebody right on this place." Sam, who had a large wholesale business in Omaha, smiled inwardly at all this fuss about a feed store.

"And, of course, we intend—Sam and I—to make this entirely a business arrangement," Lou put in blandly.

"Yes, certainly," Sam agreed. "Well, Hat?"

Hat was bewildered. She could not get it straight. She knew that she had not said anything, but Lou seemed to think that the whole thing was settled. Jen, on the other hand, was looking at her with intense sympathy. Hat was dumb, but the spirit which dwelt in her pale bulk of flesh was stiffening and protesting. She had known that they would try to put something over on her, and she was moving cautiously. She had no defense but a mute obstinacy that had got her the name of being as stubborn as a mule.

Art was beginning to regret his first impulsive approval. Every time that he was with Sam and had to witness his older brother's air of riches and assured success, resentment always crept into his heart and finally rendered the companionship intolerable. He had no recourse but to stand up for Henry.

"Perhaps we'd better consult Henry about this," he observed ironically.

All eyes turned for the first time to Henry. He was now swinging his foot as well as sucking in his breath, and seemed to fi..d this arrangement far more absorbing than the question of his removal from the feed business. His creed—never stated—was: Let 'em fight it out among themselves. He sniffed slightly but made no answer.

Art was forced to go on. "It seems to me that it's asking a good deal," he stated in his pulpit manner. "It isn't such a light thing to move a family like that even forty miles. And Henry has his business. Why should he be asked to change? A thing like that can't be settled off-hand."

"I should say not," cried Jen.

Lou leaned forward and smiled at Art. "I thought we weren't here to decide what was light or easy for ourselves, but what was best for Father and Mother Shafer. If people object to taking them——"

"We don't object to taking them!" cried Jen hotly.

"Oh, pardon me! I thought you said——"

"I said that I thought that those best able to take them ought to. And I say so still."

"Exactly."

"But when it comes to forcing Hat into——"

"Now, now, now, now," said Sam soothingly. "There's no question of forcing. It's entirely for Hat and Henry— Hm!"

He broke off and the rosy hue of his skull spread downward through his cheeks. Hat's Allie had sidled in through the door. She was a pale snuffly little girl with a wisp of light braided hair. But at sight of her they were all silent. She went up to her mother and began pulling at her skirt and whispering something.

"Whadda you want? Hm?" Hat demanded.

Allie repeated her whisper. "Can't I? *Ma*-muh, can't I?"

"What does she want?" Sam asked.

"Oh, she says she wants to go to the picture show," Hat said shamefacedly.

"Well, Marg'rut's going," Allie persisted.

In spite of Jen's warning glance, Art's hand dove into his pocket. But Sam was ahead of him. He held out a freshly minted quarter on his plump glistening palm.

"Oh, let her go, let her go," he cried heartily. "Here, kiddie, go ahead. That's the place for you. Remember what it's all about, and tell your Uncle Sam when you get back."

Allie took the quarter, got out a bashful "Thangkew" to Hat's demand of "What do you say?" and ran from the room. Art surreptitiously slipped his dime back into his pocket.

They all breathed again, but even Lou felt it was impossible to return to the old point. Fate had been personified by Hat's Allie in wrinkled white ribbed stockings and a gingham dress too short for her. Her appearance had mysteriously changed the course of the argument. Sam himself could not switch it back. It was as if the six children of Hat and Henry, with their demands and clamoring needs, came in with Allie, like the ghosts of the kings in *Macbeth*. Every one felt that Hat would not come to Lenaville. There was a silence.

"What a difference the motion pictures have made!" Art remarked ponderously.

"She's always wanting to run to them," said Hat apologetically.

Sam fidgeted and tapped his foot. He wanted to get away on the six-ten. He wasn't going to spend another night in that hotel, not with Lou along. The vision of a large leather chair at home, in which the hollows were his own, filled him with homesickness. It was a terrible thing for a man to be so uncomfortable.

"Well—suppose we get back to business," he said with determined good nature. "Now, if Hat thinks she wouldn't like to leave Hobart, of course that's her own affair. But it means that some other plan must be thought of. What do some of the rest of you think about it? Hat, suppose you suggest something."

"You see," Lou explained hastily, "the reason the suggestion about Hattie's staying was made, was because Sam and I both felt that too much of a change wouldn't be good for Mother and Father Shafer. They're pretty old, you know, and it's hard for old people to adjust themselves. They could hardly make an abrupt change at their time of life."

"No, that's true, of course," said Art, trying not to look at his wife.

"No, I think they ought to stay as near the old home as possible," virtuously agreed Jen. "But, of course, for Hat and her family to come here!"

"Perhaps it wouldn't be the best thing," Lou conceded graciously. She felt a sudden sense of unity with Jen. "The place is in frightful condition."

"Oh, it is! I don't think they ought to be allowed to live here. It's frightful for them."

"And you know it costs to keep it up," Lou reminded them. "Although of course Sam has been glad and willing to do it."

The rest were silent. Sam made an impatient gesture. "Well—Hat?" he insisted.

Hat flushed dully. She could not help feeling that they were blaming her because she had not offered to come to Lenaville. Now they seemed to think that that obliged her to offer something else. She glanced at Henry. He twisted his mouth and looked inscrutable.

"Well—I don't know. You folks better settle it. You will, anyway," she muttered.

"It's hard to know what to do. It's a difficult thing all round," said Art with solemn satisfaction. Now that his immediate anxiety was lifting, he began to feel the dramatic sense of the occasion. "A difficult thing," he murmured.

"But then these things have to come," said Lou.

"Yes, that's what life is," sighed Jen.

"Well, of course, it's hard for them," said Sam with his resolute cheerfulness, "but if you look at it another way, it isn't bad. Suppose we left them alone here through the winter and they fell or got laid up. No one might hear of it for days. They've cared for themselves and others all their lives, now it's time the rest of us were caring for them."

"And they can't possibly be happy here under such conditions," declared Lou, shaking her head. "That kitchen! Some one ought to take hold of it and give it a thorough cleaning. And I should think they'd freeze here in the winter. Boo!" She shuddered, drawing her arms in their transparent black sleeves tight to her body.

"Yes, of course, it can't go on much longer," Art affirmed gravely.

"It's a good thing they have children to look after them," cried Jen.

There was a murmur of agreement. The tension was lifted now and a pervading cheerfulness taking its place. Even Jen felt that things were going well. Only Hat looked suspicious and unconvinced.

"But still we haven't quite come to the point," said Sam, genial but bent upon business. "We haven't said just what is to be done. Now, I think we're all agreed——"

He broke off again with an impatient exclamation. This time it was Margaret in the doorway, looking at them with an expressionless stare.

"Grandma's crying in there," she observed coldly.

There was a feeling of consternation.

"Oh, pshaw!" muttered Sam impatiently.

"I thought you had gone downtown," said Jen, with a suggestion of reproach. "Where is she?"

"In her bedroom."

Margaret shrugged her shoulders and went out.

There was a hush.

"I expect I better go in," said Hat stolidly.

"Yes, yes. All of you girls had better go," Sam proposed nervously. "Hm! Pshaw!"

Lou and Jen, bustling slightly with a sense of dramatic importance that they could not quite subdue, followed Hat out of the room. The men waited, uneasily watching the brown-painted bedroom door with its knob hanging slightly askew. Sounds of an old woman's sobbing, weak and fretful, came through it, and the low soothing tones of the three women.

"Hm!" Sam murmured uncontrollably, "I was afraid we might have a time."

Lou, mysteriously important, appeared in the doorway. She made a sign to Sam with her eyebrows.

"Will you come here a moment?"

"Can't Hat manage it?"

"No. We need you."

Sam followed his wife into the little bedroom. The black walnut bed, the dingy dresser that lurched forward, where one castor was missing, the painted wardrobe, the china washbowl with raised pinkish flowers, the faint smell of bedding and musty carpet—life in the old house rushed blindingly before him.

He stepped awkwardly up to the bed where his mother lay, shaking, and clutching with her brown misshapen fingers at the edge of the patchwork quilt. He tried to pat her gnarled bony shoulder.

"Now, ma! What's all this?"

The old woman tried to jerk away from him, but the influence of Sam, the first-born and best-beloved, was almost immediate. Her sobs quieted, she fumbled for something with which to wipe her eyes. The sense of shame with which he had been laboring all afternoon caught hold of

Sam as he saw the effect that his presence still had. For years he had paid no attention to his mother except to send an occasional check, which he could easily spare. Hat had thought of her, worked for her, come to see her every few months in spite of the exactions of poverty and a great brood of children—and yet she would do nothing for Hat and was wax at a word from Sam.

She groped with her hand for his. He put it, plump, pink, silvered with hairs, over her knotted fingers with their split and blackened nails.

"She thinks we're going to do something to her," Hat announced.

"Why—you don't think that, do you, ma?" Sam asked weakly.

He bent down to catch what the old woman whispered— "planning something——"

"Why, what should we be planning?" Jen asked with a warning glance at Sam.

He scowled at her. An immense urge to get the thing over and done with, and to get away from these jealousies, undercurrents, pettinesses, came over him. He hated the way that he always found himself acting when he was among "the relationship." He wanted to get home.

"Now, ma, let's have this thing out. Will you listen— hm?"

He bent close, drawing from her a faint nod.

"That's right. Of course you will."

Her thin gray hair, streaked with brown, that was always drawn smooth and tight from the broad white parting, was wildly dishevelled. The tiny braid that for years she had wound into a hard little knob at the back of her head was slowly uncoiling like a bit of twisted wire. Sam could see a part of her wrinkled brown cheek drawn up with crying.

"Well, then, you know things can't go on always as they have been. You and pa oughtn't to be left alone this way— it isn't the thing. And there's no reason why you should, when you have children to take care of you."

"That's what I told her," Hat put in, "but she says she don't want any one taking care of her."

"Oh, now, ma!" This was the thing that Sam dreaded. But he forced his voice to its cheerful sensible tone. "Of course you can take care of yourself, but the time's come now when we ought to do something for you. You've worked hard all your life, and now you ought to let some one else do part of it. That's all Hat meant. Isn't that so?"

She looked suddenly up at him. "Tell *them* to go!" she whispered fiercely.

Sam spoke shamefacedly to Lou and Jen. "I guess you girls had better go in the other room a little while, and ma and I will talk this thing out together."

Sam gave a puff of relief when he was alone with his mother. He felt that he could manage her, if only those women would keep their oar out! He bent down close and whispered to her, so eager to get the thing over and convince her, that he convinced himself. At the same time he felt a sweet melancholy affection for her—she was so tiny, withered, silent, so true.

"Now, see here, ma, I don't like to go away off to Omaha and leave you and pa here alone. Oh, I know you aren't helpless, but just the same something might happen. Like that fall you had. You might happen to get sick, or pa might, and I tell you it isn't the thing. I don't think you will, but then you might, you know."

"Hat could come," she said resentfully.

"Maybe she could and maybe she couldn't," Sam replied judicially. "One of her children might just happen to be sick at the same time you were, and then where'd you be!

Besides, it's hard for Hat to keep coming here every little while. She's got a big family to look after and plenty to do at home, and it isn't always easy to pick up and leave."

The old woman was silent, shrinking away from the moist reassuring pressure of his hand. Dumbness was her only weapon. She felt the struggle between them. Her face grew warily impassive.

Sam went on hastily:

"Now, ma, I think it'll be better all around if you and pa would go and stay this winter with Hat. It——"

"You mean leave here! I knew you were trying to drive us out!" Her face broke up again into violent weeping. She clutched at the quilt.

Sam grew suddenly angry. "Drive you out! As if your own children would drive you out of anywhere! We're trying to do the best thing possible for you, and you make it hard enough! Here I came clear from Omaha—" The sight of his mother, frightened and whimpering, brought him back. "You didn't mean that, of course, ma. But I want you to try and see the thing from a reasonable viewpoint. Of course we want to do the best thing for you, whatever it is."

Her lips quivered uncontrollably, but she managed to whisper: "I don't want to leave here. I've always lived here—all my things is here——"

"I know it, ma, but just for this winter—afterwards we could see—how it worked out!"

He got up suddenly and walked to the window. He could see the lawn, the grass unkempt and withering out under the shaggy trees that grew too thick. The old barn, the dingy chicken yard, the old one-legged chair fallen tipsily under the apple tree—he shivered. He could not leave them here!

"We've always got along," his mother quavered. "I don't

want to be beholden to folks as long as I can do for myself."

"You wouldn't need to be. You could do there just the same as you do here." For the moment Sam conceived this to be true. "Only, in case of anything, you'd be where Hat could look after you. No, you'd help Hat a lot more than she would you. Just think of all you could do with the childen."

Still the dumb, obstinate look persisted.

"Look here, ma!" Sam exclaimed suddenly. "Would you rather come with me? I said Hat, because I knew Hat was near the old place, and that you'd have the children there— but if you'd rather come with me——"

She looked at him. "No," she said faintly.

"Well, I didn't think you would," Sam said heartily. There had been a sudden rending thought of Lou. "It's so far and all. But if you—now I tell you what I'll do. I'll see to it that you and pa have your own things at Hat's, if you'd like that better. I don't blame you." He forgot that the definite offer of her home had never been made by Hat. "There can be a room built on if necessary. I'll see to all that. And there you can live, just as snug as you please, much more comfortably than you do here——"

He broke off, for his father's shuffling steps had come to the door. The old man stood in the hallway, looking hesitatingly from his wife to Sam, with his dim blue eyes.

"What's ma crying for?" he asked.

He gently put off little Benny's fingers and came into the room.

"Run away, Ben. Grandpa wants to talk to Uncle Sam."

He was a very old man. He had great bowed shoulders, a beard like hoarfrost, blue eyes set wide apart, with the unfathomable look of the old peasantry. He wore a shapeless brown coat and slippers with tufted red flowers.

He had done many things—farmed, kept a little grocery store, been janitor at the Court House. Now he just puttered around his barn and grounds, keeping a pig, a horse, and a few bees and chickens, raising vegetables and a little corn, and living upon these things and the checks Sam sent. He had grown sweeter, vaguer, and more useless with the years. He loved his animals—had a name for each of them—and was happiest of all when he wandered about the yard with little Benny, hunting on the ground for good apples, and singing old songs in his thin, sweet, wavering voice.

"Come in, pa," said Sam impatiently. "Ma and I were just talking about next winter."

The old man stood in the doorway, with that vague, half-frightened look in his eyes.

"I guess I better get my cap," he said uncertainly. "Head's always chilly without. Do you know where the durn thing's gone, ma?"

"I see it a little bit ago. Ain't it on top of the wardrobe?" she asked in a muffled voice from the pillow.

"Oh, yes. How in time did it get up there?" The old man, who had been peering at the bed and the window-panes, got down the skullcap of black cambric and fitted it carefully over his gray head.

Sam waited nervously. The old man was much blinder than he had been when Sam last saw him, six years ago. It was impossible, unsafe, to leave him alone with the old place through the long cold winter.

"What was you sayin', Sam?"

"We were talking about next winter, pa," Sam said in his most reasonable tones. "Now, I don't think you folks ought to try to stay by yourselves and run this great place. There's no sense to it. It's hard on you, isn't it?"

"Well, I—I don't——" The old man frowned uncertainly.

"They want us to go to Hat's," his wife said in a low trembling voice.

"Why, you mean—visit? I don't know's I care to——"

"He means stay there. They're all trying to make us."

Sam gave an impatient twist. "I don't like the idea of your staying here another long hard winter. You'd have company at Hat's and be well taken care of, and—well, we'd feel better about it all round."

Pa was staring out of the window at the gnarled purplish limbs of the old apple tree. Comprehension was slowly and visibly dawning in his eyes.

"Why, I'd hate awful to leave the place," he said uncertainly, with a glance at his wife. "I don't know, we been here so long, it'd be awful hard to break away. I don't know what'd become of the beasts—they've got used to me—I wouldn't like to think of anybody else havin' 'em. Peter's been real lame the last year or so. I've kinda looked after him. I don't know, Sam—Ma, whadda you say?"

"I don't say. They've done the saying. They fixed it among 'em," she finished bitterly.

Then she reached out passionately for Sam's hand.

"Sam, I ain't sayin' it about you. I don't want to go against what you want. You been so good to us, sendin' us money and all. But I wouldn't do it for the others. And I—you gotta let me take what I want with me!" she cried suddenly and vehemently. "I'm gonna have my own things. I ain't gonna use Hat's."

"Yes, yes, ma. Of course you can take whatever you want. Take everything in the house if you want it. I'll fix all that." Sam almost laughed in a rush of relief, glad to be, in some manner, the generous provider that he loved to be. He only half comprehended that his attitude of displeasure, of impatience, had been enough to make his mother throw to the winds her independence, her home, all the things that she cherished. She had never been able to "stand against" Sam.

"I'll leave you and pa to talk it over by yourselves," he conceded heartily. "You just see if you don't think it's the best thing. You just talk about it a little."

He got out of the room as fast as he could, and let out a long breath of relief. He detested what he called "times." But he had learned in business to go through with them and finish them, and then throw them off.

The others had gone outdoors. Through the partly open door, he could see them moving about the lawn looking for apples in the long shiny grass. He knew how he would appear unconcernedly among them and say cheerfully, in an off-hand way: "Well, I guess that's settled."

But he lingered for a moment in the parlor, and his exhilaration evaporated. He remembered that he would have to tell Hat how easily he had made free of her home. Even promised to build on a room. And had agreed to let ma take her things——

Those things were all about him now. He could not look at the pampas grass sticking up absurd and stiff from the blue-painted vase. The elaborate lace curtains tied back with cords of red plush, the sea shell beside the door, the plants, the ingrain carpet, musty-smelling, and patterned with great sprawling cornucopias of roses.

"Oh, pshaw!" he muttered.

He turned uncertainly toward the bedroom door, from which he could hear a low murmur. In the intervals the eight-day clock ticked loudly in the kitchen.

No. It was over and done with. He shrugged his shoulders vigorously and put it from him.

It was strange how people seemed to take root in a place. He should think any one would be glad to leave this run-down, miserable spot. See how the steps were coming apart!

After all, he had to pay the bills, and he was entitled to some voice in the matter.

But it was too bad that the way of life was as it was.

As he went out of the house, he realized that he could take the six-ten as he desired. There were arrangements to make, but he could hustle them through in no time if he had to.

He smiled sardonically as he saw Jen's tense listening back.

Lord! He would be glad to get out of that hotel and back to his own home again.

The Robin

RICHARD SULLIVAN

Richard Sullivan was born at Kenosha, Wisconsin. He graduated at the University of Notre Dame in 1930, and later studied at the Goodman School of the Theatre of the Chicago Art Institute. After experience in radio writing and advertising, and work in his father's store at Kenosha, he became a teacher of English at the University of Notre Dame in 1937. He is married and has two daughters. He has contributed stories to *The Atlantic Monthly, Scribner's Magazine, Columbia, American Prefaces,* and other magazines.

EARLY morning. The garden lay fresh and dewy beneath the big trees. A long line of top-heavy pink tulips nodded and bobbed against a mass of green shrubbery. Over in a corner, near the birdbath, an early lilac shivered in the cool yellow sunlight. On the bird-bath, chipper and wide-awake this morning, sat a robin, splashing the tawny red feathers of his breast.

The robin was careful and proud of those sweet red feathers. He cocked his head back to slant a look down at them and cocked his head down to squint a look back

From *The Midland,* March-April, 1932. Reprinted by permission of the author.

at them. He inspected them critically and at the same time lovingly, as if red feathers were a treasure deserving both care and pride. He dipped his head to the water, and tentatively splattered his breast. Pleased with the result, he went further, half-raising his wings and splashing more vigorously. Further pleased, he made a few joyful noises and after looking gayly about the quiet garden flopped boldly and bodily into the bath. He spluttered and pecked and slapped his wings. He splashed and danced and flirted his tail. He got himself thoroughly wet. He had a great bath. Then he hopped to the rim of the basin, and preened himself dry in the sun. His breast gleamed like old red gold.

Presently he thought he spotted a worm. He cocked his head and stared, but his eyes, though bright, were never very sharp, and he couldn't be sure at a distance. So in a sort of careless nonchalant way, as if he were out for mere exercise, he flew all around the garden, watching the spot slyly, but doing his best to allay suspicion in the worm— if it were a worm. It turned out to be nothing at all. The robin had changed his reconnoitering maneuver into a flanking movement that was leading up to a surprise attack, but at the moment of lighting he discovered that there was nothing to surprise. Oh, well . . . perhaps a blade of grass swaying under a dewdrop had caught his eye. After a little hopping around and careful listening with his ear down and tail up, he found a choice breakfast, a fat wiggly angleworm, quite unsuspicious. Immediately after breakfast he found a grub, which he also ate, and a little later another angleworm. This last he took up to the crabapple tree, which was just beginning to blossom, and ate half of it there as he sat on a firm branch in a shower of pink buds. Getting thirsty, he left the other half in a safe crotch, and flew to the bird-bath, for a drink. He drank a few drops and chirped delightedly. The sun was getting warmer. The day was starting out well.

At about this time the black cat was coming down the alley. It had green eyes and a yellow collar with a little brass bell. The bell tinkled slightly as the black cat gracefully picked its way. It chose for its soft paws only the smoothest spots among the sharp alley cinders. Its lean muscles rippled as it walked, and its black coat glowed beautifully. It waved its sinuous, menacing tail. It was a large well-kept cat, and as it walked it looked lazily from side to side, as if inviting admiration.

While the robin hopped about the cement rim of the bird-bath the black cat carefully picked its way between bushes into the garden. It moved with such smoothness, such grace and supple caution, that the little brass bell had no reason to tinkle. The only sound which marked the cat's progress toward the birdbath was a faint rustling of leaves, and that was a sound which any one might have attributed to the breeze on a fresh airy morning in spring. The cat slunk under branches and flowers to a gray stone bench that lay halfway between the alley and the birdbath. Under the bench it crouched in a black furry ball with head low and unblinking eyes sweeping out cold green glances.

At about this moment the robin, who was having a glorious time of it, swung out on an exuberant turn round the garden. He circled the apple tree and wheeled in a clean low curve out around one of the big maples; then back again flying, making a loop of it. He nipped at a blossom as he passed the lilac bush. He shot up to the eaves trough of the house, and there went into a very ecstasy of tumbling about. He chirped and hopped. Glee, this was glee! This was high spirits! He swooped back to the lilac bush. He lighted, he chirped; chirping shrilly he jumped through the grass; high hops and stretched wings. He found a handful of bread crumbs that the sparrows had missed, and for a few minutes pretended excitedly that each crumb was a worm. But that game got too slow. After he had carefully stalked five or six unwiggling, unprotesting bread crumbs and had cocked his head at them and listened with his ear down and tail up, he grew impatient of the make-believe, and simply gobbled down the rest as plain bread which was incapable of putting up a fight or managing an escape. Then he began chirping wildly again. Such a sun! By mid-day it would be like summer in the garden. This was glee!

The black cat took advantage of the robin's glee. It sneaked up. Very slow, very low, very beautiful it crept from the bench toward the birdbath. When the robin was circling the maple the cat was a quarter of the way. When the robin was dancing on the eaves trough the cat was half the way. When the robin was playing worms with the crumbs the cat was three-quarters of the way. And in an-other instant it was smoothly curled up beneath a squatty little evergreen shrub that lay within springing distance of the birdbath. It was set. The black cat was ready.

The robin flew to the birdbath. He lit on the side furthest from the cat, but immediately hopped jerkily around the rim to the near side. His frolics had put his feathers in disarray; so he set to work straightening himself out. He smoothed down his panting breast with his bill, still pre-serving that attitude of mingled care and pride. In the mid-morning sun tiny metallic glints showed among the red feathers. Soon he pecked a few times, rather vigorously, under his wing. He seemed unsatisfied. Something was wrong here under this wing. A flea? He stretched out the wing full length and twisted his neck around to get a good look at the itchy spot. It was an awkward unbalanced posi-tion. The cat's tail waved sinuously upward, and its black hair ruffled silkily along the spine. The robin kept pecking.

The cat crouched its weight slightly back for a swifter spring. The robin kept pecking. He found the flea and worked justice on it in a single deliberate nip of his bill. All the soft skin around the cat's claws was snarled up ready. But satisfied now the itch was gone, the robin flew up to the crotch in the apple tree, to get the half worm he had left there.

The black cat was very patient. What it could not do one time it could another. It allowed its tail to sink and its black glowing hair to fall smoothly in place. But it kept its claws unsheathed and its legs set to spring. It was perfectly hidden beneath the evergreen.

The sun grew warmer. It hit the garden from a higher angle now, and soon dried up the dew. A couple of yellow butterflies danced along the line of tulips. A woodpecker was drilling at one of the maples, and a half-dozen sparrows were cheep-cheeping on the eaves trough. The robin, after meditating for some time in the crotch of the apple tree, chirped back at them. For a little while there was a spirited chatter, until a blue jay joined raucously in to spoil it. Then the robin excused himself from the conversation and went off to have another bath.

Two sparrows had just splashed in and out of the bird-bath so quickly that the black cat had no time for action. But sparrows were small and hardly worth action. The two little birds now sat on the rim, gray and dumpy, as the robin approached. They cheeped at him pertly and stared with their bright black eyes. He sat beside them for a moment, and burnished his breast. It gleamed red in the sun. He polished the tiny metallic glints in it. When his bill furrowed the feathery surface the soft gray down underneath ruffled lightly against his pink skin.

The black cat lay crouched for the spring. It waited until the robin stood flapping and splashing in the water. Then

—tinkle—a black flash; instantly it had him. The tinkling bell might have clanged for all the good it did the robin. The robin screamed. The two sparrows shot away. The cat clawed at a mess of fluttering feathers. Later it would bite. The robin screamed so loud that the terrified woodpecker stopped hammering the maple. The scream filled the garden. Still clawing, the cat bit. With delicate long white teeth it bit into the soft pink body. Blood came out. The blue jay swooped over the birdbath, jabbering madly. The cat arched back, sprang down. The robin hung in its mouth. The cat's tail waved high and menacing. Its cold green eyes burned over the garden slowly, and then it picked its way out through the bushes. The two sparrows who had fled chittered on the eaves trough with their fellows, and the blue jay made hoarse excited noises in the maple tree. In the bird-bath lay a few bloody feathers, floating on the water.

The black cat returned down the alley. As it picked its steps through the sharp cinders its little brass bell tinkled carelessly; its coat was glossy in the late morning sun; beneath its black sides the lean muscles rippled deliciously. It hardly noticed the slight weight of the robin, which was now growing cool between the slender sharp white teeth. As the black cat gracefully stole along it felt in such high good spirits that it could not repress a gentle, delicate purr.

Back in the garden the two yellow butterflies were performing insane acrobatics about the lilac bush. The blue jay was gone. The woodpecker had resumed his hammering, and the noisy sparrows were sitting in a chattering line along the eaves trough. The apple tree now cast shade over the middle of the garden, and the edges of the shadow-patch continuously waved on the grass as the branches above swayed slightly in the wind. The sunshine was hot. It was like summer in the garden. In a little while the sparrows settled to the grass. One of them made such a fuss over a few specks of bread crumbs he found there that the others came hopping eagerly over; but after close inspection by the group it was decided that some one had been here before them. Soon after the sparrows flew away.

At about midday, when everything was strangely quiet, another robin flew into the garden. He was very much like the first. He had the same proud and careful cock of his head for a look of inspection; the same delighted way of chirping in the sunlight; and as he sat preening himself on the birdbath his shining red breast feathers showed exactly the same color as those which now lay slowly, wavily sinking in the brown still water before him. He was very much like the first. . . .

A Preacher Goes to Texas

JOHN W. THOMASON, JR.

John W. Thomason, Jr., knows soldiering at first hand through lifelong experience, and the War Between the States from intimate family background. He was born in Huntsville, Texas, in 1893, of a family of Confederates—his grandfather was Longstreet's Chief of Staff. He attended Southwestern University and the University of Texas, then studied art in New York. In 1917 he enlisted in the United States Marine Corps, and received numerous awards for distinguished service. At the end of the World War he remained in the Marine Corps, and has risen to the rank of Lieutenant-Colonel, serving in Cuba, Nicaragua, and the Orient. He has written and illustrated *Fix Bayonets* (1926), *Jeb Stuart* (1930), *Gone to Texas* (1937), and *Lone Star Preacher* (1941).

IT IS one of those stories Uncle Jimmy Farrow used to tell, at Mr. Lee Rodgers' place on Patterson Lake in Houston County, when we sat, after supper, on the porch through summer evenings: how the Rev. Praxiteles Swan appeared in Texas and preached his first sermon at Washington on the Brazos, to the notable confusion of the devil in those parts. In his years of achievement,

From *Lone Star Preacher,* by John W. Thomason, Jr., Charles Scribner's Sons, 1941. Copyright by Charles Scribner's Sons.

they called Praxiteles Swan "the Hurricane of God." He
was superannuated before my time, but all my old folks
had trembled under his thunders, and he loomed vast and
legendary, even in the country where Sam Houston and
Davy Crockett were remembered.

Uncle Jimmy, a dried-up little fox squirrel of a man who
claimed to have served with Quantrell, and who, for sixty
years after the war, never sat in line with a window, day
or night, was a shirttail boy in Washington County in the
1850's, and saw the preacher arrive. But the actual beginnings of that career I found myself, years after Uncle Jimmy
told the tale, in an old thick book dealing with the saints
of early Texas Methodism. In it is preserved, besides other
edifying material, Praxiteles Swan's own journal of his life
and acts.

Uncle Jimmy's narrative style was of the leisurely con-
templative type, best enjoyed by persons having no other
engagements. It owed much of its effectiveness, I think, to
the setting—the deep and timeless peace of the Trinity River
bottom, the noises of the night and the woods, and the dark
shimmer of the lake under the stars. And the journal, although it recorded immense and laborious travels in a
wilderness, and fiery contests for immortal souls, is also
the chronicle of an elder and unhurried time—it is, in fact,
long-winded. Therefore, I abridge the one and paraphrase
the other.

Of Praxiteles' beginnings, it is enough to know that he
came of a regretted *mésalliance* between a Yankee school-
teacher named Swan, and Miss Cassandra Pelham, a lady
of imperious Virginia blood. He was orphaned early. His
uncle, Colonel Marius Pelham, raised him, as they say, on
his place in the pleasant Piedmont country outside of Char-
lottesville, where the Colonel lived, withdrawn and feudal,
among his Negroes, his fighting cocks and his blood horses;

drinking brandy juleps before dinner, port after, and Madeira between meals, and reading the more outrageous of the Augustan poets in the original Latin. An Army officer until it bored him, a member of the Congress until, he said, the tone of the lower house became too degraded for a refined person's stomach, and a duelist always, he instructed his nephew in the accomplishments and prejudices of the Virginia gentry; and through Praxiteles' adult life, the violent old autocrat stood sneering over the shoulder of the man of God—although I am sure Praxiteles would never have admitted this.

His uncle sent him to Princeton College for his education, because he regarded Mr. Jefferson as a nauseous demagogue, and could not abide his works; and after that he designed the young man for the law. But, unaccountably, the nephew came under other influences. In his twenty-second year, the summer after his graduation—he being then six feet and upward of lank red-headed youth—he faced his uncle in his own garden, and told him plainly he was called to the Methodist ministry.

Praxiteles records the interview at length, and it must have been of a nature to make the house servants turn gray under their dark skins and seek places of safety. He quotes his own remarks, which are elevated and improving, but his uncle's statements he barely suggests, with the explanation that they were horrid blasphemies, and he feared his aged relative to be already in Satan's waistcoat pocket. He comments sadly that Colonel Pelham was a man of honor, infatuated in the delusion that a man of honor could live a decent life according to his personal standards, without dependence on higher guidance. "In such there is no hope; they are worse than the most dissolute and hardened sinners, for whom there is at least repentance and salvation. 'Drunk with wine, as Ephraim in his fat valleys——' "

The upshot of it was, his uncle threw him out, and they never saw each other again; they came of the same violent blood. But you identify Colonel Pelham as the unrepentant sinner, a figure at once moving and repellent and somehow glamorous, which Praxiteles thereafter used effectively through fifty years of sermons. The same afternoon he departed from his home, taking some gold pieces left out of his quarterly allowance, his riding cloak, and a change of linen in his saddlebags, astride the big, hammerheaded, three-quarters-bred mare given him when a colt. He went to Baltimore.

Baltimore was the outpost of Southern Methodism, lately split away from the Northern brethren on the vexatious question of Negro slavery. I abridge his account of what he did there, and how he was ordained; and how old Bishop Andrew, a shrewd prince of the church, had him in for an interview and detailed him to the Texas mission. Because, nowhere else, the bishop said, indicating the letters and memorials on the episcopal desk, were the shepherds so sorely tried as in the Texas missions; nowhere else were the sheep so black and the wolves so bold. You conceive him appraising Praxiteles' lean length of bone and sinew, his shock of red hair, his purposeful green eyes, aggressive nose, and the thin firm mouth over the long jaw and the pointed chin, and considering that such a young soldier belonged in the forefront of the battle. Perhaps he thought of King David, who was also white and ruddy. No bishop would have wanted to be responsible for King David's discipline, and Texas was a long way off. He cautioned Praxiteles about Texas. The people were sensitive in unexpected spots, he warned, and it would be better not to refer to his calling as missionary work, or to his colleagues as missionaries. Up here, of course; but down there "be ye therefore wise as serpents, and harmless as doves." Praxiteles, he ordered, would proceed forthwith to the settlement called Washington-on-the-Brazos, in the Rutersville District, pending the yearly assembly of the Texas Conference and a permanent assignment. The pastor of that flock, he explained, had succumbed to a lung fever induced by his toils. In Texas, the bishop warned him, a minister's body needed to be as robust as his soul. His honorarium, he thought, would be a hundred and sixty dollars a year, the years his congregation made a crop. When they didn't, the Lord would provide. At the end, he blessed Praxiteles and sent him forth, quoting the appropriate scriptures.

Praxiteles neglected his journal for two months; he states, merely, that he rode down to Texas after Christmas. And he resumed his entries in early March, 1852, the day he crossed into the state by Gaines' Ferry on the Sabine. A cold rain drove on a northeast wind, he mentions, and the roads were trying to his mare, who was not now up into her bridle as when they left Virginia. He refers to great discomfort from his breeches, which were worn through inside the knees—"Mem . . . get some good woman to patch them for me."

Texas was excessively well-watered that year. He listed the creeks between the Sabine and the Neches rivers, all of them high and some of them overflowing from the rains, and never a bridge in the country, and no bottom to the roads. He discovered that his mare could swim, which was probably a surprise to both of them, when the ford went out from under in an innocent-looking brown creek east of the Trinity, and they all but drowned. He pressed on, as only circuit riders and fugitives did in those parts, resting where darkness overtook him; one night in a verminous tavern, another in a loft above a barn full of horned cattle, and once in the attic of a poor man's house—a man who received him hospitably enough, fed him bacon and greens and corn bread, showed a readiness to discuss spiritual affairs, and then, when Praxiteles disclosed his denomination, tried to eject him into the wet and stormy wilderness. The journal briefly states that Praxiteles declined to be ejected, but it contains this entry: "I had rather associate with howling savages than with Campbellites."

By Swartout he came to the Trinity, booming along at flood stage, and found a ferry, and had directions to Washington. "Just keep goin' west," they told him helpfully. "Don't turn neither north nor south. There ain't but one road goin' west."

He passed Cold Spring and Montgomery, climbed the watershed between the Trinity and the San Jacinto, with its solemn pine forests, and plunged again into bottom land, smothered under pin oak, walnut, pecan, hickory and sweet gum, every tree trailing Spanish moss, mournful in the rain as dripping beards on hanged men. Miles of the road were under water, and the occasional higher stretches marched, rutted, between rain-dappled lagoons that carried a current, more often than not. Houses were a day's ride apart, and there were no settlements, and nobody on the road beyond occasional glum mud-plastered mail riders. He spent a night in the bottom, huddled under a tree, his mare trembling and the water making noises all around. There was a panther—the first he had encountered—hunting in the neighborhood, and its squalls were dreadful in his ears. He took comfort, he recorded, from singing hymns, and felt that the Lord's hand was over him. He forded the East Fork, which was not bad, and swam Winter's Creek and Peach Creek, and late on a gray March evening he approached the Middle Fork of the San Jacinto; two days' ride, he calculated, from the Brazos. It was still raining.

The Middle Fork ran banks full, foul with floating brush. Where it lapped into the road, one stood with a sodden quilt on his shoulders and a shotgun under his arm, gazing downstream into the last of the light. That man was, in fact, our Uncle Jimmy Farrow; then a sort of roustabout for the cook on Old Man Locke's wagon train, that did hauling between Cincinnati on the Trinity and Brenham. The cook had given him a ten-gauge double gun, and told him to go get a mess of ducks, because the teamsters were promising to fry him over his own fire if he fed them any more side meat and corn pone; the high water had detained the wagon train for days and they were in the worst possible humor.

Uncle Jimmy, telling us the story, says he was watching so sharp down the river for the evening flight that he let the fellow get right up on him before he noticed. Long-legged fellow on a big gaunted mare; all he could see was a white face between a hatbrim and a turned-up cloak collar, stopping to speak to him. As he turned his head, Uncle Jimmy saw ducks from the corner of his eye, and he told the man, blast his bowels, if he moved he'd kill him.

The fellow sat there, frozen—it's not what a duck sees that scares him, Uncle Jimmy claims; it's what moves—and five hundred mallards came along the river about as high as the treetops. Right at the ford they flared out over the bank, making for a stubble field back in the woods, and Uncle Jimmy picked his correct second of time and let them have both barrels, knocking down a dozen or so. Those old ten-gauges, with thirty-inch, cylinder-bored barrels, scattered fine. The ducks fell on the land, but some were crippled, and he had to be mighty spry to beat them to the water and twist their necks; and this man dismounted and helped; had legs like a sandhill crane, Uncle Jimmy says, and a reach like a hayrake. When they had collected the ducks—nice mallards in prime condition from the winter on the Gulf Coast—Uncle Jimmy saw the stranger was just a youngster—little older than he was—and he took him to the wagon camp on some higher ground a quarter of a mile upstream.

The boys—half a dozen teamsters—were playing brag under the lean-to shelter they had knocked up and covered with a wagon sheet, and they were sullen and ugly, and down to ten gallons of whisky, which Old Man Locke was sitting on with his pistol in his waistband, and dealing out just a tin cupful at a time, before meals. Old Man Locke told the stranger he reckoned he was welcome to what grub there was, and he could sleep under a wagon; and if he was stayin', he could turn to and help the cook. Old Man Locke was rough-talkin', they said, in those days.

Well, there was nothing finicky about the stranger; first he unsaddled and scraped the mud off his mare, then he helped with the ducks. The cook had boiling water ready to scald them, and Uncle Jimmy and this man snatched the feathers right off of them, all in no time.

Here Uncle Jimmy digressed to describe at length the way they broiled the ducks; something we all knew and did in those parts, and liked to talk about, but need not here repeat. Uncle Jimmy recalls, the teamsters were in a better humor after supper. Nobody really paid any attention to the stranger until he declined the slug of bitters that Old Man Locke courteously offered him. Then they wanted to know who he was and where he came from.

He stood up, as tall as a tree, Uncle Jimmy remembers, and told them he was a preacher of the gospel, a-bound for Washington-on-the-Brazos.

"Well," says Old Man Locke, who was strong on religion himself, "you must be a Methodist. Either they're Methodists over thar, or they ain't anything."

"I am," says the preacher, "an unworthy servant of the Methodist Episcopal Church, South. The name is Swan."

"Well," Old Man Locke answered, "I'm a man that takes my religion serious. I'm a blue-light Presbyterian, I am, and so is all my folks. Young man—Reverend, I should say, though you look mighty young and mighty redheaded to be a shepherd—even a Methody shepherd—it mought turn out your luck, one of these days, to sit under ouah preacher, down in Victoria—the Elder Calvin Knox Singletree. When he talks, you can smell hell, brother—that's what you can! And the way Elder Singletree puts it, I like a religion that's a religion, not spoon vittles, or sugar-tits fer babes, but strong meat fer men! A religion, as Elder Singletree says, a man kain get his tushes into. No, young man, you're a foreigner here, and far from home, and you're welcome to yo' share of my grub an' campfire, but you're unfortunate. So are a lot of folks. Elder Singletree's religion is the only religion fer grown folks. No other kind will be preached in my wagon train. But if you want to read us a Psa'm before we turn in, I'm agreeable and the boys will listen."

Uncle Jimmy says they sat quiet while the Reverend Swan read them a scripture and prayed them a prayer; and I found the story briefed in Praxiteles' journal.

Next morning, the rain blew off and the Middle Fork went down, and they got across in good shape; and Old Man Locke sent Uncle Jimmy ahead on a mule to make some arrangements for him in Washington. He rode with Praxiteles, who, Uncle Jimmy remembers, asked all sorts of questions about everything, and they made good time, for before dark they came out on the river, and the ferryman set them across, of a Saturday afternoon.

There was not a great deal to Washington, although the orators referred to it freely as the cradle of Texas independence, the town on the great river the Spaniards call *Brazos de Dios*—Arms of God.

There were some log cabins and barns, and a few clap-boarded houses, the wide whipsawed boards cleated on over the original logs and whitewashed. Some stores were ranked out of alignment; the most elaborate building in sight, a rambling unpainted structure behind a false front, was Gadsen's Saloon and Billiard Parlors. Patient horses stood on three legs in front of it; elsewhere, dejected mules and phlegmatic oxen labored through the mud, drawing high-slung wagons. There was a cotton shed and a platform handy to the river, but the steelyards over the weighing stand hung rusty on a rusty wire, and the dull yellow sky lowered over all. Razorback hogs moved importantly across the road, or stood to scratch their ticks against the corner posts of the buildings. Everywhere there was mud; all the men wore their trousers inside their boots.

Praxiteles came up from the ferry with Uncle Jimmy and rode toward the saloon, from which proceeded loud shouts of laughter and considerable swearing in bad-tempered, drawling voices. Elsewhere, sallow men lounged in front of stores, whittled and chewed tobacco; only around the saloon was there life and movement. As Praxiteles drew in his horse and sat, undecided, looking about him, a man came with great dignity from the saloon, caromed off the hitch rail, and walked into Praxiteles' mare. He leaned against her shoulder, his hand going uncertainly to the rider's knee.

"Well, I declar'," he said, amiably—"I declar'. Gettin' to be so many people in town, a man can't make his way thoo 'em noways." He got his chin up, beamed at the preacher, and said, with interest, "I never seed you befo'. You strangeh hyar? My name's Medary; ev'ybody knows me."

Praxiteles confirmed him. Yes. A pilgrim and a stranger. The Reverend Swan. Would he be so good as to point out the tavern?

The other brought his eyes into coincidence and studied him gravely. Tallest preacher, he remarked, he ever did see. But there wasn't no tavern. Could get a shakedown, now, in Goat Gadsen's place, but nothing fitten for a preacher. He, the man continued, always slept the preachers—that is, the Methodist preachers. He wasn't a Methodist, himself— reckoned he was a kind of backslidden sinner—but his wife was the all-fired out-prayingest Methodist between the Sabine and the Colorado rivers; had a preacher in the house right now. "Come on, preacher," he added hospitably. "Come on. Come on out to my place. I'll show you."

He cast his weight against the mare and paid no attention to Praxiteles' courteous protest. He would walk, he stated. Little walk do him good. He feared he was sort of overtaken. If he'd knowed the preacher was comin', he wouldn't—this he swore roundly—have smoked so many seegyars. He then recognized Uncle Jimmy, and told him to come along, too, and lead his horse for him.

He was a very persuasive man, and Praxiteles was tired, and they went willingly, Mr. Medary hanging to a stirrup leather, and recovering an admirable equilibrium as the heavy walking brought the sweat out on him. They plodded a mile down the road, plunged into the woods, then proceeded between new-cleared land where raw furrows ran under the trees, girdled and dead, to a sprawling house in a grove of moss-draped oaks. It was as good a house as Praxiteles had seen in Texas. Its original logs had been sheathed in weather-boarding; it was roofed with cypress shingles and had a huge stone chimney at each end. All around it ran a deep porch, and the kitchen and outbuildings and barn, as well as the house itself, were smartly white-washed. Chickens and turkeys scratched in the yard, and a whole congregation of potlikker hounds boiled out noisily to greet the master. Hard behind the dogs came two little Negroes; then a couple of tow-headed children, very bashful, and a brisk, neat lady with a humorous dark eye and a firm mouth, evidently mistress of herself and others. An older girl appeared at the door, looked out, and withdrew hastily.

" 'Light down, rev'rend, 'light down!" cried Mr. Medary, now perfectly steady on his legs. "Gimme those saddlebags. Walk right in, seh; you' in yo' own house! . . . Nigger, take the rev'rend's mar'. Rub her down with a snatch of hay befo' you water her, and give her a feed of cawn in the corner stall. . . . She stand quiet in the stable, rev'rend? . . . Nigger, I'll be out to look at her, an' if she ain't bedded right, I'll cut yo' years off and make yo' eat 'em!" he led the way to the house and did the honors: "Mrs. Medary, hyar's the Rev'rend Swan—him that the presidin' elder was tellin' us was coming. . . . Rev'rend, this is Nick, an' this is Bubber, and this is Lucindy. Chillun air the po' man's blessin', rev'rend!. . . Mrs. Medary, whar's Jinny?"

They hustled him into the house. A fine fire snapped and crackled in a deep fireplace, taking the chill out of the wet March air.

By the fire in a rocking chair, with a shawl over his shoulders, sat a lean man with a rusty black store suit which was weather-stained and mottled with age. He got painfully to his feet, extending a limp hand; he had a sad sallow face, thinly bearded, and hot-tempered dyspeptic eyes.

"Hyar's Brother Grebs—Rev'rend Brother Grebs," continued Mr. Medary cordially. "He's passin' thoo, goin' up to Marshall. He was took sick."

"I'm mighty po'ly," agreed the Rev. Elkanah Grebs. The Lord's hand has been heavy on me, brother. Boils, even as Job, and a touch of the bloody flux."

The good man was vastly depressed; the ills of the spirit, he asserted, gravelled him worse than the weaknesses of the flesh. He had proposed to conduct services for the little flock in Washington; they having been without spiritual food since the late Brother Haggers passed to his reward last November. He had sent the word ahead that he would preach tomorrow, and the good folks were making ready to come in, by buggy, oxcart and wagon, from Dan even to Beersheba—that is, from as far west as Brenham, and from Anderson and Big Sandy, the other way. There would surely be young olive branches, born during the winter, for baptism, and probably couples to be church-married— maybe things you wouldn't want to keep waiting. But the Methodist Church, called Gilgal Chapel, was struck by lightning last fall and burned. The cotton warehouse was full up to the rafters. About the only place a gathering might be held was Mr. Gadsen's Saloon and Billiard Parlors; and Reverend Grebs had approached Mr. Gadsen in the matter with confidence, for the faithful those days congregated in eccentric places when the weather was too bad to sit under the trees.

Mr. Gadsen, Praxiteles was informed, hardened his heart like Pharaoh and said he wasn't going to lose his Sunday-afternoon trade for a parcel of howling Methodists; he was a Campbellite himself, and his customers would be put out with him. No, seh. He wasn't even polite about it. And while they talked within, young sinners placed cockleburs under the saddle of the preacher's mule; so that when he came out and mounted, he was flung off into a mud puddle and further humiliated. Here Mr. Medary felt constrained to interrupt. It wasn't, he told Praxiteles, as though the community was down on preachers. They treated them right well—everybody did. That was just a bunch of young hellions who'd been heating their coppers with Goat Gadsen's forty-rod—and sort of hellin' around. They didn't mean anything by it—just boys, reely.

The sad feature, Brother Grebs concluded, was that the good folks would be coming along, and no way to stop them. They'd have that haul over heavy roads—his voice trailed off sadly. Praxiteles, listening with concern, recalled something of his furious uncle's conversation—philosophic reminiscences to the effect that, coming on a new scene, the superior man always does something impressive; something to command public attention—like the time, in Natchez, Colonel Pelham, on arrival, called Colonel Marmaduke Astley out and shot him within an hour. Like the time, again, in his first term with the federal Congress, he caned the congressman from Rhode Island.

Praxiteles announced, a cold fire behind his green eyes: "There'll be services, as God willeth, in this publican's place of business. I'll conduct them myself."

About that time, Uncle Jimmy says, Miss Jinny entered the room, having primped herself up for company; she was the oldest girl in the family, peart as a red heifer, and fat as a butterball—fine a gyu'll as you ever did see, Uncle Jimmy asserted, slapping his leg. It was time she was married off, everybody was saying in those parts; and it was her own fault she wasn't. The young bucks were around her thick as flies in fly time, but she just couldn't seem to make up her mind. The Lord only knew, Uncle Jimmy recollected, how many gougings and kneeings and general ruckuses there had been over her in the settlement. The field was narrowed down to Bud Pike and Jim Pike, two cousins that farmed up the river a ways. They'd had their eye on her, and between them they whipped off the others —being, Uncle Jimmy says, as mean a pair of wildcats as ever came out of the Brazos Bottom—and now they were running each other for her, nip and tuck.

First one would be ahead, and then the other, said Uncle Jimmy; the whole community was watching it, and there were bets made every day in Goat Gadsen's Saloon and Billiard Parlors.

As for the Reverend Praxiteles, he wrote that night in his diary how he was made acquainted, at Mr. Medary's house, with a most comely young lady, Miss Jael Medary; and he notes that, before retiring, he read from the Book of Judges the story of Jael, and the decisive steps Jael took in the case of the soldier Sisera, as celebrated by the great triumphant song Deborah the prophetess made about her on that occasion. It edified him considerably. And he added to his diary: "Genesis ii, 23 & 24. Mayhap the Lord sends me an helpmeet."

Meantime, they all went in to supper.

Never, anywhere, Praxiteles reflected, looking through half-shut lids as Brother Grebs delivered a comprehensive grace, had he seen so much, or such a variety, of food on a table. Whatever else Mr. Medary did with his talents, it was evident that he was a good provider; and when the grace was finished, Mr. Medary exhorted his guests to eat hearty. A man shouldn't let himself die in debt to his stomach, he stated, and he, for one, did not intend to.

"That's right. Plenty more in the kitchen!" cried Mrs. Medary.

Uncle Jimmy remembers that Miss Jinny—only her mother called her Jael—kept looking sideways at the preacher, and he looking back at her, in a way to make you sick. He never could see, Uncle Jimmy remarked, why the women in them days took on so over a preacher. And they still did, he was told.

The family possessed an organ capable of music. It was not in tune, and the dampness had done unfortunate things to its keys, but Miss Jinny was able to coax recognizable melody out of it, and after supper, her father, who, by frequent trips out to the smokehouse—from which he returned wiping his mouth and chewing a clove—maintained himself in a state of geniality, insisted that they sing. His wife reminded him that it was Saturday night, and too near Sunday for ballads and breakdowns, especially with preachers in the house.

Mr. Medary replied that, like nothing on earth, he honed and hankered for a hymn tune.

They placed the lamps and Miss Jinny sat herself to the organ. Praxiteles admired the bronze lights in her hair and the lines of her flat back. He came gallantly near to turn the music, and made bold to recommend a noble hymn of praise, Mount Zion—No. 36. She struck the chords with confident strong hands, and he led boldly:

> "O Love divine, how sweet thou art,
> When shall I find my willing heart
> All taken up by thee?" . . .

Mrs. Medary lifted a thin soprano, some beats behind the rest; Mr. Medary amiably contributed a growling bass, far from the key; and Miss Jinny, whose voice was untrained, but sweet and fresh, came along effectively with Praxiteles' baritone. The Reverend Elkanah, wrapped in a quilt by the fire, beat time with a slippered foot.

Somebody hollered outside, "Hello, the house!" and there entered Mr. Bud Pike and Mr. Jim Pike, two of the ugliest young men Praxiteles had ever seen; when their eyes fell on him, they bristled visibly. One was tall—not so tall as Praxiteles, but tall enough—and very solidly built; he had a broad dark face and hard black eyes, and a shock of hair, well-greased, and huge hairy hands. The other was shorter and more compact, with a bullethead, little piggish eyes, and a flat face, all of him as square and stocky as a blockhouse.

No need for Mr. Medary to whisper, after introducing

them, that they were cousins—for the family favor was strong—and no need to add that they were sparking Miss Jinny—for both looked at her like she was something good to eat—and their enmity to Praxiteles, simply because he was in the room with her, was evident and immediate. He saw, also, the bright blush that rose from Jael's neck to the roots of her hair.

But when Mr. Medary added, behind his hand, that she would be making up her mind which one to choose, right soon, and that the reverend might have a wedding on his hands any day now, Praxiteles was conscious of a wave of revulsion. He realized at once that he didn't want this to happen; he was later to search his soul in prayer over the violence that suddenly filled his heart, without receiving light on the matter.

The singing was resumed, Praxiteles standing manfully in his place by the organ, while Miss Jinny appeared to be nervous. She did not incline her body modestly away from him as he leaned to turn a leaf, and once or twice her hand went up and touched his on the music. When this happened, a pleasant excitement surged in him. The two boys were glooming like thunderclouds.

The atmosphere in the room was no longer friendly; you could, Uncle Jimmy says, fair smell the blood and guts on the floor.

The Reverend Grebs announced that it was his bedtime, and he reckoned his young brother had come a long way and was ready for the shucks—"only, it's not shucks, under this Godly rooftree, brother; it's the finest goose feathers under elegant eiderdown quilts," he explained, so that Mrs. Medary colored with pleasure.

Let them, suggested Brother Grebs, have a lesson, and a sweet season of prayer before they sought their rest; ask a blessing on their labors in the morning.

Here the biggest Pike spoke his first word: "What labors, pahson?"

"Friend," Praxiteles answered him, "it is my intention to hold services at the settlement in the morning."

"Whar-bouts?" asked Mr. Pike.

"It is my intention to request your Mr.—Gadsen?—Gadsen to allow us the use of his place of business for two hours in the morning."

"Does Goat Gadsen know about it? Well, we was just ridin' on. We'll tell him what you want," said Mr. Pike ominously.

Praxiteles thanked him with the blandest air imaginable. "Do so, I beg, Mr. Pike. It is the Lord's work."

They departed without ceremony. Mr. Medary looked at Praxiteles thoughtfully, and the Reverend Grebs said he hoped his afflictions would let him out of bed tomorrow, but he was afraid they wouldn't. Nonetheless, he prayed at length and powerfully, and they all retired.

In the morning, they rode into town; the women and children in a wagon, Reverend Grebs, still feeble, riding with them, and the others on horseback.

Praxiteles hitched his mare to the rack and approached the front of the saloon steadily, his saddlebags, which contained his Bible and his hymn books, in his hand. A dozen unkempt individuals, not all of them sober, observed his approach. Within, the cheerful murmur of godless entertainment ceased. At once the door was crowded.

Two detached themselves from the knot of observers and stood out to meet the preacher—Bud Pike and Jim Pike, the gallants of the night before. Praxiteles was aware of a stiffening of the hair at the back of his neck, and a quiver along his bones, a sort of bugle call to action in his blood, for the aspect of the two was not peaceful. They were squarely in front of him, their arms hanging, but out a little from their bodies, and their faces dark and sneering —what a family resemblance they had, Praxiteles noted. He said, the skin around his mouth feeling stiff, "A good morrow to you, friends!"

"No friend of yours, pahson," snarled Jim Pike.

"That's right," agreed the other.

Praxiteles stopped because another step would have brought him into collision. "Young men—" he began.

"Listen, preacher. What would you do if we was to give you a damn good whippin'?"

"My friends," Praxiteles told them, keeping his voice under control, "if the Lord give me grace, I will bear it. But if He don't, woe to your hides!"

With that, Bud Pike slapped him—a slap at the end of a full-arm swing. Praxiteles might have taken a blow, but a slap, now— A second later, Jim Pike put his head down and charged, butting like a bull. Praxiteles side-stepped. Bud came in, his arms flailing, exactly in time to receive his cousin's bullethead in his stomach. The air went out of Bud with a great "whuff!" and the two fell, entangled, in a mud puddle. Before they could sit up, Praxiteles, his temper flaming like his hair, was upon them; he squatted on Jim Pike's shoulders, whipped a long thigh over his neck and ground his face into the mud. Bud Pike, dizzy from the impact, he seized by the stock as he came to his knees, hauled him close to, and began to buffet him with mighty short-arm punches that rocked his head loose on his shoulders. Jim, underneath him, threshed about like a chicken with a wrung neck, but never really got his head high enough to breathe.

The engagement was like San Jacinto fight in its brevity and violence and its astonishing and improbable outcome. The eagerness and fury of his enemies, together with the soft footing, delivered them into Praxiteles' hand. In time the action would assume legendary proportions, and take its place in the folklore of the region, but Uncle Jimmy Farrow, there present, swears it occurred exactly as he tells it.

It did not last long. The one was smothered and the other's face beat into a bloody pulp. But Praxiteles was conscious of a wild joy, and quite heedless of his cut knuckles. He heard, at first dimly, then with reluctant attention, the genial voice of Mr. Medary, and felt that gentleman's hand on his shoulder.

"Rev'rend! Rev'rend! They got enough, seh, sholy! Don't kill 'em, rev'rend; they's just boys!"

Giving the completely groggy Bud one last terrific backhander in the mouth, Praxiteles flung him away and rose from Jim's back, turning that one over, not gently, with his foot. Jim's face was completely masked with mud, and he made distressed blowing noises through it as he tried to sit up. Bud Pike came to his elbow, spat out a tooth and opened one eye. When Praxiteles looked at him, he lay down again, hastily. And from the saloon fifty men whooped in Homeric laughter.

"Boys, did you see his arms going? Like Old Man Weyser's windmill with the governor off in a blue norther!"

"Ol' Jim, with the reverend sittin' on his head!"

"Make way for the reverend, boys! He's a bobcat with bristles on his belly. He's a cross between a catamount and a alligator!"—this from an enthusiast well drunken, who was immediately suppressed; for the ladies were getting down from the wagons. The men stood silent as Praxiteles Swan came toward them, having retrieved his saddlebags. They made way for him respectfully; some of them touched their hats.

One called, "Oh, Dutch, get the reverend a towel an' a basin, in case he wants to spruce up!"

Behind them walked Mr. Medary, his chest out a foot,

saying to this acquaintance and that: "Reverend Swan, boys, from old Virginyeh. Particular friend of mine—stayin' at my house. They say he's a powerful preacher too."

The ladies followed. Miss Jael Medary, her skirts lifted daintily from the mud, disclosing the neatest ankles in the world, passed her fallen suitors with the effect of shying away from leprosy, but she was not thinking of them; she never thought of them again. Her cheeks flamed deliciously, and her eyes were at once speculative and tender, following the tall figure of Praxiteles Swan.

In Mr. Gadsen's Saloon and Billiard Parlors, saints and willing sinners hustled together with chairs and benches. The Negro bottle washer snatched the goboons out of sight behind the bar.

In his little room at one side, Mr. Goat Gadsen himself brought water and helped in the removal of the worst of the blood and mud with which the Church Militant was spattered; his expert judgment was, the eye where one of Bud's wild swings had landed wouldn't close altogether; he recommended a chunk of raw liver as soon as services was over. And the ladies would be glad to mend his coat, where it was split up the back. Uncle Jimmy passed out the hymn-books.

The Reverend Elkanah Grebs, assisting, said he was miraculously restored in health, and he'd be pleased to deliver the opening prayer.

"You sho'ly smote the Amalekites hip and thigh, brother," he exulted. "'The sword of the Lord and of Gideon!' And what, if I might make so bold, will be yore text this morning?"

"I'll give 'em a lesson from First Samuel, the ninth chapter—how Saul went looking for his father's asses," Praxiteles told him.

Brother Grebs knew his Bible; Uncle Jimmy says he

rubbed his hands and allowed that he couldn't do better. It was the passage describing young Saul as being "from his shoulders and upward . . . higher than any of the people."

"And I don't know what you're looking for, exactly, but I do know what you've found, brother," he added, as Praxiteles pulled his coat on and went into the bar, where the congregation was settled down.

Uncle Jimmy laughed. "Reverend Grebs, he was right about it. He married the new preacher to Miss Jinny the next Sunday morning, and Brother Swan was the first man in Washington County that got married and was not shivareed by the neighbors."

Black-Purple in the Corn

LEO L. WARD

Reverend Leo L. Ward, C.S.C., was born on a farm near Otterbein, Indiana, and attended the University of Notre Dame. He studied theology at Washington, D. C., was ordained to the priesthood as a member of the Community of Holy Cross, and returned to Notre Dame as a teacher of English. He has remained there except for a year of study at Oxford, and is now head of his department.

THERE was a darker shade of green in the corn this morning. Yesterday it was just like it had been the day before, and the day before. But this morning the fields wore a darker color as Sel Ganer looked out over the prairie from where he stood, one hand holding to an iron brace, leaning against the windmill.

Out of the prairie distances it came to him, this new mood, this subtly new color of the fields—a hint of black-purple in the corn—a new richness, a maturity, a fullness of growth in the broad oil-green blades. The wonderful languor of it all drifted into the man's spirit as he looked out at the fields through the lashes of his half-closed eyes. Vaguely he felt a sense of merited leisure, a deep, quiet

From *The Midland,* July-August, 1928. Reprinted by permission of the author.

realization of labors finished. For now the cornplowing was done for the season—those interminable weeks of plowing and plowing up and down the fields.

At last Sel Ganer remembered the white jug beside him. What he had come to the windmill for was to get a morning's supply of water before he should go out to the hayfield. He was going onto the mower this morning, for the hay was just ready to be cut. The haying would not be monotonous, endless, like the cornplowing had been. He did not mind the haying much.

He picked up the white jug by the old hame strap that was fastened to its looped handle. He had filled it a good quarter of an hour ago, before he had started to look at the cornfields—and had forgotten it since. . . . Then he moved off toward the barn to get his team for the mowing.

"You got everythin' now?" asked Sel's father, who came through the farmyard gate with two buckets of milk as Sel started to open the door of the barn.

"Yeah, everythin'."

"How's the sickle?"

"Sickle's all right, I guess. Sharpened it the other day, and hain't mowed nothin' much with it since."

Sel reached over the barn door and unhooked the latch. The elder Ganer, a little old man with soft, quiet eyes and a heedless stumbling way of walking, hurried off to where the mower stood in a corner of the barnyard.

"Guess it'll do," he said, coming back from the mower as Sel was leading his second horse out of the barn. "Could be a little sharper, but guess it'll do. Hain't got much time for sharpenin' it, anyways. We got to get into that hay pretty quick, the way it looks. Gettin' pretty ripe in places."

"Yeah, wouldn't wonder." Sel led his horses over to the other corner of the barn where the watering tank stood. And a few minutes later he was hitching his team to the mower. Then he went out of the gate with the white jug hanging from the hames of one of the horses.

As Sel Ganer rode along the back pasture lane the corn came up to the fence beside him. Once or twice his horses tried to reach their heads over the fence as they walked along, hungry for a bite of the dark green blades. He was vaguely pleased by the heavy odor of the corn and by the dark green walls that crowded up to the fence on both sides of him. He could see down the rows as he passed, and underneath, the dry gray soil was dark with almost uniform shadow cast by the big green blades above.

Once he stopped the team, raised himself on the mower seat, and looked out over the corn. He could hear the horses tearing the blades from the stalks near the fence, but he let them go on eating, while he kept gazing over the dark green field flashing in the sun everywhere about him. At last he sat down on his mower, backed the team away from the wire fence, slapped the lines carelessly on their glistening rumps and moved idly on toward the meadow.

Arkansas

RAYMOND WEEKS

Raymond Weeks was born at Tabor, Iowa, in 1863, but spent his boyhood in Jackson County, Missouri. He studied at Harvard and the University of Paris, later becoming Professor of Romance Languages at Columbia University. In 1917 he published *Ode to France,* and he was decorated by the French government for service to the Allied cause. Humor, rich appreciation of his Missouri regional background, and mastery of style mark his *Boy's Own Arithmetic* (1924) and *The Hound-Tuner of Callaway* (1927). He now lives on his farm near Manakin, Virginia.

THIS is not a story. It is not a history. It is a fact. One cannot say that Arkansas belonged to Alphonse Jaccard or that Alphonse belonged to her. They belonged to each other. In all the annals of Jackson County there is no record of a more mutual affection or of a more mysterious end. A few of the oldest inhabitants still remember their close union, their constant companionship, their disappearance in a blaze of glory.

It all began at the County Fair. The Martin hogs had won all the first prizes except one, while the Jaccard hogs had received only seconds. Tom Martin began all the trouble. As he stood looking at his blue-ribboned grunters he declared:

"In the matter of pigs we can beat the world."

Now, this was wrong of Tom. We ought to be modest in victory. Alphonse Jaccard spoke up:

"Hum! anybody can raise fat hogs! As for speed and sense, your hogs ain't nowhere!"

In judging this remark of Alphonse, you should bear in mind the long line of Jaccards and their glorious record: the walls of their parlor were hung with blue ribbons. Since the death of old Mr. Jaccard four years before, the eclipse of the family had begun. Not that no ambitious Jaccards were left; there were plenty of them—five sons and four daughters, all reared in veneration of the past. But victory avoided them. For three consecutive seasons the County Fair had left the Jaccards broken in spirit, baffled. They returned home in silence and hardly spoke all winter. They did not love one another less for their misfortunes—only, what use was there for words? Would they bring back lost glory? So you will understand Alphonse—you will understand him and sympathize with him when he said:

"Hum! anybody can raise fat hogs. As for speed and sense, your hogs ain't nowhere!"

Tom Martin answered insolently:

"I'll run my pigs against yourn this minute or at the next fair!"

And Alphonse Jaccard replied:

"Next fair, so be it! A race of yearlings!"

Thus was the gauntlet thrown down in the presence of bearded men and breathless women.

Excitement spread throughout Linwood, throughout the county. Two days later, neighbors came to the Jaccard farm to talk with Alphonse. They learned that he had gone, nor would the family say where. Tom Martin declared that Alphonse had left the country for good. But just wait, Tom! wait and watch. Fate has something in store for you! One cannot forever trample upon the unfortunate.

Now of course you wonder where Alphonse was. Where do you suppose? Five days after the close of the County Fair he was riding Bonny, his best saddle horse, through the valleys of Arkansas! That's speed for you! The valleys did not delay him long. His proud spirit was not looking for valleys, but pigs. He made for the mountains. Nothing stopped him, neither fine cooking nor beautiful maidens nor enchanting scenery. He rode with set features and indifferent eye. People marveled at this cold, handsome young man from the north country. His bearing, his horse and saddle and the three hounds that accompanied him, bespoke the gentleman. Perhaps he was a fugitive from justice? Yes! that must be it! Brave men admired him, soft-eyed women sighed when he passed. The whole State of Arkansas was his for the asking. But it was not the State of Arkansas that Alphonse wanted!

Among the cone-like small mountains of Arkansas live, as you of course know, the famous wild pigs of America. These noble beasts formerly possessed the entire northern continent. They held their own against the Indians, but the Pale Faces, with their cruel and treacherous firearms, forced them slowly into the mountain fastness of Arkansas. The pigs would never have yielded in fair fight, but their generous nature hates treachery and cowardice. They retired, therefore, more through contempt than fear.

Travelers and scientists who want to study the pig under conditions approaching, though not equaling, his former splendor, are accustomed to go to Arkansas. There they see him master of a wild and beautiful domain, all of whose peaks and valleys, rivers and lakes, caverns, forests, paths, thickets and lairs are as familiar to him as your pockets are to you. In his architecture he differs notably from the degenerate brutes called pigs which have been imported from Europe. He is long, thin, wiry, made of bones, nerves and muscles. He can run so fast as to make a dog seem a turtle. Accordingly, if he runs from dogs, as he sometimes does, it is purely out of love of running. At any moment he can turn around and shake any dog into thistledown. His sense of hearing is as remarkable as his sense of sight. His intelligence is as great as his beauty. In short, he is a pig that is a pig!

It will never be known how Alphonse managed to capture a sucking pig of this illustrious stock. That he did so and escaped alive is proof that he was a hero. He always refused to tell how he did it. We can only imagine his seizure of the tiny treasure, its squeals, his mad flight to where his horse waited, the pursuit through the mountain fastnesses of two hundred indignant and infuriated relatives of the victim, their cries and grunts and oaths and snorts and jibberings, the labored breathing of the horse fleeing from death and horror! No other man ever accomplished such a feat. The bones of many who tried it are preserved as trophies by the pigs of Arkansas.

No sow ever cared for her baby with greater tenderness than Alphonse for his little prisoner. He carried it at first in his bosom, later on a soft bed of cotton in a sack which he hung from his neck. He stopped at every cabin and house to give it warm milk, and taught it to drink from a bottle. He petted it and talked to it for hours as he rode. The little thing wept for days, and called for its mama. At last, however, it began to nestle close to his body, especially at nightfall. Alphonse sang it to sleep with old French songs which he had learned from his mother.

What saved the life of the captured baby was not so much

the care which it received as the affection back of that care, for Alphonse, when he had definitely escaped from his pursuers and had been able to look at and to fondle his captive, felt that it was the most intelligent and lovable little creature in the world. Accordingly, he loved it with what proved to be the passion of his life. They both longed for sympathy and love. They were made for each other.

Not until he had crossed the frontier into Missouri did Alphonse feel safe from pursuit and arrest at the hands of the Governor of Arkansas. What a relief to reach his native State, to be able to caress and look freely at the baby pig! He took it out from its sack, petted its curly brown hair, its silky ears, pressed it against his cheek and neck. He noted in detail its beauty, looked into its deep, intelligent eyes and, transported out of himself, he felt that only one name would fit the lovely creature: he named her Arkansas!

There was a memorable scene one night at the Jaccard house. The family had just finished supper when the beat of hoofs was heard coming rapidly. They all rushed to the door with one name on their lips. Alphonse arrived, tossed the rein to the hired man, got down from the saddle with care, holding something in his arms, caressed an instant with one hand the face of his faithful Bonny and hurried into the house. He embraced all the family, motioned to have the door and window blinds closed, then drew tenderly from the sack the mite of a piglet and exclaimed in French:

"This is Miss Arkansas! Long life to her!"

He sat down and held her in his arms. The family crowded around.

For a few moments Arkansas lay there blinking at the light and the strange faces, then she closed her eyes and tried to bury herself in Alphonse's bosom. He pressed her to his neck and cheek, humming the low song that she knew best. She did not squeal, as vulgar pigs do, but uttered a sweet little plaint, interrupted by tiny sobs, while a tear rolled from each eye. She was thinking of her mama, her brothers and sisters and brave family in the Far Country.

Needless to say, Arkansas slept that night and for many weeks in a snug box, close by Alphonse's bed. He gave her warm milk and tended her like a sick infant. If any one had suggested fixing a place for her in one of the stables, Alphonse would have said to him: "Go there yourself!"

I will not delay you with a long account of Arkansas' education, although the subject would prove of interest to pedagogues. Let it suffice to give a few details. At the age of less than three weeks, she knew how to eat from a bowl without putting her feet in it. She had inherited all of the native neatness of the pigs of Arkansas. Her feet and skin she kept immaculate, which added to her beauty, for she had a lovely clear pink complexion. By the time she was a month old, she understood French perfectly and could already speak several words, such as: "Hein?", which means: "Excuse me, Sir (or Madam), what did you say?" Or: "Allons!", which means: "If you have no objection, Sir (or Madam), let us start." Could you have done as well at the age of one month? She also knew how to distinguish from the sound of the horn the different meals—breakfast, dinner, supper. While not expansive toward visitors, she received them with courtesy and was equally polite to all. She soon began to pick up English and in time understood it quite well, though she naturally preferred French and her own language.

From the first, Arkansas was a prime favorite. The dogs idolized her. They used to run to her and kiss her good morning. They played hide-and-seek and tag with her. It was a delight to watch these games. She enjoyed almost equal popularity with the cats, chickens, ducks, geese, horses, cows and mules. They all regarded her as a princess.

But Arkansas' great favorite, her sunlight and her comfort, was, and remained, Alphonse! She worshipped him. She followed him all over the farm, keeping close behind him and talking to him almost continuously. Before she was two months old, he had taught her to start running at a signal and to return at another. Her progress was rapid.

There was on the farm only one animal with which Arkansas refused to have anything to do, and that was the pigs. She despised and hated them as coarse, swollen, dirty, loathsome, degenerate caricatures of a noble race. She never went into their lot nor paid any attention to them, although they often spoke to her through the fence.

Winter passed, spring, midsummer. September arrived, the month of the great trial! The heart of Jackson County almost ceased to beat, so intense was the excitement. There were more than thirty pigs entered for the speed contest. Large wagers were put up, with the odds favoring Arkansas, partly because of her family descent and romantic history, partly because no one was more respected and beloved than the handsome, silent young man of twenty-five, who was her master, Alphonse Jaccard, whose name stood as a synonym for honesty, generosity and loyalty.

It had been the happiest year of Alphonse's life. For the last week before the great event, he had slept in the open air near Arkansas' little house. He feared trouble. Then, too, the moon was approaching full, and he had noticed that at such times Arkansas seemed to be melancholy, that she remembered then more than at other times the Far Country where her family waited for her. She did not conceal her longing from him. On the contrary, she used to lean against his leg with a soft pressure when they stood watching the full moon rise at bedtime, and she used to say, looking off to the Southland with her nose in the air: "Ah! Ah!," which was her pronunciation of Arkansas, the Far Country.

The day for the great race arrived. All of the beauty and chivalry of the county were gathered there, as well as everybody else. The farms were entirely deserted. One of the Jaccard boys had ridden Bonny over to the fair early in the day, to be sure that all arrangements had been made. Alphonse came in a big wagon with the rest of the family, including Arkansas, to whom he had carefully explained what was to take place. They planned so as to arrive only a few minutes before the race, whereas most of Arkansas' rivals had been there for days, the judges having granted permission for all entries to become acquainted with the track at times when it was not in use.

The great race was to be the final event of the afternoon. An immense throng was present, fully two thousand persons. The grandstand was packed with sturdy farmers, their red-faced wives, rosy-cheeked daughters and brown-cheeked boys. Hundreds sat and stood in wagons or perched on the branches of trees. There was no breeze. The dust of previous races hung in a soft haze over the landscape. The squealing and grunting of the entries for the race could be heard, mingled with loud exclamations and tender cajolings of their masters and seconds.

Emotion rose to the breaking point half an hour before the race. Where was Alphonse? Where was Arkansas? The question passed from lip to lip. As for the Martins, they were there in force. Tom looked pale, as was inevitable when the reputation and the glory of the family were at stake. His father, the Major, his mother and his sister Bessie, tried to remain calm, but showed their nervousness.

At last the Jaccards and Arkansas arrived. The rumor spread like lightning: "They have come!" The families of the other entries turned pale. Finally, from the judges' stand came the signal: "Get ready, gentlemen!"

Then followed the loudest clamor of squeals and grunts

that has ever been heard at a race course. The owners and attendants dragged, pulled, pushed and drove to the track the more than thirty entries, and one is forced to admit that they—I mean the entries—were a handsome lot of porkers. Each one had a number tied about his neck and a rope to a hind foot. The rope was to be detached at the last moment, when the chief judge should cry: "One! two! three! Go!!!" The mob of the entries crowded to the inside of the track, to get the advantage. Where so much is at stake, no precaution should be neglected.

A murmur of admiration burst from the immense throng when Alphonse and Arkansas appeared, walking side by side, she being unattached by any vile and dishonoring rope. They walked slowly, conversing as quietly as if on their farm. He was calling her his treasure, his delight, his darling, his Arkansas, and she looked up at him out of her black eyes and said: "Have no fear, Alphonse!"

She paid not the least attention to the grunting, squealing horde of her rivals, but one could see that her nose curled in contempt.

It is now necessary to mention one thing about Arkansas which I have intentionally deferred. I have more than once spoken of her beauty, which was of the purest type, but I have not stated that her two left legs were slightly shorter than their right mates. This was due to one of the peculiar habits of the Arkansas pigs. Allow me to explain.

For centuries these pigs, whose social life is most complex, have recognized the principle of private ownership of property. Each family or clan owns a hill or mountain, where its members pass their time. A member of another clan is forbidden to walk or forage on that mountain, unless by special invitation. Furthermore, the mountains are cone-shaped. But this is not all: the families or clans always walk or run around their mountain in the same direction. The result of this is that all Arkansas pigs, without exception, have their legs shorter on one side than the other. Time is lacking to enlarge on this well-known fact, whose origins lie concealed behind the mists of antiquity. All Arkansas pigs are either lefters or righters, and naturally run on a curve. Any pig can run straight!

Now, Alphonse, with his keen intelligence, saw the bearing of this fact. He accordingly stole his prize from among the lefters: Arkansas was a lefter. You will readily see the immense advantage which her form of architecture gave her on a race course where the contestants had the judges, and consequently the inside of the track, on their left hand.

The fated moment arrived. The chief judge, Colonel Milt McGee, proud of his role, called in a tremendous voice: "Are you ready? One! Two! Three! Go!!!" Oh! my friends, what a race was there! The squealing, squirming mob was off, launched by violent kicks. The crowd arose en masse. Their shouts shook the hills and would have been heard clear to the Missouri River, if there had been any one there to hear them. Against a background of unsurpassed beauty a great historical event was taking place. The spectators knew this. They also knew that they were present looking at it. Accordingly their excitement and enthusiasm swept silence off the earth!

As I have said, the contestants had started in the mad race. Each one had been told to do or die. The people looked down on a surging mass of rumps, tails and flopping ears. Never since the time of the Greeks had so much vieing ambition torn along a race course. Never had contestants talked so much to one another as they ran, so intense was their excitement.

But, you ask, what of Arkansas? She and her master had taken their place on the outer side, in the most unfavorable position. At the moment of starting, Alphonse, who was bending over Arkansas, said in her ear: "Go, little treasure! Go, little angel!" And she went! She was built for it! Being constructed to run on a curve, she fitted the race track, and being thin—an enemy might have said too thin—her flight through the air caused almost no friction. She did not appear to be running; she seemed to glide through the air, close to the earth, but not touching it and not of it. The Martins, where were they? And the other entries? They seemed to be standing still, or even running backward, when Arkansas passed them. As she swept by the grandstand on the first lap, not one of her rivals had even come into sight at the bend of the track! It was only when she passed right in front of you like a cannon ball that you could catch a glimpse of her little black hoofs walking on the air. She passed as a flash from a mirror would pass, yet she kept her bearings, and, as she swept by an island of French where Alphonse and the family stood, they thought they saw her wink at them!

Oh! the love of a pig! the unequalled, the magnificent Arkansas!

She ran faster and faster. When she passed by on the third and supposedly last lap she was going so rapidly that the judges' hats blew off. She knew that the race was won, but she saw in front of her the vile mob of her rivals who were almost an entire lap behind. She gave a little flirt of her hind-quarters, just to signal to the judges that she knew what she was doing, and tore on around the dizzy track for a fourth time. She finished the extra lap amidst a frenzied scene of enthusiasm that shook the earth. With cries of "Arkansas! Arkansas!," the vast crowd surged over the track. But she did not hear their cries. She was in the arms of Alphonse, who was weeping like an infant. Ah! Alphonse! why did you not die that moment?

At last the judges, led by Colonel McGee, forced their

way to where Arkansas and the family stood. The Colonel himself wound her glorious neck with streamers of blue ribbon, while another judge tied a tuft to her tail. She received with becoming modesty these badges of victory. They all noticed that she was not breathing faster than in repose, and that she had not turned a hair. The judges also decked with blue ribbons the broad straw hat of Alphonse, the lapel of his coat, his happy mother and sister and even the saddle of Bonny.

The great sun went down through the golden dust and the crowd finally began to disperse. Arkansas and Alphonse had left the race track. She had leaped into the wagon unaided. Alphonse had followed and sat down by her. At that moment she beheld, pale and ghostly through the haze, the full orb of the rising moon. She was seen to whisper something into Alphonse's ear, to give him a single, tender glance, then to jump from the wagon and start off, running toward the west. Alphonse turned deathly pale. He not only had heard what she had whispered, he knew her—he knew her from the life lines on her hoofs to the hair on her back. With a mere wave of farewell to his mother, he leaped out of the wagon, unhitched Bonny, mounted her like a flash and was gone! The assembled thousands stood spellbound. They saw Arkansas running rapidly, her blue trophies fluttering in the air. She turned her head at times to see if Alphonse was following. Indeed he was! Never had Bonny run as then, except perhaps the night when they stole the baby pig. The throng watched them breathlessly, until at the crest of a hill they saw faintly a last flutter of the blue ribbon on Alphonse's hat; then they broke as one man, rushed to their swift saddle horses, and made off in a mad pursuit of Alphonse and Arkansas.

Ride hard, brave men and courageous boys! Gallop, horses! Cut into tatters the prairies and the fields! You do not know that the flutter of blue over the hill was the last you are ever to see of the unfortunate Alphonse Jaccard! . . .

There are those who will tell you, my listeners, that this whole affair is only a dream—that it never happened! They were not present. Do not believe them!

For months, tales drifted in from the Indians and traders to the west and southwest of us—tales of a phantom pig and a spectre horseman, of their furious course, of beseeching cries, songs and whistlings heard in the night. Piously and with sinking hearts we pieced together these rumors. Alas! there could be no doubt! Arkansas, running true to her architecture, had described a vast curve, which turned gradually toward the south, with all the inevitability of mathematics! Finally, an Indian brought in the hat of Alphonse, still decked, O pathos! with a piece of blue ribbon. He had found it in the direction of the Verdigris River, two hundred miles away! Then the most stupid among us understood. Arkansas had transcribed her inherited curve across the limitless prairies and desolate plains of Kansas Territory, down through the corner of Indian Territory and into her native State of Arkansas, carrying in her wake ¹ beloved master.

The House of the Far and Lost

THOMAS WOLFE

Thomas Wolfe was born at Asheville, North Carolina, in 1900, and died at Baltimore, Maryland, in 1938, one of the acknowledged literary masters of his generation. Experience of his boyhood and youth is powerfully expressed in his first novel, *Look Homeward, Angel* (1929); perhaps even more than his later books this work reveals his retentive memory, energy, and poetic feeling for words and rhythms. As a student at the University of North Carolina he was primarily interested in drama, and wrote three plays, in one of which he acted. He followed this interest in graduate work at Harvard, where he obtained a master's degree in 1922. From 1924 to 1930 he was an instructor in English at Washington Square College in New York City. Parts of the following years were spent in England and on the continent. The best comments on Wolfe's work are his own, in *The Story of a Novel* (1936) and in portions of the posthumous *You Can't Go Home Again* (1940).

IN THE fall of that year I lived out about a mile from town in a house set back from the Ventor Road. The house was called a "farm"—Hill-top Farm, or Far-end Farm, or some such name as that—but it was really no farm at all. It was a magnificent house of the weathered gray stone they have in that country, as if in the very quality of

From *Scribner's Magazine*, July, 1934. Reprinted by permission.

the wet heavy air there is the soft thick gray of time itself, sternly yet beautifully soaking down forever on you—and enriching everything it touches—grass, foliage, brick, ivy, the fresh moist color of the people's faces, and old gray stone with the incomparable weathering of time.

The house was set back off the road at a distance of several hundred yards, possibly a quarter mile, and one reached it by means of a road bordered by rows of tall trees which arched above the road, and which made me think of home at night when the stormy wind howled in their tossed branches. On each side of the road were the rugby fields of two of the colleges and in the afternoon I could look out and down and see the fresh moist green of the playing fields, and watch young college fellows, dressed in their shorts and jerseys, and with their bare knees scurfed with grass and turf as they twisted, struggled, swayed, and scrambled for a moment in the scrimmage-circle, and then broke free, running, dodging, passing the ball as they were tackled, filling the moist air with their sharp cries of sport. They did not have the desperate, the grimly determined, the almost professional earnestness that the college teams at home have; their scurfed and muddy knees, their swaying scrambling scrimmages, the swift breaking away and running, their panting breath and crisp clear voices gave them the appearance of grown-up boys.

Once when I had come up the road in the afternoon while they were playing, the ball got away from them and came bounding out into the road before me, and I ran after it to retrieve it as we used to do when passing a field where boys were playing baseball. One of the players came over to the edge of the field and stood there waiting with his hands upon his hips while I got the ball: he was panting hard, his face was flushed, and his blond hair tousled, but when I threw the ball to him, he said "Thanks

very much!" crisply and courteously—getting the same
sound into the word *"very"* that they got in *"American,"*
a sound that always repelled me a little because it seemed to
have some scornful aloofness and patronage in it.

For a moment I watched him as he trotted briskly away
on to the field again: the players stood there waiting, panting, casual, their hands upon their hips; he passed the ball
into the scrimmage, the pattern swayed, rocked, scrambled,
and broke sharply out in open play again, and everything
looked incredibly strange, near, and familiar.

I felt that I had always known it, that it had always been
mine, and that it was as familiar to me as everything I had
seen or known in my childhood. Even the texture of the
earth looked familiar, and felt moist and firm and springy
when I stepped on it, and the stormy howling of the wind
in that avenue of great trees at night was wild and desolate
and demented as it had been when I was eight years old
and could lie in my bed at night and hear the great oaks
howling on the hill above my father's house.

The name of the people in the house was Coulson: I made
arrangements with the woman at once to come and live
there: she was a tall, weathered-looking woman of middle
age, we talked together in the hall. The hall was made of
marble flags and went directly out onto a gravelled walk.

The woman was crisp, cheerful, and worldly-looking. She
was still quite handsome. She wore a well-cut skirt of
woollen plaid, and a silk blouse: when she talked she kept
her arms folded because the air in the hall was chilly, and
she held a cigarette in the fingers of one hand. A shaggy
brown dog came out and nosed upward toward her hand
as she was talking and she put her hand upon its head and
scratched it gently. When I told her I wanted to move in
the next day, she said briskly and cheerfully:

"Right you are! You'll find everything ready when you

get here!" Then she asked if I was at the university. I said no, and added, with a feeling of difficulty and naked desolation, that I was a "writer," and was coming there to work. I was twenty-four years old.

"Then I am sure that what you do will be *very, very* good!" she said cheerfully and decisively. "We have had several Americans in the house before and all of them were very clever! All the Americans we have had here were very clever people," said the woman. "I'm sure that you will like it." Then she walked to the door with me to say good-bye. As we stood there, there was the sound of a small motorcar coming to a halt and in a moment a girl came swiftly across the gravel space outside and entered the hall. She was tall, slender, very lovely, but she had the same bright hard look in her eye that the woman had, the same faint, hard smile around the edges of her mouth.

"Edith," the woman said in her crisp, curiously incisive tone, "this young man is an American—he is coming here tomorrow." The girl looked at me for a moment with her hard bright glance, thrust out a small gloved hand, and shook hands briefly, a swift firm greeting.

"Oh! How d'ye do!" she said. "I hope you will like it here." Then she went on down the hall, entered a room on the left, and closed the door behind her.

Her voice had been crisp and certain like her mother's, but it was also cool, young, and sweet, with music in it, and later as I went down the road, I could still hear it.

That was a wonderful house, and the people there were wonderful people. Later, I could not forget them. I seemed to have known them all my life, and to know all about their lives. They seemed as familiar to me as my own blood and I knew them with a knowledge that went deep below the roots of thought or memory. We did not talk together often, or tell any of our lives to one another. It will be very hard to tell about it—the way we felt and lived together in that house—because it was one of those simple and profound experiences of life which people seem always to have known when it happens to them, but for which there is no language.

And yet, like a child's half-captured vision of some magic country he has known, which haunts his days with strangeness and the sense of imminent, glorious rediscovery, the word that would unlock it all seems constantly to be almost on our lips, waiting just outside the gateway of our memory, just a shape, a phrase, a sound away the moment that we choose to utter it—but when we try to say the thing, something fades within our mind like fading light, and something melts within our grasp like painted smoke, and something goes forever when we try to touch it.

The nearest I could come to it was this: in that house I sometimes felt the greatest peace and solitude that I had ever known. But I always knew the other people in the house were there. I could sit in my sitting-room at night and hear nothing but the stormy moaning of the wind outside in the great trees, the small gaseous flare and jet from time to time of the coal fire burning in the grate—and silence, strong living lonely silence that moved and waited in the house at night—and I would always know that they were there.

I did not have to hear them enter or go past my door, nor did I have to hear doors close or open in the house, or listen to their voices: if I had never seen them, heard them, spoken to them, it would have been the same—I should have known they were there.

It was something I had always known, and had known it would happen to me, and now it was there with all the strangeness and dark mystery of an awaited thing. I knew them, felt them, lived among them with a familiarity that had no need of sight or word or speech. And the memory of that house and of my silent fellowship with all the people there was somehow mixed with an image of dark time. It was one of those sorrowful and unchanging images which, among all the blazing stream of images that passed constantly their stream of fire across my mind, was somehow fixed, detached, and everlasting, full of a sorrow, certitude, and mystery that I could not fathom, but that wore forever on it the old sad light of waning day—a light from which all the heat, the violence, and the substance of furious dusty day had vanished, and was itself like time, unearthly-of-the-earth, remote, detached, and everlasting.

And that fixed and changeless image of dark time was this: in an old house of time I lived alone, and yet had other people all around me, and they never spoke to me, or I to them. They came and went like silence in the house, but I always knew that they were there. I would be sitting by a window in a room, and I would know then they were moving in the house, and darkness, sorrow, and strong silence dwelt within us, and our eyes were quiet, full of sorrow, peace, and knowledge, and our faces dark, our tongues silent, and we never spoke. I could not remember how their faces looked, but they were all familiar to me as my father's face, and we had known one another forever, and we lived together in the ancient house of time, dark time, and silence, sorrow, certitude, and peace were in us. Such was the image of dark time that was to haunt my life thereafter, and into which, somehow, my life among the people in that house had passed.

In the house that year there lived, besides myself and Morison, the Coulsons, the father and mother and their daughter, and three men who had taken rooms together, and who were employed in a factory where motorcars were made, two miles from town.

I think the reason that I could never forget these people later and seemed to know them all so well was that there was in all of them something ruined, lost, or broken—some precious and irretrievable quality which had gone out of them and which they could never get back again. Perhaps that was the reason that I liked them all so much, because with ruined people it is either love or hate: there is no middle way. The ruined people that we like are those who desperately have died, and lost their lives because they loved life dearly, and had that grandeur that makes such people spend prodigally the thing they love the best, and risk and lose their lives because it is so precious to them, and die at length because the seeds of life were in them. It is only the people who love life in this way who die—and these are the ruined people that we like.

The people in the house were people who had lost their lives because they loved the earth too well, and somehow had been slain by their hunger. And for this reason I liked them all, and could not forget them later: there seemed to have been some magic which had drawn them all together to the house, as if the house itself was a magnetic center for lost people.

Certainly, the three men who worked at the motorcar factory had been drawn together for this reason. Two were still young men in their early twenties. The third man was much older. He was a man past forty, his name was Nicholl, he had served in the army during the war and had attained the rank of captain.

He had the spare, alert, and jaunty figure that one often finds in army men, an almost professional military quality that somehow seemed to set his figure upon a horse as if he had grown there, or had spent a lifetime in the cavalry. His face also had the same lean, bitten, professional military quality: his speech, although good-natured and very friendly, was clipped, incisive, jerky, and sporadic, his lean weather-beaten face was deeply, sharply scarred and sunken in the flanks, and he wore a small cropped mustache, and displayed long frontal teeth when he smiled—a spare, gaunt, toothy, yet attractive smile.

His left arm was withered, shrunken, almost useless, part of his hand and two of the fingers had been torn away by the blast or explosion which had destroyed his arm, but it was not this mutilation of the flesh that gave one the sense of a life that had been ruined, lost, and broken irretrievably. In fact, one quickly forgot his physical injury: his figure looked so spare, lean, jaunty, well-conditioned in its energetic fitness that one never thought of him as a cripple, nor pitied him for any disability. No: the ruin that one felt in him was never of the flesh, but of the spirit. Something seemed to have been exploded from his life—it was not the nerve-centers of his arm, but of his soul, that had been destroyed. There was in the man somewhere a terrible dead vacancy and emptiness, and that spare, lean figure that he carried so well seemed only to surround this vacancy like a kind of shell.

He was always smartly dressed in well-cut clothes that set well on his trim spruce figure. He was always in good spirits, immensely friendly in his clipped spare way, and he laughed frequently—a rather metallic cackle which came suddenly and ended as swiftly as it had begun. He seemed, somehow, to have locked the door upon dark care and worry, and to have flung the key away—to have lost, at the same time that he lost more precious things, all the fretful doubts and perturbations of the conscience most men know.

Now, in fact, he seemed to have only one serious project in his life. This was to keep himself amused, to keep himself constantly amused, to get from his life somehow the last atom of entertainment it could possibly yield, and in this project the two young men who lived with him joined in with an energy and earnestness which suggested that their employment in the motorcar factory was just a necessary evil which must be borne patiently because it yielded them the means with which to carry on a more important business, the only one in which their lives were interested— the pursuit of pleasure.

And in the way in which they conducted this pursuit, there was an element of deliberate calculation, concentrated earnestness, and focal intensity of purpose that was astounding, grotesque, and unbelievable, and that left in the mind of one who saw it a formidable and disquieting memory because there was in it almost the madness of desperation, the deliberate intent of men to cover up or seek oblivion at any cost of effort from some hideous emptiness of the soul.

Captain Nicholl and his two young companions had a little motorcar so small that it scuttled up the road, shot around and stopped in the gravel by the door with the abruptness of a wound-up toy. It was astonishing that three men could wedge themselves into this midget of a car, but wedge themselves they did, and used it to the end of its capacity, scuttling away to work in it in the morning, and scuttling back again when work was done, and scuttling away to London every Saturday, as if they were determined to wrest from this small motor, too, the last ounce of pleasure to be got from it.

Finally, Captain Nicholl and his two companions had made up an orchestra among them, and this they played in every night when they got home. One of the young men, who was a tall fellow with blond hair which went back in even corrugated waves across his head as if it had been marcelled, played the piano, the other, who was slight and dark, and had black hair, performed upon a saxophone, and Captain Nicholl himself took turns at thrumming furiously on a banjo, or rattling a tattoo upon the complex arrangement of trap drums, bass drums, and clashing cymbals that surrounded him.

They played nothing but American jazz music or sobbing crooner's rhapsodies or nigger blues. Their performance was astonishing. Although it was contrived solely for their own amusement, they hurled themselves into it with all the industrious earnestness of professional musicians employed by a night club or a dance hall to furnish dance music for the patrons. The little dark fellow who played the saxophone would bend and weave prayerfully with his grotesque instrument, as the fat gloating notes came from its unctuous throat, and from time to time he would sway in a half circle, or get up and prance forward and back in rhythm to the music as the saxophone players in dance orchestras sometimes do.

Meanwhile the tall blond fellow at the piano would sway and bend above the keys, glancing around from time to time with little nods and smiles as if he were encouraging an orchestra of forty pieces or beaming happily and in an encouraging fashion at a dance floor crowded with paying customers.

While this was going on, Captain Nicholl would be thrumming madly on the strings of a banjo. He kept the instrument gripped somehow below his withered arm, fingering the end strings with his two good fingers, knocking the tune out with his good right hand, and keeping time with a beating foot. Then with a sudden violent movement he would put the banjo down, snatch up the sticks of the trap drum, and begin to rattle out a furious accompaniment, beating the bass drum with his foot meanwhile, and reaching over to smash cymbals, chimes, and metal rings from time to time. He played with a kind of desperate fury, his mouth fixed in a strange set grin, his bright eyes burning with a sharp wild glint of madness.

They sang as they played, bursting suddenly into the refrain of some popular song with the same calculated spontaneity and spurious enthusiasm of the professional orchestra, mouthing the words of Negro blues and jazz with an obvious satisfaction, with an accent which was remarkably good, and yet which had something foreign and inept in it, which made the familiar phrases of American music sound almost as strange in their mouths as if an orchestra of skilful patient Japanese were singing them.

They sang:

> "Yes, sir! That's my baby
> Yes, sir! Don't mean maybe
> Yes, sir! That's my baby now!"

or:

> "Oh, it aint gonna rain no more, no more
> It aint gonna rain no more"

or:

> "I got dose blu-u-ues"—

the young fellow at the piano rolling his eyes around in a ridiculous fashion, and mouthing out the word "blues" extravagantly as he sang it, the little dark fellow bending forward in an unctuous sweep as the note came gloating fatly from the horn, and Captain Nicholl swaying sideways in his chair as he strummed upon the banjo strings, and improvising a mournful accompaniment of his own, somewhat as follows: "I got dose blu-u-ues! Yes, suh! Oh! I got dose blues! Yes, suh! I sure have got 'em—dose blu-u-ues— blu-u-ues—blu-u-ues!"—his mouth never relaxing from its strange fixed grin, nor his eyes from their bright set stare of madness as he swayed and strummed and sang the words that came so strangely from his lips.

It was a weird scene, an incredible performance, and somehow it pierced the heart with a wild nameless pity, an infinite sorrow and regret.

Something precious, irrecoverable had gone out of them, and they knew it. They fought the emptiness in them with this deliberate, formidable, and mad intensity of a calculated gaiety, a terrifying mimicry of mirth, and the storm wind howled around us in dark trees, and I felt that I had known them forever, and had no words to say to them—and no door.

There were four in the Coulson family: the father, a man of fifty years, the mother, somewhere in the middle forties, a son, and a daughter, Edith, a girl of twenty-two who lived in the house with her parents. I never met the son: he had completed his course at Oxford a year or two before, and had gone down to London where he was now employed. During the time I lived there the son did not come home.

They were a ruined family. How that ruin had fallen on them, what it was, I never knew, for no one ever spoke to me about them. But the sense of their disgrace, of a shameful inexpiable dishonor, for which there was no pardon, from which there could never be redemption, was overwhelming. In the most astonishing way I found out about it right away, and yet I did not know what they had done, and no one ever spoke a word against them.

Rather, the mention of their name brought silence, and in that silence there was something merciless and final, something that belonged to the temper of the country, and that was far more terrible than any open word of scorn, contempt, or bitter judgment could have been, more savage than a million strident, whispering, or abusive tongues could be, because the silence was unarguable, irrevocable, complete, as if a great door had been shut against their lives forever.

Everywhere I went in town, the people knew about them, and said nothing—saying everything—when I spoke their names. I found this final, closed, relentless silence everywhere—in tobacco, wine, and tailor shops, in book stores, food stores, haberdashery stores—wherever I bought anything and gave the clerk the address to which it was to be delivered, they responded instantly with this shut finality of silence, writing the name down gravely, sometimes saying briefly "Oh! Coulson's!" when I gave them the address, but more often saying nothing.

But whether they spoke or simply wrote the name down without a word, there was always this quality of instant recognition, this obdurate, contemptuous finality of silence, as if a door had been shut—a door that could never again be opened. Somehow I disliked them more for this silence than if they had spoken evilly: there was in it something ugly, sly, knowing, and triumphant that was far more evil than any slyly whispering confidence of slander, or any open vituperation of abuse, could be. It seemed somehow to come from all the evil and uncountable small maggotry of the earth, the cautious little hatreds of a million nameless ciphers, each puny, pallid, trivial in himself, but formidable because he added his tiny beetle's ball of dung to the mountainous accumulation of ten million others of his breed.

It was uncanny how these clerk-like faces grave and quiet, that never spoke a word, or gave a sign, or altered their expression by a jot, when I gave them the address, could suddenly be alive with something secret, foul, and sly, could be more closed and secret than a door, and yet instantly reveal the naked, shameful, and iniquitous filth that welled up from some depthless source. I could not phrase it, give a name to it, or even see a certain sign that it was there, no more than I could put my hand upon a wisp of fading smoke, but I always knew when it was there, and somehow when I saw it my heart went hard and cold against the people who revealed it, and turned with warmth and strong affection toward the Coulson family.

There was, finally, among these grave clerk-like faces one face that I could never forget thereafter, a face that seemed to resume into its sly suave surfaces all of the nameless abomination of evil in the world for which I had no name, for which there was no handle I could grasp, no familiar places or edges I could get my hands upon, which slid phantasmally, oilily, and smokily away whenever I tried to get my hands upon it. But it was to haunt my life for years in dreams of hatred, madness, and despair that found no frontal wall for their attack, no word for their vituperation, no door for the shoulder of my hate—an evil world of phantoms, shapes, and whispers that was yet as real as death, as ever-present as man's treachery, but that slid away from me like smoke whenever I tried to meet, or curse, or strangle it.

This face was the face of a man in a tailor shop, a fitter there, and I could have battered that foul face into a bloody pulp, distilled the filthy refuse of his ugly life out of his fat swelling neck and through the murderous grip of my fingers, if I could only have found a cause, a logic, and an act for doing it. And yet I never saw the man but twice, and briefly, and there had been nothing in his suave, sly careful speech to give offense.

Edith Coulson had sent me to the tailor's shop: I needed a suit and when I asked her where to go to have it made, she had sent me to this place because her brother had his suits made there and liked it. The fitter was a heavy shambling man in his late thirties: he had receding hair, which he brushed back flat in a thick pompadour, yellowish, somewhat bulging eyes, a coarse heavy face, loose-featured, red, and sensual, which showed unpleasantly in a mouth that was always half open. It was, in fact, the mouth that gave his face its sensual, sly, and ugly look, for a loose and vulgar smile seemed constantly to hover about its thick coarse edges, to be deliberately, slyly restrained, but about to burst at any moment in an open, evil, foully sensual laugh. There was always this ugly suggestion of a loose, corrupt, and evilly jubilant mirth about his mouth, and yet he never laughed or smiled.

The man's speech had this same quality. It was suave and courteous, but even in its most urbane assurances, there was something noncommittal, sly, and jeering, something that slid away from you, and was never to be grasped, a quality that was faithless, tricky, and unwholesome. When I came for the final fitting it was obvious that he had done as cheap and shoddy a job as he could do; the suit was vilely botched and skimped, sufficient cloth had not been put into it, and now it was too late to remedy the defect.

Yet, the fitter gravely pulled the vest down till it met the trousers, tugged at the coat, and pulled the thing together where it stayed until I took a breath or moved a muscle, when it would all come apart again, the collar bulging outward from the shoulder, the skimpy coat and vest crawling backward from the trousers, leaving a hiatus of shirt and belly that could not be remedied now by any means.

Then, gravely he would pull the thing together again, and in his suave, yet oily, sly, and noncommittal phrases, say:

"Um! Seems to fit you very well."

I was choking with exasperation, and knew that I had been done, because I had foolishly paid them half the bill already, and now knew no way out of it except to lose what I had paid, and get nothing for it, or take the thing, and pay the balance. I was caught in a trap, but even as I jerked at the coat and vest speechlessly, seized my shirt, and thrust the gaping collar in his face, the man said smoothly.

"Um! Yes! The collar. Should think all that will be all right. Still needs a little alteration." He made some chalk marks on me. "Should think you'll find it fits you very well when the tailor makes the alterations."

"When will the suit be ready?"

"Um. Should think you ought to have it by next Tuesday. Yes. I think you'll find it ready by Tuesday."

The sly words slid away from me like oil: there was nothing to pin him to or grasp him by, the yellowed eyes looked casually away and would not look at me, the sensual face was suavely grave, the discolored buckteeth shone obscenely through the coarse loose mouth, and the suggestion of the foul loose smile was so pronounced now that it seemed that at any moment he would have to turn away with heavy trembling shoulders, and stifle the evil jeering laugh that was welling up in him. But he remained suavely grave and noncommittal to the end, and when I asked him if I should come again to try it on, he said, in the same oily tone, never looking at me:

"Um. Shouldn't think that would be necessary. Could have it delivered to you when it's ready. What is your address?"

"The Far-end Farm—it's on the Ventnor Road."

"Oh! Coulson's!" He never altered his expression, but the suggestion of the obscene smile was so pronounced that now it seemed he had to out with it. Instead, he only said:

"Um. Yes. Should think it could be delivered to you there on Tuesday. If you'll just wait a moment I'll ask the tailor."

Gravely, suavely, he took the coat from me and walked back toward the tailor's room with the coat across his arm. In a moment, I heard sly voices whispering, laughing slyly, then the tailor saying:

"Where does he live?"

"Coulson's!" said the fitter chokingly, and now the foul awaited laugh did come—high, wet, slimy, it came out of that loose mouth, and choked and whispered wordlessly, and choked again, and mingled then with the tailor's voice in sly, choking, whispering intimacy, and then gasped faintly, and was silent. When he came out again his coarse face was red and swollen with foul secret merriment, his heavy shoulders trembled slightly, he took out his handkerchief and wiped it once across his loose half-opened mouth, and with that gesture wiped the slime of laughter from his lips. Then he came toward me suave, grave, and courteous, evilly composed, as he said smoothly:

"Should think we'll have it by next Tuesday, sir."

"Can the tailor fix it so it's going to fit?"

"Um. Should think you'll find that everything's all right. You ought to have it Tuesday afternoon."

He was not looking at me: the yellowish bulging eyes were staring casually, indefinitely, away, and his words again had slid away from me like oil. He could not be touched, approached, or handled: there was nothing to hold him by, he had the impregnability of smoke or a ball of mercury.

As I went out the door, he began to speak to another man in the shop, I heard low words and whispered voices, then, gasping, the word "Coulson's!" and the slimy, choking, smothered laughter as the street door closed behind me. I never saw him again. I never forgot his face.

That was a fine house: the people in it were exiled, lost, and ruined people, and I liked them all. Later, I never knew why I felt so close to them, or remembered them with such warmth and strong affection.

I did not see the Coulsons often and rarely talked to them.

Yet I felt as familiar and friendly with them all as if I had known them all my life. The house was wonderful as no other house I had ever known because we all seemed to be living in it together with this strange speechless knowledge, warmth, and familiarity, and yet each was as private, secret, and secure in his own room as if he occupied the house alone.

Coulson himself I saw least of all: we sometimes passed each other going in or out the door, or in the hall: he would grunt "Morning," or "Good day," in a curt blunt manner, and go on, and yet he always left me with a curious sense of warmth and friendliness. He was a stocky well-set man with iron-gray hair, bushy eyebrows, and a red weathered face which wore the open color of the country on it, but also had the hard dull flush of the steady heavy drinker.

I never saw him drunk, and yet I think that he was never sober: he was one of those men who have drunk themselves past any hope of drunkenness, who are soaked through to the bone with alcohol, saturated, tanned, weathered in it so completely that it could never be distilled out of their blood again. Yet, even in this terrible excess one felt a kind of grim control—the control of a man who is enslaved by the very thing that he controls, the control of the opium eater who cannot leave his drug but measures out his dose with a cold calculation, and finds the limit of his capacity, and stops there, day by day.

But somehow this very sense of control, this blunt ruddy style of the country gentleman which distinguished his speech, his manner, and his dress, made the ruin of his life, the desperate intemperance of drink that smouldered in him like a slow fire, steadily, nakedly apparent. It was as if, having lost everything, he still held grimly to the outer forms of a lost standard, a ruined state, when the inner substance was destroyed.

And it was this way with all of them—with Mrs. Coulson and the girl, as well: their crisp, clipped friendly speech never deviated into intimacy, and never hinted at any melting into confidence and admission. Upon the woman's weathered face there hovered, when she talked, the same faint set grin that Captain Nicholl had, and her eyes were bright and hard, a little mad, impenetrable, as were his. And the girl, although young and very lovely, sometimes had this same look when she greeted any one or paused to talk. In that look there was nothing truculent, bitter, or defiant: it was just the look of three people who had gone down together, and who felt for one another neither bitterness nor hate, but that strange companionship of a common disgrace, from which love has vanished, but which is more secret, silent, and impassively resigned to its fatal unity than love itself could be.

And that hard bright look also said this plainly to the world: "We ask for nothing from you now, we want nothing that you offer us. What is ours is ours, what we are we are, you'll not intrude nor come closer than we let you see!"

Coulson might have been a man who had been dishonored and destroyed by his women, and who took it stolidly, saying nothing, and drank steadily from morning until night, and had nothing for it now but drink and silence and acceptance. Yet I never knew for certain that this was so, it just seemed inescapable, and seemed somehow legible not only in the slow smouldering fire that burned out through his rugged weathered face, but also in the hard bright armor of the women's eyes, the fixed set grin around their lips when they were talking—a grin that was like armor, too. And Morison, who had referred to Coulson, chuckling, as a real "bottle-a-day-man," had added quietly, casually, in his brief, indefinite, but blurted-out suggestiveness of speech:

"I think the old girl's been a bit of a bitch in her day. . . .

Don't know, of course, but has the look, hasn't she?" In a moment he said quietly, "Have you talked to the daughter yet?"

"Once or twice. Not for long."

"Ran into a chap at Magdalen other day who knows her," he said casually. "He used to come out here to see her." He glanced swiftly, slyly at me, his face reddening a little with laughter. "Pretty hot, I gather," he said quietly, smiling, and looked away. It was night: the fire burned cheerfully in the grate, the hot coals spurting in small gaseous flares from time to time. The house was very quiet all around us. Outside we could hear the stormy wind in the trees along the road. Morison flicked his cigarette into the fire, poured out a drink of whiskey into a glass, saying as he did so: "I say, old chap, you don't mind if I take a spot of this before I go to bed, do you?" Then he shot some seltzer in the glass, and drank. And I sat there, without a word, staring sullenly into the fire, dumbly conscious of the flood of sick pain and horror which the casual foulness of the man's suggestion had aroused, stubbornly trying to deny now that I was thinking of the girl all the time.

One night, as I was coming home along the dark road that went up past the playing field to the house, and that was bordered on each side by grand trees whose branches seemed to hold at night all the mysterious and demented cadences of storm, I came upon her suddenly standing in the shadow of a tree. It was one of the grand wild nights that seemed to come so often in the autumn of that year: the air was full of a fine stinging moisture, not quite rain, and above the stormy branches of the trees I could see the sky, wild, broken, full of scudding clouds through which at times the moon drove in and out with a kind of haggard loneliness. By that faint, wild, and broken light, I could see the small white oval of the girl's face—somehow even more lovely now just because I could not see it plainly. And I could see as well the rough gleaming bark of the tree against which she leaned.

As I approached, I saw her thrust her hand into the pocket of her overcoat, a match flared, and for a moment I saw Edith plainly, the small flower of her face framed in the wavering light as she lowered her head to light her cigarette.

The light went out, I saw the small respiring glow of her cigarette before the white blur of her face, I passed her swiftly, head bent, without speaking, my heart filled with the sense of strangeness and wonder which the family had roused in me.

Then I walked on up the road, muttering to myself. The house was dark when I got there, but when I entered my sitting-room the place was still warmly and softly luminous with the glow of hot coals in the grate. I turned the lights on, shut the door behind me, and hurled several lumps of coal upon the bedded coals. In a moment the fire was blazing and crackling cheerfully, and getting a kind of comfort and satisfaction from this activity, I flung off my coat, went over to the sideboard, poured out a stiff drink of Scotch from a bottle there, and coming back to the fire, flung myself into a chair, and began to stare sullenly into the dancing flames.

How long I sat there in this stupor of sullen and nameless fury, I did not know, but I was sharply roused at length by footsteps light and rapid on the gravel, shocked into a start of surprise by a figure that appeared suddenly at one of the French windows that opened directly from my sitting-room to the level sward of velvet lawn before the house.

I peered through the glass for a moment with an astonished stare before I recognized the face of Edith Coulson. I opened the doors at once, she came in quickly, smiling at my surprise, and at the glass which I was holding foolishly, half-raised in my hand.

I continued to look at her with an expression of gape-mouthed astonishment and in a moment became conscious of her smiling glance, the cool sweet assurance of her young voice.

"I say!" she was saying cheerfully. "What a lucky thing to find you up! I came away without any key—I should have had to wake the whole house up—so when I saw your light—" she concluded briskly, "—what luck! I hope you don't mind."

"Why no-o, no," I stammered foolishly, still staring dumbly at her. "No—no-o—not at all," I blundered on. Then suddenly coming to myself with a burst of galvanic energy, I shut the windows, pushed another chair before the fire, and said:

"Won't you sit down and have a drink before you go?"

"Thanks," she said crisply. "I will—yes. What a jolly fire you have." As she talked she took off her coat and hat swiftly and put them on a chair. Her face was flushed and rosy, beaded with small particles of rain, and for a moment, she stood before the mirror arranging her hair, which had been tousled by the wind.

The girl was slender, tall, and very lovely with the kind of beauty they have when they are beautiful—a beauty so fresh, fair, and delicate that it seems to be given to just a few of them to compensate for all the grimly weathered ugliness of the rest. Her voice was also lovely, sweet, and musical, and when she talked all the notes of tenderness and love were in it. But she had the same hard bright look in her eye that her mother had, the faint set smile around her mouth: as we stood there talking she was standing very close to me, and I could smell the fragrance of her hair, and felt an intolerable desire to put my hand upon hers and was almost certain she would not draw away. But the hard bright look was in her eye, the faint set smile around her mouth, and I did nothing.

"What'll you have?" I said. "Whiskey?"

"Yes, thank you," she said with the same sweet crisp assurance with which she always spoke, "and a splash of soda." I struck a match and held it for her while she lit the cigarette she was holding in her hand, and in a moment returned to her with the drink. Then she sat down, crossed her legs, and for a moment puffed thoughtfully at her cigarette, as she stared into the fire. The storm wind moaned in the great trees along the road, and near the house, and suddenly a swirl of rain and wind struck the windows with a rattling blast. The girl stirred a little in her chair, restlessly, shivered.

"Listen!" she said. "What a night! Horrible weather we have here, isn't it?"

"I don't know. I don't like the fog and rain so well. But this—the way it is tonight—" I nodded toward the window—"I like it."

She looked at me for a moment.

"Oh," she said noncommittally. "You do." Then, as she sipped her drink, she looked curiously about the room, her reflective glance finally resting on my table where there was a great stack of the ledgers in which I wrote.

"I say," she cried again. "What are you doing with all those big books there?"

"I write in them."

"Really?" she said, in a surprised tone. "I should think it'd be an awful bother carrying them around when you travel?"

"It is. But it's the best way I've found of keeping what I do together."

"Oh," she said, as before, and continued to stare curiously

at me with her fair, lovely young face, the curiously hard, bright, and unrevealing glance of her eye. "I see. . . . But why do you come to such a place as this to write?" she said presently. "Do you like it here?"

"I do. As well as any place I've ever known."

"Oh! . . . I should think a writer would want a different kind of place."

"What kind?"

"Oh—I don't know—Paris—London—some place like that where there is lots of life—people—fun—I should think you'd work better in a place like that."

"I work better here."

"But don't you get awfully fed up sitting in here all day long and writing in those enormous books?"

"I do, yes."

"I should think you would . . . I should think you'd want to get away from it sometime."

"Yes. I do want to—every day—almost all the time."

"Then why don't you?" she said crisply. "Why don't you go off some weekend for a little spree. I should think it'd buck you up no end."

"It would—yes. Where should I go?"

"Oh, Paris, I suppose. . . . Or London! London!"

"I'm afraid I don't know it."

. "But you've *been* to London," she said impatiently. "Of course you do."

"Oh, yes. I lived there for several months."

"Then you know London," she said impatiently. "Of course you do."

"I'm afraid I don't know it very well. I don't know many people there—and after all, that's the thing that counts, isn't it?"

She looked at me curiously for a moment with the faint hard smile around the edges of her lovely mouth.

"—Should think that might be arranged," she said with a quiet, an enigmatic humor. Then, more directly, she added: "That shouldn't be difficult at all. Perhaps I could introduce you to some people."

"That would be fine. Do you know many people there?"

"Not many," she said. "I go there—whenever I can." She got up with a swift decisive movement, put her glass down on the mantel and cast her cigarette into the fire. Then she faced me, looking at me with a curiously bold, an almost defiant directness of her hard bright eyes, and she fixed me with this glance for a full moment before she spoke.

"Good-night," she said. "Thanks awfully for letting me in—and for the drink."

"Good-night," I said, and she was gone before I could say more, and I had closed the door behind her, and I could hear her light swift footsteps going down the hall and up the steps. And then there was nothing in the house but sleep and silence, and storm and darkness in the world around me.

Mrs. Coulson came into my room just once or twice while I was there. One morning she came in, spoke crisply and cheerfully, and walked over to the window looking out upon the velvet lawn and at the dreary, impenetrable gray of foggy air. Although the room was warm, and there was a good fire burning in the grate, she clasped her arms together as she looked and shivered a little.

"Wretched weather, isn't it?" she said in her crisp tones, her gaunt weathered face and toothy mouth touched by the faint fixed grin as she looked out with her bright hard stare. "Don't you find it frightfully depressing? Most Americans do."

"Yes, I do, a little. We don't have this kind of weather very often. But this is the time of year you get it here, isn't it? I suppose you're used to it by now?"

"Used to it?" she said crisply turning her hard bright gaze upon me. "Not at all. I've known it all my life but I'll never get used to it. It is a wretched climate."

"Still, you wouldn't feel at home anywhere else, would you? You wouldn't want to live outside of England."

"No?" she said, staring at me with the faint set grin around her toothy mouth. "Why do you think so?"

"Because your home is here."

"My home? My home is where they have fine days, and where the sun is always shining."

"I wouldn't like that. I'd get tired of sunlight all the time. I'd want some gray days and some fog and snow."

"Yes, I suppose you would. But then, you've been used to having fine days all your life, haven't you? With us, it's different. I'm so fed up with fog and rain that I could do without it nicely, thank you, if I never saw it again. . . . I don't think you could ever understand how much the sunlight means to us," she said slowly. She turned, and for a moment looked out the window with her hard bright stare, the faint set grin about her mouth. "Sunlight—warmth—fine days forever! Warmth everywhere—in the earth, the sky, in the lives of the people all around you nothing but warmth and sunlight and fine days!"

"And where would you go to find all that? Does it exist?"

"Oh, of course!" she said crisply and good-naturedly turning to me again. "There's only one place to live—only one country where I want to live."

"Where is that?"

"Italy," she said. "That's my real home. . . . I'd live the rest of my life there if I could." For a moment longer she looked out the window, then turned briskly, saying:

"Why don't you run over to Paris some weekend? After all, it's only seven hours from London: if you left here in the morning you'd be there in time for dinner. It would be a good change for you. I should think a little trip like that would buck you up tremendously."

Her words gave me a wonderful feeling of confidence and hope: I think she had traveled a great deal, and she had the usual, assured way of speaking of a voyage that made it seem very easy, and filled one with a sense of joy and adventure when she spoke about it. When I tried to think of Paris by myself it had seemed very far away and hard to reach: London stood between it and me, and when I thought of the huge smoky web of London, the soft gray skies above me, and the enormous weight of lives that were hidden somewhere in that impenetrable fog, gray desolation and weariness of the spirit filled me. It seemed to me that I must draw each breath of that soft gray air with heavy weary effort, and that every mile of my journey would be a ghastly struggle through some viscous and material substance of soft heavy gray, that weighted down my steps, and filled my heart with desolation.

But when Mrs. Coulson spoke to me about it, suddenly it all seemed wonderfully easy and good. England was magically small, the Channel to be taken in a stride, and all the thrill, the joy, the mystery of Paris mine again—the moment that I chose to make it mine.

I looked at her gaunt weathered face, her toothy mouth with the faint fixed grin, the hard bright armor of her eyes, and wondered how anything so clear, so sharp, so crisp, and so incisive could have been shaped and grown underneath these soft and humid skies that numbed me, mind and heart and body, with their thick numb substance of gray weariness and desolation.

A day or two before I left, Edith came into my room one afternoon bearing a tray with tea and jam and buttered bread. I was sitting in my chair before the fire, and had my coat off: when she came in I scrambled to my feet, reached

for the coat and started to put it on. In her young crisp voice
she told me not to, and put the tray down on the table, saying that the maid was having her afternoon away.

Then for a moment she stood looking at me with her
faint and enigmatic smile.

"So you're leaving us?" she said presently.

"Yes. Tomorrow."

"And where will you go from here?" she said.

"To Germany, I think. Just for a short time—two or
three weeks."

"And after that?"

"I'm going home."

"Home?"

"Back to America."

"Oh," she said slowly. "I see." In a moment, she added,
"We shall miss you."

I wanted to talk to her more than I had ever wanted to
talk to any one in my life, but when I spoke all that I could
say, lamely, muttering, was:

"I'll miss you, too."

"Will you?" She spoke so quietly that I could scarcely
hear her. "I wonder for how long?" she said.

"Forever," I said, flushing miserably at the sound of the
word, and yet not knowing any other word to say.

The faint hard smile about her mouth was a little deeper
when she spoke again.

"Forever? That's a long time, when one is young as
you," she said.

"I mean it. I'll never forget you as long as I live."

"We shall remember you," she said quietly. "And I hope
you think of us sometime—back here buried, lost, in all
the fog and rain and ruin of England. How good it must
be to know that you are young in a young country—where
nothing that you did yesterday matters very much. How

wonderful it must be to know that none of the failure of the past can pull you down—that there will always be another day for you—a new beginning. I wonder if you Americans will ever know how fortunate you are," the girl said.

"And yet you could not leave all this?" I said with a kind of desperate hope. "This old country you've lived in, known all your life. A girl like you could never leave a place like this to live the kind of life we have in America."

"Couldn't I?" she said with a quiet, but unmistakable passion of conviction. "There's nothing I'd like better."

I stared at her blindly, dumbly for a moment; suddenly all that I wanted to say, and had not been able to say, found release in a movement of my hands. I gripped her by the shoulders and pulled her to me, and began to plead with her:

"Then why don't you? I'll take you there!—Look here—" my words were crazy, and I knew it, but as I spoke them, I believed all I said—"Look here! I haven't got much money —but in America you can make it if you want to! I'm going back there. You come, too—I'll take you when I go!"

She had not tried to free herself; she just stood there passive, unresisting, as I poured that frenzied proposal in her ears. Now, with the same passive and unyielding movement, the bright armor of her young eyes, she stepped away, and stood looking at me silently for a moment, the faint, hard smile at the edges of her mouth. Then slowly, with an almost imperceptible movement, she shook her head. "Oh, you'll forget about us all," she said quietly. "You'll forget about our lives here—buried in fog—and rain—and failure—and defeat."

"Failure and defeat won't last forever."

"Sometimes they do," she said with a quiet finality that froze my heart.

"Not for you—they won't!" I said, and took her by the

hand again with desperate entreaty. "Listen to me—" I blundered on incoherently, with the old feeling of nameless shame and horror. "You don't need to tell me what it is— I don't want to know—but whatever it is for you—it doesn't matter—you can get the best of it."

She said nothing, but just looked at me through that hard bright armor of her eyes, the obdurate finality of her smile.

"Good-bye," she said, "I'll not forget you either." She looked at me for a moment curiously before she spoke again. "I wonder," she said slowly, "if you'll ever understand just what it was you did for me by coming here."

"What was it?"

"You opened a door that I thought had been closed forever," she said, "a door that let me look in on a world I thought I should never see again—a new bright world, a new life and a new beginning—for us all. And I thought that was something which would never happen to any one in this house again."

"It will to you," I said, and took her hand again with desperate eagerness. "It can happen to you whenever you want it to. It's yours, I'll swear it to you, if you'll only speak."

She looked at me with her direct hard glance, an almost imperceptible movement of her head.

"I tell you I know what I'm talking about."

Again she shook her head.

"You don't know," she said. "You're young. You're an American. There are some things you'll never be old enough to know.—For some of us there's no return.—Go back," she said, "go back to the life you know—the life you understand —where there can always be a new beginning—a new life."

"And you—" I said dumbly, miserably.

"Good-bye, my dear," she said so low and gently I could scarcely hear her. "Think of me sometime, won't you—I'll not forget you." And before I could speak she kissed me once and was gone, so light and swift that I did not know it, until the door had closed behind her. And for some time, like a man in a stupor, I stood there looking out the window at the gray wet light of England.

The next day I went away, and never saw any of them again, but I could not forget them. Although I had never passed beyond the armor of their hard bright eyes, or breached the wall of their crisp, friendly, and impersonal speech, or found out anything about them, I always thought of them with warmth, with a deep and tender affection, as if I had always known them—as if, somehow, I could have lived with them or made their lives my own if only I had said a word, or turned the handle of a door—a word I never knew, a door I never found.

Beatus Rex

STARK YOUNG

Stark Young was born at Como, Mississippi, in 1881. He studied at the University of Mississippi, and after graduate work at Columbia University and a period of private study and writing, returned to that institution to teach English. In 1907 he joined the faculty of the University of Texas; from 1915 until 1921 he taught at Amherst College. Since that time he has been on the editorial staffs of *The New Republic* and of *Theatre Arts Monthly*. His interest in the theatre has been very active; in addition to dramatic criticism and books and articles on the theatre, he has written and translated plays and has directed productions. He has lectured and travelled in Italy and has written extensively about that country. Best-known of his works in fiction is the novel *So Red the Rose* (1934), a rich and sympathetic story of the old South, in which much of his own family history and tradition is embodied.

WHEN we left Rimini we had no idea of seeing Florence. Miss Hutchinson's and my scheme was to do certain cities and towns, I to make the drawings, she to write what she called in her journalese the story. And Florence, as she said, had been sketched, painted, described, and recounted till it was black in the face; it was exactly the sort of subject we meant to avoid. There were plenty of other towns in Italy.

But it turned out after all that our best trains to the south would go by Florence and Chiusi. I begged my companion to let me stop off one day at least; there were reasons that made me want to revisit the convent at Fiesole once more before I died, if only for an afternoon. Well, she said, very well; I could have Florence this time, provided—did I remember the doctor in Molière who said if the other doctor would only agree to an emetic for this patient, he could give anything he liked to the next?—provided she was at liberty to stop wherever she chose after this. We were in Florence soon after noon, and later we took the tram that left the Duomo at four o'clock for Fiesole.

The little sister who met us at the door and was to be our guide through the convent had never seen me before, and I was glad of that. I was hoping not to see the mother superior again, but to make this visit like a stranger to the place. We saw first the chapel and then the fresco of Saint Jerome and his lion outside in the portico, where Cosimo de' Medici's stair ascended from the road below. It was a stair with a high wall on one side; on the other a solid balustrade from which you looked down upon the valley where Florence lay and, beyond that, Samminiato and the line of the hills. Up the stair, as it mounted, there were cypresses; there were two rows of them—on each step in the middle a cypress stood and one at the end near the balustrade; their shadows fell on the flagstones of the steps and on the wall, and the light under them was soft and quiet. Afterward we saw the cloister with the pots of coleus crowded on the low wall between the columns, and the arms of the Medici on the well-head, and after the cloister the court with the date-palms, the balcony where the nuns gather for recreation in the evening after dinner, and the long wall covered with yellow roses. Then we came to the garden, the geranium terrace, the cypress avenue below, the rondel with bay-trees and oleanders. The oleanders were in blossom and the whole place was sweet.

We came along the path to the olive-orchard, where a gate is and the statue of Saint Joseph. Under an olive-tree seats were arranged, where you could rest—two iron benches and some wicker chairs; and there the sister left us. It was time for benediction, she said, and we must excuse her. If we wished to come to benediction, or after benediction, we could go out by the stair; or, if we liked, there was the rose walk, halfway up the hill, to the gate on to the piazza; Cherubina would let us out.

We sat down and Miss Hutchinson lit a cigarette.

"Now tell me about your cousin," she said. "You promised you would, if we came here, though I generally hate stories about people's cousins; it tangles things up."

I said: "About Rex?"

"Yes, who was here. That's the point, isn't it—he was here?"

"Yes, that's the point."

"But, see here, why's our Saint Joseph got a Phrygian cap? I just noticed it." She burst out laughing, and pointed gaily to the saint on his high pedestal. "Considering the Phrygian significance."

"It's Phrygian, all right," I said, "but nobody'd know why. Look how quiet the statue looks in the shadow. It's in a poem Rex wrote: 'Thou art as alabaster filled with wine——' "

"To Saint Joseph, is that?" She was still gay over the Phrygian business; it involved her precious Freud.

"No," I said, "it's not Joseph; it's a love-poem."

"So? A love story! Then go on, *caro mio,* tell me about

Rex." She settled her quick little body, like a lean bird, in her chair.

It was not so easy to do, I said, making Rex intelligible, but I would try.

The first time I saw this cousin was in the spring, in Texas, two years before the War broke out. I had been in New York all winter painting. They were baroque murals that I was doing, in the grand style, all the sumptuous curves, the rich variants on the circle, the magnificence of the baroque tradition in anatomy and architecture, fruits and flowers. I finished my commission in April, and all of a sudden, one day soon after, I knew that I wanted to be in another country. New York was all very well, but I wanted to see the light flooding down from a far, bright sky, to see white roads going off over the hills, stretches of white rocks and sharp, black greens, to see the morning in that world, the full white noon, and then the breathless spring nights, with the starry mists and the tiers of bright, hard stars above that sad, sweet land.

I would go to Austin, already familiar to me, and walk about the country and paint. Miles of purple winecups and wild verbenas, the color of lilacs, would be in blossom; and the blue lupines would spread so thick in places that travellers on the train would ask if there were lakes.

"But if you are in Austin, you must meet your cousin Rex Drouillard," my aunt, who takes the family very seriously, wrote me from New Orleans. "His mother is here now for the winter with her brother, your cousin the doctor. Cousin Emma is the same as ever, still waltzing all night if she gets a chance." My aunt told me things I had heard all my life but might have forgotten about his mother and about Rex. And after all, too, she reminded me, his great-grandfather, Uncle Charles McGehee, was my great-grandfather's brother, which makes him kin. My cousin Emma

McGehee had married Henry Drouillard, a gentleman much older than herself, and the head of a great Creole family in Louisiana. Till his death she was a leader in New Orleans society. But after he died the house was sold, for they had spent most of his money. Cousin Emma took Rex, who was about fifteen at the time, to Paris with her and spent whatever was left.

Mother and son were in Paris five years, which made Rex twenty when they came back to live with his uncle. For a while he tried tutoring in French, since he was by now more French than American, and spoke French better than he spoke English; but his manner toward the young ladies was such that fathers put an end to the lessons, and the tutoring was soon all over. And yet, my aunt observed, doubtless quite shrewdly, this would shortly have taken care of itself, if people could only have a little sense. Rex had not seemed so fiery to her, not as all that; she took his behavior to be really only a French notion he had, by which you consider it the manly thing to do, when you are left alone with a woman, to make love to her. However that might be, Rex had come to the university at Austin—the French professor there had been a friend of the family— and had burrowed his way into the classes, or had it burrowed for him by this family friend, and in two years got himself graduated, just how God alone knew. He had supported himself by a little translating for the university library and by a monthly comic paper he had established and that had not only paid expenses but made a profit; it had even begun to pay for contributions—people would have gladly donated their writings for the sheer pleasure of seeing themselves in print, but Rex as editor had a taste for doing things up in professional style—when the dean of the college heard too much of its Parisian note and closed it down.

The second year Rex had an assistantship not in French, but, of all things, in political economy, which he won not so much through his study of the subject as of the professor, who was all temperament. Rex had written his mother an amusing letter about him, and how, from the time he heard him burst out at Christmas dinner on the love life of North American lizards, he knew he should get on with the economist—Cousin Emma had read the letter aloud one afternoon at a card table, and all the family had given their opinions on the subject of its propriety. His mother tells me also, my aunt wrote, that there are several young ladies who are not perhaps in love with Rex but who seem to make him silk shirts and have him to suppers.

The first time I saw Rex he was sitting at his table naked with a gilt-paper crown on his head. He sat at the table writing, with the crown on his head and a towel round his loins. His room was in a sort of outhouse in a back corner of his landlady's yard. It was a two-room place with a porch running along in front, and had doubtless once been meant for the servants' quarters. By the porch there was a locust tree in flower; the white blossoms were scattered on the floor of the porch and on the steps. It was early in the afternoon and the sun was blinding. The shade of the porch and the shade in the room were very distinct. The air was full of the drowsy sweet of the locusts.

We shook hands, and Rex, before he sat down again at his table, reached for some white cotton trousers and put them on. He had taken off the crown.

"I don't suppose you mind," he said, "but I'd better put some clothes on. I like to wear the crown sometimes, got it at a *bal poudre.*" The simple explanation seemed to serve our purposes.

I took the only other chair to be seen. There was nothing else around but the white iron bed and the table; the room was bare as only a room in Texas can be. He was tall and blond, and spoke English rather precisely, like a foreigner, but had so much of a sort of half-laugh when he talked that he sounded careless or loose. You might set this little laugh of Rex's down as shy, or nervous, or silly, or as ironical, or as defensive. Whatever it was, it did not improve the impression he gave people.

"My mother writes to me about three times a year," he said, "and I write to her about three times. But she's broken the rule to tell me you were coming. She says you're a fine painter. She adores painting. Everybody in Paris painted her, you know. Immortal Helen, and all that."

I said: "We'll pray at least that I'll be fine some day.'

"You see while she is the painted swan I'm only a good man Friday to a college professor. These are his quizzes I'm reading. It's all rot, and I wouldn't do them if the course were mine. But he believes in it, so I'm doing it."

"Well, now that, I should say," Miss Hutchinson grumbled, interrupting me for the first time and beginning to turn the emerald round and round on her finger, as she did when about to be dubious, "sounds a little dutiful and tiresome."

"Not at all," I said, "it's only using his imagination about the other man."

"My mistake. What did he say?"

"He said: 'But it gets me my six hundred bucks and I can live on that, the college year. Especially since, being a professorito now, I'm invited to all the dances instead of having to chip in. And I've gotten even a little by wearing my crown and getting the air on my skin. And gotten even this way too—' he reached over for a sheet of paper; it was a poem."

Miss Hutchinson crossed her legs.

"That's better," she said; "that's better. Did you see it?"

" 'I'll give it to you,' Rex said; 'I've a carbon. I'm that efficient.' For that matter you could see by his eyes and hands that he could show efficiency enough in case he cared to bother. In his own affairs there were spurts of it when it seemed worth while."

Miss Hutchinson turned and looked me in the eye. "And tell me—was the poem good? How was it?"

I nodded. "I know it by heart," I said.

"Well, then, say it for me."

I repeated the poem to her:

"Across the marble ledges of the dawn,
  Rose-tinct and gold, like a Venetian's hair,
  Day cometh now, and from the argent lawn
  Of Paradise leans down upon the air.

And the white Artemis grows pale and fades,
  She who with splendor drowns the unbosomed night,
  Her twinkling flock asleep, folded in shades;
  The larks singing on the hills of light.

Waken, O lovely eyelids, waken slowly,
  The dew on these green slopes trembles for thee;
  This morn is one, but thou art all, and holy,
  And holier with the dawns that are to be."

My companion heard the poem to the end without moving.

"But look, *caro mio,* poetry's the only thing I can stand rich. That's rich."

She could be very nice sometimes.

When the light had faded and I was through with my painting, I used to drop in for Rex and take him somewhere for supper—he had no regular place. Afterward we walked in the country. People along the road to Mount Bonnell used to see from their porches and little front yards two young men walking past, talking busily, one of them laughing a great deal, not very loud. Rex was not as strong as a horse, but he could walk forever, as long a time as he could talk; he had the kind of endurance that women sometimes display; a mysterious vitality fed his slight body with some sort of deathless elixir.

One night, walking, we met some acquaintance of Rex's, who joined us and began to talk about his troubles. He was a solemn-looking young man, almost at the end of his college course, and he told us that he was trying to decide what he ought to do. He had seen a student cheating on examinations, looking at notes that he had hidden in his coat pocket. Here we were with the honor system, he said, and under the honor system you were pledged not only to be straight yourself but to see that other men were straight. And yet he hated to report the chap, and get him expelled and all. What ought he to do?

"Do you remember Jeanie Deans?" Rex said. The senior shook his head. "Well, anyhow, she's a Scott heroine, and she wouldn't tell a lie even to save her sister from hanging. No, right was right, and Jeanie preferred an easy conscience for herself."

The student was silent, in consternation, I suppose, and walked along with his hand up before his mouth. I said: "Yes, but doesn't there come a point sometimes in your living, a point on whose rightness your whole existence afterward will depend?"

"My God, you're elaborate, darling!" Miss Hutchinson said, when I came to this.

"Well, how else can you say it? I mean a point where your decision goes down to your very elements."

"I get you, sweet. They're what people used to call crucial moments, morally, the sweet old things! What did Rex say?"

"He said: 'If your precious existence hangs on that moment, well, let it hang.'

" 'Like Jeanie's sister,' I said."

That was about all the religion Rex had. From his careless prattling you gathered at length perhaps that he saw life as a flux. Something on the whole pathetic, something set in darkness. Filled with little bodies of men who were confused, warm-hearted, transitory, and touching. You can give others whatever good or daring or brief audacity you have in you to give; for yourself, meantime, you can admit life's beauty and fatalism. He was a sort of voluptuous mystic.

"And the soul?" my companion asked.

"I fancy he never thought he had one."

"Whew! I'm damned devout myself. i wouldn't risk it," she said.

I said: "I don't suppose the notion of a risk of any kind was very clear to Rex."

"Well, what I'd like to know is where he thought he was headed."

"There, I suppose, he did variations on Einstein."

"Space all bent up?"

"Yes, and thought that the shortest distance between two points was in himself."

"That's a whang of a thought. But I don't skip around concerning my little soul."

"Perhaps Rex had his mother's feet in his brain."

She made no answer to that, thinking perhaps of her soul, which she must have risked plenty of times, and I said nothing more. We sat following our own private thoughts.

"Obviously there's one other department," my friend observed presently.

"You mean love? He was shy about it. He spoke of it

once. Not anybody there in Austin, not the loyal shirt-makers he lounged around with. I met one of them; she overdid the comrade note so that I wondered. But I never wondered about Rex. He was in love with a girl he had met on the steamer coming home the year before. Sometimes he wrote to her and she to him, but not regularly. They were both in love with one another. I don't know any more."

She complained of the poor data I offered her, and I continued:

After all, I said, I was in Texas for only a fortnight or three weeks at the most. Then that next autumn the War broke out and in a month Rex had left Texas and was on his way to enlist for France. I did not see him, but I had a letter from the boat, mailed at Cherbourg. He was on his way to Paris, he said, and was sorry not to have seen me; but a week in New York was so short. The rest was about seeing the girl again during that week before he sailed. I could see he had to talk of what he felt. All of it was about love. But the way he said it was satirical. All of it satirical, which was like him.

I heard nothing else from Rex, either at that time or later, when I was in camp, and then five years afterward he wrote me from Fiesole here. The letter was not very long. He had been gassed in the Argonne and his lungs were not so good. He was here at the convent rather indefinitely. The sisters nursed him; they were like mothers and saints. He had never seen goodness like that. He enclosed a poem he had written. I might like it. That was about all.

My companion threw away a cigarette that had gone out.

"And what about the woman?" she asked—"that he loved."

"Nothing."

"Not a word?"

"No, I don't even know her name."

She thought a while. Then she shrugged her shoulders. "Well, after all, he was your friend, not mine."

I had answered the letter in good time, and then, after two months, my letter had been returned to me with a note from the mother superior informing me that Rex was dead. He had died the 24th of April.

That summer, when I was in Italy, I went to Fiesole to the convent to ask about Rex and to thank the nuns for their kindness. They were nearly all English and Irish sisters, and had made their convent into a sort of home for convalescents.

Mother Theresa seemed glad to see me; we sat down in her little drawing-room, and she told me about Rex. He was a good young man, a kind heart; always in her prayers she had said: "God bless him and keep him what he is." He was considerate of the sisters' feelings, but he was not religious. He used to say that the sisters were holiest when they knelt in benediction, because then their veils hung in the best lines, and they were most human when they gathered on their balcony for their recreation, the half-hour allowed them after dinner, laughing and chattering and noisy like birds. He used to pit the saints in the garden against one another. He would come in and say that Saint Joseph was furious because the Madonna got all the flowers. He would say: "Saint Anthony is pouting this morning; he thinks Saint Joseph has had too much attention." That made the sisters laugh heartily and shake their fingers at him for his wickedness, but he only laughed the way he always did—that sort of little half-laugh.

Mother Theresa herself was grieved that he was not religious, but especially so since he was not going to live; the doctors said he would not last much longer; it was his lungs, from that dreadful war. Where could the poor young man's mother have been, leaving him over here alone like that? "His mother," thought I, "was dancing in Louisiana"; but I said only: "She doubtless had no idea he was sick; he hadn't told her."

The sisters made prayers for him, the reverend mother went on, but of course they said nothing of that to him, not liking to intrude. Then, when you could see he was not going to live much longer, Mother Theresa thought she herself must speak to him a little. "Has the doctor been telling you how you are, dear?" she asked then; that was what she said. And Mr. Drouillard said: "You mean, has he told you I'm going to die?" "Yes," she said; "God help us." "And so, mother, you think I'll be damned?" he said. And she said: "Only God can know what is in our hearts. You must pray." "No," he said, "you make the sisters pray for me—Sister Stanislaus, Sister Gonzaga, Sister Agnes, Sister Anastasia; tell them, if they'll pray for me, I'll bring them some Turkish paste, when I'm well again, from Gilli's, to eat at recreation—that's an idea, Turkish paste for nuns!" He was smiling, but had not taken his eyes off Mother Theresa's face. No one would forget his eyes.

The next morning, after benediction, when the convent guests were at dinner and Sister Agnes came to rub his arms for neuritis, he sent her for Mother Theresa, and when they came in he called them to the bed and told them that he had been thinking of religion and that he believed at last. How their hearts leapt for joy! Mother Theresa hurried the sister off to catch the priest before he should have left the sacristy. He came and was there for a long time talking with the poor young man, leaning down to hear. Then he baptized him, and said the prayer *Absolve, quaesumus, Domine,* and gave him the sacrament. Sister Agnes, who had lost control of herself, knelt at the foot of the bed crying and thanking God. In the night he died. It seemed a beautiful thing in God to grant them this blessing, that he died in the church.

When I stopped, Miss Hutchinson went on smoking in silence for some time; then she threw her cigarette on the gravel and put her heel on it.

"That's all," I said.

She began turning her ring round and round.

"That taste for paper crowns he had—that's what I'm thinking."

I did not argue the point.

"Poor devil!"

"Look," I said, "you see the lights coming on, there toward Santa Croce; it will soon be night; let's go up to Mother Edith's parlor. It's the ring of cypresses there just under the brothers' wall."

We rose and passing through the gate began to ascend the path up the hill. It wound along among the olives and fruit trees, and the vines, grown as they were in Virgil's day in festoons between clipped elms. At last there was a broader path, an incline that led into an open space. Cypresses bordered this path, and stood in a ring about the open, and climbed on up the slope to the rock cliffs below the wood of San Francesco. On the ground among the straight trunks the late golden light spread in long rays. You could see the Virgin's shrine against the rock, the dark ivy leaves about it. The edges of the leaves were shining. Under a cypress at the side of the path I saw a red-purple iris standing up from the stones; there was the white ground, the dark tree, the purple flower—the elegiac, passionate beauty.

We stood there looking down over the fading valley, and Florence and the hills.

"He's too much for me." Miss Hutchinson said presently;

"I mean putting him together. You can usually get a sort of outline of any creature, and sort of fill it in. But this beats me."

I said nothing, but lit another cigarette. She spoke again, to herself mostly.

"So he said he was converted, to make these people happy, these nuns! They'll talk about it the rest of their lives."

At last, when I had only nodded my head and still had said nothing, she turned to me. "Well, then, what about that second poem? Was it the one with the alabaster?"

"Yes," I said.

"Can you quote it too? You knew all of the other one."

"I can if you like."

"I'd like to hear it; say it."

I said Rex's poem:

> "Thou art as alabaster filled with wine,
> Wherein the sun of summer shineth through,
> Tinged with the sound of bees when the rich vine
> Shakes down its garlands in the diamond dew.
>
> Thou art a gleaming saint amid the trees,
> Whereon the holy moonlight lieth white,
> In some old garden where the centuries
> Trail their dark mantles in the silent night.
>
> And songs of lips dead long ago I hear,
> Of them whose holy dreams were fraught with pain,
> And if I have or have thee not, it were,
> O Saint and Shrine, O Life in Life, in vain!"

Miss Hitchinson waited for me to finish, then turned on me.

"But I thought you said he didn't mention the woman he loved!"

"He didn't."

"Well, what else do you think he meant by all that poem? Not that it would change matters any; look how this last poem declines from the first; it would have been the same whether this love-affair turned out well or turned out badly. All in vain anyhow, as he says. With a man like that."

"If you mean Rex was shallow, futile," I said, "I'd say no; he was deep enough—he just had no anchor."

"Well, what's the difference?" she said.

"All the difference. He gave me a lot."

"Oh, yes, and the nuns a lot."

"And, besides, I'd say Rex's story is not a love-story."

"You men are funny."

She turned away from me and stood there leaning against one of the trees, looking down at Florence, as if she were alone.

In the stillness I could hear far down in the valley a stream running, and above the cypresses the first stars had come out. Presently the night would deepen, the nightingales in the laurels down the slope would begin to sing, and the sky be thick with stars. I was thinking of Rex and what he may have thought of their splendor and certainty.

But I said only, "It's time we started," and we said nothing more till we came to the convent gate and out into the piazza.